THE WAGES OF SIN

Also by Zoë Sumra

Sailor to a Siren

THE WAGES OF SIN

ZOË SUMRA

Elsewhen Press

CHAPTER ONE

Connor Cardwain straightened up from the motionless woman's side. Spring-cool air brushed his cheeks, scented with pollen: incongruous breaths in a morning that seemed dark. "When did anyone last see her?"

His street lieutenant shrugged. His jacket moved with him, half a second late, torn at the shoulders and seams: as did his hair, fallen halfway out of its ponytail. "The chitties show she dropped off her rent and security payments yesterday afternoon. Half five or so. I hear she went out the evening with a Union merchant –"

"She was seeing one of Comet's men."

Lieutenant Tarr's eyebrows went up. "You spend that much time stalking your cleaning staff, I don't like to think what you got on the rest of us."

"Last I saw, the cleaning staff flit in and out of my private rooms. I like to know the people closest to me." He looked Tarr up and down – a button missing from his jacket, to go with the rips: he'd lost it squeezing in through the bedsit window after breaking it – and knelt back beside the dead woman on the floor.

Her name was, or had been, Merissa: she'd been nineteen, one of his older cleaning girls. A quiet little mouse, brown of skin and black of hair, one among millions. A year ago, when she'd first turned up at his back door with a scrubbing brush, he'd asked her about the broken fingers on her left hand. A man, of course: it usually was. She'd been saving to get them rebroken and reset. Now, they were broken again, and scraped so badly the skin was hanging off: resetting the bones would do her no further good.

Connor touched Merissa's chilly forehead, brushing back her familiar dark curls. Her face was unrecognisable. Her killer had beaten her so badly that blood had spattered up the meagre furniture. Below her, a few smears on the floor showed where her killer had dragged her a foot or so before giving up on any idea of moving her further.

His idea? Connor pursed his lips. It was usually a man, but two years spent with a pair of women calling him stepbrother had taught him a few lessons on female violence.

Tarr wandered across the room and with one boot-toe touched a low cupboard door, now dangling off one hinge. "She'll have kept her stash in here."

"She didn't."

He glanced down at Connor. "Where, then?"

"In my safe. Half my drift staff do the same."

Most of the furniture was overturned, as if in revenge for the attacker's failure to locate the pitifully small number of marks he might have expected to find – nobody, however crazed, would have expected a stash to be hidden in a fourth-hand table or wobbly stool. Some had landed in her blood. A trickle of that blood ran away towards the bathroom. She must have been drawing a nice amount from her merc boyfriend to rate a flat with a bathroom.

Knuckles rapped on the door, and Connor's bodyguard Marcello leant round the jamb. He shared Connor's colouring, coppery skin and black hair, but wore his hair in a fancy set of braids bound at his neck's nape rather than a plain tail: a young man's prerogative. "The landlord's outside," he said. "Wants to know if he can have the room back yet. He wants to start cleaning up –"

"She paid for the week yesterday. He gets it back in six days."

Marcello looked down at the dead woman and grimaced. Connor felt a momentary rush of sympathy. His bodyguard had grown up on the streets, a rough, tough fighting man, and had seen God knew what in his life, but he, like the late cleaning girl Merissa, was just nineteen years old. "She's not using it," he muttered.

"I am." Connor rose, wincing. He was barely into his thirties but already cold weather made his joints creak: too many fights, too much training for fights that never came. It was early spring outside, and the flat's windows hadn't fitted well before Tarr broke one of them.

"He's not a man known for niceties," Tarr said.

"Neither am I. The room stays as it is for now." Tarr nodded. So did Marcello, but he was looking down, mind elsewhere. "What?" Connor said, misgivings mounting.

"There's a woman waiting for you downstairs."

"Who?"

"She says she's one of Mistress Falavière's cousins."

Connor bit back a curse. "I told Éloise to find me a *male* cousin."

"She probably couldn't get one."

"She has fifty male cousins." And a hundred female ones. "OK, I've seen enough for now. You," he said to Tarr, "clear the landlord out of my way and stop anyone else getting in here. You," and he beckoned to Marcello, "lock the door and stay here. Which cousin is it?"

"Her name's Yasmine."

Connor touched his neural jack's connector, under his left ear, and accessed the Falavière family tree – more like a family thicket – he kept on file. Two Yasmines, on different ends of the bush: one of Éloise's twenty-two first cousins, and a removed cousin through two marriages and three non-marital relationships. He'd met the distant cousin at a wedding, though not the first cousin, as far as he recalled: they all rolled into one after a while, and as they all seemed to assume he knew who they were, they rarely bothered to explain themselves.

Outside the bedsit, in the hall, he surveyed the corridor – dingy and poorly lit, but not too dirty. The light fitting closest to Merissa's door was broken. He ducked as he passed it: it brushed the top of his head.

He jogged past Tarr on the stairs. At their foot, the landlord – a skinny man in a dirty red waistcoat – was talking to one of Connor's enforcers, a hard-bitten woman ten years Connor's senior. The Falavière cousin was off to the side, staring at the outside of the block of flats with faint interest on her face. A pair of white wings, beams of light from another universe, shimmered from her back.

Not the Yasmine he'd met: it must be the first cousin, and, like most of her family, a Spellweaver. Taller than Éloise, though that wasn't difficult in a woman from a rich world: darker than Éloise without being as dark as average, chestnut hair and deep olive skin. The wings indicated an attitude problem. Flaunting the symbol of her power on a grubby backstreet like this – too used to wearing her wings wide like a proud girl of her homeworld, or a deliberate attempt to intimidate? She was as human as any street girl on the corners around them. Connor repressed a snort. Some Spellweavers preferred to think they were better than human.

White wings, though, meant a healer. Pretty close to what he needed right now. He stalked up to her and gestured to her wings. "Are you a doctor?"

She half-curtseyed in greeting – a foreign greeting, one that didn't fit with her rough mercenary's clothes. "No. Combat zone paramedic."

"That'll do. Come with me." He turned on his heel and jogged back into the flats, pushing past Merissa's landlord, who was remonstrating now with Tarr as well as his crewmate.

"How did she die?" Yasmine said, behind him.

Connor bit his tongue. Éloise, dependable Éloise, couldn't read minds: he'd spent enough time with those of her family who *could* read minds to know that it was an annoying habit. "Hit on the head. Last night, it looks like." Marcello was still at his post outside the bedsit: Connor nodded to the young man, who unlocked the door and stood aside. "You can tell me best how long she's been dead."

Yasmine brushed past him, looked down at Merissa without emotion and bent over her. "Have you called the police yet?" she said over her shoulder.

"This is the Septième. Police don't assist the gangland. How long has she been dead?"

She drew a pair of latex gloves from one pocket, slid them on and lifted Merissa's left wrist. It was stiff. She closed her eyes and a faint white glow rippled from her fingers across Merissa's abdomen. "About ten hours."

Connor glanced at the window. The sun was climbing outside. It was close to ten in the morning – of a twenty-seven hour local day.

"She went out last night with a merchant," Marcello said, behind Connor. "Nights don't end early here."

"About ten, I said. Between seven and twelve, if you want to be precise." She looked up at Connor. "What happens next?"

Instead of answering, he jerked his head at Marcello. "Wait outside." Surprise flitted across Marcello's dark young face, but he withdrew into the corridor.

Alone with Yasmine – a woman he hadn't expected, a stranger, an encumbrance – Connor let out a breath and swore, repeatedly and fluently, till he ran out of vituperation after ninety seconds or so.

"Do you want me to take over?" she said.

"I want you to fucking explain yourself." He grabbed her shoulder and yanked her upright. Startled green eyes blinked at him: same shade as Éloise's. "Seeing as you didn't just take my hand off at the wrist, I assume you're here to help."

"I'm here," she said, brushing him off, "because your tame Spellweaver is thirty-eight weeks pregnant and asked me to cover for her. As you requested."

"I asked for a man."

She smiled. "Ella didn't want you to get distracted."

"I sleep with women too, damn it."

"How often: once every five years?" She half stepped backwards as if to study him better. "I know why you wanted a man –"

"Even Éloise took time to settle in. Even she made mistakes, at first: expected men to bow to her, expected she needed to curtsy to them. We aren't so polite here. We take liberties your women dislike." He straightened to his full height: four inches taller than her. "I need my staff. All of them. I do not need to start accumulating corpses in a corner just because some Port Logis bourgeoise feels herself insulted."

"Stop lying to me." Her tone was gentler than maybe he deserved. "You've trained your men. I won't spark conflict between them and another team that hasn't been as well-trained."

"Good."

"Because nobody who sees me will live to report." As Connor tried not to splutter, Yasmine continued, "You've begun with one corpse, though." She indicated Merissa. "I repeat, what happens next?"

Girls were murdered all the time. They expected it. Wrong place at the wrong time; getting too close to the wrong man; hazards of work, whatever their profession. An average man on the Septième sector lived to thirty-one, Connor's age. An average woman lived to twenty-eight.

"She worked for me. She had my protection. These," and he gestured to the street outside the tiny window Tarr had broken to enter, "are my streets. This, here, is a personal insult."

He'd been in his position for less than three years. Not the smallest of the men who ran the Septième underside gangs – that had passed a year ago when he opened his second permanent office and signed his first million-mark contract – but his reputation was still largely untested. Now, he was minded to protect it, even in the case of finding the killer of a woman who could have been expected to die any day.

Yasmine wrinkled her nose. "Does personal insult get a morgue? Mortuary equipment? A pathology assistant? A forensic examiner to go over this room?"

"There's a morgue in the hospital three streets away." He passed up discussing what would have happened if his minor part of a minor planet hadn't included a hospital. "I'd thought it was fairly obvious how she died, at least."

"Appearances deceive, and even if they don't, the details are critical." Yasmine knelt and peered under the low bed on the back wall. "No weapon. Cupboards? Bathroom?"

"Bathroom, maybe." Whoever'd killed her had had to walk out on the streets afterwards, and even on Mirqest at night, a man wouldn't expect to escape notice wandering about covered in blood. But when Connor looked inside the bathroom he saw no handy blunt instruments nor any sign that a filthy man had taken a shower. The cubicle was cleanish, a little grimy with use, neither blood-streaked nor freshly bleached.

"Take her to the hospital," he said, backing out of the bathroom. "I'll send a security team to check the place over."

Yasmine stood up as if she'd expected to still be wearing the loose, bright garments of her home sector rather than the Septième-style clothing she had on – dark trousers, grey shirt, leather jacket. She'd bought the trousers on the Neuvième. Merissa's blood slicked off them rather than soaking into the fabric. "What are you going to do?"

Connor stared out of the window. A quiet street, this: not a rich street by any stretch of the imagination, but respectable. "If you were a non-Spellweaver who needed to hide evidence of guilt from Spellweavers – from mind-readers – what would you do?"

She came up beside him and looked out at her new, albeit temporary, world. "There are a number of ways, the simplest being drinking so much immediately after your crime that you can't remember it."

"Surely the memory would come back."

"Yes, but here, you aren't over-burdened with Weavers. A person would only have to forget until the investigators had left." She pursed her lips. "Blunt force trauma to one's own head achieves the same effect. Dangerous, though. You could pay a rogue telepath to edit your memories, or a telempath to implant a false memory screen, but that relies on finding a Weaver who doesn't respect the rule of law."

"Yasmine Simonstone Falavière, on this planet there is no rule of law. There's the rule of the streets on which one happens to be at the time. On the rich streets, I grant you, the rule of Rafael Martinez occasionally resembles the rule of law you'd expect on the Neuvième, but that rests solely on one's social position. Right here, there's nothing but the rule of me."

She studied him, as if calculating the differences between him and his brother Logan. Connor was the shorter of the pair and was less heavily built. Maybe Yasmine would underestimate him as a result. That was useful at times. "You run Spellweavers – but your primary hire can't read minds."

"I wouldn't expect a random Septième street smart to know that. Some credulous types say Éloise could stop the sun and raise the dead."

"Stopping the sun could be conceivable for her in a few years. Not the other one – but I take the point that people might think she can detect meddling with memories."

Connor raised his eyebrows at her. "Can you?"

"Only if it's blatant." She chewed her lower lip. "Other methods: manipulating a third party into killing someone, believing hard enough that one had spent the night doing something else that it superseded the memory, or hiding the memory in among a lot of similar ones. Which, in this case –"

"Is very possible." Her eyes widened. Connor sighed. This was why he'd wanted a man to replace Éloise: women lacked a sense of realism, at times. "Young women, here, die violent, early deaths. Childbirth, sickness and murder. My mother was murdered. She was twenty-nine. I was eleven: Logan was six." Yasmine didn't answer. "On Port Logis, or any Neuvième planet, if a man had killed a hundred young women, you'd call him a serial killer – unless he'd done so in the course of extermination squad duty. People do have a lot of children in the Union, don't they? Not as many as you, of course." He let his lips crease into a sneer. Yasmine had fourteen siblings of full or half blood by her mother and five more half-siblings by her father. "Here, a man may kill a hundred young women in the course of ten years as a part of daily life – and wouldn't necessarily feel any guilt."

"But this one is different." She spoke quietly, as if finally coming to grips with where she was and what she was doing. "What does it feel like to be a demigod?"

"I'm not a demigod. I reserve that category for Gemstone pilots or Spellweavers."

"But you have the power over life and death."

"Only its investigation." He gestured to her white wings – healer wings. "You have a power over life and death far more profound than mine. I have a gun, and a business trading in guns. That's all."

"You're my employer for the next few months. You command my powers, over life, death and anything else. Speaking of employment, Éloise gave me a draft contract."

Bloody Circle Spellweavers. "Give it to me to check. Get Merissa to the hospital morgue, and come back to sign." She touched her neural jack's link and uploaded the file without comment. In return he sent her the contact details of the non-emergency ambulance and the administrator she needed to speak to at the hospital. Her eyes crossed as she read the file, but she smiled in some satisfaction.

"Understood. I'll come back to your office if there's a delay."

Connor nodded. "Do yourself a favour: walk."

"I know what the streets smell like already."

"You don't." He gestured to her to leave to await the ambulance staff.

Alone with Merissa, Connor studied her one last time, wondering if he were capable of seeing anything that might make a difference. "Can you tell me what happened?" he said softly. No new insights materialised. Just a dead woman, not much more than a girl, who should have had another ten years left. The cheap ring her boy had bought her glinted on her finger, smeared with blood from her damaged hand.

Something about the bruising on those broken fingers looked strange, though: too dark, too pooled around the breaks. Connor peered at the mess, then touched his jack's phone and rang Yasmine's connection.

"I didn't know you had my phone link," she said after a moment, sound conducted directly into his ear.

"Éloise gave me most of her cousins' jack phone details a while ago."

"That must be a large file."

"It is. Have a good look at her left hand later. She had fingers broken many years ago, but they've broken again — and I think it happened after she was dead."

"Will do. The ambulance will be here in five minutes. They didn't want to keep you waiting."

Connor rose and stared out of the broken window. Air fresher than on many local streets wafted inside. Amid squawks from feral pigeons, squeals from warring drifter children and barrowboys' boasts of fresh mangoes, low-flying engines were audible overhead: not car engines — high and whistling — but the dull powerful roar, like a thousand tigers yoked together, of a spaceplane's gravity-well drive as it flew in to land.

He shaded his eyes with one hand and peered out and upwards. It was a Cyclops — a warship: arc-wings crawling with guns over a powerful engine, giving it the best speed-to-firepower ratio of any ship class in use on the Septième. He activated his jack camera and zoomed in. Two logos on its tail: the planetary flag, shiny bright paint stripes no more than five years old, and above it in faded, chipped black, the charging bull logo of the planet's governor, Martinez.

Through glasses, the ship looked old: rusted at the join between wings and central hull, with dirty patches on its belly where oil had stained it one time too many and now could not be removed. One of Martinez's old squad ships from the days when he'd been a high-tonnage pirate, before he'd settled down and decided which planet to steal: a ship now turned over – with the same crew – to planetary police, defence or customs duty.

Connor grimaced up at the ship. He couldn't begrudge any degree of safety for his primary planet of operation. He couldn't therefore begrudge Martinez's order of a dozen brand new Cyclopes direct from their Union manufacturer to bolster the defence fleet. Had Connor been invited to play middleman in the deal, though, he and his bank account would have been gratified.

At least, this way, if anything went wrong, he wouldn't get any blame.

*

CHAPTER TWO

Several years previously, Éloise Falavière had informed Connor that if he ever dealt in drugs or flesh she would kill him. Given that Éloise was one of the more strait-laced members of a strait-laced society (in those respects: Connor had seen things on Port Logis that made his Septième head turn), he had taken the warning in the spirit in which it was intended, especially as he did not wish to force his brother to choose between blood and love.

How exactly he was to forge a lasting reputation on the Septième underside without trading in such staple commodities as drugs and flesh, Éloise had not bothered to elucidate. Connor had spent some days thereafter staring at a spiderplan of Septième trading conglomerates and economic reports from Neuvième and Treizième planets, before travelling to Port Logis, paying dutiful heed to his niece and nephew, and starting what would be a year-long discussion with his brother's stepfather about trading licences and insurrectionism.

There was money in anything if a man held his head and took his time. But whether a man shipped legal-strength weed and handmade lace from the Septième to the Neuvième or kept his business restricted to the Septième underside, whether he trafficked street girls to brothels thousands of parsecs from home or brokered protection rackets across a hundred planets, he needed contacts, a route into the power structure that would not offend – and weapons. Lots of weapons.

As a lieutenant in Meris Hardblade's employ, Connor had undertaken weapon procurement for his teams and had picked up a range of interesting information on the politics of supply to one gang or another, but hadn't had occasion to consider how guns got into gun shops in the first place. It surprised him, at first, how easy it was to order handguns, rifles and their plasma packs wholesale. Septième models weren't as advanced as Union or Federation versions but it didn't take much in the way of refinement to fire a plasma burst into an unprotected body. Neither did it take much refinement to produce cluster bombs. Cheap weapons were in steady demand on the Septième and, to his initial surprise (though not Dominic Falavière's), among a few separatist movements on the Federation's borders.

The wider underside thought of export the way Connor had once thought of it: sell what was easy – children to brothels and mines, narcotics to the rich or to local gatekeepers keen to maximise profit-to-risk ratio. Connor did run legal drugs, namely tobacco, cannabis and whisky, into the Neuvième, not that the Port Logis Customs discussed how he'd got the whisky *out* of the Federation. But his primary income source quickly became firearms.

And for emphasis, he had Éloise.

One day when her third child was barely three months old, very soon after she'd declared herself fit for work, she and Connor had been walking together through a firearms factory, Éloise with the baby tucked into her shawl, when one of the security guards had fired a pistol at Connor from less than a yard away. Éloise had caught the bolt in the palm of her right hand, handed the baby to Connor – still dribbling milk – and beaten the would-be assassin to death with a brand new six-calibre rifle and her own foot, before threatening the owner with a substantial lawsuit for forcing her son – *"clearly underage"* – to witness a killing. Something about the way the factory foundations had creaked underfoot as she spoke convinced the man she was serious, more than the lore and law banning Circle Spellweavers from lying. Connor had come away with a half share in the business (he'd since bought the other half). "Not a bad wage for an hour's work," Éloise had said once they were clear. Connor had given her enough of a bonus to buy two new formal shawls of silk and lace. Logan, upon hearing the story, had given her another child, though it had died pre-term. She had become pregnant again two months later. This one would be born in a few weeks.

Éloise was not a panacea – her grasp of eleven of the thirteen spell-threads was rudimentary – but she still had a talent for frightening people. Standing next to a bodyguard who could not be injured in any way gave Connor something of an advantage whether he was meeting suspicious resistance armies, wary manufacturers or underside chiefs. Connor had understood since he was very young, when he'd first watched his mother read a grasping despot's future in her deck of cards, the importance of using every advantage that came to one's hand. Éloise represented more than a woman: Connor's stepsister, with two adult brothers and a horde of other relations, his staff's good luck charm, his rivals' bogeywoman.

And the bogeywoman was several thousand light years away, probably drinking tea in a hot tub while waiting to present Connor with a third nephew.

It wasn't Yasmine's fault she wasn't Éloise, and a change kept everyone – including Connor – on their toes. No point considering the possibility that 'someone' had taken advantage of Éloise's absence to kill one of Connor's most menial staff members. Ten marks said whoever had killed Merissa hadn't considered her as anything more than an annoyance.

'Someone' appeared to have taken advantage of Éloise's absence to test his security, however: when he checked for jack messages on the way out of Merissa's flat, he found a note from his factory manager, Mina Jai. Instead of heading straight back to the office he drove over to the factory, taking Marcello to mind his car.

Tucked away from the city centre, in an industrial estate halfway to the spaceport with its closest neighbour a fish cannery, Connor's factory/warehouse complex was a hundred acres wide. Connor drew his car up at the fence and waited in the scanner till its lights flashed green and the gate widened for him. Had he jumped the fence, as often seemed tempting, the AA gun on the factory roof would have swivelled straight to him and started warming its particle accelerator. He preferred having its barrel facing away from him.

The main car park was next to the warehouse – the factory, alongside and linked to the warehouse by internal passages, had much more tightly controlled access. Connor swung away from the main loading door and drew up next to the pedestrian door just as it opened.

Mina Jai drew little attention: she was neither small nor large, neither smart nor scruffy, neither very dark nor overly fair. Drawing minimal attention was the way she liked life. She managed the factory – producing small arms and armaments – and its associated warehouse competently and without tolerating graft, with her only vice a prolonged tendency to complain whenever Connor imported a new good that she had to find room for in the warehouse. If he wanted to add a new production line, he'd have to do so elsewhere.

She looked mildly harassed as she opened Connor's car door for him and dropped a tiny curtsey, frowning into space past the car's nose. "Thank you for heading over," she said. "I'm not happy with any of this."

"What happened?"

"I don't know. That's what I'm least happy with." Behind her, the door beeped and began to swing shut: she waved her ring-key at it, and it froze in place. She and Connor slipped through the gap and into the warehouse.

Back corridors, these, but they were clean. Through a thin wall alongside, Connor heard the clunk of staff directing bots to move heavy boxes, and as they passed a glass-fronted door to the main floor, he glanced inside. All looked as it should: completed consignments locked in place and protected by thin force fields until required.

"I've rerun a security audit this morning," Jai said as she led the way up the rickety staircase into the office. "Everything has passed."

"Then what's the issue?"

The boy who checked the automated stock control figures rose and nodded as his bosses entered. Jai motioned for him to stay in place and pressed her finger to her private study door. It opened. She glared at it, and the expression stuck to her face as if she'd smeared herself with honey before she started.

Connor passed her into the study and took the better of the two chairs at her desk. A picture of Jai's daughter, swathed in a Huitième boarding school's blue-and-green uniform shawl, floated in midair above it, next to a firearms order waiting for batch release – Jai or the night manager

Kalysdottir had to unlock every crate that left the warehouse. Connor had reluctantly added himself to the approvals list, but no one else. "I reiterate –"

Jai closed the door. "Mister, you saw how we got in here."

"Your fingerprint."

"Yes. You, Rica Kalysdottir and I are the only people who can open the door. The same applies to eight other doors in this complex. Two of those doors in the warehousing were passed last night, at a time when Rica was over in the factory."

Oh, *perfect*. "How and who?"

She shrugged, wide and expansive. "No indication of either. Just that the doors were opened – not forced, and not via someone using a staff key, which would have left a record on the lock. Fingerprint opened, which, given Rica was five hundred yards away chatting to the shift manager, means by you or me – and I know neither of us was here last night."

"Would that I could produce a witness."

The study had a high narrow window on one side and a wide, broad one on the other. The narrow window let in fitful daylight: the broad one gave a view of the warehouse floor. Connor stood and walked to it, looking down over the concrete expression of what he was starting to achieve.

Not all his money was here: for a start, he had a secured loan from the governor, Rafael Martinez, and a second smaller one from the hefty ganglander Fai Comet, as personal security. Men killed their creditors more quickly than their debtors. Thereby, *almost* all of his money was here, bar that sitting in a bank in case he needed to repay his loans in a hurry.

Every batch of completed goods, whether sold or unsold, still in its protective packaging, sat behind force fields or in inch-thick steel containers in the warehouse below. Under the floor, two storeys down, lurked a vault coated in some of Éloise's best shield-work, holding a few crates of finished goods as emergency stores for Connor's own merc strings, hard ownership records for some of Connor's properties, and a couple of items purloined by or for him over the past two years that he hadn't needed or wanted to use yet.

"I assume you've been over the security data for last night."

"Target and Ambrose are doing that at the moment."

Anna Target, duty security chief, and her deputy, Luc Ambrose. "Send me the results. Keep an eye for anything missing. Is anything overtly missing?"

"Computer says no. Kael is checking the stock lists to be certain." She waved a hand in the young stock controller's vague direction. "But things have been – moved." She came up beside him and stared down at the warehouse floor. "Chairs out of place. A crate of 3K plasma packs that looks like it was stood on. Tiny signs that someone did something out of the ordinary here."

And it was such an ordinary operation. Connor sighed. "Whatever comes up, tell me. Anything you find missing. Any sign you find of how –" or whether – "anyone got in."

"Yes, Mister." Jai hesitated. "If you leave too quickly the staff will worry. Would you like a cup of tea?"

"Spare me from that. I'll be getting too much of it over the next few weeks."

A reluctant smile curved her lips. "I'd like to meet your new Éloise."

"She isn't an Éloise, but if you trap your finger in one of those print-locked doors, she'll be able to glue it back on for you."

"A *useful* one, then."

From what he'd seen of Yasmine? Yes, useful. Might be as argumentative as Jai if anything happened that upset her principles.

After a pause designed to fool the stock controller – currently re-checking for missing goods – into thinking nothing was amiss, Connor left the warehouse. He had plenty of work awaiting him at the office: final veto on a few new hires, three sets of rivals' company accounts stolen for him by Éloise's half-brother Calad – Circle Spellweavers had a relaxed attitude to other people's secrets, having none themselves – and final preparations for a meeting with Rafael Martinez's personal security staff five days hence. And he would definitely address all of those tasks today. He did, though, request his head of security's presence in his office as soon as he got back.

"Been busy, Mister?" Pritie Mayasdottir asked as she entered his study, gesturing to the blood-specks on his clothes. Connor grimaced. Jai hadn't mentioned those.

"I'll change before I see anyone else. When did you last do a routine inspection at the factory?"

She frowned a little. "Seven weeks ago, as I recall."

"Bring the next one forward if you can spare a few hours. There may have been a breach."

"May?"

"So far there's no concrete evidence." Evidence. "On a separate topic, we're down one in circumstances I dislike." Not a big 'one', not an important 'one', but maybe that was why she had died. "I need you to pull out all the camera records from last night from the streets round the Michael Driver Road and Long Lane junction."

"What time last night?"

Yasmine and her time of death uncertainty. "Say from around ten in the evening till two in the morning."

Pritie nodded. She was short even for a Septième woman, a foot below Connor's height, and her plump, calm exterior radiated reassurance, but she'd been known to throw Éloise occasionally in hand-to-hand sparring practice. The only other Septième-born human Connor had seen throw Éloise in training was his brother Logan, Éloise's husband, and that she probably regarded as foreplay.

"What are we looking for?" Pritie said.

"A man…" Connor hesitated. He didn't know anything. "Someone strong. I'd assumed human male, but not necessarily."

"The primary predator of the human female is the human male," Pritie murmured.

"Exactly. Far from sole predator. Could have been a strong female, could be many other species. Not Dalishian: too big, and no slime-trace on the room. Sapilian would be too small."

"Ditan?"

"Strong enough."

"Silicon does that." She smiled with little mirth. "What else?"

"He – I use the pronoun for convenience – took the weapon with him."

"Not shot?" Connor shook his head. "OK, we have an individual with a bloodstained hammer or similar. Though why he didn't just wipe it and leave it I don't know. If the DNA banks are so inaccurate that Elena Mitran's murderer walked free – and she with a million marks or so sunk into the mines – why worry about killing one girl?"

Why even *think* about killing one expendable girl? Why care about reaction and counter-play? "Maybe she hit him first. Pissed him off. Her fingers were broken."

Pritie frowned. Strands of her straight black hair wafted around her face in time with her breathing. "I'll go round to her flat later. Not, Mister, that I think you've missed anything, but you've piqued my interest. When I heard she was dead I assumed it was the usual story –"

"It may yet be the usual story." And he'd tried so hard to soften his men's attitudes that Merissa's death had startled him out of his routine. It was for their own good as much as anything else. Éloise didn't often kill in retaliation for rudeness, but other Neuvième women were less forgiving, and Connor didn't want the hassle of having to over-think his entourage for every trip to Port Logis. "But I'm suspicious. Did Yasmine look in here before meeting me?"

Pritie's eyebrows shot up. "Yasmine Alesi Matthieu or Yasmine Simonstone Falavière?"

"The latter, and I assume not. She went off to organise an autopsy. Talk to her when she gets back."

Pritie snorted. "That's a given, or I never met a Neuvième woman."

She nodded to Connor and withdrew to her holdfast downstairs, blessed with direct upload from the security cameras. Connor read and reread Harlow-Crichton's corporate accounts – less interesting than he'd first thought: why did people always pick the same way to hide their graft? Petty, foolish creatures, always making it so easy for a bright man to take advantage of them. The only true point of interest was that Harlow-Crichton was a Union manufacturer. Very small, or, as they put it, 'boutique'. Connor had expected that in the land of audited accounts one would have to be more careful. He sighed. Maybe this revealed another weakness, structure as well as psychology, a twist of practice that he could use. He'd fly over there in a few months' time when he had Éloise back beside him looking dangerous.

Life was a balancing job, a high-wire walk with oblivion below, but one undertaken carrying a string of dead weights instead of a balance bar. Money begat more money: advancement required investment, and while his factory formed a steady income stream, he'd need a further lump sum from somewhere to push forward into more income.

Dominic Falavière might be good for an investment. The White Canyon team might come through with a licensing proposition… and mice might learn to dance.

A fresh letter popped up on his desk. No subject: a note from Connor's long-term friend, on-off lover and frequent collaborator, Thakar A'syan. Connor opened it, strange reluctance slowing his hand. Nothing earth-shattering. Chit-chat about the business deal he had set up in four days' time: a little coyness about the deal's topic maybe meant he was skirting closer to the wind of what a Circle Weaver found acceptable than Connor ever would. Random chat about his staff, office and life. The kind of thing they would have discussed over coffee if they were working together: a window into a mind, a connection via mundanity. Connor had never been good at small talk: he'd preferred just sitting back and listening.

The intercom built into his desk pinged: a call directly from Pritie's office. He closed Thakar's letter and hit the button. "Got him?" he said.

"No." She sounded troubled. "No one on foot, no one on a bike, no car driver, entered the building – other than two small females, one elderly, whom I've identified as fellow residents."

And this death had not been an argument about whose loud sex had disturbed who over the past month. "When did Merissa get back from her night out?"

"I haven't seen her either yet. I'll run the recording backwards till I find her." She clicked her tongue against her teeth, one of her nervous tics Connor tried not to find too annoying. "You do realise that her boy may have realised she walked out last night with someone else."

"Firstly, he's offworld, or I'd have sent a man to drag him out of Comet's office already – or straight into Comet's holding cells. Secondly, I've met him. He didn't seem the kind to demand rectitude."

"Men change their minds."

They did, and Connor certainly wasn't ruling out the pleasant young ganglander having asked a friend to check up on his girl while he was away. Connor stared back at the accounts, numbers jingling in their columns, credits, debits, projections, actuality. The smallest thing could come to matter too much.

"Gone back two more hours. No Merissa," Pritie said. "Nobody."

This was no use. Connor stood up, packed away the accounts, and headed downstairs. As he stepped onto the middle landing he heard his office door lock behind him, too slow, as it always was.

Downstairs – the office had only two storeys – he cut right and right again into Pritie's sanctum. She had back door, front door and garage feeds of the apartment complex up on her desk, and a fourth camera on an opposite block's eaves that showed a view of Merissa's window, all four running backwards at high speed. She shifted sideways when she saw Connor, and he pulled up a spare chair beside her and joined her and her auto-software in staring at the images.

And nothing. And still nothing.

Pritie paused the feeds when the background colours began to wash with faint sunlight. "This is seven yesterday evening. She never came home."

"She was there, dead."

"And got in how?" Pritie set the feeds to wind back further. People exiting the apartment block. Merissa exiting, at six the previous evening, dressed for some decorous clubbing in the same skirt and slim crop-top in which Connor'd seen her dead. "She's not the invisible woman, Mister."

In answer Connor flipped the feeds to the start of Pritie's backwards search, and ran them forwards at the same speed. A few more residents trickling home, all of them matching up to photos of those who belonged in the flats. A delivery boy toting in a cartload of vegetables, and running out a few minutes later to wave at a passing enforcer wearing Connor's badge – to ask, as Connor knew he would, about the blood trickle coming from under one of the doors.

He paused the feeds. "It must have been a neighbour," he said, but the words did not sound convincing even to himself. Merissa had paid so much for that block because it was respectable – because her neighbours were the sort to pay the same amount for safety.

"Her date last night," Pritie said. "Did he have the skills to smuggle a dead body into a block of flats past a bevy of cameras?"

"I don't have ID on him yet. A foreigner, the street says." The drifters said, that meant. So no connection to Martinez, or to his high underside backer Fai Comet, or to the biggest gang lord native to the planet, Nikalar Saxen – unless the foreigner was one of the charity workers who'd killed a recent deal Saxen had hooked, or some government representative looking for a Septième gang lord to buy as their representative abroad. "She'd seen him the previous afternoon too. A known quantity, or so she would have thought."

Pritie hissed. "When she scooted out of the office that afternoon she had coffee with a boy with Cliff Enterprises written on his sleeve. I was in the same café."

"Were you?" The words fell out of his mouth, sourer than cherries.

Cliff, the biggest conglomerate in the UISS. Cliff, trader via subsidiaries in every item imaginable, and, in its own right, arms manufacturer. An arms manufacturer busy importing warships on its own ticket, which looked on Septième traders as mosquitoes.

Approaching a Cliff employee with questions about a murder would be akin to a mouse trying to filch a tiger's food. He couldn't even begin to try. "OK. Put out a call to any watchers we have in the city centre for anything that happened last night. Try to track Merissa from there: where they ate, what they did, who they spoke to." He'd room to hope that a so-respectable merchant with a Union paycheque to spend had nothing to do with anything. But any string of coincidences could only be drawn out so far. "Wait till you have something before you take it to Cliff."

"Why?"

He'd be happier if he *didn't* know. "Martinez is dealing with Cliff directly. A small matter of an upgrade to the planetary defence fleet."

Pritie's eyes, river-dark, watched Connor as if from a little way away. "There's no export or manufacture licence in the offing, is there, Mister?"

"No. White Canyon, I might be able to swing for something more, if they don't make that operation their water-sniff and then spit me out – seems they're nervous about getting involved on the Septième: don't see how I could sneak antimagic into their wares – but nothing doing with Cliff. It seems they don't touch the underside under any circumstances, antimagic or not."

And if he went chasing one of their boys over a dead Septième girl, they might never do so. Never tangle with an authority like that.

Connor closed his eyes. "Send the Cliff team the politest message you can manage. Information that might be of help to us, public duty, et cetera, et cetera. It may induce a bite: you never know."

He couldn't bring himself to burn this bridge before he'd stepped onto it. Not in his line of work, not as a man who liked his opportunities. But if any member of Cliff's team had decided to kill a girl just because they could – because they could never be caught, because such behaviour was tacitly accepted in this galactic sector – he wouldn't let it go, no matter the cost.

*

CHAPTER THREE

Connor cracked open his eyes. Black night stared back at him, and curtains made phosphorescent by lamplight beyond: a ghost-world and a phantasm, Mirqest's capital at four in the morning. Outside, he could hear trucks rumbling to early-start businesses, and cats howling one to another, ready to mate or kill.

A breeze brushed his cheek.

He slid a hand under his pillow. No gun. A finger touched his lips: "Be quiet," a voice breathed, though there was no voice and no finger either.

Instead of phoning via jack for a guard, he sat up in bed. His rooms were more luxurious than those of his staff, though not by much more than tradition dictated: a private suite accessed from his study, with ensuite bathroom and room in his bed for two, though he'd never yet tested the springs. A reading chair, shelving unit and side table sat in the corner, darkness infesting them. A pale ghost was sitting in the chair, staring at him.

Connor relaxed, not without difficulty. The ghost, though tall, had a female silhouette, and the hair drifting around it like spider-webs was waist length instead of shoulder-length. Faint copper tones glinted off the hair in the near-dark. "Atalanta. You could have knocked."

"Then how would you have learnt that your security was compromised?" Spoken aloud, her voice was remote and chilly, and *very* foreign – a voice from the Premier sector, the heart of the Earth Federation, and a voice several steps in social class up from Connor and his crew of ex-gutter rats.

"How is it compromised?"

"I asked Pritie to unlock your bedroom window. She did."

"She'll have assumed you didn't come here to kill me, however poor those assumptions may have been." White women made bad spies, he'd decided some time previously. Too rare in much of the galaxy other than the Premier and Treizième, and too prone to shining in the dark: Atalanta's skin glimmered, pellucid and exotic.

She made an excellent official spy, though… which was what she'd become as soon as her controllers realised she was romantically involved with Éloise's half-brother. The Neuvième's ruling Circle Weavers made a habit of finding covert spies and ensuring their careers were brief, but were wonderfully accommodating of ones who stated their position in advance.

Spy, housebreaker, troublemaker, *Guild Spellweaver*. Connor shook himself. He knew better than to taint any man or woman with the label of his or her culture. If he didn't hold anything against Éloise for being a Circle mercenary, he shouldn't hold anything against Atalanta for being a Guild patriot.

Patriot of somewhere a very long way away from here. "If you've fallen out with Calad I can give you house-room for a few days –" She was just too quiet, he realised, even for a watchful woman. "What?"

"I regret to inform you," she said at her most cold and well-bred, "that my father-in-law, whom my relatives by marriage persist in calling my stepfather, has died. You need to come to Port Logis."

Connor exhaled. Dominic, dead. It wasn't too much of a surprise – powerful Spellweavers' magic always ate them in the end, and better the physical threads than the mental ones: the insanity caused by the latter was more wearing on the relatives. That didn't blunt his immediate burst of regret.

"I'm sorry to hear it." She half-shrugged but did not reply. Some of the paleness surrounding her was her clothing: she'd covered up with grey over-garments but beneath was wearing white, the Neuvième mourning colour. "Where's Calad?"

"Heading to Port Logis to meet up with his half-siblings, I believe." Still the clipped tones, still the over-precise *words*, and Connor restrained a curse.

"You *have* had a row with him. Dear sweet angels –"

"Fewer religious metaphors, please: it's been a bone of contention." Her voice grew harsher. If Connor hadn't known her so well he would have wondered if she were crying. "I don't care how many entities he believes in, so long as he keeps his relationship with them separate from his relationship with me."

Calad and Atalanta had no children from two years of marriage. Neither of them had passed twenty years old. Calad, half Neuvième and half Treizième, wouldn't be expected to have children that early – but among Atalanta's people, marriage was expected to produce babies, and quickly. If it did not, the marriage should be dissolved to allow the partners to find someone who *could* reproduce with them. For six thousand years, women from Earth had had difficulty conceiving and staying pregnant – and couldn't welcome platitudes when they didn't.

"Gisele's position appears to have bypassed what passes for Calad's mind," Atalanta continued. "God knew I didn't think he had much backbone." Factually incorrect, from what Connor had seen. "He could at least have stuck up for his mother."

"Maybe he doesn't think there's anything anyone can do. She broke the biggest taboo there is –"

"*They* did. Gisele, and Dominic. It takes two to marry, in case you've not noticed."

"What was he meant to do for her after his death?"

"He thought of everything else: he should have thought about that too."

If Dominic had considered anything unrelated to his own wellbeing in the past fifty years, Connor would be very surprised, but he held his peace. "Well, I'll see for myself soon enough. When's the funeral?"

"Tomorrow. You're lucky you've got time to get there. It would have been sooner but Michel couldn't get off assignment any quicker."

In the dark she wouldn't be able to see Connor's expression, and she wasn't one for random mind-reading. Michel – well, his compassionate leave conversation would have been interesting: *'Last time your brother didn't turn out to be dead after all. Are you sure your father hasn't just gone missing?'*

"If I don't need to go haring off to distant planets in the middle of the night, I won't. Stay here and get some sleep till dawn."

"I'm fine."

"I'm not. I spent yesterday looking for lines on a murderer who probably doesn't even count what he did as murder, and I'm tired."

"What makes you think I was going to wait for you?"

"Putting off the moment of return as long as possible." She snorted something that might have been a laugh. "Get some rest, even if you don't sleep, and we can toddle back to the family bosom together. There's a spare room three doors down that was stoved last week."

"You know how to make anything sound pleasant." She rose. "What's your great conundrum?"

"Didn't you ask Yasmine already?"

"Dominic was her uncle. She exhibited conventional reactions."

So she had gone to Yasmine, and Pritie, first. Maybe she'd learnt something on Port Logis. "A woman went out with a perfectly nice boy and turned up later at home, dead, having never re-entered the building."

"Mistaken identity? Illusion?"

"Yasmine tasted no spell-threads on the flat." And, from what Connor's spies had gleaned the previous afternoon, the boy was no Spellweaver.

"Then I see what catches your eye." She rose from the chair, closed the window and went to the door between bedroom and semi-public study. Connor still saw shade and shadow more than anything else. He felt, all of a sudden, old and tired. Dominic had lived to nearly seventy, older than many Weavers of his skill, but half the lifespan he would have lived – on his clean, high-tech homeworld – if he'd been born with no spell-threads in his mind. In the end, would he have traded power for life? No Circle Weaver whom Connor'd ever met would admit that they would sacrifice their power: but Connor remembered Dominic, proud and erect, despite the pain eating into his bones every day, and thirsty for life – passionate in a way Connor had rarely experienced. If he'd stopped using the magic at forty, he could have lived another ten or twenty years longer than he had.

Nothing in life was free, on the Septième, the Neuvième or anywhere else. Every bill was paid in the end, even those the rich and indolent folk managed to push off onto servants or younger generations. Neuvième Circle Weavers prided themselves on paying their bills themselves. Maybe Dominic had understood and accepted it.

"Atalanta."

She stopped with a pale hand on the door. "What?"

"Who's the new head of the family?" Not *family* as in children, parents, siblings and grandchildren: *family* as in the whole bickering, quarrelsome Falavière clan. The new arse to sit on a cushioned seat in Port Logis's parliament. The new commander of a private army four hundred strong.

"They'll decide after the funeral."

"They?"

"You think you and I will be heeded?" She withdrew. Connor heard the study door to the corridor open and, eventually, close itself behind her.

He stared at the ceiling, still and dark now. A new head for the Falavières, after thirty or more years with Dominic at the helm. Two of Dominic's three sisters were still alive, Amalie and Alazais, but they'd racked up too many internecine conflicts in their long lives: same went for their first and second cousins and surviving aunts. Amalie's one daughter was no leader, but a sighing thin woman old before her time. Long-dead Gauzia had left six children who took little part in family affairs. Of Dominic's three children, Michel would have been a steady pair of hands were he not in the Union military, with loyalties divided. Éloise had the drive and grit to handle conflict, but at twenty-five, even if she were already halfway through a shortened life, she was too young to dole out orders to women past a hundred years old. Calad would never be considered. Far too young, and his mother had been his father's second wife, a taboo only a man like Dominic would consider breaking.

That left Alazais's massive brood, of whom Yasmine was one of the younger members: fifteen children by four husbands (none married: she had not made Dominic's error of marrying too frequently, or at all), and another fifteen stepchildren those husbands had contributed to the ménage in one way or another. Them, second or third degree relations, more distant cousins: over a hundred candidates were neither too young to lead nor too old to have caused entrenched conflicts.

Connor closed his eyes. Praise God he was too distant a connection even to rate consideration: running a merc gang and an arms dealership was hard work enough for him. Some relative or other – of middle years, probably female… and for a moment he remembered Gisele the last time he had seen her, smiling up at Dominic as if they were both half their age. Still a foreign girl fond of fripperies, but sheltered from older women's disapproving stares by her husband's towering reputation.

And now Dominic was dead, and Gisele's stepchildren had tolerated her more than liked her, and her son was not the man to defend her…

For half a second Connor wondered whether to hate Dominic Falavière, or whether Gisele would come to hate his memory in the end.

He fell asleep again with Gisele's vague pampered smile pressed against his eyelids, and woke a little way past dawn. A page had come in with his morning coffee, and had set it on the side table in its normal place, but was still in the room, standing staring at another object on the table, a sheet of rainbow-coloured paper folded into a 3-D letter psi. "It's fine," Connor said. "She was testing the security." The child blinked at Connor a few times and scurried out.

Connor pulled on a dressing gown, wandered to the table and picked up the paper. It glittered – the Guild's symbol, with the Guild's magic folded into it. Atalanta had shown him once how she could set a trap into a fold of paper: a mind-fuddler, or a tiny electric shock, nothing large enough for comparative electric load to tear the paper, but enough to incapacitate. As Connor unfolded the paper rainbow, his brain-fog lifted, and the morning, seeping in through the window, looked brighter. Vague sounds outside sharpened.

He dressed quickly, slipped the paper into his trouser pocket, read his overnight message feed – several, and he hoped Atalanta hadn't read them all: nothing here to which a Circle Weaver would object, but the Guild had compunctions against the more refined types of blackmail and extortion – and, after locking the messages down again, went in search of Spellweavers. He found them together, in the officers' mess, reading news reports and drinking tea. Yasmine was standing: Atalanta was perched on a stool. She'd probably forgotten to tell Yasmine that she was allowed to sit down. Atalanta was married, and Yasmine was not. Atalanta's people did not draw such a sharp distinction in manners, but Neuvième formality was insidious.

For a moment Connor visualised the hyper-competent, aloof Atalanta leading the Falavière family. He dismissed the idea. She was more foreign than Gisele and was a Guild Weaver to boot. "Which death is under discussion?" he said.

Yasmine looked up. She'd been crying. "Six people were murdered in this city last night. That doesn't include armed arguments." Her tone was unfriendly.

"Were any of them my staff? Did any of them die on my streets?"

"No."

"Then I can do nothing, and you'd do better to find whichever gang lord does own those streets."

"They *died –*"

"And *I can do nothing*." He stared her down. She was tall, like most women of her people: he was taller, though not by much. "Your cousin sent you here, Mistress, to do a job of work. If you don't like it, leave and send someone who can."

"As you wish." Sulky tones, those of a Weaver who would obey orders but little more. "I need to bathe."

"Then we'll have to leave a few hours earlier than scheduled. I told Éloise I would build a bathhouse when I had money to spare. Till that day arrives you'll have to content yourself with washing."

She sniffed, disgust wrinkling her face. "Do none of you ever bathe?"

"Only when we visit the Neuvième. Next stupid question?"

"What happens while you're away?" She waved a hand at the window. "Your streets: you said so. Do your people," and her voice took on a mocking tone, "forget what you are when you aren't here."

"Not when I'm visiting my Circle relatives." He walked to the desk and peered at the women's news page. Local news spewing local murders, per Yasmine's complaint, and other crimes. A robbery of a merchant who paid Connor for protection: Pritie would have already sent a squad. An intimation that one of the Cliff crew was having an affair with Rafael Martinez: not likely, as Martinez's kept woman, if not his wife, would have made a fuss. A rumour copied from (and, unusually, credited to) the Septième Commodity Market's news division: a potential terrorist attack on the Federation starfleet – a blown-out experimental battleship, allegedly ultra-high-tech: enough to make Connor hope he hadn't sold said terrorists the explosive used. Ten unidentified corpses, weeks or months dead, found in a warehouse across the city, notable for their right hands rather than the left missing their little fingers: an upper-crust murderer trying to make his or her actions look like an underside killing, and failing. A tiny temple of Beauty blackened from fire. City police, Martinez's enforcers, foiling an attack on a wealthy merchant's mansion.

The usual, in other words. Quieter in his area than anyone else's: that was the kind of calculation that increased a man's territory.

'*All this,*' he imagined one of the elder pirates or one of his direct competitors saying, '*and you're worrying about a dead cleaning girl?*'

Worry about every little detail: that was the best lesson in life he'd ever learned. Pay attention to the details and the big puzzle would shake itself out. In the end, Éloise's list of interdictions – '*drugs, slaves and whores*', he remembered her saying, blood in her voice and on her shoes – would be his strength. In the end, he'd have an empire the size of any on the Septième, no matter how he had to get it.

'*Petty ambitions,*' he thought he heard Dominic saying, voice full of scorn. '*Aim for what you do not believe you can achieve. Aim for the highest spot you can see in whatever sphere you choose, and in the leap, you will reach further than you ever dreamed.*'

And for a Circle Weaver, aiming high – being the best – always meant an early death. Dominic would have known, and remained unafraid.

He scrolled down the page. There, in glorious 3-D, was a

snapshot of one of the new defence ships – a Cyclops warship, one of the twelve Martinez had ordered, its arching wings spiked with particle guns and a plasma cannon gracing its belly. Connor flipped the page shut. He couldn't afford to sigh over a deal he'd had no way of brokering, whatever the percentage would have been. Better to consider an earlier shipment Martinez had bought, one brokered by Connor and originating from White Canyon, three hundred aerial mortars (one of which had fallen off the lorry: a reverse-engineered version was in the safe in Mina Jai's study – another vertically integrated export good for the future). The White Canyon link he could exploit in future. Cliff, for now, was out of his reach.

Yes, consider how to make best use of his White Canyon link. But perhaps he should also consider how in hells' names Rafael Martinez had planned to pay for not one but *twelve* brand new ships mounting quite that many guns.

*

CHAPTER FOUR

Bodies waited only for as long as no one wanted to bury them. With Merissa recumbent in the morgue and set to stay there, Connor led the way off-planet in a tiny convoy of two: *Shadowmark*, his personal Hamadryad-hull light freighter, and Atalanta's tiny hired Fey – hired, apparently, so that Calad couldn't work out where she had gone.

"Where's your ship?" Connor asked over the radio as soon as they had transited from atmosphere to zero-gee.

"Flying a tow round a few mining stations on autopilot. I hope Calad got tired and dusty before heading home."

Most autopilots could not travel through E-R Bridges from one planet to another, but there were ways to jemmy the things to permit Bridge transit. Travelling through a Bridge that way verged on suicidal, but if one's ship were empty all one risked was the money – of which Atalanta was not blessed with large quantities: the money in their marriage was Calad's. Atalanta's people had land and a pedigree, but no real wealth.

As the artificial gravity slowly wound up, Yasmine entered the flight deck, having used her cabin bunk as an anti-G couch during take-off and transition. She had changed into Neuvième casual clothes: loose wrap-on trousers and a thigh-length tunic, both of them white, with a lightweight white scarf tossed over one shoulder. Either she'd expected a bereavement while she was away or she'd bought a few dozen feet of white cotton that morning. Could easily be the latter. Connor had seen Éloise convert thirty feet of silk into a shawl and trousers with the aid of a sewing machine, a pair of scissors and some embroidery thread in the space of an hour and a half, when she'd needed to accompany him to a meeting with an easily-impressed bigwig, her children had played dress-up with her formal clothes, and the mining station where they were stuck lacked a proper boutique.

He motioned Yasmine to a chair at the nav desk, and rose from the copilot's seat – Marcello was piloting – far enough to turn on the radio. Atalanta picked up within moments.

"Have either of you had any bright ideas about the amazing teleporting body?" he said.

"I wish there were such a thing as teleportation," Atalanta answered, her voice slightly distorted from the space between them. "However. Illusion rarely fools cameras, even if there were any traces, and there weren't."

"Certain techniques can work," Yasmine said, hands clasped in a demure pose and eyes lowered. Connor frowned. Without Atalanta physically present, there was no need for that level of formality.

"Nine times out of ten," Atalanta answered, "people forget to use those techniques. Besides, we both checked for trace. Nothing."

"Did you dye your hair when you went out?" Connor asked.

"No one stopped me," she said, with an air of mild exasperation. "Not your security, not the police. Neither did 'port security hassle me as I went to my ship."

"You are a young and vaguely attractive female."

"Security staff are trained to watch out for young and vaguely attractive females on the prowl."

"In my experience they often forget." He smiled sourly at Yasmine's incredulous gaze. "When we land on the Septième again, I hope you spend at least a few minutes enjoying feeling like the less dangerous sex." Marcello side-eyed Connor at that. He'd been to the Neuvième before – maybe not often enough.

Yasmine cleared her throat. "Pritie called me while we were in phase transition. One of Eliss al'Trier's women came to her full of gossip this morning."

That could have been an interesting discussion. Trier was a racketeer new to the scene, prickly in her doings and keen to pry trade from more established names. "How much gossip?"

"The woman wanted info on your deal with Cliff Enterprises."

Connor laughed aloud. "I wish I had a deal with Cliff –"

"Because Merissa was sharing a table with not one but *three* of their team, and they all seemed very happy."

Yasmine fiddled with her jack for a moment, and Connor blinked as a photograph flashed up inside his eyeball. Yes, that was Merissa, on the far right, smiling up at a clean-cut young man just as shy and engaging. Her black, curly hair bushed around her shoulders and down her back, accentuating her thin cheeks and her prominent collarbones. She seemed happy, indeed.

If she had been happy, the other woman in shot had been downright delighted. She was laughing straight at the photographer – Trier's lieutenant – eyes shut and head tossed back. Long, straight, dark hair slicked down the sides of her face to vanish behind her back, hair that was glossy with health and life, as was her deep bronze skin. A foreigner: mostly New World by the cheek shape, but not entirely, wearing a Septième-cut shirt in too fine a cloth for her environment.

Her hand rested on a man's arm: a New World pureblood man, the oldest of the four in the picture by a good few years, with hair once short caught back into a tiny plait as if he'd tried his best to fit in to Septième fashion. Plump upper body, heavy shoulders and a few facial lines: he was smiling at the foreign woman with a degree of fondness that suggested a long relationship.

"It is worth asking," Yasmine said. "Even if you threaten to tell their bosses what they were doing: make a night on the drink seem worse than it was. If they'd only talk to you…"

"I'll try them when we get back," Connor said. "If I take you, with your wings out, they might even tell me the truth."

"Why would they lie?" Marcello said. "Why would they want to?"

"To save face," Atalanta said quietly. "The Union says it's cosmopolitan, but that can mask a distrust of foreign ways. Anyone who's been to Port Logis knows exactly how much the Union, as an entity, tolerates other people's cultures."

Given that they tried to wipe the Neuvième's out, went the unspoken addition. *Given that the Circle therefore threw them off the Neuvième, and still kills their people because of the atrocities committed at that time – acts the Union wouldn't even describe now as atrocities, during wartime.*

There was a fundamental disconnect between many

cultures: the Septième's mercantilism lay closer to the Union's ethos than Port Logis and the Circle Neuvième, between the two galactographically, was to either. So far Connor hadn't had much chance to leverage that similarity.

"Commercial secrecy," he said, "for a team that arrived escorting warships. Desire for privacy. Desire to avoid any further upset – if, for instance, one of those three backed a chair over a Kriastan's tail they'd want to dodge any publicity at all till they'd left planet."

"You'd have to get very drunk to do that," Atalanta muttered.

"Too drunk to –"

To murder a Septième girl?

"The boy centre right," Yasmine said, "next to Merissa, is the one Pritie saw her with earlier the same day."

Marcello, eyes still on the sky ahead, grunted. "If she hadn't died I bet she could have fed us a truckload of gossip, straight from the spout. Some foreign half-dick boozes with a Septième girl, she'll screw him for something."

"Not all foreigners –" began Yasmine.

"Both of you shut up," Atalanta said, sharp-voiced. "Does no one think it slightly suspicious that a very high-tech weapons team was out with a girl who was then smuggled – dead or alive – back into her apartment without showing up on a security camera?"

"Your people's tech trends even better," Connor said. "Do you know of a camera blocker discreet enough to edit a couple of people out of a picture while leaving the rest of the images flowing?"

"I don't know all technology inside and out."

Was it Connor's imagination that she stressed the 'all'?

It took the ships ten hours to fly up Mirqest's Highway to the Bridge. Connor had hoped to be asleep for the crossing. As usual he got his timings wrong and woke up to the muted hum of engines changing phase.

The warning bell was muffled in his quarters: why in hells' names did he persistently wake up for crossings? Better to look at the Bridge than not, given that he was awake anyway. He rolled off his bunk, pulled on trousers and tunic – Neuvième house-clothes rather than Septième wear – and went to the flight deck.

Marcello had gone from the controls: Yasmine sat in his place. "Didn't like not watching it either, huh?" Connor said.

"I'll hear it no matter where I am, so I might as well be the first to know it's over." She raised an eyebrow at him. "I knew you and Logan had some Augury, but I didn't realise Bridge travel was that bad for you."

"It isn't as bad for us as for Weavers." Connor took the copilot's seat and stared out at the Bridge ahead: a vast cleft in space, blacker than any night, with occasional flecks of green coruscating across it. Yasmine would see those flecks predominantly as white and blue, with tiny additions for each other magic thread she could use, and would see them as brighter stripes, like an aurora. "Consider, though, that demi-mages can't control our magic."

She wrinkled her nose. "Logan seems to work with his rather than fighting it –"

"He gets Augury bursts playing chess, on a battlefield, and, apparently, when negotiating awkward social situations with people he's never met before – though if he hadn't played some of those right, another battlefield would have resulted. But he did play them right. Even your aunt Amalie likes him."

"She doesn't like anyone, the haughty old bat," Yasmine muttered, though she kept her eyes lowered, for Amalie had been married.

"She comes close enough." The Bridge was too close for Connor's comfort, though not close enough for transit. From here Connor could see its four anchor points straining in space, struggling to maintain orbit against the Bridge's vastness – the Bridge that sought to collapse to nothing. He touched the radio control next to his head. "Atalanta? Are you going first or are we?"

He heard her sigh from a mile or so away. "I'm not going to chase off somewhere completely different on a job."

"I didn't say you would." He waited, with Yasmine slowing *Shadowmark* to a crawl, till she muttered something incomprehensible and accelerated past them.

Her ship slid into the Bridge and vanished. Yasmine counted twenty seconds, aloud, then fed a final boost out of the fusion engines and, as their ship slid up to the Bridge, threw over the singularity drive. Connor braced himself – and *Shadowmark* fell into the Bridge.

The world turned inside out. From far away, he heard a wild animal howling, desperate to rend its prey: the magic, Éloise had told him, though he'd already known. Will-o'-the-wisp danced off the ship's nose, a parody of puppetry, and Connor dragged his eyes from it and to the shielding readout. Depleting at a steady, predictable rate. The only thing that kept the magic from eating them all alive –

– and the blackness parted and the ship slid out over Port Logis.

Connor let out a breath and re-hailed Atalanta. "Shall we convoy down?" No pirates here – they wouldn't live long enough to make a single hit – but she might want to put off arrival.

"I'm not yet at the stage when this *Guild* Weaver is happy driving alone into the seat of *Circle* power. I'll convoy."

Yasmine switched *Shadowmark* to zero-gee engines and set the accelerator to reach eighty percent of their max speed, which was fifty percent of Atalanta's. On-planet radio had come online. It was late at night in the capital city, but that had never stopped Logan from doing anything. Connor opened a text feed and typed, IN-SYSTEM. CALL ME IF AWAKE. CC. Twenty seconds later his jack phone went off.

"How's things?" Logan said down his ear.

"Interesting in a number of uncomfortable ways. How's your wife?"

"Upset." The line had a three second lag due to the distance between ship and surface. It made it hard for Connor to identify deliberate pauses. "I think she's not sure what to –" The jack muted for a couple of seconds and came up again. "Sorry," Logan said. "Toddler wanting to know why I'm whispering. Ellie was already sick of having one dead parent."

"That's a strange way to put things."

"If you were expecting sentimentality, you'd – *assieds-toi.*" The last was at full volume, spoken aloud instead of murmured into a jack's delicate microphone. Connor winced and rubbed his ear.

"I thought the twins slept through."

"It's Nicky. He has episodes."

"I'll be down in ten hours," Connor said, "maybe a little less. Atalanta's with me –"

"Good. Calad went looking for her on Reacher's Crest: he's furious."

"– and so is Yasmine."

"I heard Ellie had sent her over."

Connor grunted, side-eyeing Yasmine. "She's going to a bathhouse."

Logan laughed. "I'm not surprised." In the background Connor heard him wave a jingling toy at his son. "We're at the flat. Come to ours when you get down – there are a few quarrels brewing."

"Gisele?"

"Sure, and then some. A boil between Amalie and her great-aunt flared up – the great-aunt's dead, but she had eight children all of whom had kids of their own. Dominic had had a lid on it for longer than Ellie's been alive. Now they're all posing and it's getting noisy."

Very noisy, if Connor knew the Falavières, and if Logan mentioned gloves being removed he'd be speaking literally. Neuvième folk fought honour duels as often as Kriastans. Legend said Aelin Carrow had forged the first peace between Kriastans and humans: if he'd sent his deputy, Mikhail Ablissan, to assist, Connor would not have been surprised. He'd been a Circle Weaver of the Neuvième, though not of Port Logis.

"So long as my job doesn't follow me here, I'll be happy."

"You might be unlucky. What's the problem?"

"A convoluted explanation that will wait till we're not on time lapse. Suffice it to say that I have two problems, which I thought were separate till a few hours ago."

After a longer pause than was natural, Logan said, "OK. Later. Say hi to the others."

"Will do. Tell Éloise I'll pay my respects as soon as I can." He cut the call.

As he'd spent the past five hours sleeping, Connor retreated to his study and spent the next five hours working, then gave himself another brief nap to try to reset to local time. It didn't refresh him that much. When he returned to the flight deck Marcello was back in the pilot's seat.

"You've a string more business letters," he greeted Connor. "And a garbled note from your brother. Was Mister Logan Cardwain on baby duty last night?"

"If you're not careful he'll have you looking after the twins when we land. Last time I was there they kept trying to climb into ponds, and fountains. If you let his daughter drown you'll be lucky to get a choice of which limb Logan rips off first."

And his eldest son? Connor privately added. But it had always been about Gaia, with Logan, not about Kas, and increasing numbers of sons had changed nothing. Connor would have felt sorry for little Kasimir if his mother hadn't favoured him over his sister – as a Neuvième woman was expected to do.

"When he's left off his Port Logis stay –"

"Oh, we'll have the whole lot of them back sooner than you want, Number Four included."

Marcello grimaced. "One's bad enough if the one's Gaia. Remember how she tried to fly off with Tam Waiter's shuttle?"

"I remember the yelling." Most of it from Gaia and Logan, yelling at each other, though she was three years old and barely thigh-high on him: Kas had contributed a portion, misguidedly trying to rescue his sister from their father, as had Nicky, a baby at the time, reacting to the others. "Providing my niece restricts her kleptomania to other gangs' belongings, I'll be as happy as possible."

"Oh, she didn't want to *steal* it, she wanted to *play* with it. Has anyone given her a flying lesson yet?"

"Logan –" the 'anyone' of Marcello's fancy, for Marcello shared a healthy fear of Logan with over half of Connor's staff – "says she's too short to reach the controls and he'll have to wait another year or two." Marcello half-snorted. "She'll be getting three-weapon combat training when she's five," Connor added, "why not flying?" *And Kas,* he wanted to add. *And Kasimir. To them, they are an 'and'!*

He'd no children: he had little right to call out Logan and Éloise for behaving like Neuvième parents. Sighing, he opened his message box.

Status updates, actions significant enough to require his sign-off: those things were usual. Not usual was a note from Pritie encrypted twice.

Unprecedented fuss and dashings backwards and forwards within the Cliff Enterprises team. Observed hostility between Cliff's representatives and Martinez's senior enforcers. Sudden increase in police activity throughout the capital. House to house searches, without explanation as to what the search was for: hard words between the Cliff guards standing over the new ships and the 'port defence squad. Silence from Martinez.

Connor closed the message. Maybe it was safest, for a couple of days, not to be there. For him, but not necessarily for his crew…

*

CHAPTER FIVE

Yasmine reappeared shortly before landing dressed in a plain white shawl over her trousers instead of a tunic, and drove out of *Shadowmark* immediately upon landing, in search of her favourite bathhouse. Atalanta, having landed slightly ahead of them, accompanied Yasmine, ostensibly to show her face and listen to gossip, predominantly to smoke out Yasmine's youngest half-sisters Louise and Marie. Connor's denuded and all-male party headed for Logan and Éloise's city centre flat as soon as they had completed customs formalities. By that stage it was almost noon and the sun was lurking behind a distant mountain range, a rich-world teenager reluctant to rise.

Brief autumn had long shaded into winter in this, the southern hemisphere. On Port Logis, that equated to cold enough to freeze the air on its way out of bike exhausts. The equator here was uninhabitable – temperatures hovered around ninety degrees year-round – and the poles were similarly unprepossessing. Two temperate bands, one in the north and one in the south, formed the main inhabited land, with all the cities near the coasts, in search of the mildest weather possible. The southern continental shield was the preserve of miners in autumn and farmers in spring, and, as Éloise said, a few idiots year-round. No one mentioned the northern continental shield. Port Logis, practical home of practical people, had a particular use for it.

Conifers studded the ground below amid snowbanks and icicles. Fifty feet above them Connor could see each sprig as he drove: ordinarily quiescent meadows between spaceport and capital city growled up at him, full of teeth. Around, above and below, brightly-clad local residents swathed in cloaks and soberly-clad foreigners like themselves shivering in biking suits drove about their own business, a skyscape full of happenings from which Connor felt disjointed.

"Remember to be careful of the girls," Marcello was saying to Jack Priest, Connor's second bodyguard for the trip, down his helmet phone. "If you can't look at them without wondering what they're like to fuck, just look at the floor. They'll laugh at you but they won't hurt you."

"You ever got beaten up by a Port Logis girl?" Priest said.

"Yep. Once was enough for me. And I mean, you do get lucky. I got so lucky here once I nearly got done for public ind…in…indecency, but the girl was a better illusionist than the cop. Just pretend they're all six times bigger than you, I guess."

Connor turned off his helmet link and muttered a few curses. His extra pair of hands for this trip should have been a woman. Priest was a bright man – all his crewers were bright – but there was a difference between drilling all the right bows, when to stand and when to sit, who had precedence over whom and so on, and coming here and having to survive. Atalanta, who had had a decade's instruction in Neuvième etiquette, still preferred a friendly escort on Port Logis. That was enough evidence for Connor to remain on guard.

Below and ahead, outlying homesteads became suburban mansions, and suburban mansions became city sprawl. Connor stared down at low-rise apartment blocks, shopping complexes, shrines, temples, businesses, houses, bathhouses: white-sheathed in local marble, some pretending support from black marble pillars, white walls and huge windows all shimmering in weak dawn-light. The city undulated across rolling hills, studded with snow-drenched parkland, till an abrupt halt fifty miles before the cleft that rushed down to the sea, frozen mid-breaker, congealed slush become metre-tall sculpture. Frozen in time, albeit more briefly so than Michael Sinclair d'Aubry's capital city.

Connor's eyes drifted to the city centre, and its central temple, squatting on top of a hill like a great fat owl. Sinclair d'Aubry's city, and Sinclair d'Aubry's temple, now his tomb: in eight thousand years only one grave had joined his inside the temple itself. The city's remaining dead were consigned to graveyards, near temples and shrines for the most prominent families, outside city limits for also-rans.

As Connor slowed for the run into Logan and Éloise's apartment block, the temple slid behind rooftops, and with it sank enduring myths of human inconstancy. Spellweavers spent their lives in touch with something that, if not divine, was certainly identifiable with the supernatural. It would be easy for them, perhaps, to dismiss religion with the rest of superstition. Éloise for one had no truck with it. But many of them did pray – so many, even if they saw their magic as emanating from the hells rather than the heavens, clung to God even if they considered His prophets had condemned them. Maybe it didn't have to make sense: maybe it was just another twist of Michael Sinclair d'Aubry's legacy.

Every Port Logis building had an interior garage, even the ones where it was frankly unsafe to have one, such as grain silos or chemical plants. In winter, it was far too cold even in the temperate zones to keep a vehicle outside or, indeed, to stand outside for more than a few minutes. Connor had had the key code to Logan and Éloise's apartment garage saved to his neural jack from the day they'd moved in. As he drove down to the door, it opened for him: he stalled his bike in the doorway to let the other two in, then followed them inside and clipped his bike to a handy rack. The bike beside it was Logan's – a new, souped-up Connaught. Logan, once he'd started getting money at fourteen that rated greater than subsistence level, had spent it on bikes. In the past couple of years he'd branched out to spending it on spaceplanes and children, but bikes were still an obsession.

Connor hooked his helmet to his Nexi's pillion and gestured for the other two to accompany him into the lift. "Welcome to bedlam," he muttered as the lift slowed for the top floor.

"They're not that bad," Marcello said.

"They're small children."

The door slid open. Two black-haired thunderbolts assaulted Connor's waist, squealing.

"*Oncle, oncle!*"

"You came!"

"*Nicky nous a dit que tu est au fond –*"

Connor detached Gaiety from his left leg and picked up Kasimir. "I didn't know your brother Niccolò could talk yet." He kicked off his boots in the shoe stand's vague direction, almost hitting three pairs of white leather boots.

Gaia screwed up her little hooked nose. "He can say much things."

"*Many* things." Her English would remain dire if Logan didn't stop spoiling her. "You're four and a half: you know the difference between much and many." Gaia pulled a face, unimpressed. Kas tapped Connor on the shoulder and turned big worried gold eyes on him. Connor swallowed a curse. Of course they didn't care when they were scolded, just when the other one got scolded: and when did Kasimir ever merit a scolding?

Instead of explaining he kissed the little boy's forehead and ventured into the kitchen, off the hall. No one there, just rows of gleaming appliances – how the other half lived, until he and his brother had started to become the other half. Clean counters too, with a tiny bot trundling around sweeping up, though a few toys dotted work surfaces and floor. Connor picked up a small soft ball from the closest countertop. It jingled. "Is this Nicky's?" he said.

Kas nodded. "It was ours. We gave it to Nicky. He'll give it to the new baby. Maman's having a new baby."

"I know." Ball in one hand and nephew in his other arm, he withdrew into the hall. Gaia had been prancing around the two mercs, chattering in Franglais, but stopped suddenly and dashed past Connor towards the living room. Kas squirmed, and Connor put him down and watched him scurry after his sister.

"Come in," Logan called, round the corner out of sight.

"The welcoming committee already saw to that." He edged round the door. More toys littered the black carpet, along with a couple of book readers sized for small hands. Logan was emerging from the bedroom corridor, sturdy as a tree and about as tall, shepherding Niccolò, who was toddling along on stubby legs with some determination on his little face. He smiled when he saw Connor, revealing seven or eight teeth, and held out his hands, either for a cuddle or for his ball. Connor scooped him up. "Hello to you too." One-armed, he embraced his brother.

"Us too," the twins said from below, and Connor felt a tug on his leg again.

"Don't tease your uncle," Logan said with a laugh. He

released Connor and bent to scoop up the twins. They were his mirrors, held up alongside him like that: the same messy black curls, the same hooked noses, the same gold eyes. Their skin was fairer, by a few shades, the difference of a little more milk added to the tea. Nicky, clinging to Connor, was fairer again by degrees, and his eyes were darker. He had the nose, though.

"It's good to see you," Logan added. "We could do with your good sense right now."

"Happy to provide it. Éloise?"

Logan jerked his head at the glass door on the far wall. "On the balcony."

"She'll freeze."

"She can't."

Connor set down Nicky, who toddled to Marcello and Jack Priest lisping greetings. His white tunic and trousers were remarkably clean, unlike the twins'. As Logan set Kasimir and Gaiety on the floor, and the pair settled down to play with their brother and as many of the men as they could co-opt at once, Connor pulled on the pair of Logan-sized shearling slippers deserted at the balcony doorway, slid open the door and stepped outside.

Chill air stung his cheeks and hands. He drew in a sharp breath, and instantly regretted it: ice's tongue in the air cut into his throat, a kiss no man would welcome. How *anyone* could bear this for more than minutes, he didn't know.

"Excuse me for not getting up," Éloise said from a canopied swing-seat at the far corner.

"We'll skip formalities." Connor peered at her through eyes watering in the chill. She'd been crying, and looked sick. Her white house-clothes accentuated her natural pallor. "You look awful."

"I feel it." She motioned for him to sit beside her: he did, and she laid her head on his shoulder. Warm strands of magic snaked out from her wings, wrapping round his upper body like ivy. Some of the air's chill retreated. "It's not your fault I'm eight and a half months pregnant when my father's just died, it's Logan's – well, the pregnancy part is."

"I'd imagined you had some say in it too." He slid his arm round her and held her as tightly as a stepbrother dared. She was shaking. This was an Éloise he didn't know: an Éloise separated from her ruthless side. "Listen – I don't do emotion very well. Like you I delegate that to Logan." She caught back something between a laugh and a sob. "But tell me what to do and I will do it for you."

"You don't need to do much. I haven't needed to do much: my aunts organised everything." And Gisele? No way to tell from Connor's angle whether the widow was prostrated by grief, dismissed as irrelevant, or culturally debarred from taking the lead in organising a funeral.

"Then I can be your fetch-and-carry man, your shoulder to cry on, whatever you need, while Logan's occupied with the children." He looked down at her belly. She rarely gained pregnancy weight anywhere other than her torso – something she put down to exercise and others might put down to luck. "That one looks like your business still."

Éloise grimaced. "Believe me, he's as demanding as the rest of them." She plucked at her fleecy long-sleeved house tunic. "I need to change. We have two hours. If you want to do something for me, stop Calad strangling his wife in the middle of the funeral."

"Where is Calad?"

"At Alazais's, unless he's waiting to ambush Atalanta on her way out of the baths." She manoeuvred upright. It took her a couple of tries.

"I asked Galene last year," Connor said softly, "how women stood the late stages of pregnancy. She told me to ask you, as you've had more children." She stayed still, looking down at him. Weak midday light glinted off her honey-gold hair. She looked like a portrait on a playing card. "Well? How do you stand it?"

She shrugged. "Like anything else in a woman's life. We put up and shut up." She padded to the door and back inside. Connor heard her exhorting her children in French to remember their manners and not trip her up.

Icy breezes played along the balcony, whirling loose-packed snow into the air. Connor stood up and stared over icicle-hung rooftops towards the spaceport, several hundred miles away and out of sight, the crux point of a thousand little silver flashes approaching it and receding. He could stand at the top of an apartment block on Mirqest and his view would differ in every conceivable way. Coming from Septième cities – dirty, smelly and cramped, corrupt to the core – to the Neuvième's gleaming arches was like stepping from a hell into a heaven without any intervening steps on the way: beautiful architecture, pleasant scents, honest people.

A paradise that spawned extermination squads and their like, populated by men and women who died young, either mad or screaming in pain: a paradise still engaged in an implacable conflict two thousand years after temporal empires had abandoned war as unprofitable…

Connor touched his jack phone. "Calad, talk to me," he said under his breath.

"About what?" Calad said a moment later. "Because if you *mention* my wife – I've had it up to *here* with her!"

Connor rolled his eyes. Petulant little boy. A petulant little boy who'd just lost his father. "I wasn't going to mention your wife."

"Good. She sent me on some fool chase round the sector when I didn't have time –"

"I'm at your sister's flat. She's ill. Please come here as soon as you can. She has far too many children for her present peace of mind, and we need you to help marshal them."

"Fine." He didn't sound fine, mulish more like, and Calad, Connor knew, adored his niece and nephews. He was young enough – or maybe carefree enough – to take a delight in them that Connor could not: Connor couldn't help seeing how fragile they were.

"I'll expect you inside half an hour. Where's Michel?"

"At my mother's. Why not call him?" Calad signed off.

For a moment Connor contemplated calling Michel, but he was likely very busy… and Connor smothered a curse before he could even think it. At least one and possibly all of the children could tell what people were thinking. Since he had little real idea how he felt about Michel, there was nothing there for them to pick up, at least.

It irritated him beyond what was permissible in his profession: not the constant guard on his thoughts while on Port Logis, but the underlying confusion. The man he ought to miss was the one with whom he'd had an on-off relationship for a decade, not a one-night stand.

He was shivering, and the neat potted shrubs on the balcony (Éloise's) and the bright riot of flowers alongside (Logan's and the twins') were buried in snow, so he returned to the living room. Éloise had reclined, or collapsed, on the sofa, with Nicky talking earnest twaddle to her. The twins had inveigled Marcello into a chess game. "There's two of you," he was saying as Connor entered, "and only one of me. This isn't fair." He was losing.

Logan re-emerged from the kitchen corridor with Priest behind him carrying drinks. "Your clothes are on our bed," he said to Connor. "I hope you've not put on too much weight."

"Lost a bit, but it shouldn't be catastrophic." He had a couple of Neuvième outfits but nothing suitable for a funeral. Nowadays Logan wore Neuvième gear like he'd grown into it: he fitted the sector so well, psychologically and physically, but slipped back chameleon-like into Septième modes of speech and thought when he had to. It worked far too well.

The power of the Augury thread, when used unaware. Connor stared at the deck of cards abandoned on a shelf between several pictures of the children and one of Éloise with her parents when she was aged no more than three. Unlike Logan, he could choose to activate the thread, though not what it showed him. He paid for it with headaches and nausea, but he could – usually – control its timing.

But he was no Spellweaver, able to manipulate spell-threads to his wishes – able to force images of past or future. Full Augury was a rare skill, if only because augurers lost their sanity before they had much time to use it. But the temptation lingered to thumb through Logan and Éloise's playing cards till he saw himself find a murderer.

Not that he would necessarily understand the picture if he saw it...

"Checkmate," Kasimir said from the chessboard in the corner. Connor glanced at his brother – Checkmate was Logan's street nickname – but Logan just smiled down at his eldest children in some degree of fond possessiveness.

"If you can't beat two four-year-olds you'll never make a

leader," he said to Marcello.

"I don't want to be a leader. I don't want all the," and he glanced at the twins, "*nonsense* that goes with it."

Gaia turned her limpid smile on Connor. "Your turn." Kas smiled too, like he'd never heard a better idea, and started resetting the board.

"I'm not as good as Papa is," Connor demurred.

"Please." Gaia's smile changed, less delight in it and more hope. Her face – even the attitude of her body – shifted, and Connor could almost believe her sole aim in life was his entertainment. Manipulative little besom! The same child who'd started up a man's spaceship to see what it was like to do so...

"All right –" Raw delight flooded back and Gaia bounced on her half of the chair so hard she almost dislodged Kas from the other half. Connor sighed, and gestured for Marcello to vacate the opposite seat. "I will regret this."

"Only if you lose," Logan said. Éloise sniffed. She'd picked up Niccolò and was cuddling him to her. Logan sat down beside her, retrieved his temporarily youngest son and wrapped an arm round his wife. She buried her face into his chest.

Connor turned away and stared at the chessboard. The twins, playing as White, had made a standard queen's pawn opening. Wife and husband were such loaded terms. To Atalanta's people – or to Gisele's – they meant a legal contract: from the Sixième to the Dixième they signified a permanent partnership, without requirement of formal vows, and with monogamy or polygamy a matter for the people concerned. Connor suspected Logan and Éloise were monogamous. They were both still alive.

He played a pawn to match the twins'; they moved a knight, and Connor moved queen's bishop's pawn. Maybe Logan and Éloise would one day add wedding rings to their relationship. Logan had asked her before now, and she had refused. Marriage, to Neuvième women, brought more constraints than benefits. Alazais, Dominic's youngest sister, had loved all her four husbands dearly, but had never married any of them.

But Dominic had married twice. First as, presumably, a

young and romantically-minded man. Second, because he had seen something he wanted and marriage had been the only way to get it. If Gisele had been a woman of Port Logis she would simply have moved in with him as his wife and no one would have had any objections to her, her offspring or her situation. But for a parochial Treizième girl, marriage was critical, no matter that in context it was a critical error.

The twins' white-squares bishop slid out and checked Connor's king. He blinked: he wasn't used to quite such an aggressive game, but they were young and silly, so he should have expected little else. He interposed his knight, which they immediately captured heedless to the threat to their bishop, which he took with a pawn.

"You like those," Kas observed. Connor started. The children hadn't spoken since the game began. Gaia was the talkative one, of course, and she rarely spoke to Kas, or he to her. Connor had no idea whether their telempathy extended to anyone but each other yet. It behoved him to find out.

"Pawns are useful," he said, "so one must make use of them. There is no other purpose to them."

"They're not elegant," Gaia said, and captured one of his rearguard pawns with the white queen: the pawn had been covered by the now-deceased knight alone.

"Elegance is secondary." He moved a bishop to threaten the white queen. "Utility comes first." Their remaining bishop checked his king again. He sighed. This was going to be one of those matches with very little material on the board at the end.

He turned out to be right about that, and he won the match, but not by a large margin, and due to a few bursts of recklessness in his opponents even more unexpected than his calculations. From the twins' body language to each other, most of the aggressive moves in the early and mid game were Gaia's, but the final endgame moves were Kas's.

"Play again?" suggested Gaia.

"We don't have time." Connor glanced at the others. Éloise was still on the sofa, now talking to Jack, and Logan, holding Nicky, had watched the end of the chess match. Marcello was in the kitchen area, for his voice was audible in conversation.

"All three of you need to get changed," Logan said when the twins looked likely to complain. Kas, on the chair's outside, scrambled up at the note of command in Logan's voice, and went to hug his mother – and kiss her distended belly – before scampering off towards the bedrooms. Gaia followed. Logan's eye lingered after her.

Connor rose. "I hope that boy never becomes resentful," he murmured to Logan.

"Kas? What's he got to resent?" Connor did not answer, thinking only of an obedient, admiring little face. Logan wanted Gaia's hero-worship, not Kas's…

The door to the kitchen corridor slid open again, and Calad and Michel entered.

Michel always struck Connor with an air of being, aside from his fair skin and hair, completely normal. Average height for a man of his culture, average build, neither quiet nor loud, highly competent in an undemonstrative way. It had taken Connor a third or fourth look before that competence resolved itself into something a lot steelier and more menacing. An eldest son, nearly five years' Éloise's senior – and perhaps never on perfect terms with his father.

With three tiny children in the vicinity Connor swallowed memories of the one night he'd wound up in Michel's bed, and switched his attention to Calad instead.

Calad, Dominic's only child from Gisele, was five or six years younger than his half-sister, and prone to acting it. He was nineteen, Marcello's age, and Atalanta's. Right now he looked like a sulky boy, albeit an extremely attractive, verging on beautiful, sulky boy. He was close to a pureblood New Worlder – near-pure strains still popped up on Port Logis in every other family, including Dominic and his three sisters, and Calad's mother was from Terra Nova. What she had thought about her son marrying a pureblooded *Old* World human was anyone's guess.

"Have you dunked that mood in a bathhouse?" Connor asked him.

"That'd have been what she wanted to achieve. Perverse woman…" He shook off something of his sulks and kissed Niccolò. The little boy, who had been looking somewhat apprehensive, smiled and gurgled a few words.

Logan handed the toddler to Calad and embraced Michel, who released Logan, gave Connor a similar brotherly hug and sat down next to Éloise, who, for a surprise, was looking almost as sulky as Calad.

"I'll make sure you don't have to cover your head at your own funeral. Satisfied?" he said to her.

"We've already had this discussion. It's completely unnecessary –"

Michel sighed. "This isn't about observance, it's about not getting into a blazing row with anyone," and he looked meaningfully at Calad, who spoilt the effect by sitting down on the floor to play elephants with Niccolò, "today. Can you at least go one day without starting a quarrel that will last longer than you do?" She remained silent, and for a moment looked sicker than ever.

Connor retreated towards Éloise and Logan's bedroom to change. The twins scampered past him en route with their fresh clothes on inside out. As Connor escaped into the bedroom he heard the expostulations start.

The door closed behind him and everything went quiet for a moment. Connor threaded past the bed to the window. Outside was a Port Logis sidestreet, quiet and refined, with sun awnings converted into snow shelters and the flowerpot holders hanging from the eaves every hundred yards now bearing multi-coloured lights. The open-air shower at the street corner hung deactivated, frozen solid: summer and the time to shower in one's clothes between appointments would come soon enough.

A different world in every way from the kind that had bounded his entire life just two and a half years previously. Two and a half years, and *everything* had changed.

A white silk tunic lay on the bed beside a fleece-lined cloak, a pair of wrap-on trousers and a loincloth – Septième undergarments did not fit under Neuvième trousers. Connor stripped and changed with only minor difficulty. It felt as if he were trying to go up three social classes rather than to fit in on another world.

Just as he was adjusting his (white) knife belt – on the Neuvième he'd look naked without it – the door slid open and Éloise entered. Less sick-looking, more angry: "You

OK?" Connor said.

She let out a bitter laugh. "Like most people, I hate being in the wrong." She opened one of her two wardrobes and pulled out a shawl sporting a silk central panel and filmy transparent ends. Those wouldn't do a good job of covering her hair.

"You don't have to veil if you don't want to."

Éloise stopped with twenty-four feet of fabric coiled in her hands. "That knife you buckled on?" He touched the belt. She tossed her shawl onto the bed, opened her second wardrobe and pulled out a pair of wide-legged white trousers and a white belt similar to Connor's.

"How do you even wear a belt at the moment?" Connor said. "You don't have a waist."

"I know. It's ridiculous. The fact that I need a knife at all is ridiculous. Logan likes me to wear one on the Septième, as a warning, but I've only stabbed someone once in the past couple of years – it's not the way I do things." She dropped the belt on top of her shawl. "But a grown woman, here, wears a knife unless she has nothing else to prove. As with this knife, I need to cover my head today, for I still have something to prove."

Until Dominic was buried? Connor sighed. Dominic had favoured Éloise over his sons – the Port Logis way – and maybe the favourite needed to behave herself. But Dominic had not been a religious man, though he hadn't demonstrated active antipathy to the priesthood.

"I'll let you dress." He retreated to the door.

"Connor." He stopped and looked round. Éloise was running her shawl fabric through her hands. "What's happening on Mirqest?"

"I suspect our governor is trying to defraud Cliff Enterprises, I'm beginning to suspect Cliff realises this, and someone killed one of my cleaners just before she could give me some very interesting information about all of that."

Her lips twisted into a smile. "The *fun* kind of time. I'll top up your shields before you leave."

"Thank you. I don't deny Yasmine has been useful already, but I miss you." This smile sat on her face in a more genuine manner.

He re-emerged into the living room amid a diatribe from Logan. The twins, dressed correctly by now, were looking about as sulky as their youngest uncle had on his arrival. Among the appreciative audience was Yasmine. Faint scents of rose and lemongrass wafted on the air: scents she'd applied at the bathhouse. Connor perched beside her on the sofa. The lemongrass smell was coming from her hair — oiled, conditioned, perfectly coiffed: it rippled in chestnut waves to her mid-back from a base of several plaits.

"You look about as expensive as I've seen on these streets."

She smiled. "Thank you." Her trousers were silk, like his, but heavily embroidered; her shawl was a diaphanous gauze that just about kept her decent in his eyes. Another woman who didn't take much account of temple decorum? She made more sense here than she had on Mirqest. The patina of different worlds...

Logan scooped up Gaia with a final, "It matters because I say it matters," and handed her to Michel. Connor couldn't hear the few words he whispered to her, but they didn't make her look any less cross. Eventually he put her down and, with bad grace, she passed Yasmine a cup of fruit juice.

"What would you want?" she said to Connor.

"Calypso lemon if you have any. Tea if you haven't."

She shook her head. "We have only Calypso grape, and I'm too little to bring tea. You have to wait till I've five. Calypso grape, orange juice and ananas-juice."

"Pineapple," Kas contributed from Logan's side.

Logan removed his son from his right thigh. "Or I could pour more tea..." He retreated into the kitchen. Kas glanced back and forth between his father and his sister. Gaia held out a little insistent hand, and he went to her, and they headed towards the kitchen together.

Yasmine's eye lingered after them for a moment. She had four younger half-siblings on her mother's side, from her mother's last and current husband – the first two had died and the third, Yasmine's father, had broken up with her. As a daughter, Yasmine had had the right to count herself among her father's family. She'd chosen the Falavières.

"Where's...?" murmured Connor, gesturing to Calad, who

was playing a tickle game with Nicky.

"Paying her respects to my mother. Marie took her."

"Good." Connor accepted a cup of tea from his brother. "I like to keep the casualty list to a minimum."

"Always?" said Yasmine, eyebrows raised.

"Yes. Anything else is a waste."

The bedroom corridor door slid open, and Connor rose, teacup in hand, as Éloise re-entered. Like Yasmine, she'd plaited back part of her hair, but she lacked her cousin's patina. Her shawl sat tight across her breasts, glinting in the light – maybe she'd broken tradition far enough to cross a little silver thread into its weave.

Logan emerged from the kitchen corridor, went to her, and kissed her. She leant into him for a few seconds, then pulled back. Her elder two children peeked back into the living room, staring at her: she nodded at them in weary satisfaction "They'll do. We need to go." She glanced at Marcello and Jack. "If you want to avoid any possibility of ructions, I suggest you stay here."

"What do you suggest we do for the next couple of hours?" Marcello said.

She gestured for Logan to pick up Niccolò. "Practice chess till you're better than a four-year-old." She swept out and into the corridor.

*

CHAPTER SIX

So this is what it looks like, Connor thought, staring round the temple, *to have five hundred relatives.*

The assembled Falavière family didn't pack out the central hall, but they came close. Marble gleamed under their bare feet, in white and black concentric rings: the Circle's woven knot glittered between two of those rings, drawn in dark blue marble, as if calling up to its counterpart picked out in green jade around the dome's spire.

When they'd arrived, Connor had followed the crowd to the men's chapels, anti-clockwise from the entrance, capping the transepts dedicated to the angels of Wisdom, Mercy and Victory. Gaia had tried to follow them, till Logan threatened to drag both twins off holy ground and spank them: she'd stomped away at that, while Kas had spent the next hour sniffling. Éloise, Connor had since discovered, had refused to go to the women's chapels on the pretext that her unborn child was male, and had hidden in the angel of Knowledge's transept till it was time to emerge, making conversation with two of her cousins who identified with neither gender.

Atalanta was avoiding Éloise, or perhaps the fact of her pregnancy: she'd arrived late, wearing mostly white lace, and had slid onto the bench next to Calad at the last moment after the men and women had recombined. Calad had glared at her, but her shawl's tail was arranged over her gleaming copper hair in the approved manner (as, ultimately, was Éloise's), so he'd no grounds to complain.

Choristers singing in the cantaries, icons and votive altars glowing in the transepts, gold and pearl glinting on the three altars beneath the dome's tip: to Connor, not religious by nature, it felt unreal, a stage set built for an opera for which he had no libretto. But Dominic lay dead in the angel of Transcendence's transept, and his family, a stepped white cliff, sat ranked on curved benches like froth on a seashore while the priest talked and talked: and that priest, a blue-robed harbinger, spoke of life's precariousness and the mystery of the hereafter in a way that told Connor what he already knew – death was the only certainty.

Two grave slabs were set into the floor in front of the altars, the already-dead showing Dominic the way to go: Michael Sinclair d'Aubry and Elearr de Fiorail. Sinclair d'Aubry fitted here: his Circle, his planet, his city, his temple. Elearr de Fiorail was a reminder that Septième and Neuvième were not too far apart.

His eyes slid to Gisele. She'd covered her head with her shawl, like the other women, but beneath also wore a thin white veil that covered her face. She sat on a packed front row bench, but, at a few inches' separation from the people to her either side, seemed alone.

Back his attention went to the others around him – Logan tall and steel-strong, Éloise leaning against him, her brothers and Atalanta beyond them, the children dotted between. A curious set of people who had assembled into what he, a workaday man, would have described as a family. Were the fault lines between Calad and Atalanta, even between him and Michel, severe? He didn't know, and wished he did. He wished the next card he overturned would show him what to do to hold them together.

Familial love was a weakness, for certain, but life was a string of weaknesses bound up in flesh, more precarious than that priest could ever preach. At least this weakness any potential enemy could see, so he had no need to be subtle about his defences.

He returned, as maybe he invariably would, to a contemplation of the grave slabs in front of the altars. Death was inescapable, but so, perhaps, was the fate assigned to men and women of such towering deeds. Immortality lay in rhyme and legend, nowhere else. Neuvième folk, non-Weavers or those whose threads were thin, lived for a long time, but their lifespan was not infinite. Connor glanced at Alazais, who sat flanked by two of her sons far enough round the circle for him to see her face. A powerful healer – one of the two exceptions to the rule that Weavers died early – she looked younger than her eldest son, on her left. Her hair was veiled, like all the women's, but Connor knew the dark locks beneath were barely dye-touched.

But one day, maybe long after her children, Alazais would fade and die, perhaps with some warning, perhaps with none: and in time, her descendants would forget her, and her tale would be done.

"All humans sin," the priest said, "and all will die: Scripture tells us this is inevitable, and that the two are inevitably linked. But if the wages of sin are death, be assured that God and His angels will judge us based on our deeds and thoughts, and not on the opinion of others. There is no name, no reputation, that we can take to the next world: there, we can only rely on what we really are."

A concept from Scripture's time: a concept of greater starkness and simplicity than the modern mind was prepared to process. However much progress any millennium saw, however life's living changed, the fundamentals remained the same: birth, love and death, interspersed with moments of spine-shattering fear.

Connor started. The priest had closed his prayer book and the crowd of Falavières was rising. With one absent hand he corralled his niece, who had looked set to scamper off to play with the flower petals littering Elearr de Fiorail's grave, and nudged her back towards her parents. Éloise staggered into Logan in the process of standing. For an irreligious woman, she'd been affected by the occasion.

Gisele did not stagger. She walked at the head of the crowd into the Transcendence transept, with Amalie and Alazais immediately behind her, up to her husband's open coffin. For too few seconds she lingered beside him, looking down through her veil, then she turned and walked away. Her stepsisters stood together for a moment, blonde Amalie and white-skinned brunette Alazais, two quarters of a depleted whole, then they followed.

As Connor in his turn reached Dominic's coffin, behind a handful of Alazais's children, he wondered what he would feel, what he would say if he could: but thought fled from him, as flighty as his little niece. He owed Dominic quite an amount, connections and vistas of the mind, not to mention a nose for good whisky. Maybe all he could do now was pass some of it to others.

He picked up Gaia, then Kas, so they could see into the

coffin. "Grandpère looks happy," Gaia said in what was meant to be a whisper.

"He does." Connor studied Dominic's still face before retreating, leading one twin by each hand to let Calad, carrying Niccolò, take his place. Undertaker's craft no doubt, but Dominic had the look of a man who was remarkably satisfied by the way everything had worked out...

Back in the nave Gisele paused, under the dome with light shining on her white figure. "Go to your niece Éloise," she said to Alazais, "immediately." Alazais opened her mouth only to close it again – one could not question the order of a widow or widower in mourning – and retreated past Connor and the twins. Amalie stood where she was, her severe face alight with disapproval. Gisele paid no attention, just walked away towards the Angel of Creation's transept and the exit.

Connor turned. Éloise was staggering again, slumped against Logan more than ever, and her hand gripped his so tightly that not just her knuckles but his had gone white.

Connor touched Kasimir's shoulder. "Kas. Is Maman having a new baby *now*?"

He looked up in some surprise. "Yes. I *said*."

Éloise sagged into Logan. Michel materialised behind her and slid an arm under her shoulders. One of her cousins – Raymond Mazard Falavière, Connor thought, one of Gauzia's sons – stepped up and supported her other side, easing her away from Logan. "Yes," Alazais said in some satisfaction, "get her out of here before she bleeds on the floor. She's in no condition to perform reconsecration prayers." She laid a second hand on Éloise's belly. "We just have time to get her to the birthing centre."

Éloise slapped away her hand. "And stop talking about me like I'm not here."

Yasmine came up beside Logan and took his right hand, the one Éloise had gripped. "Wait a minute. You drive faster than my mother." She led him to the closest nave bench and sat down, pulling him beside her. "You'll catch them easily – if you can pay the speeding fine..." Two of his fingers were at the wrong angle, Connor realised: the index finger and little finger both dangled cockeyed.

He perched on the bench beside Logan. "She's got a grip on her," he murmured.

Logan nodded. He showed few signs of pain, just the way his jaw and facial muscles weren't moving. "You've seen her in action: I don't know why you're surprised."

Yasmine drew her knife, grabbed the shawl tail that was not covering her head, and sliced off a few neat strips. "I congratulate you both on an excellent performance. How long has she been having contractions?"

"Since this morning." Logan winced as Yasmine straightened his little finger and twined a thin white magic thread along it. "She reckoned no one was going to postpone the funeral so she might as well keep her fingers and legs both crossed and hope –" He broke off as Yasmine strapped his little finger to his ring finger with one of the strips of shawl fabric. "You're enjoying that."

"Nonsense. Too much enjoyment has a bad effect on a woman: have you ever watched Éloise strangle a man with her shawl?"

"Only once. She doesn't often wear one out anti-clockwise, only when we're at a posh do."

"One day I'm sure the Septième will see their utility. Other one now." She straightened out the damaged index finger with a practiced motion and held Logan's hand between hers for a moment. "OK, done." With the second shawl strip she bound Logan's index finger to his middle finger. "No heavy lifting with this hand for a week. That includes your children and your bike. Try not to turn right –"

"What?"

"Try not to turn right if you have to drive," she continued. "Carry teapots and babies in the left hand, and don't use any gun heavier than a pistol. When you go to the salle, inform your instructor of your condition and do not throw any blows right-handed. No barbells: stick to dumbbells." She smiled in satisfaction and sailed away.

Logan sat back on the bench, wincing. "She didn't give you a painkiller?" Connor said.

"It didn't work very well."

Kas wormed up onto his lap. "I'll help," he said, soft and serious, and he lifted Logan's injured hand and kissed it.

"Better?" he said.

"Yes," Logan said in a surprised voice. "Kas, how did you do that?"

He shrugged. "I kissed it better, like Maman always says. It stops it hurting."

"Well – thank you."

Gaia, who had taken advantage of the fuss to go and play on de Fiorail's grave, stood up. Votive candles flickered round her ankles, close enough for Connor to fear for her trousers, but she hadn't set herself alight yet. "Can we go and see the new baby now?" She bobbed up and down on bare tiptoes. A priestess who had been kneeling in prayer at Sinclair d'Aubry's grave glared at her.

"He hasn't had time to be born yet," Logan said. In answer, Gaia pointed to Nicky, who was crying fretfully in Calad's arms.

Michel's soft voice floated into Connor's skull – Telepathy magic. *Éloise has just had the baby. Logan, you owe Alazais a new set of mourning clothes and some fresh car upholstery.*

Logan burst out laughing. This time several priestesses glared. "Send her my love, Mick," he said to the empty air. He smiled up at Calad, and at Niccolò, who had settled back down (having pulled off Calad's hair tie) and was sucking his uncle's forefinger. "He would have liked the contrast. Dominic."

Calad nodded without speaking. A few cousins paused to embrace Logan in congratulation. Connor stared up at the dome, and at the green Circle mark dancing around it. Death and life as one…

Auroral light filtering through the dome glass glinted green. *Dominic got the last laugh,* the temple breathed. *He won.*

Logan's left hand clamped round his right arm. "You're OK," he said from what felt like a long way away.

Connor opened his eyes. At first he thought he saw a celestial vision overhead, some temple icon, but then he realised it was Calad, his blond hair hanging loose about his shoulders. Atalanta and two of the cousins hovered behind, a honey-skinned pair indistinguishable from each other: identical twins, Alazais's youngest girls, women Atalanta's age or a year or so younger. "That's one of the more interesting applications of Augury I've seen," one of the twins said. "How do you do it?"

"I have no idea." Connor struggled back towards reality. "Which of you two is which? I can't tell with your wings in."

"I'm Louise," said the one who'd spoken. Marie, the other, giggled. Connor studied them. There were tiny differences in the set of their eyes and curve of their lips, but without constant reference to their pictures he'd never be able to remember which was which. They even had the same figure – must have taken near-identical physical classes. Judging by the wings was too easy a way out.

He grabbed the bench for support, and snapped two fingers at Marie, the younger twin. "Where's your sister Yasmine?"

She pointed at the Creation transept. "Finding her boots."

Fine. She could drive Logan and the children around while he, Connor, soaked his head in a basin of cold water. He rose, waving off Logan's offered hand of support, and started down the transept towards the door. It stood open. Subzero winds whistled up to the temple walls and roared upwards, deflected on pyrokinetic shields. Outside, the city lay in shadow and lamplight and frost, a stage set for a horror film.

Atalanta jogged after him, one hand holding her shawl over her red hair. "My stepmother instructs you to drive to her house," she said as she caught him up.

"Why?"

"She didn't say and I'm not allowed to ask."

Connor let out a breath. "Right, right. I'm going." He waded through the warm paddle-trough at the door, retrieved his boots from the huge shoe rack and pulled them back on. The wind-shield brushed up against his back. Icy fingers tickled his spine. "Find Yasmine and tell her to play chauffeur. You answer questions, if there are any."

"Why did I tear myself off the Septième?" Atalanta said, pulling a sour face.

*

CHAPTER SEVEN

Every time Connor drove up to Dominic and Gisele's house, whether in summer's blazing heat or beneath starlight and aurora, he pondered the gap between romance and reality. When Septième folk imagined rich Neuvième couples lived in marble-fronted houses, they were right, but Port Logis produced so much marble it wasn't much more expensive than concrete. In contrast to some of the acre-wide palaces constructed by Septième moguls less wealthy than Dominic Falavière, Dominic and Gisele's house was a sensible size, no bigger than Connor's office block. Large garage, but most houses here had large garages, for almost everyone had large families with a tendency to pay visits in winter. Tall-tipped roof, with two extra storeys' space in the eaves: all roofs here had steep pitch, the better to shuck off snow and ice. The flaps that in summer would stand wide with their power cells drinking up the sunlight now rotated every few minutes to knock snow to the garden below.

The garage door slid open as Connor descended to the house front. Only two cars sat inside: Dominic's, under a dust sheet, and Gisele's. Connor pushed his bike inside and onto the rack, and tried the door that led from garage to house. It opened into a narrow hallway, painted white and barely adorned.

A cleaning bot was squeaking in the distance. Connor removed his boots and bore right, towards the back of the house, following the sound. He stopped at the kitchen door. Gisele was sitting at the table, crying silently. She'd pulled off her veil: her platinum blonde hair had unravelled from its topknot. The discarded veil lay on the floor a few inches from a broken coffee cup and its contents, being fussed over by the bot. Dominic had spent twenty years teasing his wife about her coffee habit.

Connor stayed still by the door, with an intensely awkward sensation gripping his legs. Second wife, yes, but Gisele had spent far longer married to Dominic than his first wife Saissa had. "You asked me to come," he said in an undertone, almost hoping she wouldn't hear.

Gisele looked up. Her pale face was so tear-blotched that she must have been crying for a very long time. A full veil hid a multitude of sins. Like death?

"You usually talk to me rather than at me." She sounded tired, and petulant. Maybe a few of those tears were for herself.

Connor stepped over the cleaning bot, went to the coffee maker and ordered two more servings. He'd pay for over-caffeinating himself tonight, but he'd survive. "I assume you've seen his lawyer already," he said over his shoulder.

"Oh, that's all in hand. He'd expected to die for a year at least: he'd put everything in order." Now she just sounded tired and fed up. "Every investment we made for the last five years, we made notification. The only thing missing is a few property valuations." And there had been several properties. Plantations on Union farming worlds, shares in Huitième mining operations, a house on Sukli Ban, a private beach on a local spa world where the summers were slightly less blistering than those on Port Logis. This understated house.

"Dominic was very careful," Connor said, near-inaudible in the quiet kitchen. "He was always forward-thinking." Forward-thinking, single-minded. Not afraid to hurt his loved ones if they would gain by it.

Connor watched coffee and cream swirl into the cups, a foreign custom leaching into the Neuvième atmosphere. After Saissa died, after Dominic had gone out into the world and seen a pretty girl from far away, no man of Connor's stamp could have blamed him for also seeing a business opportunity.

Connor had no doubt Dominic had fallen in love with Gisele, despite the age gap, despite the cultural difference. But the way he'd played on that cultural difference to do what he'd done – to set up his affairs to last maybe a hundred years after his death – perhaps took an outsider to appreciate. Never mind that no Septième man would marry twice: any man who could get away with a tax fraud of this magnitude would happily do so.

"A very traditional man, Dominic," he said to the coffee

cups. Setting aside the second marriage, that was. "I assume he left his children the traditional amount."

"Éloise's children too." Now Gisele's tone smacked of defeat. "And some set aside in case Calad or Michel manage to reproduce, and for any more Éloise has. Not that she isn't trying to populate the planet on her own at the moment."

"I can see."

The traditional portion: a small one, structured to give a future generation a minimal income – enough for food, basic clothes, basic housing. Little enough that if they wanted more they would have to work for it. And the rest – of what would have been a *vast* fortune – would be split equally between Dominic's surviving two sisters and Gisele.

Gisele's portion wouldn't attract death duties – and, when she eventually died, the tradition among *her* people was to leave almost everything to their children. However many years down the line, Calad was due a sizeable windfall, which would pass to either of his half-siblings in turn if they survived him.

"He tied it all up very neatly," Gisele said, a hint of acid lacing her voice. "Everything except what I should do... Connor."

He passed her a fresh coffee cup. "Yes?"

"I want to go with you when you leave."

Connor spilt his coffee. The cleaning bot, racing to mop up, knocked against his foot: he started again, and splashed more hot coffee over his hand. "*What?*" He set his cup down on the table, almost hard enough to crack it.

"I can't stay here all year!" Gisele's voice rose, and for a moment Connor feared she might cry again. "Not going out, even to the baths, and Amalie only coming round to glare at me – and telling everyone else to stay away when I throw parties, cat that she is. I need to go outside – I need to get *out* of here."

Objections queued for space on Connor's tongue. "Gisele – I don't live in a palace. I don't even live in a *house*, just a mildly run-down office block. There are spiders. There are fleas, sometimes. Nor do I have any time to help you socialise: I work long hours every day."

"I don't care."

"My work is *dangerous*, to everyone around me. People get shot at. People get killed."

Her nostrils flared. "Damn you, do you think I've lived on Port Logis for twenty years without seeing a fight?" *Not the same, not the same*, Connor wanted to scream, but a private impulse told him the interpersonal violence often got worse on Port Logis. "I'm not a hothouse flower." Yes, she was. "I'm *fed up*. I just want to be somewhere different. Just for a little while, not the whole year." Her jaw quivered. Now she really was forcing back tears, hells and damn it. "I need to get away."

He opened his mouth to beg her not to burst out crying, but stopped before that ended in him agreeing to her ridiculous request. "Gisele, my brother's wife just had a baby: I need to go and see him. We can discuss this later. OK?" He retrieved his coffee cup, took a quick gulp – it seared his throat – and retreated towards the door.

"I could tell you to take me," Gisele said, small-voiced. "I don't want to, but I could."

"It won't come to that." It wouldn't, for he'd leave without telling her before getting into that position. "Baby first."

He practically ran for the garage door before she could say any more. As he stepped into his boots, opened the door and breathed in oil fumes he realised he was still holding his coffee. He downed half of it and set the rest on the roof of Dominic's car. "Sorry," he muttered, as mounted his bike.

The garage door opened as he inched towards it. He taxied out and soared into the night still buckling his helmet, but glanced back down at the house, at the coherent remnant of Dominic and Gisele as a couple receding in the dark. Going to the Septième? For a *break*? He could cope with foreigners but he drew the line at tourists.

She can't stay, though, a little voice wormed into his mind. Gisele had some friends on Port Logis – people who hadn't been Dominic's friends – and often went off visiting acquaintances from her girlhood, but she hadn't anything like the on-planet support network that normally underpinned a year shuttling between house and temple. In her position Connor would have put his feet up with a large stack of books, or started an interstellar gambling ring from his living room, but Gisele lacked the personality for solitude.

Half an hour driving to the maternity centre and another quarter of an hour finding somewhere to park did little for his mood. Once he'd navigated the receptionist-cum-security guard and climbed two flights to the recovery rooms, he'd almost decided to refuse Gisele – but hadn't decided what he would do if she objected as strongly as she might.

No one here would object to him leaving Gisele behind, if only because so few treated her as a married woman whose wish equated to command. But if she were a married woman she had the right to order Connor to take her away, and if she were an unmarried woman, she could go wherever she liked…

Éloise was sitting up in bed feeding the baby, with a little blank frown on her face that meant she wasn't listening to anything around her. Logan had been holding the twins over the bed to talk to their new brother, with some difficulty in the right hand twin's case (Kas) due to the broken finger, but he set them both down when Connor entered. "I promise not to photograph that fatuous smile," Connor said, "and show it to the entire underside."

"Since when did I care what anyone thought of me?" Logan embraced him, fatuous smile not fading, and pulled Connor towards the bed. "He's a cute one, you've got to admit."

Connor squinted at the baby, sucking at his mother's breast with tiny fist thudding against her clavicle. He looked like a grumpy prune, but most babies did at two hours old. "At least he has an appetite."

"He fell asleep earlier," Éloise said, still staring into space. "For half an hour. This will be *fun*." With her free hand she stroked Niccolò's cheek: he'd dozed off at her side.

Gaia stopped threading her way through Logan's legs. "What's matter?" she said.

"What's 'the' matter," he replied on automatic. "Nothing's the matter. Your step-grandmother asked my advice on something: that's all."

Éloise's eyes snapped to Connor, as alert as a merc on shift, but she said nothing. Logan nudged the twins aside and backed Connor out of the door. "She wants to go to the

Septième? Is she nuts?" he whispered as soon as they were in the corridor.

"She's lost her husband and lacks sufficient shoulders to cry on. It wouldn't surprise me if she just wants out of her house." Connor shook his head. Defending Gisele? What next?

"I hope you told her – no. No, you couldn't tell her where to get off." Another smile crept over Logan's face, this one near-vicious. "What are you going to do?"

"Run away and hope she changes her mind." Connor waved a hand at the recovery room. "You've got two children in napkins and two more into *everything*: compared to that, my problems are minimal."

"You wait."

*

CHAPTER EIGHT

Connor heard nothing more from Gisele for the remainder of the day. Between borrowing Éloise's car to drive the three toddlers back to the apartment, ferrying back to pick up Logan, Éloise and the new baby Lothair, and subsequent corralling of over-excited children, two mercs fascinated by tiny squeaky humans and an apartment full of cousins, he went to bed exhausted, and slept badly. An underside office was a busy place day or night, but at least he understood that bustle, as he did not understand this.

Yasmine, who'd stayed away on the previous evening, arrived with her bags at eight the next morning while Connor was trying to persuade the twins to stop playing with their breakfast omelettes. "Leave them to it," she said by way of greeting. "They'll finish all the quicker if they do play with their food."

"You've got no children."

"I've two sisters eight years younger than me. I remember." She kissed both twins on the forehead, poured them some more orange juice and withdrew from the kitchenette.

Connor followed her, rather than retreated, into the living room. Éloise was reclining on the sofa with the baby burbling to himself in a padded bassinet beside her. From the overnight evidence he had slept as badly as Éloise predicted. Éloise, heavy-lidded, nodded to Connor and said to Yasmine, "Just keep him alive." She spoke in English, presumably for Connor's benefit.

"That's my intention," her cousin answered.

Marcello and Jack emerged from the bedroom corridor carrying their baggage and Connor's. Niccolò threaded through their legs, ran to Connor and clamped onto his knee. Connor detached the little boy and lifted him into his arms. "Yes, I'm going away. I'll be back before too long." *When your little brother learns how to sleep, I'll come back.* He kissed Niccolò and set him down on the floor beside

Lothair's basket.

"Logan's asleep," Éloise said, unasked.

"No, I'm not," Logan said, cranky-voiced, from behind Marcello's shoulder. "You lot – go away and I'll catch a few hours." He shouldered past the mercs and embraced Connor. "She's not called you?"

'She' must mean Gisele. "No."

"Good sign."

But after another round of goodbyes and childish sniffles, and a drive to the spaceport, Connor entered *Shadowmark*'s hangar to find Gisele sitting on a folding chair by the hatch, veiled casual style with her shawl. Hovering a few feet away, almost trembling with indignation, was Calad.

"Oh, good. You're here." Behind her shawl it was impossible to see Gisele's expression, but her voice sounded like a cat in a cream pot. She stood, revealing a pair of suitcases stacked behind her voluminous trousers, and folded up her chair.

One wasn't meant to speak to veiled widows in public without their invitation. Connor turned to the veiled widow's son. "What are you doing here?"

"Accomplishing nothing, however I try."

"He's coming with us," Gisele expanded. "Not *with*, but he has an appointment on Mirqest. Quite a coincidence."

"I'm two days late for an appointment on Mirqest," Calad said.

"Then I hope you sent sufficient apologies." Connor took a deep breath and aimed at the spot between mother and son. "This is a *very* bad idea –"

Gisele nodded. "I know. It's still a better idea than any of the others I've tried. Shall we?" Chair tucked under her left arm, she picked up one case in each hand and advanced on the hatch.

The subsequent flight up to the Bridge could have proved more congenial. Yasmine, as soon as she realised what was going on, was as short as courtesy permitted with her aunt, and vanished for quite half an hour for what appeared to be a radio argument with Calad, based on what Connor heard through the closed cabin door. Gisele, in her turn, adopted formal manners towards Connor and remained veiled –

though far from quiet – when his male mercs were present.

Half a day out of life: Connor did not understand, or maybe didn't want to understand, the reasons for his melancholy. No part of his life was normal. *Normal* was for the middle classes, not for men like him and, he suspected, not for Spellweavers. Yet when *nothing* felt right – opening his mouth to call for Éloise and remembering he had only Yasmine, listening to abrupt silences between Calad and his mother over the radio instead of endless trilingual chit-chat – those echoes of birth and death disturbed him.

Abandoning the ship's controls to Jack and Marcello, he went to bed an hour before the Bridge crossing, and for a minor miracle slept through it – though psychedelic dreams still plagued him – and woke with two hours of the journey left, in no better frame of mind. Heavy-headed, he washed and dressed, and wandered through to the flight deck. Jack Priest was at the cockpit controls with the ship on autopilot. He nodded to Connor's reflection in the viewscreen, but did not rise.

A tiny prickle danced across the nape of Connor's neck. "What's up?" he asked.

"I hope nothing for us. Excess police at the 'port."

"Then let's not rile them." Connor blinked into the light ahead, willing his lethargy to lift. "Anything else?"

Jack hesitated for just too long. "I don't think so, Mister," he said. "Atalanta's ship overtook us on the Highway."

Hells' mercy. She couldn't be chasing past her husband to wind him up, surely. Given the way the pair had parted after the funeral, Connor doubted she was in search of an armistice at this early stage.

Too damned hard, that was her problem: or maybe Calad was too soft. The distinction was minimal at present. Ask her to make allowance for a man whose father had just died, and she would throw Connor the look she normally kept for storehouse rats that had pissed on her barley stocks.

But if she wasn't here either to mend or worsen relationships with Calad, she must have business.

Connor left Jack to the controls, sat down at the spare desk at the back of the flight deck and opened as many newsnets and private nets as he could find, scanning and rescanning for any mention of a Guild Spellweaver – or all the pejoratives applicable thereto – being arrested in the last half day, or being a suspect in a crime over the past three days. The only result was a snide remark related to Atalanta's appearance in the city centre three days previously.

And *why* had she been on planet? Not just to invite Connor to a funeral. No. The timing was wrong: she'd been in the city for hours and had ignored Connor's offices. She'd had other business, had traversed the city centre on the way, and must not have been able to finish what she started.

Connor realised his hands were trembling. He clenched his fists and released them. Atalanta, on business. Calad, with an appointment at the same time and same place, or close enough; one he'd missed.

This was getting *messy*, and they hadn't even landed yet.

All senses on high alert now, he dismissed his screens and joined Jack in the cockpit, taking the copilot's seat without a word. The spaceport chatter dialog sped at his elbow. Police, police. Foreign traders and local traders and the police. No shootouts. No Spellweavers of any flavour mentioned.

"How far ahead was she?" he asked Jack after a few more minutes.

"She'll have landed by now if she didn't tail off away and round the other side of the planet." Jack pointed to his version of the 'port chitchat, pilot-geared, as comprehensive as the one running on Connor's screens: wind shear, turbulence and obstacles among the issues constantly updating. "I read a row between foreigners, cops and undersiders. Nothing to do with her."

Connor grunted. "If she didn't watch where she was going, she'll be in the mess by now. New World foreign might gang up with Septième on Old World foreign."

"She's not an idiot, Mister."

"True." Connor skimmed the ID list of ships tacking down the Highway around them, and tapped on a list entry a couple of hundred miles back along their trajectory. He opened the radio comms again. "Calad, we need to liaise."

"On a one-man ship during re-entry, that's not ideal," Calad said after a moment.

"I can lend you staff as required. Go behind us into the spaceport. Play it quiet."

"My ID card says Union of Independent Star Systems, not Port Logis," he answered after a further pause. "If those are the Cliff Enterprises people in dispute with the police, they'd assume I was on their side."

"Picking sides is dangerous for you as well as me. We all meander home. Got it?" He signed off without waiting for acknowledgement.

"Ten marks says he doesn't listen," Jack muttered as if to himself. Connor, in turn, pretended he hadn't heard.

Instead he reclined into seating foam and watched the viewscreen adjust for re-entry. Contrary to some of the more vapid Union-citizen beliefs he'd heard spouted over the years, not every successful Septième trading firm was involved with the underside any more deeply than by paying them protection money. 'Union trader' versus 'Septième trader' didn't have to mean the underside – for instance, him – being dragged in.

Life throws dung balls sometimes. Believe in that. Never, ever, believe in hope, any more than in that green light in the corners.

The door slid open behind the cockpit in a drift of soft fabrics and perfume. "There you are," Gisele said from the doorway. "What's happening?" From habit, Connor glanced at her reflection in the viewscreen. Veiled: well, Jack was here.

"We'll land in an hour, maybe less, maybe a little more. There's a disturbance at the spaceport." His text feed flared up again. "Though it appears to be affecting ships taking off more than those trying to land."

Now, *this* was different. He reread the chatter lines, looking for hidden meanings or sidelines of plain-text information. Mass searches, yes, in the takeoff queue. The foreigners complaining of theft. Pritie couldn't have known when she wrote to Connor.

Calm down, he whispered to his heartbeat. A theft – well. He'd been absent from planet for two days.

"Now, *that*'s foolish," Gisele said, sitting down at the desk Connor had used earlier. "I know you don't propose to pick out their shoe colour before we land, so I don't know why you would want me to think you would make assumptions about anything else they may be doing."

Connor blinked at the view in front of him. Mirqest's surface, approaching fast. Forested hills – colonial plantations and rich folk's arborealism – and farmland rolled up to each city, with the capital approaching over the horizon, at a trajectory that would lead the ship to crash land unless Jack swung into the spaceport. Except, of course, that ship and city were approaching each other via fusion drive and planetary orbit, and only his perspective fooled him into observing that the ship approached the city rather than the other way round.

He looked back over his shoulder. Gisele had opened what looked like a few gossip columns, and was flicking through pictures of what passed for local high society. Impossible to tell whether she was checking scandals or fashions.

From the other side of the flight deck, Yasmine emerged, and stopped mid-step when she saw her aunt. She dropped Gisele a perfunctory curtsey and said to Connor, "What's wrong?"

"I hope, nothing for us." Connor squinted at the city, such a familiar approach. No sizeable fires or bomb sites that he could see. The likelihood was that his office would still be standing – and the morgue where he'd left Merissa. Cops, foreigners, underside all in a row...

Calad had named Cliff as the foreign team in the mix without prompting. He must have known Cliff was in operation on the planet. Connor, for one, hadn't mentioned that factlet to him.

Ahead, a cloud of ships puffed away from the spaceport, revealing overly neat files below: freighters and personal runabouts alike lined up for who knew what checks. Organised by someone with influence and money: Cliff Enterprises or Rafael Martinez. No one else here, not even Saxen, had enough influence to do this. An alliance between Saxen, Stig Davids and Eliss al'Trier would have required Davids and al'Trier to be on speaking terms.

Traffic Control signalled to their ship to keep circling: Jack retook control from the AI and complied. Another line of ships took off. CLEARED TO LAND, the traffic controller signalled. Jack pitched *Shadowmark* downwards towards the hangars.

Connor squinted at the ground as they descended, at scurrying security staff, traders clumping in groups to stare at the ground crews, piloted and autopiloted goods trucks drawn up in their own queues en route to their destination ships. The *ships* that were being searched instead of the goods trucks themselves. Connor frowned. Theft of data onto some team's drives rather than having been upnetted? Theft of something small, for sure, for it seemed *every* ship was being searched, whatever its cargo capacity. He didn't fancy the search teams' task, if so.

Some months ago he'd bought four hangar leases in the freight end of the 'port, including a Hamadryad one for *Shadowmark*. The 'port AI, after its traditional delay, ordered Jack to a landing strip midway down the port and from there to their hangar. Connor opened his mouth to warn Gisele, but remembered himself just in time and addressed Yasmine instead: "Better get your stuff together. I want to head home as quickly as possible."

Yasmine nodded and, though the ship was steering at a not-quite-compensated angle, headed off the flight deck. Gisele was gripping her chair arm, and did not rise. At least she'd not been physically airsick.

Jack levelled the descent and steered into the hangar as its door opened for them. Connor unbuckled his restraints and left the flight deck at a jog. Behind him, he heard Gisele rise and hurry after him. More airsick than he'd thought, perhaps.

He hadn't bothered unpacking: it took him mere moments to reach into his cabin and collect his case. Yasmine joined him at the hatch just as the engine powered down. "Are we to wait for my aunt, Mister?" she asked, somewhat stiffly.

"I've ordered a car to the 'port to pick her up. The driver's not pinged me yet." There was always a spare bike on the ship, but he'd never seen Gisele drive a bike.

Sighing to himself – people didn't change, and he would never expect Gisele to change – Connor cracked open the hatch. He stopped with one foot still inside *Shadowmark* and one on the ramp. Below him on the hangar's concrete floor stood a man about his own age. Foreigner, New World pureblood with dark hair tied back in a tiny plait, wearing Septième clothes like they didn't fit him properly. He held an over-trimmed pistol in one shivering hand. Its barrel pointed straight at Connor.

It was the man on the far left of that photograph of Merissa. The man's shoulders looked heavier in real life, muscle beneath fat, and the rest of him seemed rumpled from disuse rather than overweight.

Connor's pistol was buckled into his holster too far from his hand. He gestured backwards with two fingers to Yasmine and Marcello in a manner he hoped seemed inconsequential. "Who in eleven hells are you?" he said, voice full of ice cubes.

Instead of replying, the stranger said with a formality that did not match the gun in his hand, "Mister, where is my wife?"

*

CHAPTER NINE

Wife?

Connor was set to reply that he'd never run off with a wife in his life, but as he'd technically just run off with Dominic's, he said with a sigh he hoped sounded long-suffering, "Mister, you and I are strangers, and I don't know your wife either. I invite you to elucidate."

"I last saw her," the stranger continued in the same over-dogged tone, "three days ago. Her cousin was with us. He left the two women together –"

"Women?" In that photo he'd had his eye on the foreign woman: if that was the missing wife – did 'women' mean her and Merissa?

The door to the main 'port corridor creaked open. "That will be all," a woman's voice said from the doorway. Connor looked. A New World pureblood: taller and darker than any woman Connor would expect to see on Septième streets, with afro hair swept up into a beehive atop her head, flanked by two much younger men too nervous to be guards. She looked Connor up and down from below as if she were the one above – at a level they would have been similar heights – and said to the novice gunman, "*Approaches*, Mikhail. There are better angles available."

"I want to find Nerys," the man – Mikhail – said with the same obstinacy as before.

Bare feet pattered up to Connor's shoulder. "Ilsa, there you are," Gisele said, honey-voiced behind her veil. "I've been watching you for a dozen miles. Come inside – I want to talk to you." She sailed sideways towards Connor's private study. "Yasmine, bring tea and coffee," she said over her shoulder.

Yasmine stood staring after Gisele for a full three seconds, but turned and headed for the galley without a word. The dark Union woman reacted with slightly more equanimity. "Stay here," she instructed the three men – who were her junior in age as well as rank, Connor estimated – and she brushed into the ship as if it were Gisele's rather than Connor's. She didn't remove her boots: Union folk didn't. Maybe Gisele would start forgetting soon enough. Septième people only did so in temples.

Marcello stared at Connor as if he thought he was psychic and could explain what was going on. Jack, standing behind Marcello, made unsubtle gestures towards Mikhail from out of the man's range of vision. "Don't just stand around: get me a chair," Connor said to the space between the pair. Jack and Marcello glanced at each other, and Jack withdrew.

Connor turned back to Mikhail. He seemed far different from the photograph of three days previously: no longer jovial, but tired and agitated. A man, Connor was certain, who'd never killed, but who might take it into his head to do anything in his present condition.

Present *apparent* condition. Connor exhaled very slowly. Spend long enough on Port Logis and a man might start believing people presented themselves in some way that approached reality. For a start, Mikhail couldn't possibly be as young as he appeared – late twenties: he was almost certainly, bearing in mind the therapy methods available in the Union, in his late thirties or early forties.

Jack re-emerged from the galley corridor carrying a stool, with Yasmine behind him bearing a tray of hot drinks and a sour expression. As the young Weaver headed into Connor's study, voices drifted out past her: Gisele chattering, 'Ilsa' occasionally getting a word in edgeways.

"That's better," Connor said to *Shadowmark*'s hull, and sat down on the stool as if it were an armchair. Maybe he couldn't rely on whatever impression Mikhail gave, but the spaceport fuss and Ilsa's appearance indicated he wasn't making trouble only for Connor. "So. 'Mikhail'. Were your parents religious or romantics?"

He flushed a little – older than he looked, then, but not that old. "As my parents are dead, I can't ask them." Spoilt attitude, more than huffy.

"So we have that much in common. I can't say I ever encumbered myself with a husband, though... are you married to your wife?"

Mikhail hesitated again. "We became engaged to marry

last year," he said, a child seeking excuses.

"That's optimistic of you." All the little tingles running down Connor's neck were starting to make him nervous. "So. When did you last see her?"

"Four nights ago." The night Merissa had died. Damn. He'd still been on-planet. "I got some bad news – I left planet. Then I heard Nerys was missing, so I came back." He glared at Connor, gun hand trembling again. "And *no one* has seen her."

Assuming this missing 'Nerys' *was* the woman in that photo – one missing and one dead in the same evening could be coincidence. Could be. It didn't seem likely.

A woman significant enough for the 'port authority to near-on shut down the spaceport in order to search for her: this did not look good. But Mikhail did not know, yet, that Connor knew about the connection to his organisation.

His eyes drifted to the two younger men who'd escorted Ilsa into the hangar. One, he was sure, he'd never seen before, but the second was familiar. The other man from the photograph: the one who'd picked up Merissa in a coffee shop the day before she died. His wife's cousin, Mikhail had said.

"If you were having such a good time that evening," Connor said to Mikhail, "why take a walk? Why leave any woman in a bar in a city like this?"

"So you *do* know –"

The study door slid open and Yasmine poked her head outside. "My aunt wishes to speak to you," she said to Connor. Sounded like she'd snapped out of the sulks. Connor, misgivings not fading, stood and followed Yasmine into the study.

Gisele had unveiled and was sitting alongside Connor's chair, hands wrapped round a coffee cup as if it were a chalice. She smiled up at Connor, as reassuring as a cat, but didn't stop talking to Ilsa.

"– and I mean, my dear, what you *expected* and what you *thought* shouldn't really bear that much resemblance to what *exists*, otherwise we'd all be eating venison five days a week and then there would be a glut on the deer hide market, which would be a pity. Connor, do sit down." She shifted to allow him round to his chair. Yasmine poured him a cup of tea without asking. Maybe she'd spent the past few minutes failing to say a word.

Ilsa, in contrast, was still trying. "This is not just a missing person –"

"Oh, I realise it couldn't be, or you wouldn't be making such a fuss when a grown woman heads off whoever knows where, but how you can expect a provincial official not to draw on all his experience I'm not sure. You need to understand, dear, that there are times when nobody *wants* to know. Afterwards everything is so much simpler: wouldn't you agree?" Ilsa nodded and opened her mouth to speak. "Not really, of course," Gisele went on, "when you're wading through eighteen layers of difficulties, and doubtless all your Elder Gentlefolk threatening to make a fuss, and the *relatives*. People do have so many relatives nowadays, hmm?" She sipped her coffee. "I don't include husbands in that – they're inclined to make fusses in any event – and with such a hefty commercial element involved you are in a little difficulty: though for this particular deal I'm sure you can rely on the husband for the fine details. The hard part will be whatever comes next. There is a next coming up, isn't there?"

Ilsa nodded. Connor tried to hide behind his teacup and watch her. Initially she had seemed dragged along on Gisele's tidal wave: now she'd composed herself far too quickly. To Connor, she said, "Nerys is a critical member of our team and a personal connection of several of our delegates. We are mobilising every resource in this city to help locate her. Your cooperation in that would be invaluable."

Doubtless, and if Connor weren't to burn every trade in his life, past, present or future, he should take note of the Cliff badge on her shoulder. Yet the pressure to do so made him itch to rebel. "You turned out the entire spaceport to, I infer, search every ship for this woman. I know you had the city searched yesterday. What do you expect *me* to do when you have pull like that? I refer to you specifically rather than to your overgrown boy outside."

She had the grace to assume a little embarrassment. "My colleague – Mikhail Chester – is distraught. I apologise for his manner. As for the spaceport search, I'm aware that its chances of locating her are sparse in the extreme."

"Yet you wanted to be seen to do something. Placate your big bosses and kick Martinez's ankles at the same time. In your position – top of the heap – I'd incline myself to do the same."

"Cliff is not the galaxy's biggest defence contractor," Ilsa said.

Connor shrugged. "Biggest company that trades in arms. I'm a guppy in your waters: I don't bother myself with categorising the sharks. However, if you were hoping to leverage my hired magic, this young lady is all I have at the moment." He aimed a finger at Yasmine. "Or am I the only man in the city carting around any mind-readers at all?"

"Put not your faith in Spellweavers. No offence, Gisele –"

"None taken," she murmured.

"– but Nerys never got on with them, nor they with her. I respect her position."

In other words, Ilsa had objections to Spellweavers – probably religious objections – despite her acquaintance with Gisele, and fancied pushing the blame onto her junior staffer. More fool her. "Well, I'll continue to use mine as I see fit – including seeking confirmation of your motives."

"I had nothing to do with this."

Connor laughed, without mirth. "Mistress, you've clearly known my brother's stepmother for a few years." He indicated Gisele. "I've only just met you. I'll take my precautions." After a few seconds' poisonous pause, she nodded. Connor forced his brain back into action. She couldn't be so touchy by nature, not in the world she inhabited. Unused to seeing someone like him treat her as an equal? If so, he'd use that as hard as he could. Unless, of course, she'd assumed this attitude to cover up something worse.

"In all this fuss, I don't think we've been properly introduced." He granted her a formal nod. "Connor Cardwain, owner and CEO of several trading businesses." For tax reasons. Always tax reasons.

"Ilsa Martins, regional sales director for Cliff Enterprises."

Sales director, not a guard squad leader or the like here to hand over a handful of warships to their new owner. Another little indication that the Cyclops trade was not proceeding as normal – and that Cliff, as well as Martinez, was complicit in that situation. That, or she was here to broker an immediate upsell. She wasn't here to buy. Cliff did not manufacture on the Septième on the cheap. If only.

"Now we know each other, please enlighten me further. Who is your Lady Vanishèd?"

"Nerys Capuin. Senior account manager." Ilsa fiddled with her jack. A formal picture of the missing woman popped up on Connor's desk. Same woman who'd been in that photo with Merissa. Same happy woman, forcing back a smile even in her corporate photo, even dressed as here in pleats and furbelows. The black hair hung straight to her waist, Connor could now see, though this picture – with no basis for comparison – failed to accentuate how small and slim she was.

"She wasn't cheating on Mikhail," Ilsa added.

"According to their superiors, neither is anyone... no, that's not the key point." He wagged a finger at her. "Your Treizième boy with a Neuvième name: why did he dash off sideways at the same time his wife went missing, if he *hadn't* offed her?"

Ilsa inhaled like she'd smelt a dead toad. "I'm glad you asked me rather than him. His aunt committed suicide. He went to the funeral."

"Doubtless like the one I went to at the same time –" let her think on *that* – "the priesthood can stretch the definition of 'one day' only so far. When did the rest of you realise Nerys was missing?"

"Not for a day or more. She had informed me – very properly – that she had a private meeting that afternoon. She didn't keep it. I assumed she had travelled to the funeral with Mikhail, but he sent me a message to pass on to her when he couldn't raise her jack."

"And thus all this mess blocking 'port traffic. I see." Connor nodded towards the door. "Get him to pack away the gun before I set a squad on him. He's got a lot of questions to answer, some to you, some to me."

"Why don't you start with your own employee?" She waved a hand at the hull surrounding them. "Mikhail and Aled – who is Nerys's *cousin* – know nothing. I asked them.

Why don't you start by considering your own woman? What did Aled say her name was – Merissa."

Yasmine spilt a little tea into her saucer. Connor, clear-headed, watched the young Weaver right her cup and sip as if nothing had been said. New information: the fourth nightclubber's name was Aled, and in that information provision, Connor was one step ahead of Ilsa, as he'd been a step ahead of Mikhail. In a few hours or days, that might matter.

"Unfortunately," he said to Ilsa in his most urbane voice, "Merissa was murdered that same night. Which brings us to a very interesting situation." He leant across the desk, watching Ilsa as closely as he could. A foreigner and not entirely at ease. "If, say, your Mistress Nerys Capuin had dumped a body and high-tailed it out of here – what's the list of planets she'd most naturally have gone to?"

For the next five minutes he let her bluster wash over him, kicking Yasmine under the desk whenever she looked set to speak. He'd take it and grateful. Let Ilsa blow herself out. She still controlled Mikhail and Aled, and they were Connor's best links left to Merissa.

"OK," he cut her off when she stuttered over her words for the second time, "it's all talk. But I need that talk to start *doing* something."

"You want my help and won't give yours?"

Connor shrugged. "Perhaps if your people examine a mini-drone prototype of mine, I'd suddenly find a stack more info on my streets."

"Materiel we already sell to your competitors? That way doesn't work, *Mister*."

"Neither does threatening me on my patch. *My* staff member is dead, last seen in company with *your* staff members. Why don't you pull out your boys to answer a few questions about that little wrinkle? Can't force yourself down to the level of caring about a dead cleaner?"

"They can't have hurt her. Ask the police – Mikhail and Nerys knew enough to keep their nights out within the governor's cordon –"

"And you imagine the police'd tell the truth with *my* employee the victim?" Connor shook his head. "Off my ship, now. You've no need to stay. Neither of us can help the other. You can find me at my office in town if you need me." He rose, and inclined his head to Gisele. "I imagine my car will have got caught at the 'port perimeter. Once your friend tells security to lift the cordon," and he sent Ilsa a pointed glance, "I'm sure it won't take long to get here."

"I can drive a bike."

"Ever tried in a face-veil?" Connor opened the door and half-bowed to Ilsa, an invitation. She pushed back her chair and stood, still frowning.

"You're wrong, you know," she said.

"I'm wrong about a lot of things a lot of the time. Doesn't change the universe."

"Consider what will happen if no one finds her." Ilsa straightened till she looked Connor in the eye. "Consider the effect on business – everyone's business – if a foreign police force came and ripped this city apart looking for her."

"I've had enough experience of that to last a lifetime. No, it won't come to that. For one thing, they wouldn't want the ignominy of losing."

"When so much here might arouse their ire? You'll say they have no jurisdiction – but they might claim doings here had an effect on their people. Drugs. Slaves."

"If other people's business gets blown, I'll raise a glass to it and welcome."

She leant towards him, just a fraction, almost enough to make him wonder if he'd seen it at all. "Drugs, slaves – and arms. Accidents happen, Mister." She nodded to Gisele and went out.

Connor would have followed, but Yasmine closed the door before he could do so. "Now what?" she said. "Go back to Port Logis till they've gone?"

"If I do that I'll be short a business inside a week."

"And I'm sure there's no need to panic," Gisele said, rising. As Connor looked back at her, she wound her shawl tail back over her face. He couldn't tell whether she was smiling. "For trouble doesn't exactly flee when one wishes, and success and breathing aren't always correlated. Shall we go?"

*

CHAPTER TEN

The spaceport hadn't changed in its fundamentals. Connor hadn't changed: he kept the throttle low and eased his car through the 'port environs, past tidy chandlers and engineers' shops and strings of relatively decorous drinking holes, out onto Portside and over city air, rising high above rooftops till he could count every man's missing tiles. Bikes swarmed in the air, flitting between trucks, cars and buses, glinting gold in afternoon light. Yasmine's bike flitting behind the car, with Jack on her tail towing Marcello and Connor's bikes, was still a niggle he longed to be able to ignore, and –

"Isn't the forest sweet? You can see the logging pattern from here, like an elephant with three legs."

– no, Gisele had changed everything. "Please don't lean sideways: I'll tip the car." *Please shut up. Please.*

"All right." She straightened, almost imperceptibly, in her seat at Connor's side. "These seem smart streets." They were, for the Septième: stone and wood, traditional and well-kept, lined with trees and studded with what passed for boutiques. "Half the women think they're on the Neuvième and none of them can tie a shawl. I'm more interested in the dresses on the others. They look rather elegant."

Connor glanced down for a moment. "Mostly being worn by bourgeoises: a few with inherited money, the odd self-made merchant, a few superior tarts. The real aristocracy dress Neuvième style."

Ahead, the traffic parted, swift as a curtain-twitcher. Connor pitched the car to the left. In his rear view cam he saw Yasmine and Jack mirror the motion. "Hey," Marcello said from the car's back seat.

"Fasten your harness next time."

Gisele peered out of the window at the cavalcade beginning to pass: bikers in Rafael Martinez's old gangland stripes, surrounding a car. "Who's that?"

Connor stared past her at the car and its single occupant. "The governor's wife." Her car windows were not tinted.

Connor saw an upright figure, dark curls and face, teardrop-perfect eyes staring straight ahead: a young face, draped in gold lace, a monarch remote from her subjects. "Zolde de Priet. Forget about having anything to do with her. I'm too strange a fish for anyone in her social circle to court, and you've no status of your own here."

"Quite." Gisele watched the line of vehicles pass, faint concentration creasing her face. "I would like to know who cut her hair, though. And I'll want you to recommend me a temple."

"You're a monotarian, right? There's less here for you than on Port Logis. Here, monotarianism means angel-worship, not devotion to a prophet. Priestesses of Glory and priests of Victory have regular punch-ups."

Gisele sniffed. "Blasphemy, dear –"

"Nothing to do with me." The end of Martinez's bike trail had passed. Connor wrenched his car back into line and accelerated.

The city hall lay below and on the left, a barrack of a place left over from Union times upgraded and rebuilt over the years till one small tower alone was left from the original. Armed men patrolled its roof, and a steady stream of bikes weaved between it and a more modern tower, a tall black tower, opposite on a quarter-mile wide square – the police's overall headquarters. Northwards staggered acres upon acres of money, spewing up to the hills and their broad estates, a conglomerate of wealth as proud as anything on Ransomvale or Sukli Ban: land seized for aesthetics, insulated by distance from mines, logging sites and farms, wrapped in streets scoured of any hint of poverty.

One could tell which streets had ever had wealth by the sewer map. Connor's offices were perched near an edge of the network, in middle-income territory, closer to the centre than the precariat suburbs. Attempt to go up in class as well as in income level? Éloise's influence? Connor lacked her posture, her attitudes, her odd streak of prudery. But making others believe he could become middle-class had some value.

The streets surrounding his office looked quiet as he drove down, guards patrolling at expected frequencies, his refuse collectors street-cleaning, glimpses of his line staff strolling into small businesses to collect rent. Normal.

"You didn't mention you had a shrine just next door."

– almost normal. Connor descended as delicately as he could in the narrow confines, nudging the car's rear past the chimney of the cookshop opposite his garage and in to avoid the gun-shop sign. The gunsmith was his franchisee, a hopeful young woman who thought she was getting a better deal from him than was actually the case.

The garage door stood open for him; he lined up, slid inside and cut to a halt directly over the mechanic's pit. Yasmine dropped her bike in beside the car and jumped off to open the door for Connor. He waved off the string of officers, all men, who'd hurried in via the connecting door to greet him. "Get up to my study. Send Pritie here. And – what's her name – Irra, the runner." The men nodded and withdrew, leaving just the mechanic in the corner servicing two staff bikes. He couldn't be helped.

Gisele opened her own car door and stepped out, white shoe neatly dodging a puddle of oil. She'd pulled her shawl tail over her face again. "Do you always take an indirect route here?" she said through the muslin.

"There are a few people I prefer to avoid."

"Customers?"

"Former associates." Men and women who had wanted his wares without paying, till Logan rapped on their front doors and Éloise greeted them from alleys as they climbed out of back windows. Meris Hardblade's branch captain: he still shunned Hardblade's crewers as if the entire bundle of them had a contract out on him, which, for all he knew, might be true. One or two pirates: it was best to keep a sky quarrel in the sky and off the ground.

Gisele sniffed. "Aversion therapy isn't always a solution, dear."

Before Connor could compose an answer – before he could work out how to phrase to Yasmine what he wished to say to Gisele – the internal door opened again and Pritie entered. She cast an enquiring eye at Gisele. "Mistress Delacourte is my brother's stepmother," Connor said, trying to keep irritation out of his voice. "She needs a bedroom and a sitting room, and a female runner to play page." He pointed to Irra, now peeking round the door as if she thought she'd done something wrong and would get shot any moment. "She'll do."

The little runner scuttled to the car and hauled Gisele's cases from the boot. Gisele watched her go without interfering and said to Pritie, "I'm sure you have a multiplicity of advice."

"Well —"

"And I have quite a few questions. For a start, who runs that quite ridiculously over the top sweet shop on the corner of Abermarle Street and Hewson Way?"

Pritie whisked her out, returning nondescript answers. The mechanic had paused his work to stare: he opened his mouth, but Connor waved him to silence. Already this was beginning to infuriate him past his expectations.

Yasmine pulled Connor's less substantial bag from the car and opened the internal door for him with her free hand. "Do you want me to go to her?" she said.

"Not now. Leave her with Pritie. You go back to the spaceport and find Calad."

She frowned. "He's fine. He's had no time to get into trouble."

"He should have been here by now — unless he went looking for Atalanta. Our family has caused too great a disturbance this afternoon already. I'm not a fan of attention."

"What about Atalanta?"

He could do nothing for Atalanta. His position was precarious as it was. "Not much you can do that she can't. You're brighter than her husband. Extract him and get back here as soon as you can. With any luck she'll follow."

She nodded, and withdrew to her bike. Connor headed into the main hall, nodding to those employees he passed, and went upstairs to his study. The welcoming committee was there — a captain and two lieutenants, now listening with appreciative smiles to Jack Priest describe the Port Logis trip.

"— and, I tell you, just watching the women gives me a headache." As Connor entered, Jack broke off and stood up.

"Mind you don't watch too closely or more than your head'll hurt. Marcello wasn't lying to you." Connor seated himself behind his desk and gestured to Captain Mink to start.

This felt *right*, it felt *normal*, evaluating a list of trades made and declined while he was away, taking first view of the list of major trades he would confirm or decline himself: company news he might have missed, underside rumour that hadn't filtered to Port Logis. Here and now, memorising the latest false flag list, reading UISS troop movement charts, listening to rival theories from his lieutenants about the Union's intentions, his study seemed the centre of the world.

Circle mage-corps crewers – like Michel – would say their sense of ethics was all that prevented the Union from trying to take the Septième back. No rule of law stood inviolate when faced with strength of arms. The UISS did as it would: perhaps Atalanta would say the threat of Federation involvement kept the Union out.

Kept the Union, perhaps, subsidising arms sales to planets they wanted to prop up.

"– and we moved the branch ship to Firedrake," Mink concluded. "Minor load-out, running under the name Michael Michaelson." Connor allowed a tiny smile at that: Mink shrugged. "Doesn't matter that it's a clear alt, if folk keep guessing whose it is."

Connor nodded. "For long enough. We can re-register for the trip back." He pulled the 'port landing list across his desk and expanded it. "These ships, twelve Cyclopes."

"Came in with the Cliff crew."

"For Mister Martinez. I know. But something's going wrong with the trade." Connor opened the images alongside. Beautiful ships, on the ground: wings rearing up at each side spiked with guns he could price quite accurately and one model of which he'd even traded in the past. In the air, chasing him up a Highway, he would find them a less appealing sight. Those wings, each hosting a particle accelerator for the guns, would be glowing, and heavy blasts would be starting to pepper his hull. An average idiot could steer a Cyclops, if he had another average idiot on hand to use the gunnery platform.

"There were noises between the camps," Mink confirmed. "The noises got louder two days back."

"Cliff mislaid a negotiator and another one took an unscheduled trip offworld."

"What do we do?"

Connor steepled his hands on the desk. "Nothing now. We see if the talks restart. If they don't, we step in to broker." *And I will get the funds from somewhere to join in. Anywhere.* "If they do, we bring in more ships and trade to Saxen."

Mink opened a fresh docket and spread it in front of Connor – a sales form for five hundred rifles and fifty explosive drones not yet out of testing. "This came in this morning."

From Saxen. Connor pursed his lips. He'd had two hundred rifles just the other week. "I take it back. No more sales to his team – send any requests straight to me."

Beyond the study door, another door banged, and angry boots clattered in the corridor. "How," Connor heard Calad shout, muffled but unmistakeable, "is it in any way unobtrusive to find oneself front and centre of a crowd of merchants shouting, 'Burn the witch!'?" A pause. "I don't care! You –" An interruption. Connor could identify no words but heard distinct venom.

"All of you," he said, "leave, and send them in here." Each man nodded. Jack Priest, at the back of the room, opened the door. Calad and Atalanta were standing just outside, eyeing each other from half an inch apart. Atalanta was Calad's height or near enough – Calad looked a sensible height on the Septième, though was short for a Neuvième man – so they stared each other in the eye. In more than one of the bars outside, that look meant an impending head-butt.

Connor's line staff edged out of the study. Calad gave his wife a final smouldering stare – it made him resemble a particularly attractive emu – and strode up to Connor. Behind, Atalanta closed the door and perched on Jack's chair, as far from Calad as she could get.

"My cousin said you wanted to speak to me," Calad said, sulky-voiced.

If Connor could have bawled him out then and there, he would have done so. Beautiful nitwit (and Atalanta, he had to admit, was good-looking for a woman and, for an intelligent person, acted like a highly stupid one where her husband was concerned). "Have you rescheduled the meeting you missed?" he said instead.

"Not yet."

"Fine. Do that. Meanwhile, I have a job for you." He opened a contract form and centred it on his desk. Didn't matter what the job was, within reason. It never mattered. "Find out why Martinez is stalling his purchase of a dozen lovely new ships sitting in dock. I've never met a man who invited a deal to his door and didn't do it. He's planning something and I need to know what." He pushed the form to Calad, who signed it without even bothering to read it and walked out without a word.

Atalanta did not follow. "He's losing his nut," she said as the door closed.

Connor waited three seconds before he heard Calad walk away. That was faintly preferable to him pushing his way back in and throwing a punch at his wife, but only faintly: Calad was the type to let insults fester till they burst. "He's upset. Never mind him now – I'll keep him on a stable course. What happened at the 'port?"

She shrugged. "Nothing I haven't come to expect."

I don't tolerate it. I'll reach a point where no one else permits it. "Does it jeopardise your mission?" Sea-chilled blue eyes stared down at him. He held up a finger. "I don't care what your mission is." *Yes, I do.* "I want to know if being shaken down by 'port police jeopardises you to the extent that anyone is going to try to shake you down again, here. Note I said 'try'."

"I think not. The major risk to both of us is deportation."

Connor blinked. "I doubt you'd go quietly. I know I wouldn't go quietly. No governor who came up on the underside would deport an underside arms source."

"If he didn't need you anymore, thanks to his lovely new friends? And I would have no option but to go quietly, unless I wanted to stage a revolution on behalf of the great and glorious Earth Federation." She waggled her copper brows at him. "I will never be *persona grata* out here. I'm not Logan using battlefield Augury to infiltrate a soirée on Port Logis. My position here may already be fatally compromised. With your permission, I'll go and find out which way the flags are blowing."

Connor gestured to her to leave. She bowed as if he were paying her and, with one more quick glance at the paraphernalia on Connor's desk, slipped out of the study.

If, if, if. A man could kill himself via second-guessing. Connor stared at his desk litter. His three large sales requests; Merissa's photo with Mikhail, Nerys and the cousin, Aled; Saxen's order that Connor had declined; two open newssheets, one frozen on the day they'd all left Mirqest, the other blaring fresh headlines from Union and Federation alike; his quarterly accounts; a city map; a miniature of whisky Dominic had once given him. The latter had probably originated from Atalanta. What had she been looking at? What was she *doing here*?

Same question one always asked of either Union or Federation official – or non-official – folk on the Sixième and Septième. *Were they committing acts preparatory to invasion?* Not likely in this case with one spy the only person in play. *Were they sabotaging each other's acts?* Depended on whether one took Cliff Enterprises to be an organ of Union imperialism. Connor had heard arguments in favour and against. If Atalanta took them as de facto Union organ, she could have come to undermine their sale. *Were they seeking to profit, legally or illegally, from an interstellar power imbalance?* Atalanta had proved herself willing to do so in the past, even if only via selling Connor whisky minus export duty.

In her case, at least, he could rule out tourism.

Connor leant back in his seat and closed his eyes, trying to picture that last glance Atalanta had given his study. Maybe he'd imagined her intent. If not, he could conjure an explanation for her looking at every item on his desk, including the news reports – with their Federation gossip, however overblown – except for the photograph.

He reached out a hand, picked up the photo chip and, opening his eyes at last, stared at the four faces. Mikhail had come to life for him now, stepping as if from the screen with gun in hand, and Aled was a wisp flitting around the corners of his mind, as he'd flitted round Ilsa's heels earlier.

He had no such easy way to connect to Nerys, eyes closed and laughing straight out of the screen at Connor, a wealth of life in the image, with her hand wrapped round Mikhail's wrist as if she owned him. Maybe in that touch Connor could see why Mikhail wanted her back.

A man who could do him quite a bit of harm, whatever his boss wanted.

A man who'd seen Merissa just before she died.

Whatever Atalanta was doing, Connor would have to leave her to it. She would tell him eventually, or would not, and he had no feasible way to stop her from doing whatever she wanted. Right now, even kidnapping her husband wouldn't distract her. Let her stay busy, and she might keep Calad and the cops distracted. No one but Connor had much cause to give a damn about Merissa.

Connor stretched out a finger and circled Nerys's face with his nail. She'd seen Merissa too, just before whatever vengeful or sex-drugged malice had taken her life. Mikhail and the Cliff team wouldn't thank him for finding the missing woman: he'd lived long enough to know that. But maybe the two women had fallen foul of the same mischance…

Still staring at the picture, Connor touched his neural jack. "Pritie."

"Yes?" She sounded tired and a little distant.

"Come up here."

She knocked and entered ninety seconds later. She looked tired: shoulders drooping, strain creasing her eyes. She was older than Connor, maybe by ten years. Right now, she looked it, as Gisele, the same age, did not.

"Gisele's exhausting, but I don't think she's *that* exhausting. Did you sleep last night?"

"Not much," she said as she closed the door. "The search parties weren't quiet."

"I'm sorry." He was, but not enough to order her on a spa trip to Port Logis. "You asked about Merissa in the bars and on the streets."

She shrugged, expressive of Sisyphean effort. "One lone girl in the Septième night could vanish down any hole."

"She wasn't alone." Connor tapped the picture. "This

foreigner is the one the search parties are looking for. She and Merissa hit ground at the same time, or near enough."

Pritie's weary eyes sharpened. "One wiped, one grabbed?"

"Maybe." Maybe. But how had whoever killed Merissa known to put her at her flat, unless he hadn't been a stranger? She hadn't gone home, let alone taken Nerys to her place. Connor crushed that minor doubt and went on, "Try again. Send out a chat squad this evening and tell them to ask again for *both*. The cops aren't going to get anywhere either because they're looking just for the one, their one. We can get there first by tracing *both*. If you get any lead, follow it."

He wasn't trying to do favours for Ilsa. She wouldn't give him fleas, let alone a contract and a reward. But if he laid hands on Nerys he'd have a bargaining chip.

As Pritie withdrew, Connor poked at the photograph, at the two men's images, dark in gathering evening gloom. "Brushed me off when I needed your help, no matter how much you needed mine," he said softly. "If I find Nerys, you'll talk to me then."

*

CHAPTER ELEVEN

Connor dragged the first wholesale order across his desk. Trickier to read with the study lights on: he dimmed the lighting and tried to concentrate. Perhaps he should start assigning the wholesale lot, along with the retail orders, to his sales staff: particularly for instances like this – a reorder from a middlewoman who supplied all the retailers in Mirqest's second city via a succession of front companies. Large reorder, but that wasn't too unusual: Connor cleared the order and opened the next.

Even for offworld customers, most of his checks were automatic by now. Anyone Éloise might one day decide a Circle Spellweaver ought to punch. Anyone overtly opposed to Rafael Martinez, or to Connor's former boss, Meris Hardblade, on the off-chance that placating Hardblade would keep her teams off his. Anyone arming up for a private war that would become embarrassing for him if his client won. He used to add anything that would embarrass Dominic if it became known that his family were involved in it, but no longer. Now he just had to factor in his tenuous relationship with White Canyon. It didn't seem likely that Cliff Enterprises would add itself to the list any time soon.

One factory of his own (with or without gremlins – Mina Jai had sent him a nil-result note) did not a vertically integrated empire make… unless that factory could pull in a licence to reproduce items for a major company. There lay the quickest path to profit he could access – if, in fact, he *could* access it.

If Calad had only had the sense to stay on good terms with his wife, Connor might have crowbarred himself more of an entry into the Federation's operations than importing to them in tiny quantities. Not that a civilisation reliant on replicators had any need of more traditional manufacturing… which left the Union.

A light hand knocked on his door, and Calad stuck his fair head round it. "May I?"

"You're back quickly." He was: it was barely full dark outside.

"I was worried and I didn't want to phone you." He glanced down the corridor. "I see Maman's settled in."

"She's been industrious." And demanding. "What is it?"

Calad closed the door and leant on it. He never usually acted tongue-tied. His current state more than anything made Connor sit up a little straighter.

"I didn't get as far as the ships," Calad began. "There were quite a lot of security staff on site. Cliff Enterprises and Martinez's people. I could have talked my way in if I needed, but it didn't seem relevant."

"Then what was?"

Calad towed a stool out from the wall with one elegant leg and perched on it. "What's the relationship between Martinez and Saxen?"

"Respectful. Distant." Something that suited Connor's prudence. If Mirqest's governor and biggest local underside player had been at odds, or had discord developed between the triad of them and Comet, he couldn't have stayed, but nor would he have hung around if Saxen and Martinez had seemed too close. Beyond that, he could live with a little uncertainty. No man, even a Septième-born man, stepped onto the underside without a ton of it. "Update me."

Calad sighed in frustration. His fair hair wafted past his ears. "I'm not quite sure –"

"Yes, you are, or you wouldn't have trekked back here."

"Saxen's crew were hanging on the edge of the security cordon."

"I'm not surprised. Anything that happens here affects them: they'd be bound to take interest."

"What should their position be? Physical, psychological?"

Story time? Connor closed the wholesale orders. "Variable in the overall state of the world. Between them and Martinez I would expect their teams to be civil and cooperative –"

"Even the police?"

"Especially the police. Three quarters of them are ex-underside, Martinez's former staff. Don't assume cooperation means too much. I'd be surprised, for instance, if the two teams had clubbed together to finance the ships, except that *something* strange is going on with the finance. The Cliff team isn't behaving normally, if any Union team is ever normal."

"Hey."

"Sorry."

Calad nodded in acceptance. "There is some hostility between the teams."

"There's always an odd niggle between individuals from time to time. Do you mean that? Individual beef?"

"No. Groups on groups. Saxen's were eyeing the security guards and staying very quiet."

"Read their minds?"

"I couldn't."

"Then go back and – what do you mean, couldn't?"

"A street-witch has shields on them. I could have cracked the shielding: I'm not an expert but I'm far from hopeless at that stuff. She would have realised what I'd done, though, and warned Saxen, so I thought…"

"Thank you for thinking. Saxen could make my life quite awkward if he chose."

"I was worried more about Martinez."

"*Martinez*?"

"If he and Saxen are collaborating. If those of Saxen's squad playing games were just a small group, or if they were angry because I interfered. I'm aware you need to keep him on side even more than you do Saxen."

Connor hadn't credited Calad with the imagination to get that far. If he turned out to be right, maybe Connor would have to recalculate the use he made of him. Éloise had the brains to do more than play the grunt, but preferred the latter: Calad's primary resources were his pretty face, his charm, and his ability to slice a platoon in half without trying too hard. Undeniable though those talents were, they didn't always suffice.

Internal power games – part of Saxen's team colluding with Martinez while keeping the rest uninformed? Whatever Saxen turned out to be doing, that situation could turn very dangerous very quickly. "Get back out there. Observe. Don't trigger those shields but don't bother to keep yourself hidden. I don't mind them knowing you're watching."

He hadn't the staff numbers they did. He hadn't the experience or the contacts. But with his on-hand arsenal, he might give either big man a second's pause.

"Most importantly," he said as Calad made towards the door, "get a full inventory of their magic, tonight or tomorrow. In fact – take one of Pritie's juniors with you and stick him, or her if you're lucky, to sit and watch the physical side, so you can prioritise the magical defence list."

"Saxen's team or Martinez's?"

"Both. When you've got a handle on the 'port situation, drive to the city centre offices – for Martinez start at the city hall and police HQ – but steer clear of their private houses for now." Calad nodded. His green eyes held a question. "What?" said Connor.

"I'm not used to seeing you confused."

Not used to Connor letting on that he was confused, perhaps. "There are too many options right now. I need data. This particular data, only you can get for me."

"Or Yasmine."

"Or Yasmine, when she isn't playing parlourmaid to your mother." Calad flickered a smile at him – bright enough to lighten the evening. "What's happening with your side job?"

"It's looking dead. I can't find my contact or any word on her. I'll let you know if I have to take a detour to deal with it." He nodded to Connor and headed out.

Connor opened the wholesalers' applications again. The screens seemed to flicker and blur. Differing degrees of importance, maybe.

One of the three names sparked a memory, and Connor opened a datanet. Yes: the wholesaler supplied a pirate cartel, the AUB, that had spent the last ten years engaging in a low-level private war with White Canyon, one that threatened to spark into something bigger every so often. Connor rejected the application and stared at the other two. Consequences, consequences: where 'Thou Shalt Not Get Caught' was the primary commandment, what was left?

Risk, loss, ultimately death. The wages of sin. It was easy for Connor to pretend he was a man alone, never acknowledging a meaningful relationship other than his brotherly one, but his employees deserved a little better than his contempt.

With a sigh, he pushed away the forms. He couldn't concentrate. Darkling muses had reanimated Merissa's ghost in the shadows, running a polishing rag along the skirting: *"So what happened in the battle of Hester's Point if both sides ran out of guns and magic?"* she had said once. Connor hadn't been able to provide a satisfactory answer.

Saxen's team, Martinez's team, the Cliff Enterprises team.

Cliff had sent a negotiations team with their consignment, and apparently connected to that consignment rather than a further sale. That was one of the biggest red flags Connor had ever seen: all arms payments were strictly completed in advance of the client getting within sniffing distance of the goods.

So Cliff wanted to change the deal, or they thought Martinez wanted to change it.

Martinez: there was another issue. Gone fifty and retired in glory to play lord of a planet-sized manor. Still sharp? Going soft? Sharp might lead him, when combined with gubernatorial hubris, to think he could play games with the richest corporation in the galaxy. Utter foolishness, but many men were foolish when they believed themselves high.

A degree of softness could have led him to engage Saxen to disrupt the deal. A degree of sharpness, even trying to *prove* he was still sharp, could have led him to engage Saxen for the occasion while planning to double-cross him. In either case he could have given himself away to the Cliff team enough for them to send experts.

Experts in *negotiation*, again, not Circle Spellweavers, Cliff's first choice for expert muscle. And however Connor tried, he couldn't solve that particular conundrum. If trouble, hire Circle: it was automatic for the big Union corporations. They didn't stint on magic where this kind of risk was involved.

Which indicated Cliff was the cause of the issue, and Martinez's arrangement with Saxen – whatever that arrangement might be – was a response to that self-same issue.

Connor closed his eyes and rubbed his eyelids. Ifs, buts,

whys, maybes. Saxen's team shields, even, might be a response to whatever magic a rational man would expect a Union team would bring – if Spellweavers had only been able to get on with Ilsa's star negotiator. Connor half-laughed. Irony, if Nerys, missing, were a cause for her team's lack of magical muscle!

No. That was ridiculous. Nerys, Ilsa and the rest were *professionals*, as were Circle Spellweavers. Mere distaste couldn't be anywhere near sufficient to keep magic out of the Cliff team's reach.

So there was something else going on. A reason Nerys's presence meant the Cliff team didn't need magic to be safe? Connor himself was a latent augurer, as was his brother Logan. He couldn't control his power other than by using playing cards to induce it, and he couldn't steer it even then. A latent telepath, however, could sniff out lies automatically – including a Spellweaver's lie. A latent telempath could manipulate a negotiation in her favour with neither effort nor evidence.

Connor centred the photograph on his desk again, this time ignoring Merissa's image in favour of Nerys's, eternally laughing out of the screen at him. "Who are you?" he murmured to the photo. "Who are you, and why in eleven hells did you come here?"

Ilsa wouldn't tell him: Mikhail and Aled were highly unlikely to do so either. Unless, that was, they thought they were helping Connor find her.

He pushed away the photo. *Think.* Nerys and a throwaway mention were not enough: he couldn't base a theory on it. The only time a corporation risked that much money on the abilities of one human was if the human concerned were a full Spellweaver, preferably with thirteen colours in his or her wings –

A nasty feeling spread through Connor's stomach and up his spine. There was room for coincidence in any life. Such as a coincidence between a Cliff team turning up on the same planet as a Federation agent while an underside lord played games with a governor.

Atalanta, also, would never give him a straight answer about her doings until they were done. Calad –

Calad might not know. The squeakings of their earlier quarrel sounded, in retrospect, like she might have manufactured most of it to get him out of the way.

How to get the truth out of *anyone*…

Down the corridor Gisele's voice floated to a runner, "Don't wait for a reply, dear: it isn't done." Connor frowned. He couldn't. Could he?

*

CHAPTER TWELVE

"Magic," said Gisele, "isn't a quiet profession." As she was veiled, Connor kept his tongue between his teeth, and settled for giving the chintz curtains alongside her a meaningful glare.

They were lingering over breakfast in an upmarket café in Rift Haven, an artificial village on the edge of a group of tycoons' bucolic estates. If Connor had closed his business after his last big deal rather than reinvesting the proceeds, he might have scraped to a small house in this district: he'd have suffered dirty looks and ostracism. Here, all the money had been laundered years before, other than in the one family out of every hundred who had built their wealth legitimately. Connor probably would have been asked to leave the café, even smartened up as he was, if he hadn't brought Gisele, all in white with her filmy shawl tail wrapped round her face.

How she never dropped that tail in her tea or waffles, Connor didn't know, merely admired the artistry in the way she flicked it up and down to pass morsels underneath it. Her eyes, shrewd and assessing, followed every woman who passed in the café or on the street outside, as if they were on Port Logis and a woman's opinion mattered. Connor suspected she was making notes, though he did not know on what.

"It isn't that there's no magic about," Gisele continued, "but that it's not being used for purposes you'd consider relevant, or even sensible."

"I didn't think we'd reached the realm of faerie lights and faked artworks."

"Not entirely. Chilling a wine cellar, though? And portable painkillers – I mean, even Alazais doesn't agree with them in most circumstances, though one can't expect a healer to be sensible all the time. And to interfere with a negotiation of the type you mean – well, one of two approaches, the physical or the mental, would predominate, and there isn't much of either going on with Ilsa's group."

"There isn't?"

"No." Gisele set her cake fork on her plate's gilt-tipped rim for long enough to pour them both more tea. "She has personal physical shielding herself, and the ships have what you would expect, from what I saw in the spaceport. Not on Mikhail, certainly, or on that other boy Ilsa was towing around."

"She had two."

"I didn't notice particularly. Who is *she*?"

Connor glanced out of the window in the direction of Gisele's extended cake fork, to the sunny street outside and a short woman marching across the faux village square dressed Neuvième style in shawl and cloak, all in blue. Three other women trailed her, two in servants' clothing, the third in a grey local-cut gown. "Théodora Bramhall. Underside lord's daughter and another underside lord's widow. Money not quite clean enough to pass muster: personality enough to force it through."

"She looks rather forbidding. The one in her tail seems susceptible to it."

"That's her niece. I forget her name: she's a nonentity."

Gisele's eyes flittered across a trio of blue-robed priestesses scurrying across the square, two with Glory's emblem hanging from their belts and one of the mixed-sex Creation sect, deep in conversation. "It's not as simple, you see, as magic or its lack or even its *exclusion*. It's what one does with it. I gain you nothing by telling you what our waiter's thinking – I don't gain you much by making him serve us more quickly, with or without his knowledge that I'm manipulating him."

"Without prejudice, I feel some Circle Weavers use it as a sledgehammer."

She nodded. "Very true. Whereas the few Guild Weavers I've seen, though they aren't infallible, tend to be a little more circumspect."

Connor, for his part, had abandoned thoughts of circumspection. "Atalanta's up to something."

"She's a spy, dear: she usually is. I don't think she's taken a holiday in her life. Even during the wedding she was probably collating information."

"She's working, here, now." She would have contradicted his assumption that she was, if she were not. "There is very little here for her unless she's spying on Ilsa's team. Saxen is high underside but he does half of his trade via Mirqest."

"What is his trade?"

"Girls and boys." And if Atalanta were a working Circle Weaver she would have taken an axe to those activities. Éloise had threatened the same. "Rafael Martinez retired five years ago and has no anti-Guild or anti-Federation operations hanging over that would warrant her paying him a visit. There's nobody else major based here, and even those based elsewhere with operations here aren't known for interesting the Federation."

"Unless she's spying on you, of course."

Connor realised he had been playing with a remaining corner of pastry, and set it down at the edge of his plate in a puff of sugar. "I'm open to family about what I do. She doesn't need to spy on me."

"On all your deals? Your chats with Union corporations? Please be sensible, dear."

Connor retrieved the pastry and chewed it, trying to think. Complications: they rendered perfectly good jam as sour as pickled cabbage.

Éloise had shielded him. No one outside their family could read his mind: she received notification any time anyone inside the family read his mind, and would surely have a couple of words for him if she noticed Atalanta dipping in and out on a regular basis. And it was undeniable that he dealt both with arms manufacturers and a range of interesting arms buyers. White Canyon would be the big target. All his remaining details on his dealings with them were in his warehouse's vault – not that anyone, even Logan, knew he'd kept it. He'd just wanted a little insurance.

A Federation spy could want any number of details on the big four Union corporations. The UISS maintained a representative government, but its megacorps stood above politics, oligarchs supreme. The Federation disapproved.

White Canyon hadn't done anything interesting with Connor, from his perspective: a small order, testing him as they tested anyone, to see how much value he could deliver for them. Was a test order valuable data to a Federation spy? Maybe. It would reveal what a Union megacorp counted as small potatoes.

And why would he assume Atalanta's handlers knew for whom he was acting as middleman? His client list was, to him, a catalogue of those to whom he could get away with trading, the galactically inoffensive or those so powerful their patronage meant more than the sum total of the toes on which they'd trodden. As raw data to the Federation it would look predominantly like a list of Sixième and Septième trouble spots.

Exploitable trouble spots?

"Please don't pretend you don't enjoy this," Gisele said, muffled by cloth and waffle dough. "You're becoming important: it's worth the target signs."

There was a difference between enjoying a feeling of power – between having taken a decision to step onto the underside ladder proper, at the risk of everything he had or would become – and potentially being spied upon by his brother's stepsister.

"That's like assuming you can sidestep Michel's career. You're stuck with both of them, one on each side."

And Michel was UISS Fleet: and the UISS Fleet worked with White Canyon – and with Lionstooth, Cliff Enterprises and Kalshung – for any and all supplies, plus a galaxy of smaller weapons manufacturers; and so far Connor had seen no crossover between what he did and what relationship the Union armed forces had with its megacorps. He'd be surprised if he were permitted to glimpse that crossover.

And the twelve ships sitting lined up in hangars at the spaceport, shiny and new and half of a small Union Fleet attack squad, had nothing to do with that.

They also had nothing to do with Connor. So: "I can't rule out Atalanta being here to oversee the ship transfer to Martinez."

"Federation forces could eat a squad like that for lunch." She lifted her veil to sip her tea, as if for emphasis.

"It's still a data point – a note that Martinez is strengthening, or that Cliff is bolstering petty warlords, if the Federation cares." Checking they had a handle on cross-border technology transfer, perhaps. The Federation persistently led in the technological arms race with the Union. The Union persistently used any available method to catch up.

Newssheet rumours a couple of days before: a Federation maiden flight gone drastically wrong…

That had nothing to do with anything: Federation Atlas-class battleships and Union trade deals didn't. What sat on those ships Cliff was selling, assuming it really intended to sell them and nothing stranger were going on, was Union weaponry and not Federation cutting-edge ordnance.

He could sit here drinking tea till his bladder burst wondering if those ships had anything hidden inside. If they had, there was zero chance – zero whatsoever – that the pinnacle of Union trading, Cliff Enterprises, would let special, secret or stolen technology stay sold on the cheap to a tinpot dictatorship on one small, boring, backwater planet.

"Curiosity."

Gisele turned her head towards him. "What?"

"I can see something's wrong here. She can see the same if she tries. She's not stupid and has more than enough relevant experience. She could well be shadowing the deal because there's something wrong with it."

"I still think you're mis-estimating Ilsa."

No specification of *over-* or *under*-estimating. "Will you help me check, either way?"

"An old friend or my stepdaughter." Gisele took another sip of her tea. "You're making me a very tasty proposition, dear."

"I apologise." Not that he felt sorry.

"Atalanta. Ilsa. Saxen and Martinez on the side. Do you suspect the local patisserie too?"

"Do they bake hidden messages into pastries?"

"I've seen it done." Gisele shook waffle crumbs off her fingertips. "Saxen's Weaver is a local street-witch. I've seen the same threads all over the city."

"Calad mentioned something of the sort."

"He is brighter than he looks, dear boy: even Dominic realised that, though I'm not sure Calad does." With considerable effort, Connor did not reply. "I will need to get a little closer to some of these people."

"To ask them why they're dancing a four-step?"

She wrinkled her nose sufficiently for her veil to wrinkle along with it. "Crudité is a snack, not a tactic, and time is valuable."

The skies outside the café seemed to darken. Connor supressed a shiver. "Time's something I can't promise you, or anyone."

"Time is a weapon."

"Hmm?"

She made a dismissive little motion with one hand. "You're considering time as a combatant: other people's schedules and conditions. You don't consider what happens when one sits back and waits. Cracks widen enough for a body to... walk in."

And Atalanta, if she had any interest in his clients, would be able to do so, having spent a couple of years becoming *persona grata* amongst his staff. A woman who introduced herself on Port Logis as a spy...

He pushed back his chair and rose. A passing waiter pulled it aside to tidy. "Are you ready to head back?" Connor asked.

"Well, your comments on *time* make me wonder."

He picked up her cloak and draped it onto her back. "Wonder what?"

She tossed the cloak's tail over her shoulder with practised efficiency, covering her rumpled shawl. Surely she'd left it untidy on purpose; she'd lived long enough to know how to dress herself. "Whether you're ready – for anything."

*

CHAPTER THIRTEEN

"Hmm." Connor bent over the list Calad had drawn up for him, pretending to give it his full attention. Mid-morning light kept licking words from the screen, wherever on his desk he centred it. He'd eaten too many pastries earlier. "This particular shielding: what's its focus?"

"Some anti-telepathy. Not much: even I could crack it with little difficulty. Predominantly physical." Calad tapped the list: both Saxen and Martinez's upper echelons. "The higher rank the employee, the better the shielding. I'm not sure I approve –"

"I definitely don't. Grunts do more and know more than even they realise." On that line... "How's your wife?" he added as casually as he could.

Calad scowled, an Apollonian thundercloud. "Talking to my mother and to some spare priestess she picked up." That *had* been quick work on Gisele's part. "They're twittering like three baby birds. At least Maman's keeping Atalanta out of trouble."

"Did you ask her to do that?"

"No. I wish I had."

He was still frowning. Maybe Connor could risk a little push. "It's understandable, maybe. If you'd told Gisele you were looking into what Atalanta was doing, she could have decided to draw her aside without being asked."

Calad balled up a fist and looked like he was going to smack it into Connor's desk, but pulled the punch at the last moment. "She always told me!" Maybe he realised how petulant he sounded, for he added in a more normal tone, "Whenever she's working she always tells me an outline of what she's doing. Even if we've had a row, even if it's sensitive – she just tells me she has a job and can't give details. This time, *nothing*."

The little green-tinged bell was starting to ring in Connor's mind. "Did she ever tell you after the fact what the sensitive jobs had been?"

Calad shrugged. "Some, not all. Data snatch, mainly."

"Industrial espionage?" Calad nodded. "You're saying," Connor went on, "that if your wife were about to commit industrial espionage, you would at least know?"

"Well, what do you expect?" Calad sounded defensive: maybe he'd already had this row with Michel, another man ten years his senior. "A husband and wife are one being. It's in the wedding vows. If she didn't tell me what she was doing after that: well, even her bosses would expect it."

"I don't share your equanimity on that point."

He also didn't share Calad's newfound air of thoughtful acceptance, creeping its way across his face and into the set of his shoulders, an indication of impending détente between youthful husband and equally youthful wife. If Calad's mind were easing, Connor couldn't agree.

Federation versus Union: ultra-high-tech versus a catch-up crowd who were very, very close. Industrial espionage – particularly in the arms arena – was the biggest, nastiest prize out there. Doubtless a few of the sensitive jobs Atalanta hadn't divulged to Calad were personal espionage, and the odd assassination (though of the pair, Connor would pick Calad for the latter job).

Something worse than assassination and a lot worse than, for instance, cutting into the Cliff sales team's data lines while they were marooned on the Septième and vulnerable.

Or she might not be working at all and could have come to planet initially to vent at Connor about her brainless husband. Connor doubted it. Atalanta did very little on impulse. The only impulsive act he'd ever seen her commit was falling for Calad, and he wasn't even sure about that one.

As with warning Calad she had jobs that she couldn't discuss, she *would* have told Connor if he had been wrong in assuming she had a job at all… maybe.

His desk intercom rang. He reached past Calad and activated the speaker. "Yes?"

"Mister Saxen's quartermaster and one of his captains are here to see you."

The little green bell began to ring louder than before. "Send them up." He flicked off the intercom. "Stay here," he said to Calad, "and try to look menacing."

Calad frowned a little, but straightened his belt so his pistol was visible. His wings, gold and white, began to shimmer at his back.

"Which captain?" he said. "I hope it isn't the one I bothered earlier. Elderson."

"At the 'port?"

"Yes. And there was another at the office."

The door creaked open. Connor minimised the picture of Merissa with the Cliff team and the list Calad had given him, and straightened a little in his chair, just as Marcello entered shepherding Saxen's two representatives.

Both were short, in different degrees. One was slender, young in years but careworn, fussy in manner as if Connor's study carpet irritated him. The other, wearing captain's stripes, was broader in the beam – in a way that reminded Connor of a smaller version of Thakar A'syan – and more relaxed in posture, though his eyes were watchful.

Connor flicked a finger towards the captain. "We've met before." Once, at least a year ago, though he'd kept a close eye on all Saxen's top staff for years. "Sean Jules."

Sean Jules nodded, nearly a bow, and gave Calad a less acute but altogether more cautious nod. "Good to see you again, Mister. This is Lieutenant Michael Handyman."

Connor's eyes flicked to the fussy lightweight. "You're the one who put in for five hundred rifles and mortar kit."

Handyman nodded. "I'd like to discuss the order further with you, Mister," he said, in a voice deeper than Connor had expected.

"We can't fulfil it at this stage. There's nothing further to discuss."

"Yes, yes." Handyman looked as if he were about to perch on the stool in front of Connor's desk, but thought better of it at the last moment and straightened up. "We – that is, my employer – wanted to explore when that deal would become available. It's a matter of forward planning."

Connor leant back a little way in his chair. "Lieutenant Handyman, the drones are not yet for sale to anyone. They are not yet out of testing. As I object on principle to selling before I have anything to offer –" and to someone who had been observing his tests, though, as he'd conducted one of them in a mined-out quarry no more than nine hundred miles from city limits, it had not been the most subtle test in history – "the rifles are also unavailable."

Handyman looked set to raise an objection: Sean Jules tapped his shoulder and motioned to him to step back. "We acknowledge your position, Mister. Are there measures we can take that could repair the situation between us?"

And now the little tinkling green bell was ringing in earnest. All the gun traders in the capital bought wholesale from Connor – practically his first step in business had been to secure a small arms monopoly in Mirqest's capital, setting aside anything that Cliff, Lionstooth and their ilk dealt in directly to customers large enough. His was not the only gun factory on the planet: there were manufacturers in other cities – all of which were minority-owned by Connor through one shell company or other – but even if any underside corps fell into *every* local dealer's bad books, they could go to another planet. A hundred spots on the Septième could supply needs like Saxen's, and all were sixteen to twenty-four hours' journey away: eight to twelve hours from the supply planet's surface to its Bridge, and eight to twelve hours down Mirqest's Highway, depending on ship engine power.

Saxen, working with a street-witch, wanted weapons in bulk and in under a day.

That practically settled it. Martinez, Cliff, the ships: Martinez stalling till Saxen could mount an assault on Cliff's guards, which Martinez could then deny he had any part in, editing or deleting spaceport security camera footage if he had to. Connor held himself steady in his seat. Go check the 'port cameras for tampering? How could any man tell the difference between a tampered-with camera and one that had simply been vandalised or missed its maintenance check-up? Aloud he said, "Apologies can be accepted once they've been made. Put in a more realistic order and my team will process it in due course."

Sean Jules just nodded. Unwilling to make Connor suspicious? Too late, if so. "My boss'll send you a message in short order. He's as anxious as anyone to normalise relations between our team and yours."

Connor nodded. "I look forward to hearing from him." He

motioned to Marcello, and the younger man ushered Saxen's two mercs out of the door.

"What's going on?" Calad said as soon as the door had closed.

Connor almost voiced his concerns but swallowed them at the last moment. He'd never in his life met a Circle Weaver with a grasp of subtlety. "I have suspicions. Stay here and work with Pritie to re-up security – and try to get back on speaking terms with your wife."

Calad, who had assumed a purposeful expression, paused mid-breath like an overstuffed sheep. "I don't want her to think I'm spying on her."

"Neither do I. Speaking terms are beneficial to all concerned." Connor shook his head. "I'm going to the spaceport. Let me clear my head before I give you a new headache."

*

CHAPTER FOURTEEN

Gisele had organised a luncheon party. Connor lurked in his study, flicking through a handful of order lists without reading any of them, watching women flit past his door in clouds of silk that wouldn't seem out of place on the Neuvième: an oddly assorted collection, considering it contained an expensive tart, two priestesses, a petty merchant's wife, three petty merchants, two socialites (one being Théodora Bramhall's nondescript niece), one of Fai Comet's captains, one of Nikalar Saxen's lieutenants and a mid-ranking policewoman. Maybe there wouldn't be any teacups thrown.

He waited till the door had closed for the last time, and until Marcello was due to go on his break, and headed down the back stairs as his bodyguard whistled his way down the front ones. A few of his staff members nodded to him as he passed but they paid little attention.

Two conundrums, with one missing woman the link between them. If the spaceport could give him a hint to the second, it had a chance of helping him towards the first. If so, the origination point would be nearby…

He threaded past the kitchens and, at the back door, he stopped, staring at the alley. A mild veneer of grime clung to the paving slabs and concrete walls, set to become food for lichens and algae. Keeping to the cleanest patches of pavement, raised areas in an uneven surface, Connor walked to the end of the alley. To the right lay the office door and the little row of shops: takeaway cookshop, temple, gunsmith. To the left ran a row of apartment blocks, for as far as he could see. He went left.

If he kept going in this direction for twenty minutes, he'd reach Merissa's former flat, in a block amid fifty similar blocks. As he walked he stared at each frontage and kept glancing up into the sky. The odd security monitor fixed on the flats; the odd drone beaming images back to Pritie's databanks. It wasn't tricky to stay out of their range of vision.

But Merissa's main front door had been in a camera's range of vision, and her block's back door was down an alley that could only be entered by passing another camera.

The street began to wind, and to divide. Connor veered right and, keeping to the shaded side of the street and again staying away from cameras, cut past another few housing blocks and down an alleyway. He was out of his own territory, now: it showed. His neighbour – Stig Davids on this side – did not employ as many refuse collectors and roadsweepers as he did.

Ahead was a jerry-built bus stand. It lay just into Davids's zone but abutted Connor's and two others, and, like any such, alternated between petty war zone and truce area. Today it was on a truce. Connor eased a half-mark coin from his money belt, far enough away that he'd packed the belt away again before he passed anyone else, and wandered into the bus shelter stooping a little to hide his height. Buses were for assorted middle class strata and the upper working class. No curiosity from anyone other than a small child, about his niece's age, who likely stared everyone out of countenance: the rest were dog-tired labourers and merchants' spouses.

He waited for five minutes on one of the cracked plastic seats, hands idly folded in his lap, no more than half an eye on the dirty glass door behind which one of Davids's enforcers was chatting to, of all people, a cop. After that little wait, a bus drew down to the concrete, its destination the spaceport. Connor rose and climbed aboard. He watched the cop and the enforcer in the window glass's reflection. Neither looked up at him.

That might have been different if he'd been covered in blood and carrying a hammer. Connor wasn't convinced. Each man could have written off the incident as the other's responsibility.

Connor took a seat midway down the bus, away from the other passengers. As the bus pulled out, he watched the ground below, counting bike parks, car parks and sidestreet parking areas that had been cleared of abandoned vehicles neither by Davids's enforcers or his own, according to the side of the line they inhabited. After two minutes he stopped – more than that would not have been walking distance – and stared at the bus roof.

At night's ebb, with shadow his envelope, that bit would have been very different. Any man could park a bike on another man's roof or in another man's five square feet of garden at night without detection. That, though, was a Septième man's thought: a foreigner would have assumed he needed a car park – if Connor were to suspect the foreigners.

Suspect everyone.

A little over half an hour after leaving the stand, the bus passed the 'port fence and, presently, drew up on the edge of the transport hardstanding. Connor alighted and wandered along behind the other disembarking passengers towards the hangars. When he was sure he had dawdled to the back of the group, he peeled off and headed for the side door into the freight 'port. The same principle applied to freight and passenger termini: as he, himself, had both passenger and freight 'port passes, it didn't matter which he picked to test.

At the side door he waved his owner ID ring at the door, which clicked open obligingly. It wasn't a fancy slider but a hinged door. He nudged it wide with one foot, left it open for the woman behind him – checking first that she had an ID – and started through the corridors towards his rented hangars. Any man or woman who had a ship in dock, be it a passenger or freight vessel, would know where to go.

Or if he or she didn't care, and had broken into the 'port armed with the gumption to saunter to a random hangar as if the choice were deliberate, the same would apply. And anyone could enter the main passenger terminal, up to a certain point, without ID to go further. And drifters proved that no ID was necessary to use a spaceport at all.

He passed his ships' sealed hangars, and those belonging to a string of other undersiders, high and low, closer to respectability and closer to piracy. At the corner began the short term rental hangars. Those were, on the whole, cleaner, and their inhabitants less wary. Somewhere around here was a path between freight and passenger 'ports, intended for ground staff use but not heavily restricted. Right and then left, perhaps.

"Are you trying to run away?"

Connor kept walking. "In a manner of speaking. What do

you see here, Mistress Ilsa Martins?"

Though he hadn't slowed or shortened his stride, she caught him up within a few yards. Height and long legs. "A spaceport. Scruffy round the edges but I've visited far worse. Security staff – not many: they're mostly gawping at the Cyclopes we brought – dockers, ships' staff, owners."

"Exactly." He'd been right: the freight-to-passenger door was there, down a cream-tiled corridor that had once been white, with an AUTHORISED PERSONS ONLY sign dangling off one nail on its wall. Connor struck down the corridor with Ilsa still close behind him. A passing security guard barely glanced at the pair of them.

The single door at the corridor end was neither locked nor, when Connor pressed his elbow on the button and opened it, alarmed. Instead of crossing into the passenger zone he stood with one foot next to the door, blocking it from closing. "And now what do you see?"

Ilsa stared ahead. Connor followed her line of sight. This link led to the back end of the passenger 'port, the unfashionable end. Not many fancy-clad folk, even the middle classes seeking to swap from passenger to freight zones on business of their own without going round the long way. A cleaner was trundling down the corridor mounting a fruitless crusade against grime blown up by a thousand engines an hour, and three teenagers were lounging against the wall in the distance.

Ilsa pointed. "Are they drifters?"

"Yes." Connor withdrew his foot and the door slid shut. "Let's head towards your ships. They'll come this way in a few minutes. Walk slow."

She fell into step with him, seemingly in reluctance, keeping a good six inches between their shoulders. "I ask again, *Mister*. Are you trying to run away?"

Connor gestured to the 'port walls around them. "When did you pick up that I was here?"

"I happened to step out of my hangar – away from a disagreement that would proceed better were I not present – and saw you. I wanted…"

"To check up on me? I don't care whether or not you trust me. But." He jerked his head at a security camera overhead.

Its wires were dangling out of the unit. "A good fraction of the 'port cameras don't work. No guard challenged me as I came in. I dare say a few dockers or ships' guards noticed me, and recognised me, but in four days' time they won't remember I was here. On my way in I touched nothing with an uncovered hand. Round here, a DNA trace requires the target to have touched an object. Terra Nova might be able to do a little better, but we can't."

Whoever had left Merissa dead in her flat had gone somewhere thereafter – and had done so undetected. When Connor reached home he would be able to check how many times his own security had spotted him on today's journey: likely, few. The man or woman could have vanished anywhere in the city: this 'port trip was proof of concept only – but it certainly could have been done.

It could have been done by Nerys, if she had returned to the 'port and run from her existing life for any reason or none. It could also have been done, for instance, by one of Martinez's team if he'd kidnapped or killed Nerys to damage Cliff's efforts, then killed Merissa for seeing what happened.

Behind, the door creaked. He did not turn, just kept walking, hoping Ilsa would not break stride. The drifter kids skittered past, rats in the gloom: he let them gain a six foot head start before whistling, <Hey, you. I have a question.>

The kids – in their early teens: survivors – paused and looked back. One poked his fellows as if he recognised Connor. "What d'you want, Mister?" the largest kid said.

Connor folded his arms and, for once, tried to look taller than he was. God, he needed Logan back. "Four nights back, this 'port. A woman acting weird and a man acting weird, maybe not together." Maybe just the one. Maybe neither.

The trio glanced at each other. "There's the drift here and everywhere," said the smallest. "There's women, there's men."

"There was one bint being weird," the kid in the middle said. The other two hummed in vague agreement.

"What was she like?" Connor said.

The kids shrugged. "Just a byrd," the middle drifter said. "Pinched some clothes, chasing a ride. In the C-wing and going the wrong way."

Cyclops hangars, the kid meant: close to where Cliff had set up shop. "All yours," he said, and he tossed the child the coin he held. The kid caught it midair and the little trio scurried off.

"That was in aid of nothing," Ilsa hissed, possibly too low for the retreating children to hear. "Street gossip? I've obtained every image of that night and the next morning. There was nothing of interest."

"You didn't know what you were looking for." *He* didn't know what he was looking for. A break in a pattern.

"You can't even believe they saw anything out of the ordinary."

"I can. Clothes that didn't fit a hangar." Connor jerked his head towards Cliff's rented hangars. "Let's get back to look at the images."

Probably a drifter having stolen clothes in which to skip planet. If a young woman had come into money, faking a better social class would let her spend it on a travel ticket that would minimise harassment. The date – the same as Merissa's death and Nerys's disappearance – could not be taken as a coincidence too far until Connor'd seen the images. What *was* too much of a coincidence was such a woman seen around Cyclops hangars in the freight 'port. Freighter Cyclopes did not do passenger runs.

He strode ahead of Ilsa to the closest Cliff-hired hangar, holding one of their sale ships plus one of their four personal-use vessels, but stopped in the doorway. Too many security staff all clustered together: 'port security, planetary police, a woman from the defence fleet. Two of Ilsa's staff: Aled in the front, poised and calm, playing control man. Two of Saxen's captains: Horsefield and Elderson, all set up to play little and large, maybe having changed their minds. The superintendent of police, Leifson, a little man standing with arms folded, alongside the tall, powerful man who had been his boss for the past twenty years.

Connor took a step back and tucked himself into the doorjamb. What in eleven hells? Rafael Martinez in the spaceport inspecting his merchandise would have been one thing. Rafael Martinez in the spaceport in the centre of what looked like it might spring into an argument at any moment was something different. Connor'd seen that kind of body language before.

He narrowed his eyes to slits, the better to sharpen his hearing. "Delays..." he thought he heard Martinez saying. Saxen's pair of captains did not make moves, or expressions, that indicated they wanted to back him up.

Ilsa cut ahead of Connor, and beckoned him round and to a side hatch at her personal Hamadryad's tail. He followed her aboard what proved to be a spick-and-span light cutter optimised, he guessed by its loadout and internal lines, for speed.

"You been getting this often?" he said, gesturing to the hangar and, by association, the fracas.

"Any commercial situation has its difficulties. This is nothing different." She indicated to him to follow her into a side room fitted out with a featureless white desk. As he seated himself she laid a hand on a patch of white slightly duller than the rest. Two light-screens extruded from the desk, already loaded with spaceport security vids.

"Look all you want, but we've been over this footage," Ilsa said, behind his shoulder. "It's not significant."

Connor flipped the footage back to the night in question and sped it backwards and forwards, searching for any sign of the situation the drifters had noticed. "I repeat: you didn't know what you were looking for."

There. Ten past thirteen at night: a young woman walking into shot, purposeful stride though not fast. It was a side-on shot: her face was not visible. Straight black hair, clothes on the smart end of Septième trader wear, neither foreigners' clothes nor aristo fashion redolent of the Neuvième. The clothes nearly fit her, but not quite, and she was drift-thin. Connor frowned. A vaguely familiar drifter.

"That's not Nerys, in case you're wondering," Ilsa said, behind him. "We've viewed these images already. It's not unlike her and those are like the clothes she was wearing when she went missing. But it definitely isn't her."

Clothes a Treizième woman thought were appropriate to the Septième, however confined to a small social stratum that appropriateness went. Clothes now worn by a Septième drifter… probably. Nerys, for instance, had been thin, and thin was fashionable on the Treizième. But a Treizième visitor would have bought her outfit to fit.

"I thought," he said, "you were looking for someone who might have made away with Nerys, rather than for Nerys herself."

"I looked for *anything*." She cut off the word as if she regretted the entire sentence.

"This is definitely something."

Connor brought up a handful more camera feeds, following the young woman through the spaceport away from the Cyclops hangars. He lost her a few times when the images cut out, then picked her up again, and finally lost her image for good not far from a doorway and heading for it at quite a clip. Not a drifter who left the 'port via ship, at any rate…

He paused the camera feeds and rested his chin on his hands. "Mistress Martins, what was Nerys's private appointment?"

"I don't know."

Because you didn't want to know. Because you prefer to focus on your sphere of affairs and to leave speculation to others.

He wound back the camera feed and replayed the young woman's walk. Head down, not looking at anything around herself. That didn't fit the drift. Any drifter would take more care of herself. This was a woman who knew exactly where she was going and wanted to get there as quickly as she could short of running.

There was a shadow at the end of the corridor. Another person. Might be there for any reason of his or her own: but as the woman walked, the shadow kept pace with her.

Connor opened another feed, one of the cameras he'd already discarded. A man, tailing the woman – well, that wasn't unexpected, whether he wanted a quick tumble without asking first or just to ask for her jack frequency. Yet he did not accelerate before the woman could reach occupied areas, and nor did he slow down when she approached the spaceport exit: instead he followed her into the blackout zone at the door.

"What is it?" Ilsa said.

"She was being followed." Connor gestured to the man's image. "Ring any bells?"

Ilsa bent in to study the picture. "Vaguely. I may have seen him once. I don't know him." She squinted closer. Her lip curled in distaste so swift it must be automatic. "He's an Old Worlder. Look. The cheekbones, the build."

Connor restrained a grimace. God save him from other people's prejudice. She was right in strict relation to facts, though: he barely had cheekbones, and, moreover, he walked as if he were uncomfortable in fabric clothing. "Where did you see him?"

"I've no idea. Once, in a crowd, or a picture. I don't know."

Of all the men Connor would have expected to see menacing a Septième girl, an Old World foreigner came low down the list. They saved that for when the Septième girls had been shipped over to their planets for the express purpose of being menaced.

A representative of the flesh trade from the Federation end? There wasn't much else here he could be doing.

Connor stood, closing down the camera feeds. "I'd be grateful if you would speak to 'port control. We need some more images of where these two went, and we need info on that man – on how he arrived here and who he said he was when he entered the spaceport. I don't much care right now if he was lying."

He'd another avenue to follow up. He smiled sourly. "If it makes you feel any better, I'm going to do a more distasteful job." Yes. Saxen was one of the less pleasant men Connor'd met on the underside. His captains, though, were a better lot on the whole, and would likely have more concrete information to hand on whether this foreigner had come here to deal in girls.

*

CHAPTER FIFTEEN

If Connor'd still had Ilsa Martins stuck to one shoulder, he doubted he'd have passed Nikalar Saxen's entrance hall. She would have started squeaking with a list of reasons she should call the police, and the subsequent eviction would not have been polite. Then again, if Connor had had Éloise with him instead, he wouldn't have passed the entrance hall either, largely because his over-zealous stepsister would have razed it before he had a chance.

The HQ was an office, not a knocking-shop, but the quartet of dull-eyed young women sitting in the sparse entrance hall were all whores, the kind who'd had any intransigence beaten out of them long ago. Connor hadn't spent so long on the Neuvième that he was accustomed only to sex workers who'd chosen their profession, but still he felt himself wincing – a foreigner's wince – as he brushed past the line of girls. Maybe men bedded whores, or rent boys, simply because they could. He'd never seen the appeal.

"Sean Jules has an office back here," he said to the junior lieutenant on reception duty.

The lieutenant jerked his head at a plain door in one corner. "He's busy. Last one, though. Have a seat – Mister." He pointed to the chair at the end of the working girls' line.

"Thanks." Connor stayed standing, though, watching the women and the odd strings of Saxen's staff crossing the hall without paying the whores any attention. Maybe once he himself would have ignored such girls. Maybe, on a street or in a bar, he still did. But Merissa had been no older than these four, and Nerys, dead or alive, had looked their age.

Maybe this whole mess was so much simpler than it had appeared ever since he'd learnt Nerys's name. One girl snatched off a street, and another killed –

And smuggled back into her own flat.

The plain door opened. A fifth prostitute emerged, and shuffled to her mates with the air of a woman ten years older than she was. "Please come in," Sean Jules called to Connor from behind her. Connor lost little time in complying. His skin was beginning to itch.

He pulled up short in Sean Jules's doorway, blinking at the anatomy diagrams on the office walls and the folding cot in one corner. "You a walking hospital?"

"Medical officer," Sean Jules said with half a smile. "It's not a specialism that goes out of style."

"I'll introduce you to my new bloodhound: she's in the same line." Connor nudged the door shut. A man in Saxen's trade needed a doctor he trusted: why not train one of his captains? "Is this regular surgery hour, or are those five taking a trip?"

"The latter." Sean Jules made a noncommittal shrug. "Matter of whether they head clockwise or anticlockwise. I'm sure you get it."

"I do." Capable of bearing healthy children – suitable to be shipped to a Federation baby factory – or incapable of such, and going to the Union. Any export trade had repercussions, but maybe Saxen hadn't banked on this type of repercussion. "I realise you have to consider your boss's commercial confidentiality, but I ask this in the understanding that it will bite you all on the arse if it blows up in my face." He spread the suspected Federation pervert's image out from a handheld. "If this is one of your customers, or a customer's rep, or a tester, you'd be advised to tell me so, now. He's been hanging after women of a specific appearance, and I don't think he's hoping to paint their pictures."

Sean Jules studied the man's picture for a full thirty seconds. "He's not," he said in the end. "He rings a bell, but he's not a customer."

Connor had been far from sure that Ilsa was telling the truth about her recognition of the mystery man. Sean Jules's reaction, though, seemed genuine. Could he trust that instinct? "Where did you see him?"

"In the news." Connor blinked: *that*, he hadn't expected. "In the last week, or I'd have forgotten it," Sean Jules continued. "Some chatter piece from out-sector. It was in the laugh slot, but I remember thinking that wasn't the appropriate place for it." He frowned. "People had died. Quite a few people."

Connor perched on the folding cot's edge, trying not to breathe too loudly in case he broke Sean Jules's train of thought. More dead bodies. The wages of sin, indeed.

Sean Jules shook his head. "Sorry. It's gone. If I remember, I'll tell you. It's not work-related."

I bet you'll tell me, after you've followed up on why I was asking. No matter. Connor wasn't – much – worse off than not having asked.

"Thanks." As he rose, he caught sign of a document popping out of the wall on display: a diploma from a decent medical college on the Neuvième. "You trained out-sector?"

"Two years solid sitting in a classroom. They wanted me to add another three years in a hospital. Boss wanted me back quicker than that and I figured I'd get my on-the-job experience out here."

"Understandable." Connor's eyes lingered on Sean Jules's first aid supplies set up in neat, clear trays. "Let me know if business slacks off. I might be able to make you an offer."

Sean Jules laughed, full of cynicism. "Mister, no matter what your fancy contacts think, this business never slacks."

"Not unless a man wants it to. You never know."

He left Sean Jules turning over meanings and counter-meanings in his head, and headed out into the street. The five sad-eyed girls were climbing into a car, headed for the spaceport and a foreign life, almost certainly to die abroad.

Saxen's empire could fall tomorrow and Sean Jules could make sure he came out a major winner from it, however much was already tucked in his personal accounts. The Circle, in the unlikely event it chose to intervene, would find too little to pin on him. If he chose to have daughters, they wouldn't spend their lives looking over their shoulders. Connor couldn't say the same for Saxen.

He wasn't going soft. Circle ideas of justice were about as far from soft as a man could go. *Cautious*, he could say.

Back at the office, he evaded the last of Gisele's departing lunch guests and, bypassing Yasmine's curious glances, holed up in his office with a newsnet. After ten minutes or so he abandoned the net, called Pritie upstairs and explained what he needed.

"Two weeks' worth of images?"

"That just means it'll take a while." Connor pulled up the best still of the spaceport tail he'd found. "This man, and a smallish story involving at least three deaths, probably more. It's all linked. Circumstantial, so far, but if you can find the news story I can make it a direct hook-up."

"Hmm." Pritie copied the still to her jack and stood frowning into midair for a moment. "Am I in a race?"

Against time, Connor nearly said, but he checked himself. Against Sean Jules, or, if he spilt secrets to his boss, Saxen's organisation. Maybe even against Ilsa. "I think so. I can't say who with."

She nodded. "I'll run it as quickly as I can."

Connor grimaced to himself. Probably too late, after bringing Sean Jules's attention to it, but: "Try to keep this bit quiet." She raised her eyebrows, but nodded, and left.

He wasn't even sure why he'd said it. Maybe his absolute certainty that – although faced with Ilsa's equal and opposing certainty – the woman on the camera had been Nerys. Maybe an instinct or something below that, an urge to follow the money, and the knowledge that in this instance a foreign man, a Federation man, represented quite a lot of money indeed.

So did those shiny new ships sitting in the 'port.

Hands moving almost independently of desire, Connor opened a screen on his desk, snagged a stylus from the box in his top drawer and began to write. Cyclopes. Twelve of them. Martinez's tonnage had already more than matched that of any two other operators on the planet. Now, did he exceed *all* other operators? Not when one counted every rich household's single armed personal ship. But he might now out-ton the entire local low underside, and Mirqest was not a high underside playground. Fai Comet had put paid to that five years ago, with the sole exception of Saxen, who'd been born here, and Comet himself rarely visited.

Twelve new Cyclopes and their *purchase price*. The last few years' tax revenue he could glean from official documents: he opened a few. The discrepancy between funds Martinez wanted to spend and funds available for him to spend was significant. Connor narrowed his eyes to slits, remembering the 'port, remembering the smell of cordite in the air and the numbers of Saxen's crewers in the corridors. Some of the pictures he'd taken would show those crewers. He pulled up the images on his desk.

He scrutinised each picture by line, noting squad composition and weaponry, and, at the end, dropped his stylus with a quiet whistle. Saxen's numbers in the freight zone rivalled official 'port security and outweighed the Cliff team by at least fifteen to one. Cliff had powerful weapons... on too few people.

In none of the photos showing Martinez and Saxen's teams in the same shot had they been looking at each other. Connor closed his screen and stood, huffing a sigh. Conclusions, for once, escaped him.

He'd been staring out of his window at the smoke plumes puffing from the shrine chimneys opposite for a while – he didn't know how long – when he heard the door swing open behind him. "Yes, Gisele?" he said without turning round.

"You're never in one place for more than five minutes," she said, vague accusation in her voice.

"I told you I wasn't going to be on holiday this week." He looked back. She'd shed her veil: two pins clipped back her pale hair, ready to have gauze drawn over it in the space of moments, and she wore one of her simpler white shawls, possibly having intended to impress the priestess. "Did you have a good time?"

"A useful one, at least."

"Hmm?"

"I kept Yasmine out of your way." She crossed the room to stand beside him, and gestured to the shrine outside. "You were right about perspectives on monotarianism. What makes you so sure Ilsa's lying?" Connor, catching up too late, hesitated for just too long. "You needn't try to spare my feelings," Gisele said. "Old friend or not, I'm not blind. But you have to admit it would be a very clumsy lie. A woman the dead spit of Nerys, in a place Nerys was expected to be: Ilsa would be a fool to deny it, which, as she isn't a fool, indicates to me that she was telling the truth."

Connor's voice box caught up with his brain. "You're the telempath: you can diagnose lies. I can't."

"I wasn't there, dear: you were."

"Fine, fine." Wait till she had time to talk to Ilsa again. Just wait, and be patient. "It strikes me that if someone had a beef against Nerys – or a fetish for women of her appearance – this other woman could be linked to what happened. I don't even know how Ilsa is so sure it isn't Nerys anyway. That footage isn't clear." Though, with Merissa involved as well: "I suggested to Saxen's staff that someone's been snatching short, thin women with black hair. One of our missing pair resisted, and was killed. One didn't realise what was hitting till too late, and got picked up."

Leaving aside Merissa teleporting into her own flat, that would do fine.

Gisele uploaded the spaceport photos from Connor's desk top and studied the images. "I suppose procurers could look like anything," she said after a few moments.

"He might want short children for all I know –"

A car dropped out of the sky to the street in front of the office, followed by six bikes. Connor just had time to process the police livery on vehicles and drivers before a red alarm light started flashing on the wall.

"What have you done?" Gisele said, curious rather than accusatory.

"Nothing." No. That wasn't true. He'd poked around in other people's business. "Stay here unless the fire alarm goes off or the roof explodes." He drew his pistol, dropped it onto his desk and headed out into the corridor. There was no point running.

He heard the shouting before he hit the stair head: shouting, and some crashes. No gunshots. Keeping his pace leisurely, he started down the stairs. Damn Logan for knocking Éloise up when he had. Damn himself for diving into the wrong situation.

The entrance hall was full of armed police. Yasmine, her white wings so bright they neared blinding level, was staring down a roaring sergeant from a foot away. From the look on her face she was set to sever one of his limbs. She might survive that situation, but not all of Connor's employees would…

Two of the junior cops levelled rifles on Connor as he reached the stair foot. He ignored them and inclined his head to their inspector, who was standing in the centre of the hall like he owned it. He'd once worn an underside lieutenant's stripes: maybe he thought he ought to own it. "If this is about my 'port taxes, I've paid up. I even got a receipt."

The man glared up at Connor. Now, which excuse would he trot out? Unlicensed trading? Connor had every licence he needed, and didn't trade in products that couldn't be licensed. Import from the Federation wouldn't fly. The import end was legal. Claim that one of his customers didn't have the proper licensing to buy from him? Maybe not. Most cops were ex-underside, but they'd been out of the game long enough to grow soft. Rich people's enforcers, now. He'd even paid them off this month.

"You're harbouring a Guild terrorist."

Connor blinked. For two years he'd half-expected Atalanta to bring him unwelcome presents. This timing, though, was startling. And suspicious.

"Really. What is she believed to have done?" The inspector hesitated. A gunshot, startlingly loud, barked from a nearby room. Connor steadied himself and continued, "She hasn't committed any crimes on Mirqest. She hasn't indicated that she is going to commit one, or even wants to commit one. I'd be delighted to see any evidence you hold that she has such intentions."

Movement flickered in his peripheral vision, to the left. Slowly and deliberately he turned his head to look. Pritie and Atalanta stood in the security office doorway with a pair of guns trained on them, Pritie looking unaccustomedly afraid, Atalanta glaring like she'd heard Connor's comment.

Not much shooting. Why the lack of shooting? Why not storm in here and kill everyone they saw? *Éloise*, a whisper crept from inside Connor's head, twin to the treacherous desire for her to stick close to him and leave Logan behind.

He had no right to grow in any way accustomed to a gift like hers. Any situation like the one they had turned sour in the end: any such advantage reversed and hit a man's arse before he knew where he was going with it. But right now, he'd take the police's fear of ricochets over a stack of dead mercs.

No more dependence.

He strode over to Atalanta as if he rather than the inspector owned the afternoon. "You own a distillery," he said softly to her, "not a yoghurt factory. I'd thank you to grow a face more suited to the one than the other." Over his shoulder, he said to the inspector, "If there's a case to answer, arrest her, and all her thirteen spell-threads. Otherwise I suggest you find a reason to pull her in before coming back."

The small of his back was itching. By rights, one of the cops should shoot him any second. *I mean it*, he wanted to call. *I have to make a stand.*

"OK, all of you," the inspector barked after a chilling silence, "*out.*" With assorted glares, the police officers marched out of the front door, not stashing their guns – guns that Connor had supplied them – till they were outside.

Connor made a slow three-sixty turn, catching the eye of every man and woman there – willing them all not to make a sound, not to retaliate – and as his squad sniper Khayam broke tableau to pull the door to, dangling off one hinge though it was, Connor shouldered between Pritie and Atalanta and headed through the door behind them.

The security office was a wreck. Notepads and computer parts lay scattered all over the floor, and the main data hub had a couple of neat gunshots straight through it. Connor bent and picked up a casing fragment. Scorch-marks caressed his hands.

Whatever's going on, I'm close. Or someone thinks I am.

"They knew what they were doing," Pritie said, behind him. "Otherwise they would have shot everyone rather than make a line for here."

"I agree."

The police: Martinez's captains and lieutenants in charge, enforcing for him as they had done for twenty years. Connor hadn't been convinced the governor cared one way or another what he did as long as the supplies kept coming. More fool him. Any underside lord kept tabs on his turf, whether or not that underside lord had bought himself some respectability in the interim.

Connor picked up Pritie's fallen chair and motioned for her to sit. She did not move from her position braced against the doorframe.

"Are you hurt?" he said.

"No." She gestured back with a shivering hand. "Atalanta was here. She…" She shook herself, moved inside the room and closed the door.

"Now sit down," Connor suggested.

She did. "I was trying to get rid of her," she continued, more quietly.

"Atalanta? Why?"

In answer, Pritie tapped the skin beside her ear, where her neural jack lurked. "I ran the search on jack. Slower but more discreet. He's an engineer, Mister."

That was a surprise. Connor'd expected 'modelling agency manager' or 'film talent scout'. "What kind of engineer?"

"Astronautics." Her chin sank onto her hand. "About a week ago, a Federation battleship blew up in testing. All hands were killed."

"I saw the news story."

"Then maybe you'll have some ideas for why its engine's chief designer – a top secret engine, I'll add – appeared a few days ago on a Septième dunghill."

Oh, dear God. "How long after the explosion?"

"About two days. Two and a half, perhaps. He's listed as a missing person." Pritie aimed a finger at the door. "And who do you think just might be on the hunt?"

She came to Port Logis with me, Connor wanted to say. But Atalanta had been Dominic's stepdaughter: she could hardly have avoided the funeral if she ever wanted to return to Port Logis in her life, for the avoidance would have been seen as worse than being a Guild Weaver invading a Circle grieving party. "OK. Don't talk to her about this. There's a chance she won't read your mind."

"She will if she's working."

Working, Atalanta would do almost anything. "Then steer clear of her for an hour at least. I'm going to –"

"Talk to me?" Arctic accents, in the doorway. Connor sighed. The upmost upper classes were a mystery to him even on the Septième: he'd never have a chance of understanding upper crust foreigners.

"Pritie, go look at our defences," he said without looking round. "I want a full damage report. Atalanta –" He turned at last. His brother's stepsister was leaning on the doorjamb. He'd rarely seen anyone look quite so pissed off without them breaking anything for emphasis. "Anything you'd like to share?"

"Don't throw this back at me." She sidestepped to allow Pritie to pass her – which she did just slowly enough not to seem like she was running away – and closed the door before continuing, "You're making a mistake."

Connor perched on the edge of Pritie's desk – the only piece of furniture the police had left upright. "Why not enlighten me? If it's classified information, I think I already know enough that you'd be obliged to shoot me. So." He gestured to the chair he had righted for Pritie earlier. She didn't move. "Come on. I'm not meant to sit while you stand."

"I wasn't born on Port Logis." She sat anyway. The scowl had gone, but her eyes were two lapis lazuli orbs, unknowable. "His name is Hasan Saeed. He is listed as missing and his employers want him home."

"The Federation starfleet." She did not reply. "But someone made a mistake: someone didn't slap down a journalist hard enough, and they reported his walk-away too close to another report – that of a spaceship blow-out. What happened to the ship, Atalanta?"

"Classified."

"And if I ask the woman whose name is *not* Atalanta?" He leant a little closer to her. Somewhere inside was a woman he might possibly know.

She shook her head. "I'm not a technician. I wouldn't understand the explanation if anyone gave it to me – assuming anyone knows yet: accident investigation takes time if one's to do it properly."

"Yet this guy's wanted for possible sabotage, which means the high-ups think the problem was connected to the engine." She didn't argue. "And any guy who'd pull a plug on a *Federation* experiment – especially pull it in a way that gets people killed – is likely to be dangerous."

"Yes." She glared at him again. "Also intelligent, wealthy and well-connected. Are you starting to see the difficulty yet?"

Connor held in a breath. What connection this had to

Nerys's disappearance he was starting to sketch out in his head. Massive astronautics contracts, brokered by Cliff Enterprises, did cross the Federation/Union divide – with restrictions. Maybe Nerys had once got close enough to sniff a project no outsider should have ever seen.

"So get out into the city – I'll give you an escort if you want one – and pull out a few spell-threads…" Her face had creased into a frown. "What?"

"He's employed in an *extremely delicate* situation. His shields protect him from Guild Weavers as well as Circle Weavers. Let's assume for a moment he is definitely still here – something of which I'm not certain. Not only could I not read his mind if he were in front of me without significant effort and personal risk, I can't locate him at a distance greater than ten metres or so. Think of it as my probes sliding straight off him."

At any other time Connor would have enjoyed some quiet reflection on of inter-Federation politics and cross-departmental espionage. Outwith the Circle Neuvième's no-secrets-possible society, it was an understandable move, but if he knew any details he would be able to leverage the weaknesses. Not today. "So we need to go back to old-fashioned detective work."

"There's no 'we' involved. I have to find him myself."

"How? Break into the cops' surveillance stations?" A fractional hesitation in her eyes: "Let me rephrase," Connor said. "Were you planning on breaking in there *on your own*?" No answer. Connor caught himself just in time not to throw up his hands. "You might not appreciate this, but I'm your stepbrother. Forget the commercial side –"

"You don't want to forget it."

"I'll take what I can get. What we *have* is two significant, and linked, problems. Will you at least consider that we would *both* come out of this better if we worked together?" Faint consideration brushed her face. Connor held out his hand. "Hunting partners?"

After a full minute she reached out her hand and shook his. "Deal."

*

CHAPTER SIXTEEN

Ascertaining what Atalanta had already done or attempted proved to be a particularly aggravating form of game. Yes, she had a login for the surveillance stations, obtained via mindreading a police officer. No, she'd been unable to use it to remote access: she hadn't been able to replicate the system details well enough to fake entry. Yes, the login still worked (information confirmed by one of Pritie's juniors, Katrice, a teenage drifter Connor had hired after finding her watching whores undress on a feed she'd cut into their brothel's cameras). Yes, Katrice could replicate the environment, but when she wormed inside, it transpired that past days' security media was filed strictly off-network.

That left a physical infiltration to access the surveillance history directly.

In an ideal world they would have waited a day to prepare, but from the evidence of the visit Saxen's pair had made earlier, the police might be too busy for any sort of meeting if Connor delayed it too long. There was only one rush plan available that looked anywhere near coherent.

While his crew prepared their kit, Connor checked the sunset time and, at an appropriate interval beforehand, made a phone call to the spaceport and a second one to police headquarters. He hadn't expected to get through to the chief superintendent directly – and didn't – but the man's secretary was surprisingly obliging.

Inside Connor's study were four mercs ready to go, the minimum staffing level Connor had considered safe: Pritie, Marcello and Jack, plus Yasmine, Connor's explicable shadow. Any more and they would have looked like a strike team or, more aptly, a distraction.

Nothing is meant to go wrong.

Swallowing private misgivings, Connor surveyed the foursome. "Jack, when we arrive, you will stay with the car." He nodded. "Where's Atalanta?"

"Having a row with my cousin," Yasmine said from her

seat by the door.

Fuck them both one after the other. "Fine. We leave when they're finished."

Pritie's lips flattened into a line but she said nothing. Yasmine rose and skirted up beside her, and said, "I agree with Pritie: do we *have* –"

"Yes." Atalanta, Connor trusted to make her move precisely on time. Calad would also turn up on time if only by dint of sticking close to his wife to continue the row.

Two minutes later Atalanta materialised in the study, bright-eyed and silent, with Calad hovering behind her, his cheeks flushed. Connor dialled ten minutes onto his jack timer. "Go," he said, "and move carefully." His voice came out curt and clipped. The pair of them slid out of the door and away. Connor closed his eyes. *Please just go. Please. We'll miss the light.*

First one, and then a second, bike engine receded into the evening. Connor set the timer running. The rest of them waited in silence. Connor's stomach was tingling. Never, never, could he trust the magic to warn him of an upcoming problem. He wouldn't trust its answer if it did.

On ten minutes, he gestured to the other four and started down the stairs. Hums of regular office business filtered from every doorway. Connor fixed a supercilious scowl onto his face, pushed open the garage door at the stairs' foot and marched to his car. Yasmine and Jack climbed into the back, and Marcello into the front passenger seat. Pritie mounted her own bike and headed out of the garage the moment its door opened wide enough to admit her. Connor drove after her into the golden hour more slowly and with deliberation.

It took him twenty minutes to drive across increasingly upmarket precincts, plazas and parks to the police's dark headquarters tower in the city centre and to park outside. Pritie's bike was already strapped to the headquarters' bike rack. Connor climbed out of the car, shook his head at the bike as if in frustration, and strode to the door with Marcello and Yasmine shadowing him as closely as they dared. Jack hung behind, on guard, managing to look more like a chauffeur than a getaway driver.

Inside was a flurry of people and conversation. Pritie was

leaning over one of the interview counters in dogged conversation with a duty sergeant. "I told you they're not interested," Connor said as he passed her.

"Interested in what?"

Connor turned. Mikhail Chester was standing in the station doorway behind him. Bang on time, which Connor had only been able to factor in given his experience of Union social mores. "Police brutality complaints. Irrelevant to us or to anyone. Come on." He gestured to Mikhail – whose foreign accent and expensive jacket were giving the scattered officers pause – to follow him.

"I'd thought the city centre would have better security," Mikhail said in an undertone to Connor as they approached the chief superintendent's door.

"Think how much worse it could be." Connor nodded to the chief superintendent's secretary – a uniformed policewoman he had last seen on her way in to have lunch with Gisele – and pushed open the door. He gestured to Yasmine and Marcello to stay outside. Mikhail sidestepped in the way of men who were only used to sliding doors, and followed Connor in.

Karl Leifson, the harassed-looking little man behind the desk inside, had been paging through a file before Connor entered, but set it aside and nodded to the pair. He was greying and thin, with a slight tremor in one hand that might have been down to drink. It had actually been incurred when he stopped a blow heading for Rafael Martinez's neck, back when he'd been Martinez's captain in charge of enforcement, before the one-time pirate lord decided to make himself into a rich-world name.

He would never have agreed to meet just Connor Cardwain. Mikhail Chester, though, was a different matter. Walk in with a foreigner, it seemed, and one could do anything.

Leifson motioned to the two plastic chairs opposite his desk with his tremoring hand. His non-tremoring one turned a page on his handheld. Best hope he wasn't checking Connor's list of suspected offences. Even a list of occasions one police force or another had bothered to investigate him would be very long. "Misters, welcome," he said in a tone that offered none.

"Though we have no progress to offer you –"

"I have." Connor pulled a handheld from his pocket, opened Saeed's photo and passed it over. "I got you a suspect. Federation citizen, on planet illegally."

Leifson's eyebrows went up. "Mister, I've had cause to use *that* line twice. One was a drift kid with no previous and the other was a Union joyrider with more money than my whole department."

"The line's there so you can use it. We caught him on a 'port camera trailing some woman the living spit of Nerys Capuin. He probably has a thing for them."

Police forces saw enough perverts to fill the local jails three times over, and if any man tried to stop them – or woman, for Connor knew Éloise had tried – he'd be busy for several years. Potential killers were another. Never mind this runaway engineer almost certainly hadn't killed Nerys, or anyone else on this planet: it would do as a fake story till someone, anyone, had hold of him.

"Right." With a sigh, Leifson towed a new page towards him across the desk and opened a form. "I'll stick his picture into a drone and send it up, in case it does any good. Do you have any ID on him?"

"Not confirmed. We got a possible name on him from a foreign news source." Vague enough to sound helpful, but simultaneously might not help Leifson's staff too much until they'd found the man, and certainly wouldn't help anyone else – for instance, any of Saxen's staff, or the governor's personal guard – who came asking for info.

Leifson frowned. "I don't get involved in out-sector crime."

"What a good thing you can pick him up for something you have reason to think he did here." Mikhail started to fidget. Connor half-raised a hand to hush him. "He was sighted at the spaceport, but we don't have full visuals of the way he went as he left. We wish to request access to the city security images."

A shutter fell across Leifson's eyes. "Not possible."

Mikhail leant a little way across the desk. "On Ransomvale, you'd pull them up before a lawyer organised a warrant."

"This isn't Ransomvale." Leifson shut his screens with a

single swipe of his good hand. "Thank you for your assistance, Misters. I wish you good day."

Connor rose with a nod just too brief to be polite and tugged Mikhail out of the office when it looked like he would stay to argue. "It isn't worth it," he murmured as the door shut behind them. "Push him now, with nothing more than a picture as your backup and no authority, and you'll just get a knock on the hatch at three in the morning and a man with big fists explaining what not to say to his boss." He didn't look at Leifson's secretary at her desk a couple of feet away. Instead he gestured for his bodyguard and his Weaver to follow him out.

"You can't mean to *leave* it –"

"I can and will. Any number of other ways to get the same information: they're just slower."

He pushed open the connecting door to the main front office. Pritie was still with the desk sergeant, rolling her eyes as if she'd repeated herself six times already. Connor beckoned to her as he passed, but said to Mikhail, "We go the most direct way, this is what we get. A great big stash of nothing. You go back to the 'port authority and ask them, or get Martins to do it, or – or call some fancy lawyer straight from Ransomvale and get him onto Leifson. I'll push to the edges of my authority and grab all the information I can."

"It shouldn't work like this," Mikhail muttered under his breath.

"Like what? Piecemeal and antagonistic? That's the way things are." Connor forced himself to shrug as he opened the front door. "Life could always be worse. I don't get on too well with the governor and the cops, but neither do I get on too well with Comet and Saxen. As long as they all stare down each other, I'll survive just fine in the gap between."

"You're as bad as any of the rest of them." Mikhail, blinking in sudden warm sunset light outside, spoke as if he'd glimpsed an angel's vision. "You just happened to walk onto our side."

"I'm on my own side. You dragged yourselves into my orbit when your wife got my cleaner killed."

Hurt stained his eyes. "You don't know that's what happened."

"It's getting obvious. I trust the experience has given your crew enough of a distaste for the scenario that they don't repeat it." He gave Mikhail a cursory bow and walked away towards his car.

The sun was sinking past the nearby rooftops. Amber light, witching light, bathed the city streets, precursor to fire or to worse. Connor settled into his car seat and, as he drew up a city map on the dashboard with his territory marked out in red, checked the time.

His slow exit with Mikhail had given Leifson more than enough time to order the right data files retrieved or deleted. Any action commencement would mean Atalanta and Calad knew what to take. Eyes still on his map, mind elsewhere, Connor counted seconds, calculated upload speeds, plotted security sensor freezes. This police station was as secure as anywhere on the Septième. Wager everything on his infiltrators not being Septième –

Just past his car's rear bumper, a quartet of bikes settled to the concrete, heralds to a car that skittered down at an improbable angle. Connor craned his neck round. A pair of Saxen's high-ups – a senior lieutenant and a captain – vaulted out of the car and marched towards the police station door with the bikers flanking them.

Jack Priest gestured to the newcomers with eyes raised. Connor restrained a curse. He *couldn't* go back inside. He *couldn't* go back towards Calad and Atalanta.

"Yasmine," he said, "escort Pritie out of there. I don't care what you need to say to do it."

She retreated without comment. Connor itched to dig his fingernails into his palms. *Not as planned. Not as planned.*

For the trigger that he *had* planned was coming into view across the car park, two minutes too late to pull strings in the right way. Mikhail, alone, armed with a lawyer on jack tangler straight from Ransomvale – which was to say, heavily armed – but heading into a palaver too great for him to control.

For a couple of frozen moments Connor contemplated leaving him. Yes? No? Yes, surely. He'd set all this up once: he could do it again.

Twenty yards and a million miles away, Mikhail pulled

open the police station door as if its hinges were a personal insult and vanished from view. Connor pushed himself out of his seat and jogged across the car park as if he'd dropped his spare hair tie in Leifson's office. *Look casual. Feel casual.* Whatever the situation, never look upwards towards the window Calad and Atalanta had intended to force.

He paused in the station doorway. Yasmine had her wings out, one of them dangling in a constable's face, though he seemed too frightened to object: she was speaking to Pritie in a low voice, gesturing to the door. Pritie was ignoring her. Mikhail had stopped, irresolute, partway down the hall towards Leifson's office. He'd switched his lawyer to a viewscreen projecting out of his neural transceiver: the man seemed engaged in a conversation with a female police sergeant at Mikhail's side, though Connor was unsure whether the lawyer could see the scene or only hear it. Any second now they'd all devolve into a jurisdictional debate. At least when Éloise had been on secondment to the Port Logis police force for an assignment on the Septième, she'd kept her nose clear of domestic police.

Holding Mikhail at bay was a racket of an argument ahead and out of sight. Connor elbowed past a couple of cops and grabbed his arm. "Get clear of here, now."

Mikhail blinked a foreigner's surprise at him. "I thought people would be more subtle about demanding action with menaces."

"Usually they are. This is an unusual time."

Mulishness flitted across his face and dissipated, replaced by earnest endeavour. "Mister Cardwain, I am not going to let any dispute get in the way of *anything* that helps me find Nerys."

"Getting shot in crossfire would be a pretty good way of ensuring you never do find her." Connor shook his shoulder. "Just come out and wait –"

The voices ahead peaked and abruptly ceased. Connor froze, listening, not sure what he wanted to hear. If only he had Logan towering beside him. If only he had Éloise.

If he continued to rely on Éloise he would not remain a man.

Deep inside the office, a gunshot spat. Didn't matter who

had shot whom, not now: didn't matter that the car park, their escape route, was growling with fresh engines. *"Run,"* Connor said, shoving Mikhail towards the door. Behind him Yasmine grabbed Pritie's arm and started hustling her away. A police officer made as if to stop her: her wings brightened, and the man fell back.

"We had nothing to do with this," she called over her shoulder.

"That won't help," Connor said under his breath. No. For he'd put them all in the wrong place at precisely the wrong time. *Never tangle with authority.*

The four of them tumbled out into the car park into a jumble of bikes and noise. Connor, frantic energy beginning to burn at the back of his head, squinted up into the sunset lingering on nearby office blocks and city hall. Half a squad of Saxen's mercs, guarding cars and bikes, swung heads Connor's way: Connor pushed Mikhail leftwards towards the spot where he'd parked.

His car was missing. Connor stumbled to a stop, staring like a wounded donkey at the empty spot. No car. No Marcello and no Jack. Just a few police officers, scrambling from official bikes fresh-dropped to the car park, reaching for weapons and looking for suspects, and squealing in the air: yet more bikes approaching. Whether they were police or not, Connor didn't want to find out.

Pritie and Yasmine split, Pritie taking a defensive spot on Mikhail's left and Yasmine on Connor's right. Connor grabbed Mikhail's arm and broke into a run, pulling the other man along with him. Mikhail, albeit a little heavier than Connor, stumbled but couldn't help but follow.

"Where are we going?" he panted.

"Away. You're unfit." *He* was unfit. Past thirty now and spending too much time behind desks and too little in a gym.

Concrete chips plumed off the wall by his head. He heard the gun-crack a second later. Pritie, the shortest present by most of a foot, muttered a curse and raised one arm to shield her head: Yasmine, at Connor's side, stopped and glanced backwards.

"They're not following," she called.

Not if 'they', police and Saxen's staff, intended primarily

to attack each other. Connor didn't slow his run, no matter how badly Mikhail was flagging: Yasmine caught them up and passed them seconds later. *Fucking* Weavers.

Another gunshot flashed past Connor's shoulder, close enough to singe his jacket collar. Mikhail's high panting edged higher still, fear-tinged. Up above, the new bikes squealed closer and closer, now joined by an even higher buzzing: tiny drones, carrying explosives. Drones of the type sold by Cliff Enterprises.

A tiny corner of Connor's mind, the corner that kept him calm in firefights, repeated over and over again, *Get away. Get away. Keep your head and get away.* Gradually, neuron by neuron, Connor swallowed the blinding panic running up his spine and faced that tiny thought, and as his feet thudded on concrete and his ears tried to track each successive gunshot, he asked himself, demanded of himself, why?

Not *why* the firefight. *Why* did his hindbrain ache so hard to get away from the police tower?

Pritie waved sideways at a tiny alley. Connor yanked Mikhail round the corner and held him against the wall with Yasmine and Pritie covering them. Here, out of sight of the police station, the little compulsion cut out. Cursing the Augury thread, cursing his luck, Connor said, "We need to keep moving."

"I *can't* – I –"

Cataclysmic boom behind him. Connor tensed. The city seemed to freeze, in motion and sound. Then a second crack, eardrum-endangering, roared overhead.

Connor threw one arm over his head and pulled Mikhail to his knees, as if he thought that would benefit either of them. The sky was collapsing. Thunder-dense booms ripped the air, again and again.

With a faint whine, Connor's car lurched down from the sky and stuttered into the alley. The closest door cracked open: in the rear. Connor hauled Mikhail up and shoved him inside, then yanked open the driver's door.

"Move," he said. Marcello, at the controls, shifted sideways far enough to allow Connor to climb in beside him.

In the back, Pritie pulled the door shut on herself and Yasmine. Three crammed in the front, for Jack was in the front passenger seat: three in the back. No Calad, and no Atalanta. Connor kicked the car into the air, staring out of the windscreen for the faintest glimpse of red or blond hair.

The police station was smoking. Opposite, the city hall lay in cratered ruins, with one wing standing like a drunkard over the wreckage. All across the city, in every direction, more flames leapt into the evening, and through the car's closed doors Connor heard repeated *crack-phut* from gunfire.

Hands trembling on the controls so hard the car barely hung steady in the air, Connor traced the city with eye and mind. Blazes near gangland offices and police stations: governmental offices, defence station, anyone who could dispense justice.

"Is it over?" Mikhail said, voice quivering, from the back seat.

Flames, maybe, from Connor's offices. Certainly at the 'port authority offices. Anyone and everyone who had thwarted a wannabe-plutocrat. "No. It's just starting."

*

CHAPTER SEVENTEEN

Many years ago – when Connor at sixteen had thought himself a grown man, and had been unwilling to reconsider upon viewing evidence to the contrary – Meris Hardblade had launched her first raid on Sanctis Merovir's territory. Revenge for insult or seizure of opportunity following a momentary lapse in Merovir's concentration: Connor had never been sure which. He'd talked himself into a gun team, and Logan too. Hardblade's staff had taken him for eighteen and Logan for sixteen, till they'd checked the pair's ID cards much later.

Over a decade on, he could still taste dust on the air, clogging his throat, and could smell burning corpses set for a personal pyre, gun-blasts their firelighters and charred roof-struts their wood. Children, drifters, had lain in the street, decapitated or dismembered in the mess.

Now, as he drove, threading as fast as he could through angry bikers towards his office, he saw battle lines drawing up in the streets below. Allied ganglanders pulling together defences against whatever came: hit squads swarming unwary outposts, with little care whom they struck: police fleeing, mugging passers-by for civilian clothes and abandoning their uniforms.

It's done, Connor wanted to cry out of the window. Transfer of power, simple and brief. There was no need for Saxen to push his hand any further.

Except, of course, that there was: except that raw power answered only to power, and whoever in the higher political echelons Saxen had bribed or blackmailed, he couldn't bribe the whole city and its low underside. In some few tableaux below Connor spied a stand-off, especially between Saxen's allies on the low underside and their respectable but well-armed neighbours. The rest of the city was starting to sink into a hideous patchwork of massacres and compromises.

Take a gun, or a knife, or a grenade. Use it for its intended purpose: to kill. Kill in such a cacophony and such a firestorm that one seemed invincible: the aristocracy of a cheap HV drama brought to life, of a brass section exploding over strings, of a thunderstorm in sentient form.

Connor steered round a blossom of anti-aircraft fire – not aimed at him, but flashing in his direction – and accelerated towards his office. From his limited angle he couldn't see much damage in his city quarter. *Please*, he realised he was whispering to some angel or none inside his head. *I've no stocks on site. Let him realise that, and leave me alone.*

Fat chance of anything going anyone's way right now. A miniature flood of bikes was clustering his streets, centred on his office. As he drove closer, individual people became recognisable from what had begun as a fly-like cloud.

"Do we go in shooting?" Jack said, beside him.

"With this many of us playing this many of them?" Connor touched his jack phone and called Sean Jules's line. No answer.

The wrong man's reaction: an optimistic man, one who believed the world would work to his benefit. Connor cancelled the call and reset the line. Static buzzed down his ear for half a minute, as he slowed the car to a crawl and crept along rooftops closer and closer to the office.

The jack phone popped. "This is a surprise," Saxen said down Connor's ear, too loudly. "Impeccable timing you have."

"What do you want from me?" Silence in response. "I suspect you could stand one fight the less. I could certainly do to avoid it. So – what do you want?"

After another long pause – long enough for Connor to fear he'd taken the wrong approach – Saxen said, "Get that woman out of the street."

Instead of asking what woman, Connor nudged the car closer to his office, and peered down. His mouth went dry and he fancied he tasted blood at the back of his throat. Gisele – veiled, but definitely her, a figure all in white with pink wings arching over her shawl– was standing in the street outside the front door, between Saxen's crew and it. Eight or ten of Saxen's people lay prone on the grubby pavement outside the door, splashed with engine oil and a little spring drizzle. Gisele appeared to be speaking: impossible to be sure from this angle and with shawl chiffon over her mouth, but with the way her hands were moving it seemed a fair assumption.

He wasn't paying Gisele and had no control over her. That wouldn't wash with Saxen. "Give me five minutes," he said, "and I'll call you back." He cut the line and accelerated again.

In a J-swing more reminiscent of Logan than of the more cautious mercs who'd taught the pair of them to drive, Connor dropped his car past Saxen's hovering bikers and up to his garage door. The door stayed firmly shut. "Stay in here," Connor ordered the others, "except you, Yasmine." He cracked open his door. A handful of gun barrels rotated towards him. One man, not the closest or the one Connor'd clocked as the biggest danger, folded to his knees, gun spilling from his fingers.

"As I was saying before that man so rudely interrupted," Gisele continued to Saxen's captain Horsefield, who was standing a few feet from her with his copper cheeks and ears reddening by the moment, "you need to learn to *knock*, and acquaintance with a priestess or two might improve your perspective. I always say that travel broadens the mind, and the same is true of a more *spiritual* journey." She cocked her head towards Connor. "Wouldn't you agree?"

She was giving him an in, he recognised over the panic he was forcing down inside him: an in that she hadn't granted these unconscious men on the street. They hadn't needed to raise a hand or a weapon to her: by Neuvième law and custom, speaking to her out of turn had been enough. This was not the Neuvième.

"I think," he said, fighting his larynx to achieve something approaching a steady voice, "we would do best to go inside and talk this over with a cup of tea." He scanned Saxen's team. Two of the lieutenants were women, as was a grunt merc toting a rifle Connor would be inclined to hand straight to his brother. "You three," he said to the women, "– and you," he added to a fourth merc, a Kriastan he belatedly IDed as a small female rather than a warrior male. "Please step inside. I've spoken to your boss. We'll leave the door open," he said to the captain before he could protest, "and we'll stay in view." Before anyone else could speak, he offered his arm to Gisele and led her inside. Yasmine followed.

Lips clamped on a *what-were-you-thinking*, he half-bowed to Gisele as soon as they negotiated the lintel, and released her arm. "Mister Saxen and I," he said to the lieutenants, "are in the process of resolving our differences. Clear the hall." This last was to the cluster of his male mercs who'd sited themselves just out of firing line from the door. "My brother's stepmother would like to explain something to these ladies."

"There's no need to be sarcastic, dear," Gisele said, unwinding her shawl from her face. "*Quite* a commotion for minimal result, and I doubt that whatever you may do will have much of an effect given the soundtrack. You forgot the cream," she said to the wide-eyed runner girl who was sidling up with a tea and coffee tray. "It's in Mister Cardwain's personal refrigerator."

"My fridge is locked." His fridge was used only for storage of delicate chemicals, or so he'd thought. Connor snatched up his teacup almost before Yasmine had finished pouring out and, while his bodyguard handed cups to the bemused lieutenants, sipped. It was almost hot enough to blister his lips. He needed the pain. He needed to concentrate.

Gisele aimed a satisfied little smile at her coffee cup and said to the lieutenants, "It isn't that I *blame* your boss, so to speak, but when he *could* have promoted Minerva Connaught instead of sending your current squad captain – it's not like he could introduce himself, now, is it? – options really need to be considered. She actually asked me about the conventions: she must, I suppose, be visiting Mister Martinez's wife, though she really should have warned her *colleagues*. Wouldn't you warn them?"

The lieutenants side-eyed each other. "She did go to the house," one offered.

Gisele nodded, smile widening like a cat's whiskers. "Of course she did. There's a distinction to be drawn between necessary and unnecessary unpleasantness. Business is business, as my late husband always said, with just an added level of complication when one deals with politics. Politics, I often think, is an invention specifically designed to make lives difficult: as much as religion was designed to make lives simpler. I would take both of them with a pinch of salt. Or sugar." She added another half-spoon of sugar to her cup. She never took sugar normally. It would have been preferable, Connor thought, if he'd previously laced the bowl with arsenic. "Especially, I think, when priestesses begin to moralise over other people's lives. I'm becoming quite tired of that sort of thing. Not murdering, of course, I can see, and so many of the stanzas warning one against magic have been erased over the years – my son has made quite a study of it – but when it comes to the right way to eat meat, I lose all patience. If I wanted to know how to eat meat I'd ask a cook."

One of the lieutenants was starting to grin, and not at the sight of Yasmine coaxing tea into a Kriastan tankard. "I have to say," she said, "our boss has little truck with priestesses, and not for just that reason."

"Wise of him," Connor grunted. The caffeine was going to his head and his lips were tingling. Gisele, so calm, so ridiculous, with that smug expression on her face as if she weren't living through a coup and as if she knew where her only son was. Maybe she saw all this as part of the tour, a developing-sector porn show put on for her benefit as if by a set of dancing girls on a stage. Free from consequence and free from guilt.

"Every time I hear a priest blather about guilt," Gisele said with a pointed little glance up at Connor, "or justice, I hear a good dose of live-as-I-say. If justice is for God, let God dispense it. People are far too broken to attempt the same." She drained half her coffee cup in one swallow. The Kriastan female snorted, and inhaled a slurp of hot tea as if accepting a challenge. Perhaps she was young, or new to the world off the Huitième. The grunt merc certainly was young: trying to hide smiles at the conversation, and distaste at the tea's bitterness.

Connor drained his still-hot tea, moved a few feet away and touched his jack phone. "She's inside, and making friends with a couple of your staff," he said a few moments later when Saxen answered the call. "I have only one car on site at the moment: I'll bring back your sleepy staff in stages. Just tell me where."

"If you think a taxi job is going to mollify me, you're highly mistaken." Saxen spoke as if he were bidding in a whist game, unconcerned. "Send the woman with them."

"How?" The line was silent. "She's a Circle telempath. She could edit both our memories of this conversation to remove that order without us being aware of it. If we even remember this discussion, she'll want us to. Besides –" He shouldn't push it, now, but if he lived, it would be worth the risk. "She's wearing white, with her face veiled, and her wings are glowing like a set of club lights. In your position I'd regard the recent events as a departmental intelligence test."

"Be that as it may," Saxen said, voice like cream and about as trustworthy, "you and I have an existing arrangement –" *not to be eaten by a lion*, sour as lime juice squeezed over ripe mangos – "that needs updating."

"In what way?" Warranted fear, so much worse than unwarranted, started warring with Connor's stomach. He tried to concentrate on Saxen's voice.

"I have a lot more responsibilities now. I need more staff. They need outfitting." His tone shifted: crisper, like biting into a crab claw. "I've sent a team to your main warehouse. Go there and ensure your staff hand over anything my captain wants."

And now the alarm bells cranked to maximum. The explosive prototype was still at the warehouse. "I'll drive over now. Which captain?"

"Elderson."

"I'll meet him in fifteen minutes."

"You're being particularly reasonable."

Connor restrained a shrug. Saxen couldn't see him and none of their employees could hear the conversation. "I can smell the air. You're in an unassailable position. We both gain more if I cooperate with you."

"We'll see."

Connor took a deep breath and turned back to the women. Gisele was shepherding the lieutenants to the door, still winding her shawl back round her face, talking all the while. Connor edged up to her.

"– and take a cupful of advice, as my mother always said," Gisele said to the leading lieutenant as they reached the door. "It's more use than peppercorns, especially if one finds oneself in an unpleasant position. Do drive carefully."

"We will." The lieutenant was still amused: it echoed in her voice despite the solemn expression. Gisele stood, watching the scene as serenely as a statue, as the mercs began to drive away.

"If you mean to make a fuss," she said to Connor over her shoulder, "I advise against it. Yasmine, shut the door."

Her niece obeyed. "Pritie and the others are still stuck in the car," she said to Connor.

"I haven't forgotten."

Gisele dropped her veil again, revealing an expressive frown. "I don't think capitulation is a positive move, dear."

"Who said positive? I'm trying to save all our necks, including yours." He swallowed another *what-possessed-you*, and a few whys and wherefores. "Yasmine, I want you here with spell-eyes on the perimeter. Pritie will be in charge."

"This is not a good move."

"I don't have any choice."

Leave? Even if he evacuated all his staff, which he seriously doubted was possible at the moment, he couldn't retrieve his stock, or the White Canyon deal copy stuck in the warehouse vault. And nor would he take his reputation. Call it capitulation if Gisele liked – call it anything a married woman wanted. For once he was out of moves.

Outside, he heard his car slide into the garage, and a few seconds later Pritie entered the hall via the connecting door. Her face was bleak. "We can't survive this."

"We might if I'm careful. Stay here and maximise what we have."

He edged past her and into the garage. Jack was helping Mikhail out of the car. Connor gestured for him to hurry and for Marcello and Khayam, one short wiry figure and one tall thin one, to get inside.

The garage door still stood open. Connor swung to it, right

hand closing on his pistol butt, when he heard a car engine whine outside, but when it dropped to the street he saw it was a Harcourt B3 with the Cliff Enterprises logo on its flanks.

The driver's window slid open. "I heard my cousin's husband was here," Aled said, leaning out.

"He is." Gesturing for Jack to bring Mikhail over, Connor walked to the car and bent closer to Aled. "That must have been an interesting drive you had." The young man shrugged and nodded. "What's happening at the 'port?"

He grimaced. "Lockdown for all exiting vessels except goods haulers – those who can prove they're haulers. There's been one crash already when an incomer ran out of landing strip."

"The idiot," Connor muttered. Not the pilot, but Saxen.

Aled sent him a sardonic look. "It's lucky our boss isn't easily threatened."

"Get back safe. If you get stopped by Saxen's teams before you're back in your bubble, Ilsa might find her resolve threatened a little." Jack piled Mikhail into the car's rear seat. Connor stepped back, and Aled gave him a little salute and peeled away.

Connor retreated to his car and climbed in the driver's seat. "Where are we going?" Marcello said as they drove back out of the garage into the evening.

"To do something foolish."

If only Logan had been here: idea generator as much as strongman. Hells, if Dominic had been alive Connor would have phoned him, and never mind the call charge. The skill set to handle Neuvième and Septième politics wasn't too dissimilar.

Or Thakar. Or Michel.

Never mind any of that lot. Atalanta and Calad were here, somewhere. Éloise might be the closest thing he'd met to unkillable, but Atalanta ran her close. Connor gripped the car's controls a fraction tighter, tracing patterns in the fires below. Smoke and overglow masked all star-patterns overhead. Wherever Atalanta was – on the reasonable assumption she wasn't already dead – she would surely return to the office and assist with its defences. If she could be persuaded to flash her wings, she'd become an even more reliable bulwark, but…

And if she'd only read minds at random like a Circle Weaver, he could send her a warning: do not resist, do not take the high-minded route. Survival, now, was their fundamental. He stared into the sky, dimming with encroaching dusk, day-bright in places from shellfire. *Calad, if you can hear me, tell her to be careful. Gisele, if you can hear me, warn them both.* No way to know if he'd been heard.

No cops processing the street speed guns' auto-reports meant no speeding fines. Connor accelerated. With little enough traffic in the air he reached the holding warehouse's perimeter in twelve minutes flat and had time to warn Mina Jai on the way. The car's dash, normally a steady drip of traffic reports and news of missing cats, spewed local news faster than Connor could read. Seizure of defence and security assets underway. Martinez's wife begging to be left alone, as recent events had prostrated her: capitulation from the Martinez camp, then. Outspoken local aristocrats and nouveaux riches – Elian de Priet (Martinez's stepfather, no less), Sai Kabison, Daelle Henry, Théodora Bramhall – declaring Saxen's 'coolness under pressure' was grounds to support his future administration.

From the fussing at the gate, Saxen's captain Elderson had beaten Connor by a good fraction and his entourage was arguing with the chief of security, Anna Target. As they were outside the perimeter, the AA gun was still powered down. Connor slowed the car, took a delicate circuit near the gate and, when no one looked up, backed off and slowed to a crawl. "I'll run over the canning factory roof next pass," he said to the two men in back. "When I do, jump out and take up observation points. Yes, you'll come down smelling of fish."

Khayam unbuckled seat restraints and rifle without a word. Marcello said, "Is this going to be OK, Mister?"

God, I hope so. "If it isn't, I need you to alert the office staff and call my brother." He dropped down low to the duck-tailed roof over the cannery. Both rear doors popped open and the two mercs thudded out. Connor waited for the doors to close and then drove on at his earlier approach speed. All he could hear, for these few seconds, was his own breathing, and the car's soft whirring underneath.

Attitude was key, and he didn't even know which attitude to take up. He dropped the car to the concrete in front of the warehouse and climbed out almost before it had settled onto its skids. "Let them through," he called to Target. "Jai knows about this."

The chief, who had seemed set to mount a fruitless defence of Connor's property, lowered her rifle. A string of Saxen's bikes slid through the perimeter. One biker peeled off and landed beside Connor: the captain, Elderson. He was tall, and heavy in the shoulders, but Connor could have said the same for most underside high-ups. The aristocracy of bodyweight, beginning in childhood.

"Ready for my shopping list?" he said as he pulled off his helmet.

Connor restrained any signs of irritation. He couldn't afford them, even when the man was talking like captain outranked leader. "I'm aware you have requirements. Come inside and we'll go through them."

He retrieved a handheld from a jacket pocket and passed it to Connor to read as they walked to the loading bay door. Most of it he'd expected, such as the five hundred rifles and the set of explosives from the day before. Pistols. Flares. Plasma packs. Maybe some of the pistols would go to a few existing cops who swore loyalty. In three months there'd be nothing to show anything had ever happened: no distinction between Saxen's existing crewers and the new hires. Maybe Elderson had been promised control of the new police force.

Other items were more esoteric. "I don't produce stun cannon. I'll have to order them for you." Stun grenades, he had. Stun grenades, he didn't want to admit to having. He tapped the last item on the list, the explosive. "I told your colleagues this morning – this isn't in production yet."

"Isn't it."

Jai hurried up to the main warehouse door, fear visible in her eyes but well in control of herself. She nudged the loading door up another few inches to admit the two men, and said to Connor, "I need an hour to run batch approval."

"You haven't got it." Connor glanced at Elderson. "I think

you haven't got an hour."

"I'm not hanging about here that long!" he said with a huff. "What in hells do you mean?"

"For a non-pre-ordered shipment," Jai said, over-precise and irritable as if she'd been disturbed in the middle of her evening meal, "either I have to spend an hour running second approval, or Mister Cardwain and I have to release the order – one crate at a time." She squinted into mid-air as she surveyed the list. "I suggest you find seats."

Elderson glanced at the warehouse foreman, who nodded and gestured to a drifter flunky to bring a chair: Elderson snorted and turned away to mutter something to his lieutenant. Connor transferred the list from handheld to his jack, and said to Jai, "I'll start with the rifles." Ten crates of fifty. "You get the flares and then start on the pistols." She nodded. A faint question lurked in her eyes but she said nothing. Connor gestured for two warehousemen to follow her: "Pull them over as they're released," he said. They nodded, glanced at each other and headed after Jai.

Each crate could move on its own jets and the warehouse hopper could pull up five at a time. Slow this down. Gain time to think.

The foreman had got the hint, for two more warehousemen trailed Connor down the line as he unlocked crate after crate. Fingerprint on the sensor and lift the lock. Not tricky, but he delayed each one ten seconds longer than he needed, trying to think.

Capitulation led to more. For how long: years? Forget making a name as a man rather than a flunky, then.

As he reached the last of the rifle crates, Jai fussed up the row, unlocking the pistols adjacent. "They'll want more," she murmured.

"Yep." Connor didn't look at her. "And doubtless we'll keep churning out more, and some we'll still be able to sell to other people. And our staff will survive."

She glanced back at Elderson and his team, and Connor's team: a few warehouse staff directing the released crates outside, the rest standing in a huddle muttering to each other, and the security team off to one side, heads together, whispering. They still had their rifles. Connor's remaining staff were unarmed, and were outnumbered. But she and Connor hadn't released any of the new firearms' ammunition yet.

"You think –" she whispered.

"I –"

"Hey." Connor jumped. Elderson, peering at the pair of them, with a grunt at his either shoulder: "What are you doing?" he said.

"Unlocking your crates," Connor said over his shoulder.

Elderson frowned. "So hurry it up. What's the problem?"

"There's no problem. Every withdrawal requires two stages of authorisation: as I already said, you didn't give us time to batch-approve the second stage, so Captain Jai –" such she ranked, on the underside – "and I are authorising your withdrawals the only other possible way."

"Then do it quicker. It's already dark, for God's sake."

Jai straightened and turned away from the next crate in line. "Maybe cut out the attitude? We're handing over our stock to you –"

"Attitude. Huh. Is that what I have?" She opened her mouth to argue further: he smiled. "And you got a fingerprint. That's all."

His pistol was in his hand. Connor, bare-handed, reached for his arm: one of the grunts shoved him sideways against a crate. Elderson fired. Point-blank range. Jai didn't have a chance to scream, just folded up, half her face missing.

Target grabbed for her rifle. Still sprawled on the floor, Connor opened his mouth to shout to her to stand down. Too slow. Elderson's lieutenant fired from seven feet away, straight at the security chief's stomach. She doubled over and fell with a choked little gasp.

Connor stayed frozen in place, barely breathing, an attitude mirrored in his employees including (thanks be to God) Target's deputy, Ambrose. Elderson bent to Jai's splayed body and lifted her limp right hand. "Should stay warm for a little while." He raised eyebrows at Connor. "Do the fingers need to be attached for this to work?"

Lie. Do it. "I don't know." *Damn you.*

"Let's find out." He drew his boot knife, set the saw blade and sliced off Jai's index finger. He held it to the closest crate. Its lock flashed green and it popped open. Elderson grinned. "Nice." He gestured to one of his squad mercs. "Cut off the rest of her fingers and let's hurry this up."

He swung to Connor, an ugly grin twisting his face. "Those explosives. What did you say? 'Not in production', I think it was." He raised his eyebrows. "How many fingers did you want to keep?"

Connor's heart was thudding in his chest so hard he could hear little else. "I was telling the truth. I have exactly one prototype. Nothing else."

"Then let's have the prototype. Where is it?"

"Locked away in the office." He gestured to the high window overlooking the loading area.

"So go get it." Elderson mirrored Connor's gesture.

Squeeze the anger, squeeze the pain. Hold it tight. Hold it till it became knife-hard. Connor rose, and made to pass Saxen's troops and head for the office.

Elderson held out a hand to stop him. Tally one more little meaningless slight. "Pistol, on your belt. Drop it." He did so. They were in an arms complex: Elderson was after the status hit, not the weapon retrieval. "Luka will go with you." He nodded to a grunt merc who rivalled Connor's height and outweighed him by at least a stone.

Connor shrugged. "Where else am I meant to be going?" He pushed open the door into the side corridor that led up to the office, and gestured for the merc to hurry up.

Continuing capitulation would mean his death along with that of everyone else on site. Too many people had died already. Continuing capitulation, ultimately, was pointless if it didn't produce results.

He glanced back at the grunt puffing after him through the corridors. No point even starting to feel sorry for the man. His captain was an idiot. A bright man didn't serve a stupid captain for long.

"Don't you train?" he said to the grunt, keeping his voice loud, as he headed up the stairs two at a time.

"I work out," the man said in a defensive tone. Connor looked back. For half a second he spied a sheepish expression on the grunt's face, but when he saw Connor move he dropped it in favour of mulish arrogance again.

"Hmm." Connor opened the door and paused in the doorway. The stock control boy was in the outer office attempting to hide behind his desk. Connor pointed to a dimmer crevice between desk and security cabinet and turned back to the grunt, blocking the doorway. "You should see a specialist sometime. You might gain something."

The stock controller was as hidden as he could get. Connor strode across the office – now in full view of the windows: he didn't look down – with the grunt close behind him. He opened the study door with his thumbprint.

Jai's study: her scent was still on the room, and her picture chip – deactivated – sat on her desk. Connor pocketed it as he passed. He bent to the safe, watching the grunt in the reflection off a polished wall section. Not making any moves.

One drone sat in the safe, quiescent and innocent, a little ball an inch across. Connor picked it up and pretended to fiddle with its battery, using his left hand: with his right, he typed the Cliff hangar address at the spaceport into the drone's homing field. Address it to Ilsa? No – Mikhail: MIKHAIL CHESTER, he wrote. Attach a shipping form for a sample. Yes, the detonator was definitely disabled. It wouldn't do in the current climate to cause any misunderstandings.

Swallowing his remaining misgivings – he had no time for them – Connor rose and turned. The grunt still stood in the doorway: he stepped aside as Connor approached. "That's it?" the man said, peering at the drone.

"Would have been more in a few months if your captain had let me keep it. Still." The blueprints were on his jack. They'd stay on his jack unless Mikhail and Ilsa could prove plagiarism.

"Whatever. Go back down." Connor allowed himself a sneer before walking back towards the staircase holding the drone in both hands. The stock control boy was still behind the desk. The grunt was still very close behind him. Too close.

"I meant to ask," Connor said over his shoulder as he started down the stairs, "what are your team being paid?" They'd gone well past the window. If Elderson were watching he would have seen both men walk to the study and both walk back with the drone.

The grunt laughed in genuine mirth. "Mister, you –"

Connor pressed the drone's ON button. It hissed away, searching for the exit, auto-tracking towards its programmed destination. As Connor turned, the grunt wasted half a second staring at the escaping drone. Connor grabbed his belt, yanked him downwards, and as he tumbled past, gripped his neck and broke it.

Bodyweight and ability to win a hand-to-hand fight were not identical. The Neuvième had underlined that for Connor. Elderson's team couldn't have travelled much.

The stock controller had crawled out from behind the desk with a little pistol in his hand and was staring at Connor in wide-eyed horror. "Keep that," Connor said, pointing first to the pistol and then to the exterior wall. "You may need it. Head out and tell any of mine you see alone to run. Go home or go to my city centre office." The boy nodded without a word, and scurried past Connor and off towards the closest fire exit to the truck park.

He might escape: he might not. It mattered to Connor more than it did to Elderson, so maybe he would be lucky. Cursing the world, Connor hurried back down the staircase.

At the foot, he paused. The air smelt the same as before: oil, steel filings, etching chemicals and glycerine. A deep subterranean growl from the generator. A steady hum from the air cycler. A distant whining from the AA gun's accelerator on the roof. A more muffled echo, the invaders' shouts and orders, and a battering sound from the direction of the factory proper.

A warehouse full of guns, and he couldn't access any of them: all locked down or past doors he couldn't afford to leave open behind him. He skirted down the corridor towards the dividing zone between warehouse and factory, away from the warehouse floor.

He continued past an exterior door to the truck park, imagining he saw devils on its other side, to the tiny canteen's rear entrance. However hard he listened he heard nothing inside. He edged the door open: the canteen was empty. He retrieved a knife from the utensil drawer – damn if he wouldn't install a lock soon, to forestall stabbings over sexual jealousy at least – and instead of heading out of the door at the far end of the canteen, which would take him round a circle back towards the warehouse floor, he climbed onto the serving counter and loosened one of the foot-and-a-half square thick plasterboard ceiling tiles.

If he'd been any larger, say, Logan's size, he wouldn't have fitted. As it was, he snagged his sleeves and one shoulder on the ceiling brackets and clattered his head on an air duct. Flat on his face inside, breathing through his nose to avoid inhaling dust, he nudged the tile back into place with one toe and crawled ahead, balancing on hands and knees on metal cross-braces. In another time he might have wasted a few moments wondering how ridiculous he looked. Current inner insistence overrode it.

Working sideways, he made for a glint in one panel elevated to his left. It shifted when he tried it, and gave onto the air cycler's maintenance hatch. Dashing dust from his mouth and nose, Connor climbed up the ladder at the best balance of speed and silence he could manage. He paused midway at one of the intake points and peered out through the vent grille onto the warehouse floor, still holding the rungs.

Two corpses had been enough for the rest of the warehouse staff, who were scurrying about packing the unlocked crates onto the back of Saxen's team's bikes – parked outside, just visible through the open loading bay door – and into the one car they'd brought. Connor gripped the inner door handle, but changed his mind and began to climb instead, towards the roof. It wouldn't be long before Elderson asked for more. It wouldn't be long before he realised he couldn't get more with only a fingerprint, not without a note into the factory's net as well, and at that point, he would either start shooting or would go to find Connor, and would realise what was happening.

Inside Connor was still raging: at Saxen's pride, and his own, too confident in his own usefulness. Take nothing but that could be bought: hold nothing but that could be stolen. The underside way. He'd needed to learn to think the Port Logis way, to be able to operate there: fatal error, perhaps, to fail to switch back quickly enough. Fatal for him and for his employees.

He paused, left arm wrapped through a ladder rung, listening to the clatters from the warehouse as if they came from another world. If he did nothing more now, they were all as good as dead. Elderson had proved that over the past five minutes. Faulty premises and poor starting conditions. But if Connor acted again, they'd die all the quicker.

Not if he ordered his cards just so.

He'd reached the ceiling hatch to the rooftop air cycler. Cautiously, he raised the hatch lid, but the cycler house was empty. Its door stood a fraction open. Connor climbed out of the hatch, unhooked the knife he'd filched from the kitchen and laid an ear close to the door crack. Someone was on the roof, and he doubted it was one of his crew. A man sent up by Saxen to disable the AA gun?

He had a spare pistol power pack in his jacket. He slid it from his pocket and set it next to the crack in the door, then retreated back to the hatch.

Inside the walls he would have no phone signal. Ninety percent of the way back into the hatch, he set his jack phone to Khayam's line.

"Yes, Mister?" Khayam said moments later, clear enough to make Connor's neck shiver. Uncanny valley: it felt as if every little sound could betray him, though no passer-by could hear Khayam speak.

"How many on the roof?" he said in his softest undertone.

"One. You want there to be one less than that?"

Too obvious. "No. Where's the captain? Lydian Elderson. Big guy covered in stripes. Highlights in his hair." His heartbeat was loud in his ears. He might have one chance to make this work.

"Getting in a car with a whole stack of boxes, Mister."

"That'll do. Kill his car under him in ninety seconds when the distraction hits."

A man had to switch sides in public sometimes. He knew that. He just hadn't planned on making a switch when jammed on a maintenance ladder ninety feet in the air.

"Ready," Khayam said after what felt like an interminable ten seconds.

"OK.   Good luck."   Connor cut the call and reset for Yasmine: she answered immediately.

"You've a vulture or two circling," she said.   "Not all owned by Mister Saxen."

"Get ready to repel attacks. *Repel.* Also prep some very aggrieved messages: be as foreign as you want."

"That's a new line."

"Significant development shift coming up. Be ready for it."

"Mind warning a girl *what* development?"

For all he knew, every phone conversation in the city was being monitored. If so, he'd already said enough to risk his office staff. "Every action has a consequence and every life has a repercussion."

Outside, the roof guard's footsteps were coming closer, a consistent crunch of steel toecaps. Connor fumbled in his money belt for a coin. His finger pricked on a halfpenny, and he teased it out. Time was, he wouldn't have wasted even this. Time was, he wouldn't have taken a risk like this.

Time had come to a head: so unnecessary. Greed and corruption he could understand, but every man had a limit. Maybe he was starting to understand his limits.

Left-handed, he aimed and threw the halfpenny at the door-crack. The guard's footsteps paused. Connor ducked into the hatch mouth, knife raised and aiming at the plasma pack on the floor.

A gunshot blazed a hole in the plasterboard wall a few feet from the door. Connor, ears ringing, kept his legs braced within the hatch. The door shivered, nudged by a rifle barrel. Connor flung the knife at the plasma pack.

As he did so, he dropped into the hatch, letting himself slide down a few rungs. The guard fired at the door and hit the plasma pack. Heat scorched the top of Connor's head. The ladder shook. He grabbed hold, left-handed, just as the explosion's noise slammed into him.

Steel slid through his grip, bruising as it went. He couldn't catch hold with his right hand. He shoved out his left arm and jammed it into a rung. Immediate horrendous wrenching forced a scream through his teeth.

His right hand was shaking and sweat-coated. Blind and

near-panicking, but no longer falling down a ninety-foot shaft, he grabbed at the rungs. Nausea clawed at him. No time for that. He wrapped one knee through the ladder and, before he could talk himself out of it, pulled his left arm free. Pain washed over him, ocean-deep, and for a moment he thought he would black out.

Concentrate. Concentrate. One-handed, he struggled down the ladder to the first refuge point and collapsed sideways into it. One arm. No gun.

He looked over the edge and almost gagged at the sight of the remaining seventy feet of ladder below him. Spaceflight had never looked as unforgiving as that long drop.

Down, down. His left arm wouldn't cooperate but after an agonising few moments he tucked it inside his jacket, cuff to armpit, and swung his legs over the edge and started to shimmy down.

No bounty for Saxen's troops other than what Connor and Mina had already ordered out of storage. No way of getting *anything* else out of storage, unless Rica Kalysdottir turned up for her shift and got a gun in her face instead, as Elderson would have worked out by now. No possible entente.

He paused on the ladder, fingers sweat-slick, counting tendons in the knuckles of his one usable hand. Saxen had taken out half the police force and, from what Aled had said about the state of the spaceport, must have suborned or taken over the planetary defence squad. Loyalty, firepower, yes: he needed more weaponry, but Connor had more on hand than any team could haul away inside a day. And Saxen would have known that before he sent Elderson calling.

Therefore, his plans for the rest of Connor's sale stock could only be two. Guard and withdraw later, or destroy.

He was still fifty feet from ground level. Logan might have risked jumping it but Connor was neither certifiable nor sleeping with a Spellweaver on a regular basis. Instead of continuing to struggle down the ladder he braced his back against one side of the shaft at right angles to the ladder and his legs at the other side, and rock-chimneyed downwards, right hand close to the ladder in case he slipped. He didn't.

Six feet from the ground he swung his legs down and dropped the rest of the way. He could hear, now, an engine whining overhead. If he could hear it in here it must be both heavy-duty and close. The high pitch meant an atmosphere vehicle, not a fusion drive. Tiny mercies.

He shoved open the maintenance door. Anna Target and Mina Jai gaped up at him, accusing with blind eyes. Outside, engines growled louder, a giant riding on a hurricane.

On the warehouse floor he was out of phone blackout. Two missed calls on his jack phone. One was from Marcello. He selected call-back as he stared at the loading bay door. Too far.

"Mister?" Marcello squeaked down his ear.

"What's inbound?"

"Two armoured vans."

"Then *run*. You, Khayam, anyone of mine still outside and breathing."

"All the breathing ones ran already, except the ones still shoving their way out of the factory. Mister –"

Connor could no longer make out individual words over the squeal of incoming engines and auto-AA fire from the factory and warehouse roofs. The walls were starting to shake. He shouldn't have put such a heavy cannon on this roof. Door, two hundred feet away. Vault stair, ten feet. He ran for the stair mouth.

As he crested the stairhead and ran down the first steps, the roof groaned overhead. Cannon becoming cannon fodder. Connor didn't look up. Vault door, ahead, locked to his fingerprints. He'd be safe inside the blast doors, beyond some of the best shielding Éloise Falavière had ever cast. That, or he'd die so quickly he wouldn't have time to know anything about it.

A tearing, shrieking crash ripped the air overhead. Connor flung his good arm over his head and kept running.

The stair treads shivered beneath his feet. He grabbed the handrail with his right hand. With a rumble and a squeal, the staircase gave way under him. Connor, flailing, realised he was dangling one-handed ten feet above the basement landing. He let go.

His feet hit the floor and he skidded in a blood-smear. Stumbling, swearing, he took a couple of strides towards the door ahead. No further. A weight crashed down from above and struck his left shoulder, sending him sprawling. For a moment he stared at a splintered human femur on the floor a few feet away, protruding from the staircase's wreckage. He just had time to think, *that's not my leg, and this isn't hurting too much: maybe my shields are in better shape than I thought*, and then the world went dark.

*

CHAPTER EIGHTEEN

"Connor."

Tiny whine down his ear, like a jack malfunctioning. It mangled concentration, distorted depth and sense of time; he tried to move his hand to his ear to cut off the sound. Nothing happened.

"*Putain de merde*. Connor."

Hands, hooked under his shoulders and moving him. Nausea upending his stomach. Someone turning him sideways so he could vomit.

"How in eight hells is he alive?" a voice said way overhead.

"My cousin." The closer voice bore a hefty Neuvième accent. "Keep him still."

Warm wind brushed through Connor's bones. Odd things, bones: tucked deep inside layers of meat and sinew, or poking out of bloody flesh as if mimicking a streetside grill deep within a slum, stray cats split with a makeshift cleaver. Light and dark, contrast and clarity, like glimpsing a hidden world that had been present all along.

A chill seeped into him, then warmth again, peaks and troughs in an endless sea. The darkness did not clear. Once he tried to open it, push it aside like a print-locked blast door, but nothing happened. Instead of persisting he lay back and tried to piece his mind together, piece the *world* together. The more he thought, the closer he reached the inescapable conclusion that he had centred operations on the wrong planet.

Midway through planning an office move, his thought slid sideways into phantasms, Nerys and Merissa dancing hand in hand round a flower trough to the angel of Glory's piping. As the music faded, he realised he was waking.

Shadows fluttered overhead and around: he opened his mouth to roar them aside, but no sound emerged. One of the shapes, a still form he'd taken for a rock, raised a hand, and the fluttering ceased.

Connor opened his eyes. The ceiling overhead was glitter-streaked, but was recognisably *his* ceiling, in his bedroom at the office. Fingers twined into his squeezed his right hand. It seemed an anchor, re-found certainty distracting him from the pounding kettledrums inside his skull.

He slid his eyes sideways. For a moment he saw only outlines, a shadow-man against the lighted window. *Michel*, he thought for a fevered second, but the shadow unfurled: shorter and broader than Michel, much darker-skinned, with black hair bushing at his neck in its loose tie. Warm affection spilt from his smile, and Connor, though it seemed nonsensical, felt himself at home at last.

"Thakar," he croaked. "How long?"

"How long were you stuck under a pile of joists, or how long have I been holding your hand?"

"Both." Dust itched at the back of his throat when he spoke.

"I got here an hour or two ago. Street talk says you're dead." Something of the gentle reassurance on his face maybe aimed to say he hadn't believed it, even for a second. Connor distrusted the look.

"Dead means no one's looking for me." He tried to sit up. Nausea gripped his belly again and he closed his eyes, fighting it.

Thakar rested a hand on his chest, feather-light, but it was enough to press Connor back into the bed with the power of a determined elephant. "Take it easy. You can play dead just fine where you are."

Connor tried to answer, and maybe did, but by the way the shadows lengthened as he framed his reply, it took him an hour or more to do so. Thakar's fingers remained nestled in his. Some chirruping about his head sounded like Yasmine, or maybe one of her relations. Éloise. Éloise and Logan, not here. He'd grown far too used to having them here.

He opened his eyes again. Sunlight outside was shading into late afternoon's golden blossom: a whole day since the coup? Yasmine was hovering over his bed, squinting at a text screen: abstracted conversation, in Septième English and Neuvième French, twittered from another screen floating alongside. Sideways glances and a mop of honey-pale hair over skin nearly the same shade: Yasmine's sister Louise.

"It's Marie, and you need to go back to sleep." Without meeting Connor's eyes Yasmine selected a globule from his nightstand and advanced on his upper arm with it.

"If that's knockout drugs, I'll sack you."

She was fair enough to flush. "It isn't, and I might need to resign anyway with the way I screwed this up."

Thakar squeezed Connor's hand. "If you guys need some alone time, I'll push off and take baby sister with me." He motioned to the screen with Louise-or-Marie still flickering indistinctly, to Connor's eyes, on it.

"Please don't," the girl on the screen said – Marie for definite: Louise wouldn't have added the 'please'. Maybe to do with Marie being the youngest. Courtesy's baggage. She seemed to be craning her neck to see Connor, as he was to see her: wide-eyed and yet assured, a child in adult's clothing. "My step-cousin Logan asks how many people you want him to hurt. My mother wouldn't let him call," she added with a note of regret.

Would that your uncle was still alive, then, Connor nearly replied. Aloud he said, "Tell him to dunk his head in a snowbank and I'll call him when I'm officially alive again. He's to *stay put*. I can't work my way out of this with him clomping around: he's never been any good an actor."

Disappointment creased Marie's cheeks. Thakar sent Connor an indulgent smile and said, "Nice to hear that knock on your head didn't damage your sweet nature."

"Never. Marie, thank Éloise for me and tell Logan not to worry." He waved a hand to shut off the vid screen and shoved himself to a half-sitting position. It took some effort.

Yasmine held the globule to his wrist and grabbed his shoulder. "Stay down."

"Did someone name you head of the family while I was asleep?" Talking hurt less than before but made his head swim. His field of vision was dancing, streamers coruscating in front of his eyes. Must be a painkiller, maybe mixed with some sort of stimulant, racing through his bloodstream. "Are my shields down?"

"Extremely weak. Éloise is good, but not *that* good. You took a hit from a close-range missile and several tons of steel and concrete – and nearly got crushed against the vault shields, too."

"The vault shields are what I'm worrying about."

"You needn't," Yasmine said. "They're still running. Saxen couldn't even get down to the door until he stole the diggers we used to retrieve you. Pritie threatened him with a lawyer on Logan's behalf. He's put armed guards on the site but they can't achieve anything."

Connor closed his eyes. His last view of the vault danced in front of his eyes, door not just locked but barricaded with descending floor beams. Absolutely secure in every way. And an armed guard squad between him and it? If he could walk – assuming he could walk – maybe he wouldn't be able to drive over there.

"How long since the warehouse hit?"

"Twenty hours or so."

"OK. Armed guards displease me, in context. If you don't want me to get up, find Calad and tell him –"

"You can't send my cousin Calad."

"Why not?"

"Because he was attacked in the middle of the night by a group of Saxen's men looking for that engineer, Saeed."

*

CHAPTER NINETEEN

Despite Yasmine's attentions, Connor's arm and back still hurt, a low, dull ache that ate into the bone. A good soak in a Neuvième bathhouse might ease the pain. Connor had no bathhouse, no R&R time, no trade stock, no money and even no immediate prospect of escape from the planet.

He still had a brain. Plot his potential moves, steps on life's chessboard: it began with information.

After struggling into a Neuvième house tunic he'd dropped on his pillow the day before and bodging a tie round his hair one-handed, he opened a news net on his jack. Local news had become naked propaganda. The SCM's news division had met its match in recent Mirqest events: wildly speculative in many respects, but detailed enough in others to make Connor suspect that a journalist had been killed or, if a drone or bot, destroyed mid-report-broadcast. The basic facts were accurate. Martinez dead. His former captains killed. Political transition in progress, negotiation expected to be forthcoming, commercial protections in place as usual – the one death song for any Septième coup was disruption of trade, something Saxen didn't seem to have forgotten.

The word was out: the word, and, from that, the impulse towards movement.

Impulses were such tricky things. Connor centred a gossip feed in front of his eyeballs, the same one that had cheerfully heralded Théodora Bramhall's championship of Saxen the day before. A journalist – a young, pretty woman, the type calculated to appear non-threatening on the Septième – had snatched a few words with three or four of Saxen's captains: chatter about their futures, their plans. Their existing fleet strength. The planetary defence fleet strength. Martinez's beautiful new Cyclopes, now Saxen's.

Impulses were dangerous.

Footsteps on the stairs meant Thakar was on his way back from a cigarette break. Connor closed his jack screens. Thakar, humming a snatch from a five-hundred-year-old ballad, poked his head back into the bedroom: "You don't look good," he said.

"I'm breathing. I'm upright." He wasn't, but emphasised the words by swinging his bare legs out of bed and clambering up. Thakar caught him before he could stumble. He brushed him off. "I'm OK. How many people saw you at the 'port?"

"Four teams at least. It wasn't much past dawn, but I know I was clocked."

One foot after the other. Walking was easy when one got down to it. Connor walked, one foot after the other, first to a chest of drawers to retrieve a pair of Neuvième-cut wrap-on trousers, which Thakar had to help him into, then into his boots, waiting by the bedroom door, and then out into the study with Thakar guiding him like an addled parent. "Fancy going out and acting upset?" Connor said. "Saxen's going to be scrambling for any news he can get. I'd like to give him a lie for supper."

"I doubt my acting skills there." He was quiet for a moment as they exited to the upper landing. "No, I don't think I could pretend – truly pretend – you were dead. If you can give me a pretext, I'll pop out and spread word you're likely to die soon, but if you were, I wouldn't have wanted to leave you."

And Thakar'd really thought Connor was dying. Connor watched his profile in the shadows, requiem for another time. "I'm sorry."

"Don't be. I came because I wanted to."

Came when he'd been mid-deal, if Connor was any judge, based on street talk and his own calculations of the previous week's activities. As Thakar paused on the landing, waiting for Connor's lead, Connor leant over and kissed him. He'd forgotten how hungry he was for this, how well he *remembered*: the taste of Thakar's last nervous cigarette behind the mint he'd sucked to rid his mouth of it, the feel of their day-old stubble brushing together, familiar sweat-scent beside him and a strong shoulder beneath his, strong arms embracing him, surrounding him. He ached to give in to that embrace.

A light step behind made Connor straighten and turn.

"And the pair of you have more time-critical things to do than necking like downstairs servants," Gisele said with some acidity. Connor opened his mouth to answer, but closed it again as he saw she was winding her shawl over her face. "I hold no brief for my stepdaughter either, for that matter, but under the present circumstances you can't expect me to be pleased. I told you earlier to pull your socks up." The latter was to Thakar, who stood watching Gisele like she was another species, one that didn't speak English with any great fluency. "Contracts or no contracts, I at least remember my duty – even when *contacts* are more interesting. Connor, whatever you do, don't start without her. You'll only have to repeat yourself." She tossed her white shawl tail over her shoulder and disappeared into her rooms.

"'Her'? Atalanta?" said Thakar.

"I don't think so." Too many women. Atalanta, Ilsa, Yasmine, Gisele herself. Éloise at least had been straightforward, even when she'd been working against Connor's interests.

Down the passage, the door to Calad's bedroom stood open, as if dropped by a woman used to sliding doors. Gisele wasn't quite that absent-minded. Instead of allowing himself to carry on questioning motives, Connor edged to the door and stuck his head round it.

"I knew you weren't dead," Calad slurred from the bed. His platinum hair, same shade as Gisele's, was fanned over the pillow, and his eyes wandered around Connor's outline in a manner consistent with heavy morphine dosage. Yasmine, hovering over him, frowned at Connor and laid a finger on her lips.

"I knew you'd bounce if you ever hit the ground." Connor limped to Calad's bedside and studied him. Dark bruises on his face: a nose broken and reset. What had been a puckered scar on his cheek was closing and repairing itself, skin layer upon layer. Somehow that only emphasised how deep it had initially been. "Which of us, I wonder, got abandoned for the other most often over the last few hours?" Yasmine rolled her eyes.

"The Healing thread's busy," Calad said. "It won't make too bad a mess of my face." Not compared to the way his face would have looked without the Healing thread. "Just let my pride recover, and my ears now Maman's left me to it, and I'll be good. I'm good."

"You're delirious." Maybe. "What happened?"

A shadow clouded Calad's eyes. "We didn't know what was happening." Him and Atalanta. "We had a row." *Why am I not surprised?* "Something hit me. I don't remember –"

Connor squeezed his shoulder. "Then don't try."

"They wanted the engineer. I need to tell you…"

"I already know. Stay here and rest."

Yasmine shooed Connor aside and extended a white thread towards her cousin's head again. Thakar had stayed in the doorway, concerned eyes on the others: Connor returned to him and towed him back out into the corridor. "Do you know where Atalanta is?" he said.

"No. Heard her making a fuss a while ago but I wasn't paying much attention."

"That could make this tricky."

It wasn't incredibly tricky, once Connor had calculated that the guard shift had just changed and Thakar had tracked down the previous rotation to find the pair of young ex-drifters who'd been covering the front door. Atalanta, they said over an interview in Connor's study, had stormed out of the office no more than half an hour previously. Opinion differed over whether she had bothered to wash Calad's blood off herself first. The guard staff had been somewhat distracted by updates to the betting pool on whether or not Connor would live out the day, and hadn't seen where she went.

"She's not hard to find," muttered Thakar.

"Unless she doesn't want to be found." Connor made to stand, but Thakar's hand on his shoulder stopped him.

"Leave now and Saxen *will* clock you're still walking. I'll go looking."

"OK. But come back when it gets dark or if she turns unpredictable."

Thakar sent him a curious look. "That's caution, even from you."

"I'm meant to be dying: I wouldn't be surprised if someone made a shot at my streets. And I don't trust Atalanta in a mood like that."

He shrugged. "Fair enough. And you're right to worry: Comet's crew, for one, were clattering round their place when I drove in. I might have nudged them off just by being here."

"Not them. I'm concerned about Meriden or al'Trier. Comet's crew are busy."

Thakar took that as it stood and beckoned into the corridor. His page Joshua, a morose ten-year-old with white skin and curly dark blond hair, stepped out from a shadow and hurried up to him still packing away a book. He nodded to Connor without smiling. As Connor had threatened to kill him at their first meeting, his lack of enthusiasm wasn't surprising.

Joshua pattered out and downstairs, his footfalls fading to nothing in seconds. Thakar counted five and followed him. Connor watched him from the doorway, battling indecision. If Thakar'd wanted an armed escort he could have asked – but that wasn't to say he shouldn't have been given one without asking…

His arm was aching harder. Rather than inject a painkiller or call Yasmine, he retreated to his chair and tucked the arm on his lap for support. His study had been left untouched since the previous afternoon. Life had become more complicated since then. Solve one riddle and find three more.

Keeping the lights off – his headache had faded, but not gone – he opened a fresh screen and accessed the spaceport takeoff and landing lists. Ilsa's primary Hamadryad was still on the concrete, as were two of her support ships, but the last, a Fey, was gone. Allowed to leave? Shot down on exit? Perhaps Saxen wanted to avoid foreign trouble more than to court it: perhaps he wanted to twist Ilsa's arm – or a higher-up Cliff boss's arm, far away. There was room for Connor to hope that by the time Saxen realised his error, it would be too expensive to correct it.

Two ships belonging to an unostentatious petty trader named Karl Volta had passed the Bridge a little while ago and were due to land in five hours. Connor set a jack alarm for half an hour before their arrival time. Now, he needed Atalanta back to meet up with that ship. He might have to settle for borrowing Joshua from Thakar: it would make a point about collaboration's value – but Atalanta would make a better one.

He closed the screen and rested his right hand under his chin. Two messages from Logan, one text and one voice, were waiting on his jack. He knew without checking that the voice one would be a panicky series of threats and the subsequent text follow-up, sent long after Connor'd been pulled from the rubble, would be closer to a jocular scold. Hopefully someone had already told Éloise about Calad's incident. Perhaps even Gisele or Yasmine had done so. He didn't want to speak to either of them at the moment: he wanted to think.

Most of the puzzle pieces were in front of him now, a children's game mapped out in gunfire and blood. Nerys, Merissa, transformed from a confusing tangle to a near-simple solution. If either had been alive now, Connor would have offered her congratulations, or whatever else an indebted, struggling undersider could afford. As it was, dead women didn't need to be paid.

He was turning over several options for the immediate future – ones that did and did not involve Atalanta's cooperation – when his study window, which had been locked, slid open. "You're needed," Joshua said softly from the wall outside.

"Where?"

"One of the bars on Camber Lane. The one with the wooden roof."

Six streets away, just past the edge of Connor's territory. Connor glanced past Joshua's dim figure to the sky outside. Reddened by encroaching night, with intermittent street lamps flickering. No buses, no goods vehicles, and few cars and bikes. The night sounded broken. "I'll come. Be ready to escort Thakar back here – and stop picking my locks."

"They're bad locks," he thought he heard a mumble drift to him on the wind, but Joshua was already gone. Sighing, Connor rose and closed the window. One more hole to plug.

He touched his jack as he limped out of the study. "Pritie, try to find a locksmith. Also, I want doubled patrols in all of my streets. Pay overtime as necessary."

"It's not the overtime," she answered, with some reluctance. "Men on double shifts see shadows and miss the reality."

"Then hire more men and women. Promise them cash and a few Spellweavers to goggle at. Try any ex-cops who haven't gone to Saxen, gone to ground, or been killed."

"That won't be many."

"Anything's good."

"OK. I'll reroute some of our existing patrols and I'll let you know what I'm able to rustle up."

"You sound tired." Tireder than he'd known her: more so than when he'd fought his first turf war in charge. But she'd had Éloise and Logan to cover her, then. "Get someone to spell you for a few hours so you can sleep."

"I've no spare staff."

"Then I'll cover you myself if I can't find someone."

"That'll backfire if anyone else finds out, Mister."

"Right now I don't care. We're dead or we're good depending on much more than anyone caring if I cover for my security head. Three hours' sleep out of the next five, Mistress Mayasdottir."

"Five?"

"I need you wide awake then."

"I understand." Her pause before speaking told Connor she had indeed understood.

He staggered down the stairs with enough difficulty to make him regret this particular necessity. One floor down, at the garage entrance, Marcello was waiting, face covered in scratches and penitence.

"How many riots?" Connor asked.

"Eight that I've heard of. One was in Hardside. Saxen didn't bomb that one." Connor licked his lips. Support messages from the likes of Henry and Bramhall had indicated Saxen had the contacts to go with his brains and chutzpah, but a riot in Hardside, not far from Rift Haven and at the edge of the rich suburbs, meant he hadn't played everything right.

Connor glanced around the hall. The squad guards on the door kept eyeing him like he'd been resurrected. At some point he'd have to get round to asking Yasmine what he'd looked like when he was brought in. With a wave of acknowledgement to the guards, he snagged one of Logan's Neuvième weather-cloaks from the rack by the door.

Marcello was still behind him, shadow-close. "Stay here," Connor said.

"I –"

"It's Spellweavers, not gunhands, this time." He wrapped on the cloak, pulled the hood over his head and headed out.

His crewers' eyes clocked him in the gloom, as, he was sure, did others: lookouts and runabouts for any one of a dozen different agencies. Let them speculate. A tall man in a cloak with his head covered. Everything was speculation. Even Saxen: let him hear a rumour or two. It might stall him.

The wooden-roofed bar on Camber Lane was low on patrons, just a couple of regulars perched on stools nursing porter while a subdued barmaid swept up broken glass. No Atalanta. Connor withdrew from the bar and stood in its doorway, eyes sweeping the street: within half a minute he spotted Thakar, a dozen yards down the street in a shadowed doorway with his hands in his pockets, apparently dozing on his feet. As Connor approached, Thakar cocked his head towards him without looking.

"She's shifted in there," he said softly, pointing to the bar two doors down from the one Connor had tried first. This one was dark-painted and had an oak tree sign swinging above its door. "A stack of guys inside headed out after she went in. Can't imagine why."

Connor patted his shoulder. "I'll take it from here. You go back to mine."

"Sure?"

"Yes. Leave Joshua here to watch me if you're worried. You needn't be – when I leave I'll have her on my six."

"If that's meant to make me feel better –"

"Point to what else could hurt me then. Point to what you or anyone here could do if she takes offence." He crossed the street and entered the pub, hood still up.

The taproom was empty with three significant exceptions. The first was a bouncer, hovering near an internal swing-door that likely led to the kitchens or cellar: he waved a hand at Connor to leave as soon as he saw him, but made no other move. Atalanta was leaning over the bar, standing on her tiptoes on the wooden floor to do so. One of her wings, extended and erect, was jammed into a side groove of the metal security shutter hanging from the eaves, stopping it from descending. The other was twined into the shutter and was snapping its segments into small pieces one row at a time. Her left hand was wrapped round the bartender's throat and she had pulled him too onto his tiptoes, towards her, till they were eye to eye with faces an inch apart, although the bar counter separated their bellies. A bottle of Mortlach, its label misspelt, sat next to Atalanta's left elbow.

"When I said whisky," Atalanta was saying in a clipped tone, "I meant *whisky*. Water, barley, yeast and time: not methanol, food colouring, corn and glycerol, with a side order of bacterial scum."

Connor walked up to her, careful to approach from one side rather than directly from her rear. The bartender eyed him, frantic terror in his expression. "She means the stuff under the bar," Connor said, full of as much reassurance as he could project. He wasn't sure which of them he needed to reassure. Atalanta neither released her hold nor looked at Connor.

The bartender flapped a hand under the bar and, on his second grope, came up with a bottle of Lagavulin, almost certainly one that Atalanta had smuggled off Earth on Connor's behalf. It bore an import mark, though no export mark.

Atalanta loosened her grip on the barman's neck. He staggered back a few steps, rubbing his throat. Connor gestured for glasses, which the man passed with a trembling hand on an arm as far extended as possible. No thimble. Connor poured two measures by eye – a single for himself, a double for Atalanta – and, with both glasses balanced in his shaky left hand, grabbed Atalanta's elbow with his right and pulled her to the closest table. She fell more than sat into one of the chairs. Connor seated himself opposite her and handed her the double whisky.

"Did you look for this next door? Or did you drink them out of decent stuff and come looking for more?"

"The latter. All they had in was half a shot of Auchroisk." She grabbed her glass and drank like it was water rather than fire-water. Connor sipped his. The peat went straight to his nostrils and it was all he could do not to spit. He'd have preferred something lighter.

He tipped his shot into Atalanta's glass. She didn't appear to notice, staring instead at her hands on the table top, one clinging to her whisky glass, both callused from bladework and gunplay, with blood traces still visible under her short, neat fingernails.

"There's no shame or weakness in realising you – care for – a man," Connor said quietly, "even if that man happens to be your husband." She didn't answer, but he thought he saw her fingers grip the glass a little tighter. "Do you want to tell me what happened?"

"Saxen's crew happened." Her voice was shaking. Her voice never shook.

"After the explosions…?" prompted Connor.

"We went to ground." She shrugged, one-shouldered. "Standard operating procedure. We knew our jobs were both sunk, at that point: we took cover, and waited till the fighting had moved well away from us: didn't want to go straight to yours in case we caused more trouble than we were worth. By the time the streets were clear it must have been long past midnight. I heard a bigger explosion at one point – that must have been Saxen blowing your factory up. I'm sorry we missed that." Connor, unsure how to take that comment, did not reply.

"We talked. About what was happening, what we should do. It became clear that we had – a – a conflict of interest." Understatement of the decade, unless Connor was mistaken. "That led to an argument. We headed in separate directions.

"I don't even know why I turned round." To give him another piece of her mind, doubtless, but Connor didn't answer. "I realised the street smelt wrong – I went to shadow – I – I heard him scream. He got a thread drawn just as I came round the corner: he probably would have killed them on his own."

"He wouldn't have got to safety on his own."

"If he hadn't started out on his own, it wouldn't have happened. We easily fought them off as soon as there were two of us."

"You don't know that."   No: they might have been shouting at each other too loudly to notice anything else.

Another couple of would-be drinkers had wandered in and were casting the pair of them curious looks.   Whether Atalanta's foreign red-and-white appearance or Connor being alive and upright was their topic of concern, he didn't know, and nor did he ask.   Instead he returned to the bar and its still-shivering bartender.

He gestured to the Lagavulin bottle sitting on the bar, and to the ruined security shutter dangling overhead.   "I'll take the rest of this.   Send me the bill for the shutter."   He dropped a handful of coins on the bar – north of fifty marks: well under the retail value for a near-full bottle, though above the wholesale price – and returned to Atalanta.

She was still sitting huddled into herself at the low wooden table, sipping her glass as if she tasted nothing, but she looked up at Connor as he reseated himself, and she seemed a little more aware of her surroundings than before.   "Were you still intending to appease him?" she said.   "I may have put a hole in that plan."

"No, he saw that one off when his team dropped a warehouse on my head."   She winced.   "The warehouse still contained quite a lot of plasma packs," he continued, watching her face, "too many for Saxen's troops to haul away before destroying it.   I think he wanted to blow whatever was left as a scorched earth tactic.   Maybe even cause blowback and drill a hole into the vault."

"Did he?"

"No.   I would have been vaporised if the seals had gone.   No, Éloise's shields protected it – but there were deaths."

"I think I understand," she said after a quiet moment to herself.   "I'm not at my best."

And she didn't mean having drunk enough single malt whisky to put three grown men under the table.   Connor uncorked the bottle and splashed a little more into both their glasses.   "I need you to come back and tell Calad you're taking care of this."

She pushed her chair back and half-stood.   "Connor –"

"I need you to do it," he continued, "because then he'll believe *someone* is taking care of it, and will rest.   After that I need you to cover Pritie on the security desk for three or four hours while she sleeps. She hasn't slept in thirty-five hours or so, and I need her alert – I need *everyone* alert – in about five hours' time."

"Why?"

"To start a nice little dose of payback."

Her chin rose, and he thought he saw the haughty moralist from afar. "Everything's about revenge, is it? You're as bad as a Neuvième fishwife."

"No, I wouldn't chase down a man's daughters long after he was dead in order to prove a point. I stake my position in a world that is not as you or I would wish it to be." She didn't move, still staring at him in something between hatred and contempt. He waved his hand at the closest exterior wall. "Out there, you assume everything wants to kill you. It's how you were trained. I do so too: it's how I was raised. In what I will do, I will render it slightly less likely that a few particular sources will try to kill us in future. That's all."

"You would remake the world," she said, quiet and flinty, "as you see fit –"

"Not I. I leave such notions to Circle Spellweavers. I take maximum advantage of the way the world *is*." He leant back in his chair, as if relaxing, though his heart still hammered and the chair creaked beneath him. "And to that end, I step forward in the darkness until such time as I wish to be seen. Will you walk with me?"

Silence, or near-silence, in an evening taproom: when she nodded, Connor thought he heard a bell ringing in his mind. "Thank you," he said. "Two questions."

"I credit that you could have asked them earlier and I would have answered."

"Did Nerys Capuin pass you information on the Union starfleet suppliers, and when did you find out Calad was trying to liaise with her?"

"Is she dead?"

Blood still on Atalanta's fingers: blood dripping off Connor's, what felt like a lifetime ago. "Yes."

"She did give us data. We always considered it questionable, but we never caught her in outright falsehood."

"Don't tell me the Guild doesn't scan its agents' minds. A

Union-born merchant in Federation territory –" Atalanta didn't speak, but her silence was itself a kind of answer. Trying to maintain plausible deniability? Or something else?

Ilsa: she'd said Spellweavers – Circle ones, she had meant, for a woman of her class didn't acknowledge the Guild – didn't 'like' Nerys. A Weaver who refused to join either Circle or Guild? No. In no corner of the galaxy was that a survival trait, and Nerys, till her final mistake, had been a survivor. A magician, conduit for uncontrolled magic, as Connor had suspected? No. Something rarer.

"She was a null. Immune to magic, voice tapping, security cameras, the whole caboodle." Atalanta nodded. "So you had no clue whether she was intentionally a double agent –"

"Or spying on us instead. And neither would Union Intelligence, if they asked her to use her position to watch us, know whether she was really their creature or if she'd gone over to us. Merchants and spies have always been intertwined." Atalanta shrugged. Her copper hair danced in the light, picking up the same tones that lurked in her quarter-full whisky glass. "I doubt anyone in the galaxy trusted her, including her employers at Cliff, but the only mistake I ever know she made was picking Calad for her Circle contact – which I would have stopped if I'd known about it before yesterday, for his sake as much as anyone's. He's too easily distracted for this work."

"As you told him, doubtless, before you parted company last night… Were you running her?"

"No. I was in a position to observe her handler. This once, I was sent to contact her in a particularly peculiar situation." The missing engineer. Connor hid a grimace. Perhaps one day he would learn neither to think nor to care.

"Thank you. You've patched just about my last hole." Atalanta's presence to begin with: Nerys's passages. Only one question left, and with any luck, his theory for that one – Nerys's killer – would fall clear within hours.

He stood, drank the last few drops in his glass and picked up the Lagavulin bottle. Atalanta downed the remains of her last shot and followed him out of the bar.

Connor stood still in the doorway for a moment or so, sniffing the air, trying to smell anything other than smoke and peat. These had never been his streets. Crews not his patrolled the night, baring teeth at Saxen's new enforcers: eyes he didn't own watched him from the dark. He pulled his hood up again. Let the street keep wondering.

Atalanta dropped into position at his shoulder like the paid lieutenant she was not. She could barely be more recognisable if she tried: as a Spellweaver, as a Federation citizen, as Connor's relation. Connor left his hood up anyway. Any bit of confusion he could cause, he would take.

The eyes lurking in shadows fled as he and Atalanta moved away from the drinking holes. In their place, a deeper darkness oiled the night: dull rumbles marking ongoing skirmishes, flares of light in the distance. Too many participants – Saxen's enforcers-cum-new-police-corps, underside gangs, and marauding gunhands of no fixed grouping who might be near-adult drifters, sacked ex-cops or anyone up for a fight.

Too many participants, with too many targets. The few fallen enforcers on the corners were not Connor's men and women. The raided shops, the firebombed apartments, the drifter children wailing in the night, were not, or should not have been, his concern.

Part of Connor's brain, the part that, deep down, understood Logan's lust for violence, itched to bid Atalanta to light a wick in the Lagavulin bottle, if only so he could throw it in defence of a few of those innocents. But he couldn't afford to do so: not when a more thorough, more satisfying takedown awaited him if he could only concentrate long enough.

It was all about greed, in the end. Saxen had had the ideal setup running: solid trade, no trouble on his radar that Connor had been able to detect, safe environment, reasonable relationship with the local despot. A push for more, lust for power, sparked by envy or fear – proximity to the power embodied by Cliff Enterprises – and an entire social edifice had fallen. Connor had no mind to stay crushed beneath it.

*

CHAPTER TWENTY

Thakar wasn't in sight back at the office, which led Connor to worry until he realised one of the guardswomen was griping about Joshua filching her half-read technothriller. He left Atalanta to offer some brusque sympathy and went in search of Pritie.

"Are you *sure* we should let her in here, Mister?" she said after he had explained that Atalanta would be her sleep cover.

"I want her to feel included."

Pritie sighed. "OK, I see where you're going. Please don't ask me to think about it."

"I don't want you to think, or to worry, about anything." *Certainly not about whether I'm going to double-cross Atalanta. I haven't decided that myself.* "Just get some sleep."

She nodded acceptance. "Mister A'syan's in your study. I hope that was acceptable." She side-eyed the whisky bottle for a moment.

"Yes, it's fine." It certainly ought to be fine. God damn it, he was second-guessing everyone this week! Surely he could trust Thakar, if no one else.

Trust only family, or a paid-up Circle Spellweaver…

Atalanta was outside in the hall. "Not saying goodnight to your husband before settling in here?" Connor said. The words sounded snide before they were halfway out of his mouth.

She flushed, dark stain spreading up her pale freckled cheeks, and glanced at her dirty boots. "He's probably asleep."

"Depends if the morphine's worn off and no one's gone to top him up." From a woman who could read minds, and habitually read her husband's… "Are you not in contact with him?" More hesitation. Connor rolled his eyes. "For the love of all the angels in their little heavens, go and talk to him. I've seen you do more frightening things."

She fixed him with a beady glare and he fought to keep his back straight. Never mind he was ten years her senior and running a company – she had skills he didn't, contacts he didn't, *a very beautiful husband* (who was as dim as a candle sometimes, but maybe Connor could have forgiven him that. Maybe). He could win a staring match with her.

He counted five seconds' silence between them, then ten, then twenty. Before it hit thirty, she broke away and marched off upstairs. He followed more slowly. The ache in his arm had slid deep inside the bone, and was radiating down his back and across his buttocks: an itch he could not scratch, a weight he could not relieve.

He didn't, couldn't, follow her into Calad's bedroom, but retreated into his study, closed the door and leant on it, not sure whether he needed physical or emotional support. The past couple of days' exertion, mental and physical, was catching up with him: sheer exhaustion pried at his foundations, and he drifted for a second, lost as matchwood on an oil slick.

"Hey." Connor jumped, nearly dropped the whisky bottle, and looked round. Thakar was rising from the comfiest chair Connor left out for visitors, the one he used to put people too much at their ease: he'd been sitting in the dark, watching life go past outside the window, maybe comparing its new pattern to that pre-coup.

"Pritie told me you were in here." Connor's voice was less even than he would have wanted, less matter-of-fact. "I hope you've got all you wanted."

"Nearly." Thakar flicked on the lamp on Connor's desk. It threw him into alto-relief, a temple icon, the angel of victory, or of beauty. If Calad would have made a better angel of beauty, Connor wasn't currently inclined to push a comparison.

Thakar rose and approached him, peering in the warm light. "You look like shit."

"This is my thinking face."

"It's a cross between your knackered face and your bloody worried face. Sit down." He gestured to the comfy chair.

"Lie down, I think." Thakar nodded, and steered Connor through into his bedroom: he sank onto the bed, on his right side, trying not to feel as if he were adrift.

Thakar hauled off Connor's boots, tossing them one after

another into the corner. "What is that?" he said, pointing to the Lagavulin bottle.

"How I calmed Atalanta down." He gestured with the bottle towards the shelf by his armchair. "There's a couple of coffee mugs over there."

"Got 'em." Thakar retrieved the mugs, blew a little dust out of each and removed the whisky from Connor's tentative grip. He uncorked it, sniffed, and drew his head back swiftly. "God, that's powerful."

"It's even sharper on the way down. Try some."

"Don't mind if I do." He splashed a shot into each mug, passed one to Connor and sipped from the other, but recoiled at once. "Oh, now. This is to be taken carefully, I see."

"It is." Connor sniffed his mug and drank a little. Fire slipped past his lips and into his throat. He'd had too much already: his head would start to swim if he wasn't careful. "This won't help me think. I've got too many balls in the air at the moment."

Thakar perched on the side of the bed and ran a hand along Connor's upper back, smoothing out a tense knot Connor hadn't realised was there. "How do you get into these messes?" His voice was soothing, near-hypnotic.

"It wasn't the Spellweavers' fault this time, or Logan's." He let his eyes drift shut. "Foreigners' arguments prompting sensible Septième men to do stupid things. Right now I've little option but to play along with the rest." He leant sideways into Thakar's hand, willing his neck muscles to loosen. Some tendon in his shoulder was clicking, just too soft to be heard. "I see it on Port Logis – I see it here. Attitude issues."

"Hmm?"

"The way a man believes the world works is determined by his history. I go to Port Logis – I make mistakes because my assumptions about the way the system functions are wrong. Neuvième Weavers come here, they make the same errors in reverse, or they try to impose their system on us. It doesn't work. It never has."

At its worst... had that imposition led to the war? There were and always had been enough able diplomats at the top of both Union and Federation to comprehend each other's motives: but when the Sixième, Septième and Vingtième paid the price, maybe they reasoned that the potential gain – colonisation and servitude of up to quarter of the galaxy – was worth the risk.

If so, both governments had failed, in the end. The Federation had had more to risk, perhaps, for it needed an immigrant population with which to breed. The Union had succumbed to greed, pure and simple, and one might say it had ended with the upper hand: for while the Circle was not controlled by the Union, and in turn kept its worst excesses in check, it would not brook Federation political or military presence due to the Federation's links to the Guild.

Yet taking the Circle for granted and taking Circle vassal planets for granted had led the Union to that grave pit on Port Logis and to a stream of deaths that persisted to this day. Perhaps there were a few Union families who could be sure their lineage did not include a single person who had flown or directed combat against the Circle Neuvième. Port Logis rumour said Dominic had checked Gisele's family back three thousand years, not just two thousand, before he married her: wily man, Dominic Falavière, but proud with it. He would never have married…

… have married…

One final missing puzzle piece, and here it was falling into Connor's hands and sliding into place of its own volition in the darkening evening. *'Impossible'* became *'well, what's left?'*, and he stared up at the ceiling lights' golden glow overhead, as enraptured as a broken-winged moth.

Thakar's fingers stopped moving. Connor shifted his shoulder backwards, searching for the pressure again. "Easy," Thakar said, as indulgent as of a child genius. His fingers traced a line down Connor's spine. "Did you just have a revelation?"

"In a way." One that didn't affect Thakar, or anything he needed Thakar to do. "If I'm still alive this time tomorrow, I'll follow up on it."

"That bad?"

"I risk your life – the lives of everyone here – every moment I stay committed to what I'm doing."

Thakar's hand drifted to the tender patch of skin below

Connor's ear. "It's a path we both chose."

"As did almost all my staff. That doesn't make it easier. I win if I come out ahead *and with few deaths*."

"You need to learn –"

"I'm learning. I wish I could do so at my own pace – though that's a thought for a different man."

Thakar took another swallow of his whisky. "I'm glad you realise that. I thought for a moment one of these Spellweavers had addled your brain."

Maybe they had. Maybe he was growing infected with Port Logis ideals: though 'soft' did not fit the Port Logis mindset, 'inappropriately idealistic' sprang to mind. It would account for his antagonism to Saxen. The man was just behaving as any Septième man would in his position: Connor, another Septième underside leader, had no right to criticise him.

Or perhaps he was the only one who had that right.

"Mister Saxen," he said, "has mostly left the rich crowd alone. Maybe it's pride; maybe he doesn't want to slap down on a rebellion; maybe he lacks the ability to do *everything*, and is picking his battles."

"So?"

"With the minor exception of those new Cyclopes, I think he's weaker than he wants anyone to realise." Connor tilted his head sideways and back, and stared up at Thakar, sprawling beside him with a mug tucked into his hand, face tilted on one side like a comedy-and-tragedy mask. "So we present him with an ally to bolster his cause."

Thakar smiled. "You got someone in mind?"

"Yes, but I don't know if he'll go for it rather than starting a straight-out fight. We'll have a shot at convincing him later."

"How much later?"

Connor checked his jack timer. "About five hours, we invite him over. I may need to send Joshua with a message to confuse him." He took another drink of whisky. "Not yet, though."

Thakar laughed. "Oh, *convenient*."

"Looks like." Should have been. But a guilty shadow hung in the corner, weighing Connor down more than the pain in his back and arm and the difficulty of what was to come.

"I slept with someone else."

Silence for a moment, as they both let the echo die away. Connor let it, wondering what Thakar was thinking, discarding some possibilities, weighing others. He'd realise Connor meant a man. Neither of them considered occasional liaisons with women as significant.

"Do I know him?"

Sharp blood-tang and smell of destruction in a shot-out warehouse. "You've met once."

"Was it good?"

"Yes." It had been good. Raw desire was one thing: sheer sinful lewdness another. He'd occasionally, usually with Thakar, had nights like that, when sex had felt so good it hurt, when he'd been buried so deeply in another man – or had that man buried so deeply in him – that he didn't know which way to breathe anymore. That one night with Michel, he'd found it again. Loyalty, shame or fear, stopping him going back?

Thakar laughed, deep in his throat. "And you're thinking I'll be pissed off because you spent one night, when we were God knows how many months and how many light-years apart, having fun?" He slid his arms round Connor from behind, and now Connor felt his erection, mirroring his own, pressing into his back. "I wish I'd been there to join in. I wasn't. Now, why don't you show me what you did?"

"I'm not capable of more than quarter of it," he mumbled, but his crotch was aching harder than his left arm and he reached out to tow Thakar round to face him. Thakar shifted sideways, and Connor, half-twisting to follow, ended up sprawled on his back with his left arm dangling useless to the side and his right hand flailing at his fly.

Thakar brushed his fingers aside and popped Connor's fly buttons himself. "Impatient?" Connor said. Too dizzy to sit up. That whisky had gone to his head, or maybe the fact of his own survival, a day after he should have died.

"I've missed unwrapping you." Thakar paused in the act of pulling down Connor's trousers for long enough to kick off his own.

"Come back," Connor panted.

"I always come back."

Half a second later they were kissing again, whisky spilling from the one mouth to the other till Connor felt he was drowning. He was weak. So weak, to want so badly it felt like a need, to ache quite this hard for the touch and smell of another man. Damn his sore arm. Damn his fingers that would not close all the way. His cock was so hard it hurt.

He kicked off his dangling trousers – he'd not dressed in undershorts earlier, and was glad of it – and gripped Thakar's erection with his good right hand. "Easy," Thakar said, half a groan. "I'll not hold it if you're not careful."

"I don't care."

Thakar sobbed a laugh. "Missed this..." He squirmed round till he was half on top, and took Connor's cock into his mouth. Connor gasped. The world shrank to the fire in his abdomen and the panting urgency between the pair of them. Thakar's tongue, playing up his cock, almost *burnt*, and Connor cried aloud. Want and need collided, and he couldn't control it.

This couldn't last, could *never* last, and that more than anything else hurt.

He came, too quickly to warn Thakar: his hand tightened on Thakar's cock, and he felt hot semen trickle over his fist. Thakar let out a hoarse cry, Connor thought: he'd fallen away from all sound and sight, sinking back into the bed, spent.

Bliss persisted for a few seconds, warmth and release, before Connor's arm and back started aching again. Thakar rose and moved away, replaced by a light draught, and Connor murmured half a protest before he heard him start rooting in the laundry basket. "I'll never again say you're too tidy," he said, above and to the side. His strong hands descended on Connor's abdomen again, this time wiping him clean.

"Thank you," he slurred. Drunk on Lagavulin or on oxytocin: he couldn't tell.

"No charge." The bedroom lights lowered. Thakar tumbled back onto the bed beside Connor, nestled up to him and pulled the eiderdown over them both.

*

CHAPTER TWENTY-ONE

It was the witching hour, deep in the early morning, the apotheosis of night blowing a necromantic kiss. Neither asleep nor quite awake, Connor lay in the dark listening to Thakar's soft snores and counting the ghosts in his head.

Exhaustion had seeped into his bones, near-paralytic, yet his brain would not stop moving long enough for him to rest. Central to his meanderings was his complete certainty that no woman could bludgeon herself to death.

The same question Thakar had asked him earlier flitted across his brain: how had he got into this? A chance sequence of events, when viewed from one angle: a meeting, a coincidence, a corpse. Yet, as Connor half-dreamt in the darkness, drifting on whisky fumes, he meandered towards the conclusion that a great deal of this had been planned, and not by him.

Let other men wallow in frustration. He had no time. The alarm pinged on his neural jack, and he touched his jack phone. "Atalanta."

"What is it?"

"Time to move. Wake Pritie and head out. Don't start glowing till you hit the hangar."

Her faint hiss of disgust boomed down his aural nerve, as loud as a nearby rattlesnake. "Showing off –"

"– equates to getting attention. We can't afford any nastiness now."

"Fine, fine." She ended the call.

Connor let himself lie still for another glorious minute, warm and safe, then swung his bare legs out into the night. He shivered as he tried to rise. Dizziness swam behind his eyes and he sat back down on the edge of the bed.

Thakar blundered out an arm and, on the third attempt, grabbed Connor's thigh. "You had a roof dropped on you the day before yesterday," he said, heavy-voiced. "Lie down."

"I've got half an hour to get dressed. As shaky as I am, I'll need it."

"I'll hold you up in the shower."

"Fine: you'd best get up too."

Thakar clambered out of bed with a string of *sotto voce* grumbles. "Later on," he said as he tugged Connor sideways into the ensuite, "I hope you don't miss that extra fifteen minutes in bed."

"So do I."

They washed each other in the shower, not as husbands might but as mercs who'd known each other for a couple of decades, shieldbrothers and friends. Once out, Connor let Thakar use the hair dryer first while he rechecked the spaceport landing lists and local newsfeed. No new disturbances big enough to be noted amid the massive disturbance already going on.

Inside fifteen minutes from rising they both looked approximately presentable, though Connor's hair was still slick within its ponytail and Thakar's clothes were crumpled. Thakar called a night shift runner for tea and coffee while Connor tidied the office. Not *too* much: he didn't want to look over-prepared, more as if he were taking an advantage he hadn't expected to get. Open the odd non-business-critical screen, leave one old teacup on the shelf by an aspidistra Éloise had insisted on buying him. Hide that damned photo chip...

"What's the difference between breakfast tea and afternoon?" said Thakar.

"Minimal from what I can tell. Don't say that to a Neuvième man." Thakar's jacket had fallen down behind the desk. Connor tossed it to him and followed up with his wallet, which had fallen out of a jacket pocket. "I don't think anyone else will notice, either."

"Except that new bodyguard of yours. Where is she?"

"I needed her rested. She's got a lot of work to do overnight."

Outside, an engine purred up to the garage door. Ten minutes before Connor had expected it – Atalanta must have taken advantage of a lack of police on speeding duty. Connor grabbed a couple of business notepads, leant into his bedroom and tossed the pads onto his armchair. Now he could bless the hair-dry he hadn't had and the extra few minutes in bed he hadn't taken.

"I wish I'd stuck your trousers in the press last night," he muttered.

"That won't matter." Thakar dimmed the lights a point to emphasise how much he didn't mean that. "You could always lend me some of yours if you're worried."

"You're too short and you squat too heavy a weight –"

Someone rapped on the door: a runner, most likely. Connor dropped into his desk chair, gestured Thakar towards the closest armchair and called to those outside to enter.

As the door swung open, Connor opened his mouth to greet his guest, but closed it again as an alternative to gaping. Two women stood in the doorway. The first sidled uncertainly into the room, peering around herself, nervous in the extreme. Her hair and mouth were veiled by her shawl tail but Connor recognised her at once, teardrop-shaped eyes and a forehead fringed by escaping black curls: Zolde de Priet, the wife – widow – of Rafael Martinez.

The other woman, little more than a girl, moved with confidence born on a Septième street, eyes bright and calculating. Connor did not know her, but he'd seen her once before, vanishing into Gisele's private emporium. Then, she'd been dressed in five-hundred-mark pink silk from out-sector, with a gold chain draping her copper-honey neck and glossy, straightened black hair tumbling down her back. She was wearing a white shawl now, like de Priet, though was unveiled.

A kept woman and Martinez's wife: *Martinez's* kept woman, likely. The whore looked about nineteen. The wife, he knew to be five or six years older.

Connor gripped his remaining self-possession. On the Neuvième he couldn't have spoken to a veiled woman, but Zolde de Priet probably didn't know that and certainly didn't look capable of stabbing anyone. "Please take a seat." He motioned de Priet towards the most comfortable chair. She sidled to it and sat as if it would eat her. The whore – a street girl once, surely, a street girl who'd hit as lucky as she could get – perched on the adjacent chair, as if the two were allies now, no matter their previous situation.

One of his runners – Irra: Gisele had Connor's staff well

trained by now in levels of appropriate behaviour – edged in with a tea tray and set it on the desk. Zolde lowered her shawl from her mouth. She wasn't wearing cosmetics, and seemed younger even than her husband's paramour, a child about to cry. It set Connor's senses on alert. Could any woman in her position be quite as guileless as she seemed?

"Dana says you can help me," she said, with the smallest of hand movements towards the overpaid whore.

"I'm a helpful man in the right circumstances. These look to be those circumstances."

She looked set to answer, but voices in the corridor – female voices – caught her attention, and she started like a rabbit. Good actress, or best actress?

The door slid open again: "This has become quite an event," Gisele said from behind her veil. "I should have ordered éclairs." She unwrapped her shawl with a glance of mild disapproval at Thakar, and pulled one of the spare folding stools out from under Connor's tangler control hub. Her companion – the senior priestess who had turned up at the same party as Dana – bobbed a curtsey to Zolde, and another to Connor, full of far too much energy for this hour. Her eyes were glinting with excitement, a first-time conspirator.

Outside and downstairs, more engines whined, approach and retreat, like angry crickets. Irra was pouring tea, eyes sideways and hanging off Gisele's shawl tail. "Thank you," Gisele said, accepting a cup. "Quite pertinent as things go. Now, fetch two more chairs: I don't think my son will be joining us."

"Just your stepdaughter." Some of the past days' confusion must have leaked into Connor's brain. He had to accelerate.

Thakar, who'd spent enough minutes staring at de Priet now to twig who she was, cleared his throat. "Well, I can see those present have a joint desire to take Mister Saxen down a small peg." He spoke quietly, for he was close to the window, though it was closed.

Connor nodded. "We're just missing one."

Heavy boots crunched on the landing. Zolde jumped again. Dana's hand slid inside her shawl. "It's quite all right, dear," Gisele said to an area between the two younger women.

"You'd be surprised how many people share your sentiments."

The door opened one more time. Atalanta, a faint but unmistakeable multidisciplinary aura floating round her shoulders, stood side on in the doorway, motioning another man to enter ahead of her. The newcomer was powerfully built, not over-tall, exuding a faint air of the rhinoceros. A couple of captains lounged behind him, nowhere near at attention: rough, tough women who'd seen most of everything.

This could go downhill quickly if Connor wasn't careful. He hadn't bargained for de Priet being here. "Mister Comet," he said, "welcome. I'd like to introduce you to Mister Martinez's wife, his unofficial wife, my brother's stepmother, and one of our high priestesses."

Comet gave the women a cursory nod. "What scheme you're building –"

"– is predicated on information I would like to share with you. Please take a seat. I promise you this will be good." Irra squeezed back between Comet's two captains holding one chair in each arm, just in time for Connor's invitation not to sound like a bad joke.

Comet sat, with no air of relaxation, more of a compressed spring set to go off in Connor's face. Behind him, Atalanta closed the door, with the captains on the outside and herself on the inside. Connor restrained a sigh. Well, she would hear everything at some point: now wasn't the worst moment for it.

"I'm going to take you all back a week," he said, as much authority in his voice as he could muster. "Mister Martinez had brokered a sale from the UISS's primary arms manufacturer, of a half-squadron of twelve new Cyclopes to run lead on planetary defence. Any one would have been formidable, but all twelve plus the existing fleet would equate to one of the strongest fighter wings on the Septième outside pure pirate gangs – especially as Martinez, an ex-pirate by profession, knew how to organise a sky wing. It's a situation that always worries the underside. Saxen was already smarting at a contract he'd lost when a group of UISS anti-slavery activists teamed up with the local priesthood to push him out of a deal. There are always more deals to be had – but he saw the new ships coming in, and worried.

"At about the same time, deep in the Federation, a training flight of a new ship went wrong." He glanced at Atalanta. Her face was impassive. Long might it stay that way. "I don't know the details. I hope I find out one day. The ship's engine was a new design with a revolutionary level of power. And one of the engineers working on that ship went missing straight afterwards. Word was, he wanted to defect – to anyone who would pay him – and a man answering to his description was seen in Mirqest's spaceport a day later.

"It takes a special sort of mind to assume a Federation defector would run to, as opposed to through, a solitary planet in the Septième – albeit one with a governor not doing too bad a job – but when one of Saxen's spies reported back to him that the engineer had been spotted here, he panicked. He didn't make what should have been a logical connection: that the engineer wanted to go home with a UISS weapons manufacturer." In the background, Atalanta hissed, like an angry kitten.

"But he couldn't jump straight onto the UISS ship," Connor went on. "He didn't trust anyone, even his contact, for *she* knew she was being watched by someone from the Federation's covert ops – and her Union backup hadn't arrived. So the contact snuck the engineer into the city, and he disappeared.

"Meanwhile Saxen stocked up on as many conventional weapons as he could. He bought directly from me – not enough to make me suspicious, at first, but later enough to make me wonder if he was planning a hijack. He bought drone-bombs from the UISS crew, something they mentioned when I offered to sell something similar to them. He cleared out six gun shops over in Secundus, enough for their supplier to come to me for a full restock. The moment he had the goods – he attacked." He inclined his head to Comet. "I'm aware you had a very good friend in the police force." *The husband you never married,* he whispered inside his mind, *for an underside lord can't marry another man's retainer. Damn the world.*

"After the coup," Connor went on, "Saxen cleared out my warehouse of as many finished products as his crew could carry, and blew up the rest to stop anyone else getting them. He's now significantly better-armed than any of us here could have planned for. But the foreign engineer is still missing – and Saxen wants that man's brain in his service. He's always been in the business of trading in people."

"So do you want us to find him?" Dana said.

"No. Let Saxen keep that as a distraction. No – we are going to pull the sheet from under him. He's on top of the world right now: we are going to prove him weaker than he wants to think. Then, as soon as it gets light, someone other than me – as I'm meant to be bedridden – is going to propose to Saxen that, given his difficulties holding one city, he can't hold the Heights or the plains or the rest of the cities or, in fact, any little tiny part of the planet without help." He looked at de Priet. He hadn't assumed he would have her to hand. He didn't know if he could rely on her. It should have been Comet. "You. You've got a family name to sit on, and whoever is left of Martinez's crew and the police force to call upon."

"Me?"

"Yes. Now. Our major issue is that we are, collectively, outgunned by a very large margin. You," and he half-bowed to Comet as if to a Neuvième man, "have more firepower than Saxen even post-hijack, but it's off-planet."

"I have eight ships in orbit of other planets ready to Bridge-hop here."

Connor nodded, but said, "With twelve new Cyclopes just changing hands, plus the rest of the defence squad however clapped-out, plus the armed freighters Saxen already ran, they won't be enough to intimidate. Do you have any crews active on Firedrake?"

"Three."

"Then that makes eleven. They won't get here in time to intervene physically if we need it but they'll be able to sit in our orbit space looking visible." The Firedrake Crest had short Highways: a ship could be prepped and at the closest Bridge mouth inside five hours. "Please try to pull more ships and crews on planets with Highways seven hours' travel at maximum. Thakar, you too."

"I have two ships at Firedrake," Thakar offered. "Not the

best-armed, but they'll do for something. More elsewhere."

"Thank you. I have one at Firedrake with the rest less easy to access."

"About forty of Rafael's police are in our house," Zolde said with the faintest of tremors in her voice. "The steward convinced Saxen's men that no one was there."

Maybe. "Good."

Atalanta cleared her throat. Her eyes looked like a stormy sea, peril meant for Connor. "Those twelve new Cyclopes. They are on contracted sale to Rafael Martinez, not to Nikalar Saxen."

Connor shrugged. "Possession. Law. Nine-tenths thereof. Doubtless a hundred lawyers would stand up and say they're Mistress de Priet's, but Saxen has them."

"Can he use them?" Connor, blank-brained, raised his eyebrows in question. "Are they on DNA lock or brainwave lock," Atalanta pursued, "till Martinez activates them? Which he won't be able to do."

"This isn't the Federation." More was the pity, in this respect.

"The ships come from the Union. Their tech is nearly as good and they have heard of lawyers."

Connor turned to Gisele. "Please talk to Ilsa for me. Find a way to get those ships jammed if at all possible." Gisele. Oh, dear. He glanced back to Atalanta. "How's Calad?"

"Ought to stay in bed for another two days. Will be able to get out of bed tomorrow."

"We'll need him to look decorative. He's good at that. We'll have to live without him doing a mincing machine impression."

"Wait a second." Comet leaned forward. "Are you or aren't you planning to wipe this fucker?"

"Define 'wipe'." That stare was overpowering, one from a man whose money and influence bought him almost anything he wanted. Connor had to endure it. "We can kill him quite easily, once we pull off his shields – he has the city street-witches in his employ. Afterwards, his captains – and he has several very competent ones – will rally his crew and take us down. We must undermine him first, to the degree that the captains won't act to avenge him and the rank-and-file will either freeze or be ready to go over to us. Then we kill him."

There was a long pause. Comet eventually said, "How do we start?"

Some of the pressure within Connor's neck eased. "The first task is whistling up ships to sit near the Bridge until we need them to look like you're bringing a flotilla – to threaten or to bolster: we let him decide their purpose. Then, there are two particularly difficult steps to follow, and we have to do so without being identified, for you have to approach him tomorrow as an ally. The first step involves disabling as many of those new Cyclopes we can in any way we can, whether by manual sabotage or –" he inclined his head to Atalanta and Gisele – "taking advantage of their security systems. In the last event we may be able to steal a couple before Saxen's crew realise what's happening."

Thakar barked a laugh. "OK. That should be nice and easy."

"Not too hard." Only *very* hard, unless the ships' inbuilt security could be made to cooperate. Car or bike theft was easy, a business spanning every sector of the galaxy: spaceplane theft was a degree above. "The second necessity is to get into my warehouse's vault."

"That vault that is underneath a pile of wreckage and guarded by a squad of Saxen's men," Atalanta said.

"Precisely. Saxen may not even know the vault is there but he's keeping an eye on the ruins for something – he must want salvage. I'm sure he won't break into the vault itself – I paid Éloise enough for its shielding – but his guards will need to be removed before they can call for backup."

"Can that wait," Zolde said, "till our backup ships arrive?"

"No. They can't be here till mid-morning. We must sabotage Saxen's orbital defence capability before those ships come into traffic control range and we ought to evacuate the vault before Saxen realises anyone is moving against him, which he will as soon as we start to disable or steal ships."

"Not necessarily," Comet said. "If your friends," and he nodded to Gisele, "can make the disabling trick look like an accident, we buy more time. Without them – whether or not he realises they were jemmied – Saxen will see he can't fight."

"Nine hours," Thakar said. "Can we do this?"

The door creaked open again. "Yes," Calad said from the doorway. Connor stared up at him. He was leaning on the doorjamb to stay upright, dressed in loose trousers and a few bandages. His facial bruises had passed through purple to green already. "I heal quickly," he said, but he staggered as he attempted to move away from the door. Atalanta dropped her statue impression and hurried to him, slipping an arm round his torso to hold him upright.

"You ought to be in bed," Gisele said, faintly scolding.

"So should we all." Calad let Atalanta deposit him on her stool. His eyes on Connor were bloodshot but steady. "Atalanta and I can get into your vault with one sniper to cover."

"And your fingerprint, Connor," Atalanta added. "Whether or not attached to the rest of you."

Maybe that was a threat after Connor'd kept her in the dark. If so, she had a long way to go yet. "I can arrange that. Now." He looked from Comet to de Priet and back, both of them frozen-eyed and grieving in their own ways. "No deviation. No petty vengeance trips. And we will *ruin* him." And first the woman, and then the man, nodded.

*

CHAPTER TWENTY-TWO

Ilsa, Connor understood from Gisele's flutterings, hadn't wanted to help. Gisele gave her no option short of stuffing her head in an antimagic field. Their telempathic conversation took most of an hour, which time Connor spent cataloguing their on-planet forces and moving those around on a mental chessboard. He could only stretch them far enough to win were his opponent about as skilled a chess player as his niece and nephew. Sadly, Saxen was a little better than that even setting aside his materiel advantage.

But what did he *lack*? Connor leant back in his office chair, room still darkened, and stared out at the street lamp opposite mounting its nightly assault on the gloom.

Saxen lacked magic on tap, from what Calad and Yasmine had seen: personal shields he had, as had his senior captains, but they'd been bought on an ad hoc basis from the street-witches and he had nothing protecting his installations, and no offensive magic. He would lack legitimacy in his doings if Connor's team could successfully torpedo the approval given to his power grab by the planet's upper crust. The priesthood had made some loud denouncements in the past hour. That might be a risk. From what Connor had seen, the man *craved* legitimacy. An underside leader shouldn't want that: someone in Saxen's position – or Connor's – should want as little as possible beyond what he could reach.

But maybe the type of man who became an underside lord was doomed to dissatisfaction. Connor stared up at the sky, its veneer of light pollution draining all starlight. Reach for those stars and fail. How much did he want that he did not have? Security: whatever he gained in life, he would not have that one thing that poorer men in richer worlds could take for granted. Thakar: the higher they rose, the less likely it became that they would be able to spend the years together.

He shook his head and rose. Thakar had taken Fai Comet down to the garage to supervise a bike and car engine check that needed no supervision: Connor suspected the two were sizing up each other's mentality more than anything else. They'd never, to Connor's knowledge, come into direct contact. Comet was a sizeable player on the high underside, but had not moved in the same worlds as Connor and Thakar.

Instead of joining them, Connor went down the corridor to Gisele's sitting room and knocked on her door. It opened before he could finish the knock. "You aren't my stepson," Gisele said in mild reproof, "no matter how you behave."

"We'll have to find a way round that. For one thing, this is my office. How does it look?"

"Doable." She motioned him to one of the over-stuffed armchairs she'd dragged in here. She was frowning, faintly, a tiny blemish on a painter's fancy. "They aren't fingerprint-locked. Martinez insisted."

"Did he want them to be stolen?"

"Ilsa thinks he might."

Connor felt his shoulders sag. Not via collusion with Saxen, for sure, but Martinez had been prepared to steal his own incoming ships to enable him to claw back some of the money. It wouldn't have paid long-term dividends, but in the short term, if he'd been able to balance the payment to Cliff against what extortion he could perform with the ships, it would have been a ridiculous – and plausible, and effective – display of bravado.

"Fine. We hack –"

"Ilsa consigns you all to your several hells and refuses to speak to any of you again. She has called for armed assistance to get herself and her staff off this planet. I don't know when they'll arrive, but it won't be too long."

Connor pulled one of the cushions off his chair, tossed it onto the adjacent sofa and sat back again. A man couldn't think on too soft a chair. "Any more bad news?"

"With the ships she has on the surface now, she isn't confident of her ability to fight her way off-planet if the hack on those ships doesn't work. As a result, she wants you to host the hack –"

"Fine. Now all I need is to make sure Pritie has the hardware."

"– and is sending Mikhail to conduct it."

Connor jerked upright. "No. Not him."

Gisele blinked at him. "Why not?"

"I think he killed his wife."

She stared at him for long seconds, gloom and glimmer sculpting her face. "He exhibits nothing but distress over her disappearance."

"Which I would expect an intelligent man to do faced with a nosy Spellweaver."

"He hasn't let out a single guilty thought –"

"No, not where you could hear it, but neither has anyone else. I, at least, expected you to tell me if you heard anything." She nodded. "Well, then."

Looking at her, he wanted to voice his full suspicions, but he couldn't. A woman who'd lived under such scrutiny for so long –

"Oh, don't be absurd." As never before, a hint of a Neuvième accent lingered in a few of her usual Treizième vowel sounds. "I'm not a cushion, I'm a telempath. So. You think he checked her family background, found a skeleton, and killed her – rather than smuggle her into the Federation – before a death squad could get to her."

Connor exhaled. "I've found no better solution."

"You gave one an hour ago. Vanishing with that engineer –"

"I was bending the truth for Atalanta's benefit. I didn't want her poking about." He sighed. He didn't know even now whether that was true or not. "Please just keep a close watch on Mikhail. Did Ilsa say when he was coming?"

"She said he would slip out when he could. Her hangars are being watched."

Connor's palm itched to slap into his forehead. "Right." He rose, sketched her a brief bow and jogged out of the sitting room, already pinging his jack for Khayam and another merc, Micky Parker.

The pair met him by the garage door. Khayam looked his usual phlegmatic self but Micky was brimming with suppressed excitement, a young man's energy overfilling its bowl. Both bowed to Connor as he approached, just a little deeper than had been their habit in previous weeks.

"A man from the Cliff squad is trying to sneak over here," Connor told them. "I invite you both to spend a moment thinking about his likelihood of managing it." Both pulled expressive faces. "Go find him en route and make sure he arrives. This is what he looks like." He sent both of them Mikhail's picture, cut out of the photo from the bar. Both nodded in acknowledgement. Neither asked how to find one man in the dark in a city of millions that was equipped with a new and trigger-happy police force, just bowed – deeper again – and headed into the garage.

Connor waited a count of ten and followed them. Thakar and Fai Comet were cloistered at the back amid workbenches and machinery, hunched over a glowing 3D city map that lay open between them. "Do you want to move somewhere more comfortable?" Connor asked them.

Comet shook his head. "I don't like your window angles."

"Normally I have nothing to hide."

"That 'normally' is at issue. What's normality?" But he shifted so Connor could see the map. Spaceport, Connor's office, Comet's branch office, Connor's ruined warehouse, de Priet's house, the city hall: all were highlighted on the map, linked by filament-like police patrol paths like magic threads.

"Old routes?" Connor hazarded, pointing to the patrol routes.

"With some observable variations," Thakar said. "Minor so far." He tapped on a few square inches of map: poorer suburbs and city-centre slums that had been beholden to no lord but Martinez. "It's getting noisy round here." Connor restrained a grimace. Any new turf king who hadn't taken the time to grow organically would need a brief demonstration of his intent. Connor'd always preferred the steadier approach.

It was a distraction, though, practically arranged to order by his opponent. Any free card was worth having. "Has Joshua come back from my warehouse?"

"Yes. Saxen's borrowed your crew's diggers, and sent in a bevy of guards for them. Not sure if he thinks you dropped your wallet –"

"He could turn over that earth a dozen times and not penetrate the vault."

"Either he doesn't know that," Comet said, "or he wants you to think he's stupider than he is. Pick your poison."

Dirty yellow lights burnt in the corners and overhead, stinging Connor's eyes. The map glowed blue and red. Augury's green tint was nowhere to be seen.

I will not draw a card. I will not. If the magic had chosen not to visit him this week – well, who could trust magic?

"Can you send Joshua out again?" he said to Thakar.

"Yes. He's well."

"Send a message to Saxen's captain Sean Jules, from yourself. Imply I'm permanently out of commission and you're orchestrating a takeover before Logan gets a chance. Ask him for a commercial chat."

"He won't bite at this hour."

"Tell him the morning may be too late. I want to see what he'll do. I suspect the vault dig is a sham and if Saxen needs to move crew from anywhere, that's what he'll pick to weaken. He hasn't unlimited gunhands – unless he's been retraining bedroom girls while I wasn't looking – and he must know approximately how many police are unaccounted for."

Comet cleared his throat. "How long do we try to keep them alive?"

"I was serious about setting up de Priet as his 'assistant'. That so, she needs a grunt squad. The ex-cops'll do. *All* of that, I meant."

"Did you also mean it when you said we need into that vault?"

"Unfortunately, yes." *Absolutely. It's the most important bit of all.* "Hence, we need more data on Saxen's reactions."

Comet would have answered, but a deep dull rumble, nearer than the ones that had punctuated the night so far, interrupted him. Every squad merc and lieutenant in the garage reached for a weapon as one. Thakar, at Connor's side, rocked back into a relaxed hand-to-hand stance. Connor held still. Comet for one would misunderstand if he went for a weapon. He was one of the old school, a man who disapproved of leaders doing all their own killing.

Another boom rattled the roof tiles a few floors overhead. Someone flicked the garage's lights off. "Lights back on," Connor said, voice raised just far enough to carry. "This is an innocent office. We are not to look like we are plotting anything, even in a matter of our lighting levels. Understood?" No one answered, but Jack Priest, on guard near the garage door, twisted the lights up again.

Connor peered back at the map, pretending to scan for advantages he could take, instead looking more at the patterns in streets' outlines. As he counted boulevard-to-backstreet ratios, his mind moved into a different rhythm: reloading times, fire rates, drain on a pistol's 2C battery, auto-flick speed of a Hauer & Kalshung twelve-bore rifle. How much damage such a rifle could do to an unarmoured body.

Overhead and outside, the roars and blasts retreated by fractions, and Connor stopped calculating how quickly he could draw the pistol under the workbench. "Your branch office here," he said to Comet. "Have they given you a recent update?"

"Nothing happening. I share the street with Merovir, Ironbender and Marshall. Not surprising if a wannabe doesn't want to spook the big crews."

No, Connor thought, staring back down at the city map. The shock was aimed at little people. Crews like his, small or localised: petty traders, small shopkeepers, the Septième low bourgeoisie.

Engines drew up outside the garage door, and voices flurried within the main office: Connor nodded to the other two and headed back through the internal door. Mikhail, protesting in elevated registers, was being ushered into Pritie's security office by Micky. Connor sidled up to them and, when Mikhail had his full attention on Pritie, murmured into Micky's ear, "Where's Khayam?"

"Making a noise. I think my bike's going to die."

"If we're all still alive in two days, I'll buy you another. Thank you." Gratification illuminated his face. "Get a cup of coffee and go back to the garage. You may need to repeat the run the other way round."

"The other one's going to handle that, I think."

Connor stopped him with a finger on his forearm before he could back away. "Other one?"

"A second Cliff guy left their hangars. Playing distraction: it didn't work too good. Not sure where he is – or who he is

– or if 'is' turned into 'was'."

"Maybe they've more brains than I thought." Why let a second staffer loose into the night now? That made no sense…

As Micky ambled off to the kitchen, Connor edged into Pritie's office – its reclaimed furniture didn't fit the space – and watched Mikhail as if he were watching a murderer. He looked more like death itself, bag-eyed and crumple-clothed, though the latter might be down to his unceremonious arrival and the greyish tinge to his skin might be due to bad food.

Pritie let her gentle platitudes tail off and turned away to confer with her junior, Katrice. Mikhail swung to Connor as if flailing for conversation. He looked worse closer up. Tremors in his eyelids mirrored those in his hands. The bravado with which he'd stood on Connor's ship ramp a few days ago had all but evaporated. Maybe if he returned home, immersed himself in a familiar lifestyle and a social system he understood, he might return to functionality. At the moment he was far from that.

And he had to perform a systems hack, now, or half the city – Connor's half – might die.

"Do you prefer tea or coffee?" Connor said. "I'll send for some."

"I never want to take a breath on this stinking planet again."

Someone would have helped him with that if Connor's men hadn't found him. Someone else might yet help him with that in days to come. "Doubtless. How did you get out of the hangar?"

He glanced down at his grubby boots. "Ilsa opened the sewage pipe on our auxiliary Fey," he said to his toes. "While she was calling for 'port authority staff to make Saxen let in a plumber, I went out the back door."

"Not bad." A child could have seen through that at once, but the Cliff staff had *tried*, and that meant Mikhail was likely to at least try to help. If Ilsa had wanted rid of him as a hindrance she would have sent him out the front and wouldn't have bothered stinking up one of her hangars. "Did you see who followed you?"

"Someone's been following me the whole time I was here."

The words came out all in clumps, a petulant, paranoid child's response. "When I went for the funeral it stopped. Every other second, someone's been there. Poking into what is no one else's business."

"Who's been poking?"

Katrice pushed back her screen. "We're set."

Mikhail took the seat next to her and rotated the light-screen towards himself. Connor settled on the edge of the desk behind the pair. Katrice passed Mikhail a transceiver: he clipped it to his forehead beside his jack and started mouthing words under his breath. Connor watched his reflection in the glass cupboard opposite. Lip-read, lip-read: he couldn't make out a single word. Maybe he wasn't working in English.

On the screen, the lights flickered from a blank dialog to a string of base 2 code and from there to a net layout. Connor relaxed. "OK," he said, leaning forward, a little. "How many is this?"

"One. We do one at a time."

"I can get another ready in a moment," Katrice ventured.

Connor gave her a thumbs-up. "Not much fancy business with the first ones," he said to Mikhail. "Just disable them as quietly as you can."

"How?"

"However you want. Hells, change the passwords if you want. Make the damage simple and unnoticeable till a man tries to get in or to start them."

Mikhail slid the command select along the net and mouthed a couple of words into his transceiver. "Next," he said to Katrice.

She passed him a second and a third ship's access prompts, and Mikhail widened them again. More options flashed up on each: he selected one from the first screen and pushed it aside, then inputted a series of fresh commands into the next – fork bomb into the registry. "This isn't the best idea," he said over his shoulder to Connor.

Well, it was the best one he'd had. "Why not?"

"Two reasons." He took the fourth access prompt, shifted the ship's command input to a different spot on the control net and made a vicious little stabbing motion at the screen.

Katrice winced. "Firstly," Mikhail continued over his shoulder as the tech girl passed him a fifth control feed, "it'll be really obvious that someone from our team did this. Not from where, hence Ilsa turfing me out, but that it was us."

"She called for backup. You're going to be fine."

"Secondly," Mikhail continued as if Connor hadn't spoken a word, "it's too easy." He shifted the prompter down the next ship's net. "Too clean. Too nice."

"Hey," Katrice said with a glance at Connor, "he said –"

"He's your boss, not mine." Mikhail leant forward half an inch and stabbed at the new screen. It folded up and sank into the desk.

Connor gripped Mikhail's shoulder. "What did you do?"

Mikhail shrugged him off. "Left a note. Let's have the other command prompts." He beckoned to Katrice. She did not move. "Come on," Mikhail snapped. "I brought a stack of ships fifteen thousand light years to sell to a man who intended to spice the deal: I lost my wife along with the commission: I'm having a little take-back."

"I lost the link," Katrice said with a resigned air.

Mikhail stood and made as if to leave. Connor blocked his path. "Did you disable those ships?" Mikhail pushed past him and stalked off leftwards, away from the front door, but heading – knowingly or not – towards the back door.

Connor, breath burning in his chest, turned back to Katrice. "Get back in control of those ships. I don't care if you get spotted."

She shook her curly head. "The command link's gone."

"Then find another way." He darted out of the security office door and ran after Mikhail. Out of the corner of his eye he saw Marcello materialise out of the mess doorway and jog after him.

The back door stood ajar. Connor burst through it, and stopped, staring into the night. Alley cats and demented rats were pursuing each other out in the dark, amid squeals of midnight music: gunfire rattled its flame-dance many streets away. Mikhail was not in view.

Marcello skidded to a halt beside Connor. Even his bodyguard taking him more seriously? "What was he driving when the boys found him earlier?" he said.

"Hire bike he'd grabbed on his way out of the 'port. They found him swearing at the clutch. He drives a Colobus 3M normally, he said." A trace of respect accented Marcello's face. "Micky gave him a tow and dumped his bike in the next street."

"Which street?" Marcello pointed towards Bathgate. Connor broke into a run. Oily paving slabs underfoot threatened to trip him. Too old and too damaged for this.

"Hey, Mister," Marcello called after him. Connor ignored the shout. Glints off broken window glass alongside his head heralded a Weaver behind him: Yasmine, detached from Gisele. Fuck all Weavers, except the one Connor already had.

He stopped at the corner and peered round. The street seemed a vid tableau on pause, brick and concrete frozen in time. No Mikhail, and no hire bike: he had expected the latter absence. A couple of street kids were peeking out of an alley partway down the street, shying like nervous cats. "Where did he go?" Connor called to them. A thin hand pointed up Bathgate towards the city centre. Connor touched his jack for a moment but withdrew his hand in indecision.

Behind, Marcello ran up to him, swearing at the slippery paving. "Go back," Connor said, "for a bike."

"I can call it."

"Do that."

As Marcello fiddled with his ring-key, a bike whined behind them, and Yasmine drove at walking pace round the corner and up to Connor. Her shoulders were glinting white. "Wings down," he said. "We run on the quiet. Where is he?"

She popped open her visor. "He stole a bike. It wasn't difficult."

It rarely was. "Then –"

She grabbed his arm from a foot away. "They're leaving." Who was leaving? "The Cliff ships," she expanded. "They're leaving."

"Leaving Mikhail behind? What about the decoy man they sent for him?"

"Half the spaceport just exploded, Connor."

Mikhail, a command prompt, *whatever he had wanted to*

do to those ships. With ice dripping down his back, Connor stared at the sky. Somewhere up there were stars. Somewhere out there was Terra Nova and a corporation so remote from his own doings it seemed like another universe.

Somewhere in this night was a paranoid gang lord trying to finish a step nine-tenths of the gang lords on the Septième would kill to take. And Mikhail had just broken his serve.

"Track him." Yasmine's eyes narrowed to slits and her shoulders started glowing again. Connor backed into the closest wall, pulling Marcello with him. Other bike engines whistled overhead, and in each sound Connor fancied he heard calamity.

Out of the dark behind them, Marcello's bike emerged on its lowest thrust level. Marcello reached out and grabbed it, legs pedalling sideways to stay clear of its jets. Connor grabbed Yasmine's shoulder. "Where is he?"

Yasmine shook her head and straightened in the saddle. "He's heading south-west. Not in the trouble zone yet, but nearly there."

"Go. Find him."

She rose into the night and was gone in seconds. Marcello shoved his bike's handlebars at Connor: instead, Connor mounted the pillion and gestured to Marcello to drive. He could have driven, despite the ache in his arm. Definitely. But if Marcello drove, he could watch the sky instead.

Marcello slung on his helmet without even buckling it properly and rose in a wide spiral. As he accelerated to what felt like a crawl, no more than thirty or forty miles an hour, Connor switched his neural jack to camera mode, low-light vision, and screwed his right eye – still on normal vision – shut. Now to zoom the image.

Ahead, the city centre was a patchwork of flame and chasm, chaos-tinged, but he spotted Yasmine at once by her wing-light. She was following a blacker, lower-flying speck, gaining on it slowly, perhaps aiming not to startle.

But ahead was a semicircle of flashes, a theatre of death, and the black speck was heading straight for it.

A shout lurked in Connor's throat, though it was useless there. Marcello was tacking the bike backwards and forwards across the sky, staying close to rooftops, not quite in stealth mode. Too far from Yasmine and Mikhail. Too far.

The black speck stopped and looked back and, of its own accord, accelerated. Fleeing from the white-winged Weaver at his back. And straight ahead was the mob, ready to pounce on *anyone* they saw as a threat to Nikalar Saxen's rule. And as Connor watched, the little dark speck blundered forwards for a few more feet, turned his bike's nose towards the ground, and blazed up in a fireball.

He got my prototype and he didn't give it back to me –

Plasma fire barked up, ground-to-air in a neat parabola, cutting just in front of their bike's nose. Marcello hauled them sideways and down, evasive action. Connor squeezed his legs tighter to the bike's sides, crushing the night against his brain.

With all the circling they'd done, they weren't more than quarter of a mile from the office. Connor poked Marcello in the shoulder. "Land," he bawled towards the younger man's ear. He dropped to the closest empty street at once, and Connor dismounted. "We walk back. Too much AA fire."

Marcello pulled off his helmet and clipped it to the seat. "What about the bike?"

"Send it home on autopilot." Men were starting to spill from nearby alleys into their street. Connor grabbed Marcello's arm and hustled him inside the closest open bar.

Ten or fifteen pairs of eyes stared at them, bleary from a night of bad news and worse beer. Connor yanked Marcello through the taproom with a wave at the barman, and into the back corridor, scented with sewage and some rather intrepid soap.

"Where are we going?" Marcello said.

"Finding a back exit. It's too obvious but it was all I could think of."

"You know he thinks we're shagging in the bathroom." Connor glared at him. "Sorry, Mister: I guess 'shagging' isn't an appropriate word."

"It isn't." Connor elbowed open a door with a NO ENTRY sign hanging loose off one nail in its centre. It opened on a small cramped storeroom and a thin, pasty bar worker snorting a phial of something or other. He gaped at Connor, words mumbling past each other out of the sides of his mouth. Connor nodded as if he was meant to be here, and pushed past him to the storeroom's goods hatch. Marcello nudged him aside, shoved the hatch open and scrambled out into the darkened backstreet, then pulled Connor through after him.

Through oil-stained alleys they jogged back towards the office. Connor's jack buzzed, three messages incoming at once. He ignored the first two and opened Pritie's: CALL ME. She'd omitted a 'please'. That was worrying.

He rang her jack: she picked up within half a second. "There's one Cliff ship still in dock," she said with no preamble. "A one-seater Siren runabout I'd trust only for in-system work, but it's a good model. It might have a singularity drive. They must have left it for Mikhail."

Such a waste. Such a waste. "What's Saxen doing?"

"Sent a crew skywards after the Cliff team. A few of his old escort ships and half the new Cyclopes. He's withdrawn most of his team from the warehouse site to bolster 'port security."

"Get a line on his team movements everywhere you can –"

"Will do, Mister, but I'll start with a line on the team he's got moving up to our front door."

Connor stopped, and grabbed Marcello's arm when the younger man threatened to head too far into the lead. "Where, exactly?" he said to Pritie.

"Driving down Spice Street."

The main west-facing frontage. Connor and Marcello were in an alley at right-angles to that frontage, slightly to the south. "We're coming in the back door. If anyone asks, I'm in bed and too ill to talk." He cut the call and, finger to his lips, beckoned Marcello to the next corner.

Here, pressed against lichen-stained walls with the scent of algae heavy in his nostrils, he heard bike engines separate from the rest of the city noise, descending towards the office. Connor peeked round the corner. Five or so bikers, flying in a V. From here he couldn't identify the top man in the centre.

A pinkish glimmer flitted across the door. First a wing, then a white-draped ghost, emerged in the doorway. From his vantage Connor couldn't hope to see what Gisele was doing. Instead he darted across the street and into the alley down the south side of the office. Ducking into the side doorway, he pressed his thumb to the sensor: the door cracked open for him. Marcello followed him inside, into the sparse back stairwell next to the kitchens.

"Go eavesdrop," Connor told the younger man. As he jogged off towards the front door, Connor took the back stairs two at a time and ran into his study. He reset his jack line as he went.

"You OK?" Thakar said a moment later.

"No. Could you come upstairs? Bring Comet." He signed off, took a deep breath to steady himself – it didn't work – and entered his study. The lights activated at once on motion sensor. Connor hit the override and, as soon as the light cut out, went to the window.

Trust Gisele. Trust Gisele. No: no man could trust a Circle Weaver whom he wasn't paying. Connor now knew how much he could trust the one he *was* paying.

Below and along the office frontage, the pink light withdrew. The bikers, it seemed, did not, remaining in their loose semicircle around the main door. Connor would have heard if any of them had flown away, but it was impossible to see whether any one of them might have entered the building.

Behind him, the door opened. "Connor?" Thakar said from the corridor. "What are you doing here in the dark?"

"Spying. The light switch's on your left."

Thakar found it after a little fumbling, and twisted it up. As he did so, Connor retreated to the bedroom doorway. "I'm not up," he said to Thakar, and to Comet, behind him, "if anyone wants to talk to me. Gisele's coming up here with a message."

"She should have called you," Comet said with a faint frown.

"It's her first week on the underside –" Connor broke off. In the distance, he heard Gisele's high fluttery voice: the words were unclear, but she was engaged in conversation, and not with a merc, a servant or a relative.

He slipped inside the bedroom, closed the door and set his ear to the panel. One day he'd allow Pritie to bug the study:

it would make eavesdropping so much simpler.

Inside the study, the door to the corridor opened. "– and I mean, dear, what do you expect anyone to do?" Gisele said, a little muted but distinct. "We all have a certain range at our disposal, and it's inevitable that we use it. Most people do want to survive. Not all, and I did feel sorry for him, but most do. Survival leads us all to interesting places. Doesn't it?"

"I've rarely met a man whose calculation of his own survival was rational." Connor frowned. Sean Jules: he'd taken the bait earlier than anticipated.

"Come on," Thakar said. "We don't all do stupid things."

"And, as you're acting a dying man's heir – nice of the boys on the door to try to hide that, but I got the picture – I ask you: are you sure you're not doing a stupid thing?"

"That," Thakar said, pregnant with venom, "is a little way above you."

"Please. I know where I stand. I'd like to know where you stand." It sounded as if Sean Jules were shifting on his feet. "And is this a new tie-up or something we'd missed? Mister Cardwain's primary legacy blew up with him."

"Contacts don't explode, boy," Comet said with some sarcasm seeping into his voice. "You saw the Cliff Enterprises team in the spaceport."

"I saw 'em, sure enough. The ones who blew up –"

"You see 'em do that? I didn't. When you stick your head outside your offices, you'll see *no one* messes with Cliff – and I smelt a deal going on, them and Cardwain."

"That couldn't have come to anything," Sean Jules said after just too long a pause.

"Why not?" Comet countered. "You snatching other factories? You want a Union team floating overhead, now they see what might go into and out of those factories and how much cash they could make from it?"

Connor felt his lip curve in amusement, but the smile fell away as he wondered whether Comet could ever be *right*. Not with that, surely. But just close enough a lie…

"I'm sure my boss knows what he's doing," Sean Jules said with a chilly, prim air. "What concerns me right now is whether we should consider you gentleman as participants."

"Everyone participates," Thakar said. "You. Me. Mister Comet here. The street girls at the corners. The bullyboys in bars and alleys. We all have a spot. What you do with yours is up to you. If it were me I'd take a good smart step back."

"I –"

"Take a look at it sideways. One tinpot planet in a backwater, and your boss acts like he owns the stars. He might have a stack of dirt on the planet's high-ups but he doesn't have enough dirt on every big name in the sector to hold anything else."

Connor frowned again. He opened the text field on his jack and sent to Thakar, WHAT DIRT?

Thakar kept talking, and Connor fancied some of the intent was aimed at him: "A man in his position – sending boys and girls all over, not all of whom come back – feels in a position to take what he wants. He misunderstands when he forgets that not everyone *cares* who knows who they screw or who they kill. You're taking a line spun by bourgeois and priests, and trying to fit it to the Septième underside."

"That's not my line."

"Then what is? You don't believe the firepower argument, not against any three high underside teams."

"I don't have to. We only need to out-fight those we don't offend, like any scenario."

"Then you aren't doing very well," Gisele said. A faint squeaking followed, as if she were fiddling with something. "Here. Nice 'port tower images: your boss's ships pursuing some Cliff Enterprises ships – after threatening their occupants so much that they fled."

"They blew up –"

"How? Your people were watching them, dear. But paranoia always tells in the end, doesn't it?"

"Hold *on*."

"It always tells," Gisele repeated, serene as a flower. "I've seen it time and time again. Now, a flight up your Highway – a pursuit – and what do you think will happen in an hour or two? Just time enough to get out of the gravity well where they won't cause much fallout damage – assuming, that is, that planetary enforcers are on hand to destroy the larger pieces of wreckage. If they aren't: well, Cliff will blame your boss for failing to take proper precautions. Cliff Enterprises is a mutual company with a proud record of social and environmental protection." Footsteps, as if Sean Jules were trying to escape. "Please don't go, dear," Gisele continued. "You don't want to spoil the surprise."

"My teammates are pursuing what they think is a light-armed pleasure yacht –"

"And if they're foolish enough to believe that, do you really need them?"

"We paying stupidity tax now, Mistress?"

"Life is a series of stupidity taxes." A rustle as Gisele seated herself. "Now, let's be reasonable, hmm? You came here with a deal, or so it looks."

"I came here to talk to Mister A'syan."

"And I'm here," Thakar said. "If you didn't bargain for an entourage, that's nothing on my account."

"Fine," Sean Jules said. "We don't want any more of a fuss than necessary."

Thakar grunted. "Strange way to go about it."

"The gunsmiths opened their doors just as wide as we wanted, every time," Sean Jules said with a faint note of complaint in his tone. "We just provided a reminder that cooperation is a virtue. We genuinely did not know he was in the warehouse before we blew it. I don't want to let that blow any chance of an understanding with whoever's left."

"Or you don't want Mister Cardwain's stepsister taking a wander over here to tell you how to behave?"

"What happens will happen, with her. I never met a Circle Weaver who took against a man over a contract fallout."

"Then," Gisele said, "how would you classify the situation on Port Logis at the end of the war?" She laughed, high and tinkly. "At mothers' knee my people hear it was a contract misunderstanding. Circle Neuvième claims it high treason. Which do you think?"

"I think it behoves a man to take care."

Connor, still braced against the door, stumbled. Ghosts moved in his head: Dominic dancing with Gisele at Calad and Atalanta's wedding, pale pink and silver wings drizzled around them like flurries of blossom blown from a tree too soon.

He knows you're alive and listening, he thought he heard

Gisele say, deep in his mind where he thought he'd had secrets. *He thinks Thakar and the staff are too calm and that I wouldn't be allowed to see a male stranger without a relative present. A bit garbled, but it got him to the right conclusion.*

Connor waged a brief war with his leg muscles, and won. What, then, he wondered, could Sean Jules's motivation actually be?

He came assuming he could dictate. He's now in search of a dignified exit.

Right. That could be fixed. Connor flexed his fingers on the door panel.

Don't come in just yet. He removed his hand and waited.

"I'm not satisfied," Thakar said beyond the door, "with your reassurances. Connor and that warehouse, for a start. Your colleague must have known he hadn't got out."

"You don't need to trust me on that."

"Good thing, in all," Fai Comet said. "Trust on the underside's not a commodity in high demand. Especially not where trading, any trading, is concerned. So why did you and your team expect Cardwain – or any weapons trader – to trust in your teams, given how much firepower you were piling up?"

"Look out that window," Sean Jules countered, "and you'll see how it's panned out. We're in. Moneyed. On the up and past the bar."

"And no man walks out onto the underside with expectations of anything other than disaster." A far-off booming sound accented Comet's words. Window glass rattled. "So. Your boss was deliberately aiming for Cardwain."

"You said yourself," Sean Jules said quietly, "that contacts don't explode."

Outside, an alarm began to wail, low and throbbing, cutting through the city streets like invasive mould. The warning for low-flying space combat. Connor hadn't heard that sound in anger before: he'd thought it lost outside of war films.

He pushed aside the bedroom door. Thakar's faint surprise met him, eyebrows raised on his broad face, hair drawn back like a pair of wings framing his face, as he'd arranged it earlier when they'd risen together. "He knew I was alive," Connor said with a brief, angry gesture towards Sean Jules. "No point pretending much longer." He shoved a couple of screens sideways off his desk – he'd *tidied* in here a couple of hours before, damn it – and activated the intercom. "All hands, remain in position," he said into it. "The closest shelters were damaged yesterday in the coup. There's nowhere to go. Stay here: our shields are your best hope." He turned off the intercom and sent Sean Jules a sour look. "If that manoeuvre with the shelters was intended as stick to whatever carrot Saxen intends to dangle, it backfired. The survivors will remember. Petty misfires don't rule a planet. Or were you planning on hovering around, mopping up the mistakes and pulling prestige points where you could?"

Sean Jules did not answer. Connor went on, "Killing me for my trade would have been one thing. Killing half a city on less than the promise of a shadow is idiotic. Who do you think my contacts – my major, non-familial contacts – are?"

"You've imported for White Canyon. You've imported for Dowler-Mall."

"Little doings. Children's games." Oh, how sweet it felt to castigate the biggest trades he'd ever pulled. He straightened to his full height – feeling Logan's absence now: feeling himself the taller for it – and poked a fingernail into Sean Jules's thorax. "Congratulations on blowing the biggest contract you could possibly have taken from me!"

A thunderclap pealed behind him, shockingly close. Connor put his left hand to the desk and bit the inside of his cheek as pain rifled up his arm. The lights flickered off, came back on for long enough that the other faces imprinted onto Connor's eyeballs, then went off and stayed off.

Looked like Gisele had been wrong in her guess that Cliff would avoid low-level damage. Maybe Saxen had sprung a surprise while the ships were still in atmosphere. Maybe they were all about to die.

Connor thrust the window open. Be damned to it all – he didn't want a building to land on his head twice in two days. Overhead, chem-trails glowed in the sudden city dark, heralding ships ablaze with light jockeying together against the stars.

Outside, bikes roared away, a swarm of bears rather than bees. "I did warn you, dear," Gisele said in the dark, as chatty as a parrot. "This was never likely to end well. Did you really need them, even as a smokescreen? Paper shields – lawyers' paper – would have served you better."

Connor twisted back round. His left arm still ached: he felt sick. Gisele was standing with her back to the door into the corridor, wings aglow over her head, chin tilted up so she could look Sean Jules in the eye. She'd had to lean like that to look up at Dominic. The memory cut into Connor's skull deeper than the nausea rushing up his arm, and he sat sideways into his desk chair, trying to make it seem like he hadn't fallen there.

"Go back home if you want," he said to Sean Jules. "Tell Saxen whatever you wish. But know that you've already made a string of mistakes tonight and your crew's mishandling of a foreign squad was the worst of the lot. You'd better plan what you're going to say when the Union warships land."

Overhead, the aerial squealing had swung out towards the ocean. Alarms still wailed in the streets. "If he knew you were alive," Sean Jules said, "he'd bring you on side."

"If or when you tell him I'm alive he'll try to ruin me. The world might already think he's done that. He won't have the power to do anything worse. Go, now. I'm sick of the sight of you."

Gisele sidled away from the door. Sean Jules stared at Connor for a long moment, then dropped him a neat nod and withdrew.

The door swung shut on him. "Are you sure we shouldn't kidnap him?" Gisele said once his footsteps had faded to nothing.

"It stopped mattering as soon as he clocked I was alive and hale. Let him stay rattling around the city in supreme confusion: it keeps him off-balance, and he's one of Saxen's best." Connor closed his eyes. Éloise would have made it her priority to kill every one of Saxen's team, for pimping if nothing else. Life was easier without an inflexible ethics library on his shoulder.

His jack pinged: incoming call. He diverted it to the desk

radio and answered, "Yes?"

"Movement," Atalanta's remote accents answered. "Squad E in area six –" Saxen's crew on the ruined warehouse site – "and squad A in area one."

Connor rose, shoving back his chair. The remains of the old police force had showed their head at de Priet's mansion. He couldn't drive over there – he had to go to the warehouse.

"You go to area one," he said to Comet and Gisele. "Get a hold on them before they do something stupid. Thakar, you hold the fort here."

"We can handle area six," Atalanta said.

That's what I'm afraid of.

*

CHAPTER TWENTY-THREE

Connor had jogged down the stairs and into the garage before the implications fully settled in his mind: this was useful, or he wouldn't have left his study except to retreat to bed. First problem was that he only had one car on site and, while he couldn't drive a bike properly at present, he still didn't trust Gisele to bike in this city in a face veil.

"Mister Comet has a car," Gisele said down his jack phone. He hadn't noticed her call his jack.

"Where?"

"In your garage."

Connor pushed open the internal door to the garage. Yes, two cars were parked on skids over blackened concrete, Fai Comet's behind Connor's, beside the open door to the street. Connor's men were flitting in and out like spectres, outlines drawn in charcoal and flame. Connor squinted outside. Those fires were drifting closer and closer to the public garage on the corner of Minor Lane and Bathgate. "I'd start driving if I were you in case that fire outside gets any worse. I don't have time to see you off." He reset his line to Yasmine's and gestured for Khayam and Marcello to get into his car.

Marcello climbed into the driver's seat without being asked and backed the car round for Connor to get in the right rear seat. He ignored the implicit invitation and climbed in the right front next to his bodyguard. Khayam jumped in the back instead.

"This is quite familiar," he remarked as he settled into one corner.

"I know what I'm doing this time," Connor said over his shoulder. Khayam reserved any response.

Marcello eased the car past men and vehicles and into the air. At last Yasmine's answer-call light popped up on Connor's eyeball reader. He exhaled, loudly enough that she would hear it as a sigh, as he blinked at the flames licking the streets below. Had Saxen bothered to pay the city firefighters to come out of hiding? "Silence, Mistress, is not always golden."

"I'm on my way back to the office." She sounded deflated, lost. "Mikhail's been killed."

She had had to admit it: the end of one of Connor's hopes, and the destruction of one of his few certainties. Now, if he were to place any further trust in her: "How?"

"He triggered an explosive on purpose."

You herded him into a firefight. You could have saved him by interposing yourself. "Then get to area six and do a little better for me there."

Half a pause while she worked out that that was the ruined warehouse/factory complex: the area Atalanta had offered to cover. "I'll meet you there."

"Don't be late." He signed off and stared out of the window.

There were only so many explanations for a Circle Weaver herding a barely-armed man to his death. He didn't like any of them.

Armoured cars had flown high over the city all day, firing incendiaries and mortar shells wherever they saw fit, and their departure had only left the sky clear for the high atmosphere skirmish. Marcello now inched the car into chaos. Scorched ruins marked the edge of free territory, chasm-deep breaches in the city's heart, brushed by fresh flames and glimpses of a netherworld. Even here, street children tiptoed round the ruins or curled up against the most stable walls. They had nowhere else to go.

Lights blazed at the spaceport every minute of every day, but now it seemed, from Connor's vantage, a vortex's central hub, with vehicles spiralling into it at every angle. Marcello had turned the car's external lights to zero and now slid them along just above the damaged rooftops. A car approaching the 'port would be one among millions. A car going anywhere else was suspect.

Connor pursed his lips. He could hope that the fuss at the 'port – aftermath from the Cliff team's departure; desperation in rich folk, petty merchants, and bourgeoisie trying to escape; floods of drifters ship-hopping in even greater numbers than normal – would be more than Saxen could handle with the staff he had at hand. Had he bribed all the 'port staff already, that queue of cars wouldn't exist.

Unless he'd bribed them to keep the exodus slow...

Marcello dropped the car down into a sidestreet and held it in place, engine inhaling and near-silent, while a convoy of someone else's bikes – anyone's guess whose – sailed past overhead. "Do you trust her, Mister?" he said quietly.

Faces flitted across Connor's mind: Yasmine, Atalanta, Gisele. "Which one?"

"Mistress de Priet."

That was an easy question. "No. No more than she does me. Tonight we need each other unless or until we find a substitute. If she were playing a double game with Saxen, Gisele would have warned me."

"Would she, Mister?" Khayam said from the back seat. "You're not paying her."

And there sat the crux of it. He wasn't paying Gisele, or Atalanta, though in the latter case if he had paid her he wouldn't have been able to use that as a reason to trust her: and though he was paying Yasmine, and had Circle doctrine to back up that he *could* trust her completely, he knew full well that she was playing a double game.

Maybe that was what really had him on edge. For just over two years he'd had the unvarnished luxury of fully trusting another human being. He'd poured a fragment of his soul into Éloise Falavière, forgetting that she was an individual who could walk away from him at any moment. And she had.

Connor shook his head, shut his eyes and tried to come up with one good reason for Saxen to accept a deal with de Priet absent the night's sabotage. Her money? That he could take. Her family's position? Better, but not enough.

Consider Saxen's senior captains. Lydian Elderson; Arkash Lauder; Michael Sara; Michael Sean Jules (first forename abandoned twenty years previously); Vian Horsefield. No top-tier female staff. Connor'd listened while other people made snide remarks to him about it, notably Rafael Martinez but also Éloise Falavière. Whatever the reasoning, that glass ceiling indicated a psychological blind spot that would prevent Saxen from seeing de Priet as a meaningful ally – or as a meaningful threat.

Probably.

Outside, the bikers were long gone. Marcello made to move the car on. Connor waved a hand at him, and he set the engine back to idle.

"We're not far from the perimeter," Connor said. "Khayam, in a moment we'll find you a perch." That might take a few minutes. Most of the surrounding buildings had suffered when the warehouse went up: intact masonry came at a premium. "Atalanta and Calad should already be in position near the site, waiting for a signal. When I call them on I want you to cover them."

"Yes, Mister."

"Distractions are occasionally necessary. I don't trust Saxen's squads to stay away." Not when the man appeared to have lost his handle on common sense. "Marcello, you are to stay in the driving seat under all circumstances. I'll need you to extract me in a hurry." He touched his neural jack. "Yasmine."

"Yes?" She sounded subdued. Well she might.

"Shadow us. Ten feet." He switched off his jack and gestured to Marcello to take the car up.

After a few minutes' nosing, the car's systems identified an intact apartment block two hundred yards from the warehouse and in its sightline. Marcello slid the car into its roof, Khayam dropped out next to a chimney, and the car slid away again.

Connor's palms were itching with the wait, providing minor distraction from mounting backache. Outside, the sky still coruscated, low-level combat slicing the air, approaching and receding with low, irregular rumbles. There had been no second ground strike that he'd heard. He *would* have heard it, that tearing, creasing crunch, a calamity beyond imagining. Its mere risk made him feel naked, more so than he had when collapsed at the base of a staircase with the world caving in above him.

Maybe this was why he did not pray. Acts of God were overrated when compared to acts of humanity.

He leant forward, staring out of the windscreen at the ruined factory/warehouse complex below. Three digging machines stood abandoned at the perimeter, pails streaked with mud: rifts scored the rubble, over the vault. Maybe the diggers had stopped when they realised they could not penetrate the vault shield: maybe not. Connor set the car's systems to scan the dangling remains of the upper storeys, at the north end of the complex where the exterior wall had survived the initial blast. Yes. That area was unstable.

"Who was watching this all day?" he said, voice deadening against the near-motionless car's upholstery.

"Mister A'syan's Joshua, for a while. Two of our runners at different times."

"Did any of them mention EMP?"

"They wouldn't have recognised EMP if they'd seen it." Marcello twisted towards him. "That's it? That's the key?"

"EMP would have worked if Saxen had tried it. I don't know if a man who buys his magic retail rather than wholesale would have realised." Magic as electromagnetism: EMP as a brief antimagic bomb. Éloise – in response to experience with longer-than-instantaneous antimagic – had programmed her shields to re-erect after an EMP hit, but a smart, quick man might have broken into the vault while they were still strengthening again.

Connor switched his jack to Atalanta's phone line. "Sightline on enemy?"

"Four guards on machinery, five on the site and perimeter."

He'd seen no more than three guards on the entire site so far. Blinking into the shadows, Connor waited and watched till he spied a fourth man – near the questionable wall. He grimaced into the night, and opened a party line. "Atalanta, start at the north wall and move inwards. Calad, start at the diggers." His crew had hired the bloody things: he was damned if he'd let all of their use – or all after retrieving him – fall to Saxen.

No acknowledgements came – he wasn't certain in retrospect whether Atalanta had spoken to him with her voice or her mind – but his straining eyes captured faint movement, white-skinned humans in a dark night camouflaged only with a few oil blotches. He fingered his gun. If he'd only been able to leave the car and join in...

Pain rippled up his left arm. What in *hells*? He clapped a

hand to his elbow and clamped his jaw shut, battling nausea.

That was a reminder, Yasmine's voice sank into his head. *That's what it feels like when I'm not concentrating. Do not get out of the car. Medic's orders.*

He'd have to get out of the car in the end… but he sat back against the cushioned seat and waited, eyes still flicking across the blast site. Calad, injured Calad, was out there. Long ago, when Connor'd glanced at Port Logis society and seen only the veneer, he had heavily underestimated how much damage Calad could do in the space of five to ten seconds. Now, maybe Calad would risk overestimating himself…

Connor leant forward till his nose was two inches from the windscreen. Near the diggers he could see far better than across the torn and twisted warehouse wreckage: while the rubble lay in shadow, gargantuan and menacing, lights shone faintly in the diggers' cabs and at their tails, and flooded out from their noses, clearly illuminating two guards.

As if all attention were meant to be there.

He reset his jack line to just Calad and Atalanta. "Where's the catch?" he said.

Calad didn't answer. *I still count four and five,* Atalanta's spicy voice tickled into Connor's mind. *Not every error on an enemy's part is a trap.* Connor bit his lower lip. Not so easy, not so easy…

One of the guards, on a gentle patrol, approached the nose of the closest digger. Its gold-and-white headlamp moved on balletic feet and struck. Knife to the guard's gun shoulder, pistol shot to his only mate within sightline, then Calad slammed into the first guard, flinging him to the ground, stunned.

Calad came up with a pistol in each hand, one firing under the digger's belly, the other firing over its nose. For half a second Connor closed his eyes. The lack of brain power was *almost* forgivable in these circumstances.

From the darkened warehouse remnant, gunshots rippled, and the young Spellweaver rolled under the digger and out the other side – towards the last couple of digger guards. In sparse shadow Connor half-saw Saxen's pair waving to each other, attempting to withdraw to a defensive spot. Khayam must have seen it too, for a shot flashed over the site, striking one man: he went tumbling to the ground, dead or dying.

Now Connor could curse the lights on those diggers. They'd killed his night vision. He couldn't see the main site and had lost track of its guard squad.

From above and behind, Khayam sent a shot over the site. In its afterglow Connor saw four men crouched together within the wreckage, guns raised. One missing. Atalanta.

Four men, four rifle barrels. They spat in unison, two towards Calad, two towards Khayam, who was way out of range. One man stood too high in his perch. A shot struck him in the back of the head. His fire-burst cut out and his rifle fell from his hands, cartwheeling over the wreckage. The other three, suddenly aware they had an enemy behind them, dived for cover.

Connor let his shoulders relax, just a little. Three versus nine on the ground and active would have been ridiculous odds if two of the three hadn't been superhuman. A man could get far too used to this: the hoarding of such power, and its display.

Calad was still between two of the diggers, unmoving: the last digger guard was behind the second vehicle. Connor couldn't see him. He touched his jack. "Calad, report."

He's popped a rib, Yasmine answered. *He and I are trying to reset it.*

They had room to hope Atalanta and Khayam could keep the rest pinned down: Saxen's perimeter and site team now knew Atalanta was *somewhere*, and their failure to locate her would increase their fear and paranoia. "Drive round the diggers," Connor ordered. "Their last guard is back there."

Marcello eased the car into motion. "Want me to start shooting out the window?"

"No. I'll play with windows myself."

His only answer was a grunt, but Marcello paused the car just out of sightline of where the digger's guard had gone to ground. Connor wound down the window. Time for instinct to trump magic.

"I guess you're feeling quite isolated right now," he called, keeping his tone as conversational as possible. "What with your backup taking off, and –" he was becoming *sure*, more so by the minute – "their replacements running late, I'm surprised you've stuck around this long."

Neither movement nor sound answered him. Too still and too quiet. Connor continued. "Yes, I'm really surprised you're here. Not dropped and run yet. You'd be a fool if you weren't afraid, and I don't think you're a fool, so... there's a benefit to loyalty. It's a two-way street, though. You to him, and him to you." He paused again, listening to the night and to the car buzzing beneath him. "Where's your backup?"

A long pause where no one spoke or moved, long enough for Connor to fear that he'd miscalculated, long enough to hear sirens whistling in the darkness and wonder how close they were. Then he heard a clatter, and saw a shadow-movement, less than real, the diggers' last guard running away into the sidestreets.

Connor motioned to Marcello to advance again, towards the cleft in the wreck. This he did, keeping close to the ground, albeit inexpertly. Connor bit his tongue. Logan would have kept no more than six inches between car floor and top of twisted girders: Logan would have slid the car between those two fallen roof segments – each ten feet across – rather than hopping over the top begging to be hit. But Logan wasn't here, and not every man knew by experience or instinct how to keep safe in the air.

He motioned to Marcello to stop just out of sightline of the holed-up perimeter guards, and called out, "Your last buddy took the smart way out. I guess you called for support as soon as you heard our first shot – and nothing came. Nothing's coming to *help* you. If anything comes, it'll take you out along with us."

Connor switched to jack and opened a party line to Yasmine, Khayam and Atalanta. "Don't shoot unless they do," he said. Someone, possibly Yasmine, drew in a breath. "Maybe don't shoot even if they do," he added. "Not if they're firing wild."

Neural jack muted again, he called to Saxen's crewmen, "So give this a try. Toss out the guns. Three rifles, six pistols."

Seven pistols, Atalanta said.

"Make that seven pistols. Someone brought a pocket gun?" Connor amended. "And stay right where you are. And you'll live. Do you want to see the sun come up again?"

He waited. Maybe he imagined he could hear whispers on the wind. Then, out of the darkness, he heard ten thumps, one after another, clattering away along the wreckage.

"We ditched 'em, Mister," a man's voice called.

Connor reactivated his jack. "Atalanta, Yasmine – anything else?"

"Looks good," Yasmine answered. "I'll tell you if we see a change."

Instead of answering, Connor motioned to Marcello to drive down. A brief squealing of car engines – a brief, "Son of a whore!" from Marcello – and the car tipped nose-on into the ruined stairwell, the galaxy's slowest and dullest fairground ride. Connor hadn't enjoyed fairground rides even before acquiring a niece and nephew who were addicted to them. He gripped the seat back with his right hand, released his belt via neural jack and pressed his weakened left thumb to the car door control.

High and piercing, a whistle rather than a squeal, a nearby engine was approaching.

Connor hit his jack again. "Atalanta, get Saxen's men out of there. Don't argue. I want them away and safe and knowing you and I did that for them." In his peripheral vision he saw a shadow streak across the wreckage above – the first time he'd had sight of Atalanta all operation. "Yasmine, get Calad out of the way. Khayam – eyes on the incoming. Slow them down." He hung up. "Marcello," he said, "turn off your neural jack."

"What?"

"Do it. Put the car on manual."

The car nose now hovered three feet above the basement floor. Connor's door was another couple of feet up the side. Cursing himself, cursing the world, he let go and dropped to the floor. The shock of landing crunched into his feet and all the way up his spine. His boot-soles slipped on a streak of blood and he nearly fell.

Neither of them would have known what was happening at first: then the man would have shivered as the bombs fell, and congratulated himself on his lucky positioning, and waited for the door to be opened, and waited, and waited. The lights would have gone out after a couple of hours. Maybe he wouldn't have had the heart to kill himself. Connor hoped not.

He looked up. The car seemed perilously close to the debris edge, its jets stirring up a small tornado of dust. It would start to stir more than dust soon. Connor blundered in half a run to the vault's blast door. Wreckage groaned overhead: the car shifting in place. Connor pressed his forefinger to the lock, then his thumb.

The door popped open. Foul air rolled out: breathed and rebreathed and scented with faeces. Connor hung back for a second, breathing bomb site dust. He'd no flashlight. Guided by his car's lighting he edged into the vault.

Hasan Saeed was lying beside the second stack, with his head pillowed on folded arms, as if he'd hoped he would die in his sleep. Here and now, he didn't look much like his pictures, from journalists or 'port cams, more like his luck had run out. Connor grabbed the closest shelf. He needed support. Blood on his fingertips, in a wrecked apartment. Blood and bone crushed beneath an avalanche of falling joists outside. Louise and Marie, side by side in the temple, and one alone on a vid call. Faulty perspective leading to an error in reasoning.

The White Canyon hard documents were on a shelf next to Saeed's head. Connor stuffed it into his inner jacket pocket. He'd promised weapons to his allies: he needed something to show for this trip. Ten new rifles didn't weigh much. He slung them over his shoulders one at a time. Saeed twitched, semi-fresh air's blessing. Connor bent and tucked his good right arm under Saeed and lifted.

He stopped partway back to his feet, breath sobbing in his throat. He couldn't rise. Pain lanced down his back. Too heavy: he couldn't do it.

Instead he reset Saeed on his feet, and slung his own right arm under Saeed's left. The man was boneless, rocking on his feet, semiconscious at best. Connor started hauling him towards the door. Five feet. Three.

At the door he paused, staring out. Marcello still held the

car in place, nose down, that tantalising distance from the ground.

The vault door started swinging shut behind them. Connor pulled Saeed forwards out of its path. Above, wreckage groaned and shifted, and Connor thought he saw Marcello's hand waving frantically through the car windscreen.

Five feet, again, but this time five vertical feet. He could haul himself up five feet, easily. Haul himself up, and leave Saeed.

Instead he dragged the fainting foreigner forwards a few more steps. His car door yawned open overhead. Stooping, he got Saeed's weight onto his good shoulder again and shoved him upwards.

He got the man's dead weight barely three feet into the air. Swearing, restraining sobs, Connor crouched, eyes on the blood smears on the basement floor. *Fuck* Logan for not being here to do this. *Fuck* Éloise –

Above, the car jerked sideways and dropped another six inches. Connor swayed back on his haunches, head millimetres from the bonnet, trying to shield Saeed with his free, injured arm. *We're going to die. Both of us.*

Marcello's right hand, near-disembodied, reached out from Connor's car door. Fear or proximity to success flooded Connor's arms with adrenaline, and he shoved Saeed upwards again. Marcello's hand closed round the man's upper arm and, between his pull and Connor's push, the pair heaved him into the footwell.

Connor vaulted up in after him and pulled the door shut behind him. "Move!" he said. Marcello had already started the car upwards again.

Saeed was twitching in the footwell, rocking back and forth in the tiny space. "Where're we going, Mister?" Marcello said, glancing from black sky and ghost-lit ruins to Saeed with his nose screwed up.

"Away from here. Lose pursuit as first priority."

"Pursuit." Marcello repeated the word, letting it settle on his tongue. "Mister Saxen or Mistress Atalanta?"

"Careful around Weavers if you're going to make leaps of judgement. Out of here, quick." Connor switched his jack back on. "Khayam."

"Yes, Mister?" His voice was faint, punctuated by *phuts* from his rifle.

"In case you were playing with that incomer, take him down now. We're clear."

One hand shoving his seat restraint shut, Connor kept his eyes left, on Saxen's armoured car's entry vector, rippling with plasma fire. Couldn't think about Khayam, or even Calad, so exposed: couldn't think about risks to his car's delicate engine and the chance of it going down with himself, Marcello and Saeed on board. Just hope. Just hope.

Another *phut*. A bolt spat out from the tower and slapped into Saxen's armoured car. It brought its nose round, angling its gun towards Khayam's firing position. Khayam got off a shot first. This time it smacked into the car's engine casing. It fell away in a spiral.

The Spellweaver trio had been on the ground – and unless Connor's ears were lying, another couple of cars were on their way. He touched his jack. "Yasmine?"

"I'm with Calad. He can't drive."

"Give him to Atalanta –" with as few recriminations as possible, Connor hoped: his chances of escaping all blame for Calad's relapse were scarce, but better to push the issue down the line by a day or so – "and you follow our car. Tell her to collect Khayam and split off the other way. We mustn't both be followed." Neither group could afford to be followed.

"Yes, Mister."

*

CHAPTER TWENTY-FOUR

Merissa's old apartment block lay silent and dark in the tracer-strewn city night, its residents holed up or fled. Connor directed Marcello to park as close as possible to the front door, and hung back while he and Yasmine carried Saeed out of the car and into the entrance hall. He couldn't move the car: there was nowhere safe to move it to, so he left it where it was – locked and powered down – and, using Merissa's keys, let the party into first the unlit corridor and then the flat.

The blood was mostly gone, cleaned up after Pritie had taken pictures and declared she wasn't going to make a fool of herself over the scene any longer. Yasmine bade Marcello dump the semiconscious man on the bed and sent him beetling around looking for water, salt and sugar in the dark. Connor sat back on the rickety stool that had once lain in a river of blood, waiting. For once, he could afford to wait.

"How long have you known he was in there?" Yasmine said over her shoulder, hands busy loosening Saeed's clothes.

"I worked it out while I was laid up yesterday afternoon." The advantages of being slightly feverish. "Believe me, this was the first opportunity I've had to fish him out."

"Hmm. I could have – never mind."

His night vision was sharpening. He peered at her in the tiny twinkles coming through the window panes from fires far away. "Least said soonest mended: or are you finally shedding your preconceptions?"

"I've been trying." She stopped moving for a moment. Faint white light played across her shoulders, mark of a Weaver who was concentrating hard in order to stop her wings bursting into a beacon. "You can't hide him from Atalanta forever."

He wouldn't have to. "Let me worry about her. Just revive him."

Marcello dumped salt and sugar on the bedside table and started measuring doses into a water cup using Yasmine's faint Weaver-light as illumination. Yasmine continued, "When we go back to base –"

"Me. You two are both staying here." Yasmine looked back and frowned at him. He shook his head. "I can drive a bike five blocks. Marcello stays here with you and the car, for now."

She didn't answer, but picked up the glass of makeshift rehydration fluid, tilted up Saeed's head and started dribbling it into his mouth. Connor stared at the black damp patches on the darkened ceiling. A shell of a life, a shell of normality.

Saeed muttered something less than a syllable. Yasmine withdrew the glass and he made a tiny motion towards it. She set it to his lips and he drank, consciously, deeply.

"Stop," she said, and withdrew it again. "Not too much at once." Connor thought Saeed nodded. It was hard to tell. The night was intense and Saeed's skin was little fairer than his own.

"It's good to have you back with us, Mister Saeed," he said. "My name is Connor Cardwain." Saeed turned his head towards Connor's voice: Connor saw his eyes glint in the gloom. "She mentioned me, I gather."

"She did." Saeed's foreign voice was rusty, most likely with a day's hollering at the vault door. "Where is she?" Connor did not answer. "Is she dead?"

"Yes." Saeed drew a breath but said nothing. "You were quite lucky," Connor continued, as evenly as he could. "For a man caught up in a coup d'état, you're on your way out of it as healthy as possible. I'd like to introduce two of my bodyguards – Yasmine and Marcello: Hasan Saeed, astro-engineer." Saeed nodded up to the others, a little tongue-tied, it seemed. "Now," Connor went on, "there comes the question of getting you out of this coup d'état. I gather Nerys offered you a trip to a Union system. I can achieve that. I can also place you outside the Union – in the Circle territories – if you prefer neutral ground."

"I want to stay alive," he whispered.

"As the crewers on that ship did not?" Saeed was silent. "What happened to the battleship, Mister?" Connor said softly. "That beautiful, new, experimental Atlas-hull battleship? As a man who worked on it, I'm sure you were horrified."

"It was a fiasco." He was angry, or Connor was no judge: bitter with tears he could not shed. "The drive was overclocked. I told them. With another half a day I could have recalibrated the accelerator, rebooted the whole system and re-upped the generator. But, no, they had to proceed on time. Five hundred men and women died because a petty overpromoted sergeant-major preferred timing to accuracy."

Connor gave him five seconds before replying, "It must have been atrocious. A betrayal of your hard work." Saeed didn't answer, but gave a tiny grunt. Connor continued, "So you contacted Nerys. You could trust her, for no Weaver, Guild or Circle, could read her mind." He half-saw Yasmine turn her head to look down at him. He didn't have time to explain. "But when you got here, she wasn't able to collect you without attracting attention from a Federation intelligence officer. So she sent a body double to meet you and keep you hidden in the city till the pursuit had moved on; and the body double had access to her boss's secure warehouse. Hiding in the vault, slipping in and out for food: it would have worked perfectly – if not for the coup, and if she hadn't been caught outside the vault at just the wrong moment."

After maybe a minute, maybe two, Saeed said, "I don't care where I go. I have no family to protect: I just want to prove I was right."

Connor rose to his feet. "The Circle Weavers of Port Logis can keep both the Union and Federation off you. They've been doing it for millennia: it's enough practice. You can take your research and testing any way you want from there." He patted Yasmine's shoulder. "Mikhail's Siren is parked in the spaceport. It should fit both of you if you breathe in."

"Hold on –"

"That's an order. Any man on his first Neuvième outing needs a Spellweaver escort. I sure as hell did. Give me your bike key – you'll need the car to get to the 'port." She handed it over. He forced it onto his right little finger and retreated towards the door. "Marcello, keep these two safe till they get off-planet. I want them away well before dawn.

Drop the rifles off at my office afterwards."

Yasmine followed him to the door. "They'll ask me, as soon as I pass Port Logis's Bridge," she said, visible in the darkness only as a faint mage-white outline.

Ask what? Her part in recent events? Let her admit all. "On what?" Connor said, fighting to keep his voice cool.

"Your opinion on the new head of the family."

Connor blinked. That didn't matter an inch right now – except, of course, that it did, to anyone not stuck in a warzone, anyone with a future. "I get an opinion?"

"You're a family member. Everyone gets an opinion."

"Democracy." As he said it, it began to make sense. Election of a representative: a family forming as much of a democracy as the average underside gang and considerably more so than the average Septième planet. "Éloise. She's smart enough to speak for us and tough enough to keep everyone in line, and she'll be dead the next time it comes up for grabs."

"OK. I'll put her in as your vote." She seemed set to turn back to her patient and courier charge, but paused. "Maman and Aunt Amalie always said men were soft. Don't prove them right. He should never have been born, you know that."

He had as much right to live as I have. You have no idea whether a war criminal fathered my however-many-times-great-grandmother – and neither have I. She would never back down on this, no more than any woman of her upbringing would, raised to kneel to Severity's icon. He couldn't expect it of her. Killing Mikhail as surely as if she'd handed him the mini-drone herself… "There's a question of convenient and inconvenient timing. Unless you stripped his mind for the verbal bypasses to those Cyclopes first?" She shook her head. "And he could have helped me clear up what happened to Merissa, once he started thinking straight. That chance, I can't forgive you denying me – nor can I forgive you not telling me what was going on as soon as you knew it yourself." He backed into the corridor, closed the apartment door and leant on it, fighting exhaustion, fighting a pointless little string of tears.

Farewell, Merissa. She'd been intelligent and discreet. Nerys must have seen the same qualities in her when they looked at each other over cocktails scant days before. A photograph, a moment frozen in time: now, three of the four in that photograph were dead.

Connor shook himself back to reality and tiptoed to the corridor end. He paused at the top of the stairs, listening. On a normal night the car would no longer be at the foot, unless one of his guard squads had passed by at just the right moment to stop it being stolen. Tonight, it could draw Saxen's gunhands to them.

His car and Yasmine's bike, the latter a lightweight Lyrebrand model popular among Neuvième and Dixième women, were still outside and no vigilantes were hovering beside them. Connor, staring into the dark, saw no watchers. Yasmine's helmet was too small for him: he pulled out some of the padding till he was able to cram it on, then scrambled onto the bike and started it up. Instead of heading home, he lifted its nose into the air and swung northeast towards Martinez and de Priet's mansion.

*

CHAPTER TWENTY-FIVE

Connor pulled the bike to a standstill, peering into the night. He'd extinguished its lights, but saw all the better thereby. No mansion on the lakeshore strip ever entered total darkness. There were always security lights, lights in the servants' quarters, parties going on till all hours followed immediately by early business calls to other planets. De Priet's house was no exception. Lamps burnt in the courtyard, down the manicured footpath, on the car landing strip by the garages, in what was probably the kitchen block, and in the guard house in the garden. A handful of men in Martinez's old gangland colours stood dotted about the grounds on guard, doubtless accompanied by twice the number of guards invisible from Connor's vantage.

And on the outskirts, outside the grounds, Connor counted at least eight of Saxen's squaddies, armed and watching the house. They made no movement, either out of respect or due to orders not to attack yet.

De Priet had *left* the complex earlier, and presumably had returned – or at least Connor had had no alert from Fai Comet or Gisele that the plan had already gone south…

He moved the bike back a little way – Yasmine had been right when she advised him against activity: his arm hurt like a sledgehammer had hit it, but there was nothing he could do about that at this stage – and, from a mile's distance, made a slow circuit round the perimeter. He watched the skies rather than the house, leaving the bike's camera to record his progress, and when he passed his starting point he settled back to replay the vids.

The camera footage revealed more of Saxen's men, some trying to be unobtrusive, others not. At no point was there a gap in the perimeter wide enough to admit a bike unheard. After a couple of minutes' decision-making, Connor drove to a less impressive neighbouring property, left the bike on a roof next to a fire escape, and walked back to de Priet's house and through a shaded garden gate. None of Saxen's troops challenged him.

In the grounds, he made straight for the closest household guard and identified himself in an undertone. Less than a minute later he was inside the house.

He'd never been admitted before, even when he'd sold the household guards some of the same rifles they were carrying now (K2s by Nexi, a White Canyon subdivision more noted for adding its name to bikes and cars); as he walked through the corridors in a steward's wake, he took note of the furnishings. Little touches of opulence were mainly displayed in items that were expensive yet not gaudy: quality carpets, high art. It spoke of taste, though whether on Martinez's part or de Priet's – or some designer's – it was impossible to say.

The steward led him up the stairs and through a heavy door to the left at the top. It opened into a sitting room that would have seemed wide and airy in daylight. Now, with all its curtains drawn and a few dim lamps burning, it was a draughty cavern. Comet, Gisele and de Priet were clustered round a table well away from the door and the windows; the mistress, Dana, was embedded in an armchair a few feet away, smoking a cigarette in a long thin holder. She gave Connor a lazy salute as he entered, but did not rise. Comet nodded to him, a little distant and preoccupied. The other two women did not look up.

"It doesn't matter what kind of offer I make," de Priet was saying, "if the ships don't show up in the sky in time. We need to look like we have muscle to offer."

"They're here and here." Comet stabbed at what Connor could now see was a 3-D system map. "The police response is key." He shifted sideways to make room for Connor to pull up a chair, which he did one-handed.

At another time he'd itch for the access this setup gave him. Right now, the thought of focusing on anything but survival seemed too difficult.

The underside's great men and women did not shirk from the difficult…

Connor collected himself and focused on the map. A race, now, pure and simple: starships versus the dawn.

They weren't going to make it.

"Adjustments," he said. "Contingencies."

"We've no time," Comet said, shaking his head.

"We need to make time. Can the ships accelerate?"

"Only if we lose any pretence of non-hostility."

"I ask myself what Saxen suspects." Connor leant back and studied the map again, trying to see it from Saxen's angle. "He'll know by now that some of my staff returned to the warehouse site. He'll assume we got something from there, but won't know what."

"What did we get?" de Priet said.

"Some more weapons. Not enough to make a difference." He tapped the map. "He may assume we think as he does – in terms of brute power alone – and miss our play for a softer route to power." He nodded to de Priet. She seemed more in control of herself now, her determination more acute. "Or he may decide to hit millionaires' row too."

"He doesn't know he can win that fight, dear," Gisele said softly. "He's more cautious than you portray. He picks fights of which he's sure."

A new assembly of the possible. Thakar, earlier: '*He might have a stack of dirt on the planet's high-ups...*' "He's not stupid. The most likely thing he'd use is sex scandals. How much would that be held to matter?" The latter he addressed, with a bow, to de Priet.

"Thou Shalt Not Get Caught." And round and round they all went... "If one man thought only he were affected, it would have more impact on him than if he knew his neighbour were affected." She snorted, the first sign of inelegance she'd demonstrated. "They're all as bad as each other. I could give you a full list of all my neighbours' peccadillos."

"You could?" Comet said, looking up.

She shrugged, faint self-consciousness flitting across her face. "I kept an eye on people for Rafael. He liked to tease people just enough to make them know that he knew."

"Great. Draw up a list and we can hand out a few more little reminders of who's really in charge."

"I'll fill in any you miss," Dana volunteered.

De Priet nodded to her, just a little, but said to the air between Connor and Fai Comet, "This fits with keeping the same hold on the aristocracy that Rafael had. It doesn't fit with playing nice."

Dana squirmed round and waved her cigarette at her. "They can play nasty for you." She indicated Connor and Comet. "You can keep playing nice. Who's to say you told them what to say? Carrot from you and stick from them."

It took them a valuable half hour to hammer out a rough backup plan based on several interesting data points on de Priet's neighbours. Gisele curtsied herself out of the room – secure in her ability to walk past any guards in the city – and as Comet drew aside to ask Dana some pointed questions about her inside knowledge on the high underside and a few richer merchants, Connor was left with de Priet.

A few hours had transformed her from a frightened girl into a budding battler. She even seemed more awake than earlier, though he doubted she'd slept. "Do you have someone other than us to back you up?" Connor said, hoping she would name a friend, or a parent.

She waggled her hand in an uncertain gesture. "Father told me to go home. I told him I was too upset. If I called his steward, she'd come over and help me. She was young when my grandfather retired, but she remembers." Her underside grandfather, she did not say. Connor pursed his lips. Maybe the father would make trouble if he thought the daughter was returning the family to a life they'd abandoned.

Maybe one day Kasimir or Gaiety's children would do the same.

"But she'd come."

"She was my grandfather's page. She'd come." De Priet's eyes wandered to the wall nearby, to a picture of herself with Martinez, and another with her holding a giggling baby girl. The child had died, Connor recalled, and there looked to be no other imminent.

"I'd look over your contacts list again," he said, "including any more leftover ex-undersiders your father has knocking around his place. You'll need them at your back, and you'll need any aristocrats you can muster at your front."

"I will. Rafael talked about how important that was. How he would play this woman against that man, and him against someone totally different. He had one person, other than me, he trusted completely, but he would never tell me who."

"It wouldn't do you any good. He's dead now. The only thing that does do you any good is that Mister Fai Comet trusted the same man." Connor stared at the wall pictures. Sentiment had no place in their world: that didn't stop him feeling it, but it helped him confront it. Martinez, living to nearly twice the Septième's average lifespan, and a woman two generations removed from what the underside meant. Too far? The way de Priet was acting, she might be stuck between too far to understand and too close to realise she didn't.

"He took me seriously," de Priet said quietly. "My likes, my dislikes, my talents, what I could do to support him. I don't know if he was ever proud of me. I was proud of him."

It was an epitaph, in its way: and Connor again thought of Dominic, and of Gisele, another wife half her husband's age. The brief thought crossed his mind that Dominic Falavière and Rafael Martinez might have gone on quite well.

But Dominic had made careful plans for his death.

"Did he give you contingency instructions?"

"They were with the police. There are letters with the lawyers, but they're too frightened to speak to me."

"By morning, they'll either comply or they'll throw you on the dust heap too. It rests on whether they," and he gestured to the incoming warships on the map, "hurry up."

She linked her arm into his and drew him back to the map. "You don't think they will."

"It's my job to fear they won't, and to plan accordingly. I have three Spellweavers –" One? Two? Four? Did he have any that were truly beholden to him at the moment? "They won't stretch far enough to save us." Yasmine despatched to Port Logis, Gisele neither his employee nor anyone else's, Atalanta liable to a temper tantrum as soon as she realised Connor had crossed her, Calad too injured for active duty. Definitely couldn't save everyone.

De Priet sighed. "Part of me doesn't care if I get killed tomorrow. I've – lost –" She didn't say 'everything', maybe realising what Connor's reaction would be to a woman ensconced in luxury saying just that, but she continued, "I want to fight. I don't want him to get away with it."

"Don't you? How long are you prepared to push that out?"
She stared at him, uncomprehending. "If he runs, are you
prepared to follow? If he hides, are you prepared to search?
If he buries himself in the deepest dunghill on the Septième,
are you prepared to have children – " Her expression shaded
towards a deeper night than he'd yet seen in her. "Yes, more
children, and send them to find his children after you're
gone? That's a determination born of hate. I've seen it. I've
been where they live it. It isn't pretty and it certainly isn't
godly. Personally I don't think it's good for business. You'd
do better to stick to the plan." Her eyes sparked as Connor
spoke, but she was the one who looked away first.

*

CHAPTER TWENTY-SIX

A faint purple mist was beginning to spread along the horizon, deepening and reddening by infinitesimal degrees. Connor had stopped aching to bite his nails long hours ago. Now he just waited, staring from his rooftop vantage at the ruined city centre spreading out around his office.

"More coffee?" Thakar said, behind him.

If he had any more coffee he'd spend the whole morning pissing, and that would not be convenient. "No, thanks."

Thakar grunted acknowledgement and came up beside Connor, resting a light arm round his waist. Together they stood contemplating the city centre.

One of the city hall's wings was, per street talk, too dangerous to enter – it had killed three drifters who tried – but the other, the one furthest from Martinez's now-demolished office, was intact. Saxen had taken up residence there, per yesterday's news bulletins. Assuming he was *still* there, he'd be an easy target no matter what weapon they used…

Ifs, maybes, watch-outs, you-fools. De Priet and Comet would head to the city hall in two hours, with ships in the sky to prove their case. Comet at least had the clout off-planet to make Saxen hesitate to murder him, but Connor had, at one point, thought the same of himself.

Risk it all on Saxen's desire for legitimacy? That wouldn't work if he kept any aristocrats on his side. Overnight, Gisele and a squad of Pritie's juniors had woken aldermen, merchants, haut bourgeoisie and aristocrats, bankers and burghers, and had explained the position to them. That most had already had similar visits from Saxen's crew clouded the issue, but most who had been willing to lend Saxen their name before the overnight sky-battle with Cliff were starting to change their opinion. Connor had not received a report of Zolde de Priet's conversation with her father. He suspected the elder de Priet was incommunicado, if alive.

One had repelled even Gisele entirely: Théodora Bramhall,

who had announced her backing of Saxen within an hour of his coup. With her continued approval, and that of her satellites, Saxen wouldn't feel he needed de Priet's backing to force himself a compliant upper crust.

Over a third of the city's names, those with their own guard squads and their own armoured ships – those men and women who threatened to bridge the gap between aristocracy and low underside – reacted to potential liaison with Fai Comet with glee. For the rest, the more staid souls, Comet's name was not enough. Fear of Éloise and subsequent desire for alliance with Connor was clearly not enough. Where names like Bramhall went, there the others would eventually go.

Connor gave Thakar's waist a gentle squeeze. "I need to borrow Joshua."

Thakar's eyebrows rose. "You got your own runners."

"So you can take one of mine if he gets shot. I haven't got as good a sneak-thief on my personal staff." He had some in a couple of petty street gangs who answered to him and operated with his protection, but right now, he needed a more personal degree of loyalty.

"You've got at least one," said Thakar. "She's my height with a devil's temper."

It took Connor a moment to work out Thakar was exaggerating – faintly – about the height part. "Atalanta? I don't…"

"She's your brother's stepsister. If you can't trust that, what are we all?"

Thakar had no idea how badly Connor'd pissed off Atalanta this night. *Atalanta* didn't know it yet. If she found out while they were alone together…

The hell with it. "Fine. I'll take both of them. Atalanta won't admit her skills are suited to thievery."

"She broke-and-entered your office less than a week ago."

"She didn't, she – who told you that?"

"Pritie."

"Never mind. Just get Joshua to me round the top of Angler's Walk, near the turn to Balder Way."

Three quarters of an hour later, and wishing he'd had some extra caffeine even if not coffee, Connor eased his bike into an alley by the side of Angler's and Estmarch, local money's stratosphere on the city edge, and walked in shadow to the end of the street at its corner with Balder Way. The bike was from his common pool and thus expendable. If he lived another twenty-four hours, he'd think about pool funds then.

Atalanta was perched two floors up on a broker's office's exterior, unblinking under a street lamp till she was near-indistinguishable from the marble and sandstone statues on the office corner. Connor suspected he'd imported some of the marble from Port Logis. No riots in these streets, and no reprisals: yet no movement either, at an hour when twenty-something rich folk should still have been staggering between cocktail bars and private casinos.

He whistled upward to her: not a drifter's whistle-speech but a soft command. She jumped down to the street and fell into step beside him.

"How's Calad?" he asked without looking at her.

"Back in bed."

"I'm sorry."

She snorted, horse-like. "I'm not. He's –" She cut off and was quiet for a moment. "I am sorry."

"If the first one was your fault –" It wasn't. "– the second was entirely mine. I knew he was hurt and I utilised him anyway."

"A risk is a risk. He and I know that."

A risk was not a certainty. Connor kept his eyes ahead, on the silent main street, on the apparently deserted sidestreets they were passing – on the tiny signs of private guards' presence in the dark. On an average night, guard squads walked the street under the lights, rather than standing in the shadows watching every movement. Their alertness itself might mean trouble.

A risk was not a certainty: Connor's certainty that Calad wouldn't be able to handle the warehouse assault, and that Atalanta, full of guilt already, would sidetrack to him as they left. That she would give Connor a clean run away with Saeed.

Sidestreets shifted from dainty mews to chintzy lanes until all of a sudden the boulevard opened onto apparent countryside: the rich's private estates, growing larger and larger till the biggest reached a hundred square miles across.

Luckily their destination wasn't quite that far away. Connor kept himself close in to the hedgerow. Every estate had a private security team: he didn't want to cause trouble.

"We are paying a call on Mistress Théodora Bramhall," he said to Atalanta, "acute accent incorporated as she thought it looked elegant. Long term detractor of Rafael Martinez, her father and de Priet's grandfather having been on bad terms, and her husband having lost ships to Martinez: called Saxen to congratulate him as soon as he blew up Martinez, and appears his most rock-steady upper-crust supporter. Refused Gisele's overtures earlier in the night. Has the brains and the experience to work out what we're doing and warn Saxen. Has the arrogance not to do so till morning. Large bank account inherited from father and husband and enhanced by her own activities on the underside." He'd always hated dabblers. "Large guard squad, large staff of servants."

"And you couldn't put together a plan that didn't involve me?"

Connor stopped in a beech tree's shadow. "If we wanted to mount an armed assault on the place, I'm your project planner. When we tried to subvert her, I had a hand in that. Unobtrusive entry is more your line, and Joshua's."

. He crooked a finger behind his back. He heard nothing, but felt a breeze stir. "Getting into this kind of house isn't my area," Joshua said softly from behind him.

"No: it's Mistress Falavière's." He half-heard Atalanta sniff. If she didn't want to be referred to as Falavière she should have followed New World naming customs upon marriage rather than Old World. "She'll plot us a way in. Your job comes later."

He drew closer into the hedge and gestured through a gap in the foliage at a house semi-visible in the blushing night, at least five further miles from the hedgerow, set amid banks of trees. Its façade was easily half a mile across. "The barracks is attached to the main building: there are outposts in the woods and at the footbridge."

"Footbridge?" said Atalanta.

"This gate gives onto a stream."

"Winding through the estate looking cute? Well-stocked with fishing punts?"

Twenty minutes later with the sun still well below the horizon, the three of them, varying degrees of damp, tied their punt to a bollard alongside half a dozen others, emerged from the stream bank near the back of the house and ducked into a depression next to a cellar door. Atalanta slipped away down the side of the building, and Joshua, taut and silent, leant out from Connor's shadow to watch her go.

Connor surveyed the boy: white, but not as fair-skinned as Atalanta, with dirty dark blond hair cut in a child's mop that he'd oiled behind his ears into an approximation of a man's ponytail. Street child, with street instincts, but a child's easy-to-read face. Connor didn't have to ask when Atalanta began to scale the wall near the edge of the wing, for it showed in Joshua's wide eyes: her pauses echoed in the boy's arrested breaths, her disabling of security sensors in his mimed whistle, and the moment she slid open a window and slipped inside, in his tiny, suppressed hiss. Connor leant back on his heels and waited.

Ninety seconds from Joshua's hiss, the cellar door cracked open, and Atalanta beckoned the other two inside. Connor pointed to her, and to the flagstones in front of the door. She nodded, and when Connor and Joshua edged past her and in among a maze of wine bottles dusty enough to have been part of Bramhall's paternal inheritance, she stayed on the door.

The cellar marked the divide between kitchen block to the left and residence to the front and right. Servants were stirring in the kitchens, clanging in the distance and producing the morning's first pastry-smells. Connor hurried ahead and to a thin grey door at the wine cellar's head: it did not move when he pushed against it, but opened to Joshua's delicate touch. The boy stepped aside and Connor led him through into what appeared to be the main residence's vestibule. The night was dark, but the towering grey walls swallowed what faint light there was: Connor made for the staircase and crept upwards, pressing himself into the walls to minimise shadow-cast and concentrating on every tiny sound.

They were cutting this very fine, and he had no time to get lost. The one time he'd sold a few hundred plasma packs to the estate guards, his delivery crew hadn't entered the main house. He paused at the top of the stairs: left or right? Same principle as de Priet and Martinez's house: follow the most expensive décor. He went left.

His wet feet sank into the dark blue carpet with every step, leaving clear prints. If any one – servant, family member, guard – crossed his track, he would be followed at once. Behind, Joshua walked in his footfalls, soft and light.

Walls rose tall on each side, draped in paint and tapestry, a gloomy statement of capital. Periodic caverns sank into the walls to either side: music rooms, games rooms, an aviary redolent of guano. Deeper into the house they sank, further and further from their cellar entrance.

Finally, a bedroom corridor: dirty shoes and empty alcohol bottles waiting for collection outside doors. Too many doors. They didn't have time to search blind. Connor beckoned Joshua into a doorway's nook, and waited.

Two minutes, five, till Connor's neck was itching with the utter certainty that the guard squads would turn up any second; and then a servant emerged ahead, a boots girl not much older than Joshua, weighed down with dirty shoes collected from further back down the corridor. She was dressed neatly enough, but was pinch-faced, thin, and short. Drift-bred.

Connor waited till the boots was passing him, then reached out a hand and clamped it over her mouth. She squeaked into his hand but froze still, not dropping a single shoe.

"Recognise me?" he whispered. She shook her head, silent. "Look again." She did so, and her eyes widened. "I'm not here to hurt your mistress. Which is her bedroom?"

The boots jerked her head backwards. "Third left," she breathed.

"Good. Come to me if you have trouble here and need more work." He waited till she'd walked a way on, and jogged down the corridor to the door she'd indicated. Through open doors of empty rooms, the blackness outside was beginning to shade to iron-grey.

Joshua caught him up at the door. "Guards coming," he murmured.

Right. "This is the room, or should be. Get gone. You know your job." Joshua gave him a look of mild disapproval, and scooted back along the corridor towards the living rooms and vanished into shadows.

Shaking his head, Connor clicked open the bedroom door. He'd half-expected central locking to have cut in when the guards started searching for him, but the door opened without drama. Inside was a curtained antechamber, with a door leading off its right wall to, when Connor investigated, a body servant's sleeping cubby: just big enough for a narrow bed, a small chest and, at the back in shadow, a slim dark door. The bed in the cubby was empty. Connor withdrew to the antechamber and tweaked the heavy blue velvet curtain aside.

Bramhall's bedchamber was the size of Connor's garage, though considerably dimmer and stuffed with oversized oaken furnishings that at this hour felt haunted. The bed was in an alcove well away from the window, draped in more velvet, heavy and ostentatious. Connor squinted in the near-darkness. Two shapes in the bed. Flip a coin. He drew his pistol, skirted up the left side of the bed and pressed the gun barrel down.

Right person. Bramhall: he couldn't see, but he heard her swear, unmistakeable hoarse voice, struggling. He pushed her back into the pillows. "Stay quiet," he said, and at the sound of a thump on the far side of the bed – the redoubtable lady's companion falling out – said, "You stay there and stay silent."

For a moment he could only hear three sets of breaths, theirs uneven and fast, his steady. The guards would be here in minutes. Where were they? "You on the floor," he said to Bramhall's sleeping companion, "turn on a lamp, low."

Lights twisted up in the bed's headboard, revealing Bramhall silently glaring up at Connor as if she were twisting a carving knife in his guts. Across the bed, her body servant was huddling into a blanket, stricken-eyed.

Connor forced himself to smile. "Not fun when people walk into your home and help themselves, is it?" Bramhall sneered but did not reply. "We could have company here any minute," Connor continued. "I suggest you tell them to leave us to it. I shouldn't be here to threaten your virtue… which is rather the point."

"How did you get in?" Bramhall said in an undertone.

"Opened a door and walked in. Not difficult."

She shot a glare sideways at the body servant as if it were the girl's fault that the two of them had been ambushed by a gunwielding maniac. "The safe is downstairs. If you want its contents I expect they will be guarded by now."

"No." Connor shook his head. "There's a bigger prize in play. At first light you're going to call Nikalar Saxen and tell him you can't support him any longer without him getting some backup – that you draw the line at him antagonising a UISS corporation."

Bramhall laughed, closer to a bark than anything else. "Are you *mad*? Saxen has –"

"Saxen risks every man and woman on the planet thanks to his antics against Cliff Enterprises. Saxen *hasn't* broken into your house without a whiff of inside help. If he's suborned any of your staff I suggest you get rid of them. I've been to Zolde de Priet's house tonight: her servants are a better lot."

"De Priet?" Her flinty stare did not leave him, but he fancied it had become a touch more thoughtful. "Are you her creature?"

"No. I represent a cohort of concerned citizens. She shares our concerns."

He tapped Bramhall's forehead with the pistol. No need to add clever comments about his ability to break back in if she didn't comply. Instead he said, "Saxen can't protect you on his own. He can't protect himself on his own. If you want a better future, tell him you want him to drag up some extra muscle. I guarantee you'll end better that way."

"If you're planning to involve Zolde de Priet, recall that her husband died despite having all the experience she lacks."

"We'll get her a crash course. Anything to relieve us of the possibility of a few UISS fleet vessels appearing overhead." He half-smiled. "Your niece. Anna, I think I heard? If you continue to risk all our lives, we might decide that we'd do better with Anna controlling your fortune and whispering in Saxen's ear."

He backed to the doorway, gun trained on her. Neither Bramhall nor her servant moved. Connor felt behind him for the curtain and ducked through it.

Instead of entering the corridor he darted into the servant's cubby and tried the tiny door at the back. It gave straight onto a plain stair leading downwards. Connor padded down the steps and, after listening at the door at their foot for as long as he thought he could get away with, cracked it open and peered out.

Kitchen: deserted bar one sleepy girl stoking a cylindrical bread oven. She didn't start as Connor clicked the door shut, just said over her shoulder in a voice loaded with fatigue, "Five more minutes till the coals are hot enough. She wants early snacks, there's grapes and pears –" She turned as she spoke, and froze when she saw Connor.

For his part, Connor could do without having tandoor coals thrown at him. "Wine cellar?" She pointed at a side door. Connor took it.

Another unadorned corridor, grimy with years of kitchen helpers' oily feet scuffing its flags. Connor took it at as fast a run as he could, ignoring the side chambers – stores for cheeses and dried food, sleeping quarters for food preparation staff – and pushed open the door at the end. Back in the wine cellar: Atalanta was near the rear door, clutching a pistol that glistened in three magic colours.

Connor motioned to the door. "Move if we're clear outside."

"Joshua?"

"Behind. Go."

Atalanta pushed open the door and ran the few paces down to the stream. She paused at the bank and unhooked one of the punts from the bollard, before clambering in. Connor climbed in after her, pushed off the bank and let them drift out onto the stream.

"Can Joshua drive one of these things?" Atalanta said in an undertone.

Connor held up a hand for silence and lay down flat in the punt. Atalanta, glaring, copied him. No sound from the little boat, moving with the current: too many guardsmen making too much noise looking for a car or bike in the grounds.

When the current had carried them away from the voices, Connor murmured, "Bramhall isn't the type to be swayed by an early wakening with a gun in her face. She'll castigate half her guards and set the others around her in a tight shield."

"So?"

"The security system runs as a combination. It's not just DNA of those permitted or not permitted in the house – it's DNA plus identification as a human over about four and a half feet tall. Houses like this get through so many drifters that if they plugged them all into the scanner, they'd never stop. So Joshua doesn't show up on the scan. He never did, never could. Bramhall will get out of a meeting with her security chief and find all her personal rooms have been ransacked and no one can find the culprit – not her guards, not her servants, not her security systems. If that spooks her enough to comply, all well and good. If she calls a Spellweaver as a last resort, to smoke out the problem, Gisele will ensure the street-witches can't oblige. She will go herself and frighten Bramhall into making that call."

Atalanta didn't answer at once. Overhead the sky was shading pink at the horizon. "You'll get him killed," she said in the end.

"Then I'll owe Thakar a page. Joshua knows the risks."

"He's ten years old."

"I hadn't flagged you for turning sentimental." The punt was well out of the estate now, approaching a bridge. Connor stayed low as it slid under the arch and then sat up. If anyone had a sniper rifle on him from far away, he'd be very surprised. Dead, but surprised. "You grew up around boats. How do we stop this thing?"

*

CHAPTER TWENTY-SEVEN

He had no excuse to go to the city hall, and every reason not to go, therefore he couldn't. Do everything right. Still Connor stood staring out of his window leaning on a painted walking-stick – actually one of a pair of hiking poles he'd once borrowed from Dominic and forgotten to return – as if there were still room to pretend that he was injured.

Out there ninety miles across the city was Fai Comet's car, containing Comet, Calad (ostensibly hired away from Connor), Zolde de Priet and Gisele (ostensibly de Priet's chaperone). That car would have left de Priet's mansion as the sun brightened in the sky, heading for the city hall and Saxen squatting drift-like in its least damaged wing: heading to Saxen as a beacon and a face-saver. A partnership, as proposed by Comet, between the three of them: himself, de Priet and Saxen – a power boost for Saxen, social and material, that he couldn't have hoped to get with dawn breaking over a ruined city.

He had to trust. Trust that Comet wouldn't stab Saxen in the front until the man had time to announce the partnership to his staff, at which point either he or de Priet or both could stab him in the back. But Saxen would announce nothing if he realised Connor were lightly injured and still moving pawns on the chessboard. Connor moved back and, once he was well away from the window, stowed the hiking pole by the door, buckled on his gun belt and headed downstairs.

Take an uncertain world and present *certainty*. That was what a ruler rather than a bully did. Maybe the truth had sat in the dead-eyed girls waiting for transport three days ago, and on the manner in which Saxen's ambition had spread.

He had seized momentum and allies: in the end it would matter whether he had any *friends*.

Atalanta and Marcello were waiting in the garage, playing canasta with mismatched card decks in the half-light over one of the workbenches. They looked up when Connor entered: Atalanta collected the cards into her jacket pocket, and

Marcello scooted to Connor's car and opened the driver's door.

"Thank you." Connor edged round him and inside.

Marcello opened his mouth and shut it again. He resembled a giant baby. "Don't you want a getaway driver, Mister?" he said after a couple of attempts.

"Later, yes." Connor closed the door, fastened his belt and set his hands on the controls.

Dull fire rippled up his left arm, throbbing deep into the bone. Connor relaxed his arm and re-extended it. The fire flared again.

Too late to swap seats, for Marcello was climbing into the front passenger seat. Too late to admit his exhaustion, his pain, his overwhelming desire to go back to bed (with or without Thakar, preferably with, but he'd take anything right now) and let the others finish the job. He couldn't do that. Perhaps he'd already ensured Saxen had no future. He, Connor Cardwain, had a future out there in the Septième sector. It would run from him if he slept.

He eased the car into motion – Atalanta, still settling herself in the back, let out a small squeak – and, once the garage door swung open, accelerated out and into the sky. He'd made the tight left-and-yaw turning out of this garage a hundred or a thousand times by now: he did so again, automatic movement. Skin on his left arm screamed.

Below and less than a mile away lurked the ruins of the closest overnight battle: a relic in the middle of a wreckage-ring, twisted metal from a spaceplane amidst bricks, breeze-blocks and girders. The dead were not visible. That seemed an omission. The dead should be remembered.

Ninety miles: a hair's breadth in a planet's dimensions. When Connor looked, he saw city borders straggle out in the distance into plantations and farmland, scarred in places from mining, protected in others by money. Secundus lay another thousand miles south-west, far over the horizon, just as hedged by green land and by its moneyed class. A change in the wind and the green would go. Connor restrained a snort. Short-sightedness might kill farmland and forests both, but the choice was between them and a skydome over each city and homestead. Oxygen was such a harsh mistress.

He meandered along like a weekend driver past crack-frontaged offices and roofless tenements till he neared Saxen's offices. From above and half a mile out, they looked untouched. Too much to hope for that the Cliff ships would have dropped half a spaceship onto the roof as an accentuation of Saxen's mistakes, but the plus side was that the office staff would still be in position.

Once a hundred yards from the office, Connor slowed further, and dawdled near an intact hotel. "Atalanta. Is he inside?"

"Yes," she said after a moment.

I will not ask for those playing cards. I will not. "Good. His office, or a bedroom?"

"Office."

Connor slid the car below roof level and edged along alleyways till he drew up near the rear door. Cameras would have clocked his arrival. If any cameras were manned by those who'd give Saxen a straight answer, Connor would have cause to worry. He doubted it.

The back door stood ajar. Two drifter hires, a boy and a girl, were outside sharing a cigarette. They gaped as Connor climbed out of the car and passed them into the office, but they did not move. Atalanta, close behind Connor, did not spell them into quiescence. Let the brightest kids run. They deserved it.

Inside he paused, getting his bearings. These were kitchen and storage areas, not the more formal hallways he'd seen before. The kitchen was open to the corridor on the right through a wide arch, a cavern that offered little warmth or sustenance, and the storage rooms on the left smelt of must and mice. Ahead and leftwards would lead towards the main hall, most probably. Connor struck towards a likely-looking door.

"Next one," Atalanta murmured, sibilance sliding into his head half-spoken and half-projected.

"Thank you." Connor reached for the next door handle with his left hand, thought better of it, and swapped to his right. "Tell me if he moves." He felt more than saw her nod.

Through the door, the hall's stillness felt eerie: none of the bustle to which Connor was accustomed in an underside office, no hires or fires hanging around, very few mercs passing, all of whom ignored Connor and Atalanta as if they couldn't see them, for the very good reason that they couldn't. Connor began to breathe a little more freely. Maybe Cliff had done it – given this crew something bigger to think about, something to stoke their fear.

There was no dragon outside Sean Jules's surgery door. Connor nudged it open and peered inside. Sean Jules was at his desk, flipping through a notepad that looked like the appointment book he'd been using when Connor had visited him earlier.

Connor edged into the room, with Atalanta following. She closed the door behind them. Connor cleared his throat. "Good to see you." Sean Jules started and swung round in his chair. Connor continued, "No, really. I'm glad to see you're alive. You deserve it, if anyone does: not that survival and deserving such have any connection."

"You shouldn't be here," he said in a low voice. Connor bit his tongue to keep back a smile. Perfect.

"Calling you would have been even riskier. You never know who's listening. Like this, we can talk in private." Sean Jules, eyebrows raised, gestured first to Atalanta and then to the door and, by extension, the rest of Saxen's staff. Connor smiled openly at that. "Allow me to introduce Mistress Atalanta Falavière, my brother's stepsister. She's discreet, and ensures others' discretion."

Sean Jules sent Atalanta a look that reeked anti-Federation prejudice, but said, "Good for you both."

Connor settled on the edge of the medical cot. This was better. He could rest his arm on his lap. "Allow an older man to give you a piece of advice."

Sean Jules snorted half a laugh. The age difference between them was minimal, if any. "Shoot it, Mister."

Connor gestured to the notepad. "You've got the right idea already. Let this be your catalyst."

He shook his head. "I can't leave."

"By every underside tradition, it is your right as captain to walk whenever you want. If I mishandled my dealings I'd expect to lose my captains. Demand your cut, and go – and take that notebook. It might prove useful."

"Yeah, need to remember which kind of girl the governor of Ilamena likes to sleep with… Cardwain."

That said it all: he'd left, in his head, already. "Sean Jules?"

"Did you deal with Cliff? About that runaway man?"

Connor didn't see Atalanta move as much as observed a stiffening out of the corner of his eye, a preparation, prowling cat with prey in sight. "No. Saxen antagonised Cliff when he should have known better. That was all."

"In his defence –"

"I'd stop trying to defend him, if I were you. It won't help you much in future." Connor rose. His arm began to throb again. He'd have to ask Calad to top up the spell Yasmine had left on it. "The remaining captains." The key. "I wouldn't warn them you're going."

"I need to tell Horsefield and Elderson, at least."

"No, you don't. Pack, fly off however a man can at the moment, and take enough in-hospital training on the Neuvième to get another certificate to glue to your wall. That's my advice. Then come back if you want, and do as you will thereafter."

He turned towards the door. Atalanta was standing in the way, a temple statue, with her jacket pocket hanging a little way open. One of the playing cards had tumbled out of it and to the ground. Connor bent and retrieved it. Seven of swords.

As he touched the card its face blurred. Connor screwed his eyes shut. Best to see nothing. Better to see nothing than see an outline, a shadow, a woman bursting through the doorway, hair as black as the night in her eyes hanging loose and wild around her head.

Fingers brushed his: Atalanta, retrieving the card. Connor cracked his eyes open. The grey morning re-intruded. He waved a limp hand at Sean Jules and stepped out into the hall. For a moment he feared Atalanta wouldn't follow him, but he heard her move behind him, a few seconds after the sound should have come.

He knew Horsefield no better than any underside lord knew his competitors' captains, primarily by a list of his distinguishing vices. Elderson, though…

It was news enough that Elderson had survived the warehouse collapse, even if it were to be expected that Saxen would have cleared his staff aside. Further news that Sean Jules respected the man enough to want to warn him of his actions. Respect: might that include fear? No. There'd been none of that vibe in Sean Jules's voice.

So. A useful man, in Sean Jules's eyes, and his eyes seemed to Connor to be clear. There were two options left.

Connor opened his jack database, selected two images and transferred them to Atalanta. "I asked Sean Jules's help earlier, about Saeed," he said over his shoulder. "He wasn't any help. Meanwhile, we need to find these two."

For a moment, the silence did not warm, but then she drew in a heavier breath. "Horsefield is upstairs," she said. "The other – Elderson – is on assignment."

"Lead me to Horsefield, then." Without reply she passed Connor and jogged up the steel-girder stairs in the hall on her tiptoes. He followed more slowly. Maybe he should hurry. Maybe she wouldn't be able to keep them hidden forever.

"It doesn't take much effort unless we're noisy," she said over her shoulder as she turned a corner and mounted the second flight. "We do show up on cameras."

Then Saxen would work all this out later. Best pray 'later' was too late. He nodded to her, and she pointed the way down the corridor at the next stair head, well-lit but near-silent, and to a door just along it. He'd done this too often already today, though now the walls closing in on him were functional pale plasterboard rather than baroque gloominess.

The apartment past the door was bare: not austere, but as if Horsefield cared little enough for his surroundings that he spent no energy arranging them. He was lying on top of the bedcovers, fully dressed bar his boots, his breathing stertorous. Connor crossed to his bedside and shook his shoulder.

His eyes snapped open and his right hand darted sideways under the pillow. "There's no need for that," Connor said quietly. "I just want to chat."

"You could have booked an appointment," Horsefield answered, keeping his voice low.

"Why would I do that?" In the absence of a chair, Connor

rocked back against the wall, lounging at what he hoped looked like ease. "It's been an interesting few days."

"It has." His eyes were watchful but his expression held little surprise. Maybe Saxen already knew Connor wasn't dying. Maybe he and his captains had already discussed what to do if Connor came calling. Maybe, maybe, maybe.

"And today is an interesting day too." Connor crooked a finger in the vague direction of the city hall. Best to assume Saxen wasn't coming away from the city hall having killed all Connor's allies in search of Connor himself. "'Mister' Saxen, beleaguered and low on materiel, is being offered a deal right now. I suggest you support the idea if he asks you for your opinion."

"The best deal for you, I guess?"

"The best deal for this planet. It may or may not be the best for me: probably. I have options, though. I have money in the bank –" Very little – "and plans for a snug base on Firedrake –" Plans that currently existed only as scribbled notes – "plus a string of export links out-sector." That, at least, was true. "If this trade doesn't see me in its immediate future I'll open a casino that never loses. I have opportunities outwith Mirqest." He raised his eyebrows in polite enquiry. "Do you?"

"Hey –"

"You've a share in your favourite two breweries, a sideline in a whorehouse, a wife tucked away in a respectable street. You want to keep that?" Connor shrugged. "The city goes for all-out six-way war, you lose everything. I've lost as much as I can here already – my further losses are minimal."

Horsefield was quiet for a minute or so, long enough for Connor to ache for a seat: he kept glancing from Connor to Atalanta as if he wondered whether he could play the one against the other. It would have been possible, if he'd known the lever, but… "What's going on?" he said in the end.

Connor exhaled. The pressure in his chest was beginning to feel overwhelming. "With Saxen's elevation, there's a gap in the upper gangland for an ambitious racketeer to fill. As you can clearly see, I'm bedridden –" Horsefield snorted – "so Mister Fai Comet has decided he wants the action. Nobody here is in a position to confront him – he and Saxen saw to that many times over the years: I was the last possible threat – so Comet's in. He has ships, people, and money. More of all of those than Saxen, since that foolish manoeuvre he pulled last night."

"Hang on –"

"So Mister Comet is visiting Mister Saxen now, to propose that Saxen take on a partner who can bring the city's upper crust on side – who can control the rest of the cops, and who has a handle on the civil service operation already." Connor gestured to the window. "Out there are a hundred thousand men and women whose job it is to keep this benighted city running – or however many aren't dead already. Do you know what they do? Do you know how to replace the dead ones most effectively? Saxen doesn't know it well enough. Now, he has someone who has the vestiges of an idea. If you want to keep your amenities, you'd best follow her lead as if she were your boss – and you'd best persuade your fellow captains and your lieutenants that their interest lies in following her too. It does, you know. As soon as those three shake hands, only one of them will be dispensable to the city, and that one will be Saxen."

"Who is she?"

"Zolde de Priet."

Horsefield laughed with more astonishment than mirth. "Her? She's a twenty-five year-old aristocrat with no more brains than a cat."

"Cats have plenty of brains, and as well as the civil service she has the police – beat cops, detectives, secret police – whoever you didn't kill. She can reclaim order outside the underside zones. If Saxen doesn't accept her input there'll be a counter-revolution within a week, and she'll end on top of the heap anyway." Connor pushed off the wall and made for the door. "A hundred of the upper crust, each with one or two ships and a crew of household guards. Can your team, alone, crush that now? I won't help. I'd send in any bourgeois or aristocratic relatives I can rustle up to make a peace of sorts between my team and theirs."

Horsefield shook his head slowly. "You're an *arms dealer*. You'd *profit* from a good little counter-revolution."

"I profit from warfare. I prefer that fighting to take place a long way away from me. Call it cowardice, if you like: I call it good sense."

He nodded to Horsefield, more grudgingly than he had to Sean Jules, and retreated into the corridor with Atalanta. "Where's Elderson?" he said.

"Guard captain at the SBC offices. Nothing to steal…"

"They do." Connor, eyes flicking to each side, listening and even *sniffing* for approach, led her back downstairs. "You're thinking in physical terms. Think in terms of contacts, guard ships around the sector. Think of gold deposits sitting in highly secure and highly secret locations many sectors away – even in uninhabitable zones – and think of what could be done to lever some of that into bank funds for a particularly persistent warlord."

"And the other banks?"

"I'd assume they were in the same position. Given time, and not much of that, they would have coughed up enough for Saxen to have bought those ships from Cliff if he hadn't antagonised them off-planet first."

When she didn't answer, he looked back up at her over one shoulder. She'd stopped on an upper tread and was watching him, mouse to a snake rather than her usual mongoose impression. "Did he offer them a downpayment?"

Connor shrugged. "Do you care?" When she still hadn't answered after ten seconds, he turned and headed for the rear door by which they'd entered.

When he peered into the kitchen from the corridor, he saw only the girl who'd been outside earlier, now standing over the sink contemplating a dirty skillet: she did not look up as Connor and Atalanta passed the doorway. Back outside, they hugged the wall under a security camera, listening for engine trails. Marcello had parked in too close an alley. Saxen's empire, its foundations a-tremble, still spread around them. *Take care.*

Now they might be spotted, a man and a woman running to a grounded car in the early light, scrambling into its back seat and being driven away too quickly, and Connor thought he might have heard a shout behind as he closed the door: but he made no comment to Marcello, just let the young man drive at Atalanta's instruction. Exhaustion dragged at the back of his neck, a weight almost at his personal max. When had he last used the gym? He'd never been as fond of training as, say, Logan or Thakar. Best he learnt.

Best assume he didn't have Logan or Thakar to back him up, again, ever. However much he wanted it.

"I may need you out of the car when we get there," he said to Marcello. "It's not your muscle, it's your shoulder stripes." He glanced to Atalanta, beside him. "Unless you want to flash your stripy wings instead."

"Right now I prefer that to any thought of the car being stolen."

"There's a first time for everything."

They drove in silence for another few minutes – time passed quickly at a cruising speed of a hundred and fifty miles an hour – till Marcello said, "We're coming up on the site, Mister."

Connor squinted ahead. They were well into the city's high-end now: glass and granite shone in the pale sunlight. Even here were dark clefts where bombs or overhead cannons had struck, the latter by accident, the former by design.

Take a gun, or a knife, or a grenade. Use it for its intended purpose: to kill. Kill in such a cacophony and such a firestorm that one seemed a child, a child whose stock in trade was screaming loudly and being obeyed.

Connor blinked into the morning. Skyscrapers reared below, pantheons of wealth: the SBC's logo, gilded and grand, shone from the upper storeys of one tower straight ahead. "Atalanta, where is he?"

"Checking roof guards."

"OK. Marcello, land on the roof. No more equivocating."

Marcello decelerated enough to pull the car into a sharp descent spiral, tight across the roof, almost low enough to tear off its belly on the asphalt: he swung it sideways across the rooftop door to the stairwell, blocking off escape, side on to Elderson and his stunned guard crew, framed against the parapet. Through the thermaglass windows Connor heard the captain shouting to his mercs to fire. The car shook.

Atalanta cracked her door – on the car's right, the far side from Saxen's team – and rolled out onto the roof. Her gun spat thrice: one blast under the car, two blasts over its bonnet.

War-shouts cut out, replaced by cries.

Connor, already halfway towards Atalanta's open side door, switched direction and opened his door, on the left of the car, instead. "We won't need you after all," he muttered to Marcello, and he stepped out of the car with pistol in hand.

One of the mercs was down, clutching his right hand, its fingers burnt till white stumps showed through burnt flesh. The other squad merc, her weapon reduced to a pile of slag on the asphalt, was dragging her mate towards the fire escape. Elderson was upright. His left hand was still wrapped round his rifle butt. The rest of the rifle was absent. Atalanta, wings ablaze, advanced towards him, ignoring the two grunts. He backed away, stumbling a little on the seared roofing, leading Atalanta further from his juniors.

"How the fuck did you get out of there?" Elderson said over Atalanta's shoulder to Connor, his voice a breath from steady. Yes, he was good, maybe as good as Sean Jules thought.

"How does any man survive anything?" Connor skirted Atalanta's closer wing. Her wings were bigger than she was, making her seem Logan's size: if he ignored the glow and the white skin it might feel like his brother still had his back. "You've had a busy few days."

"It happens," Elderson said with a shrug. "What do you want?"

"Restitution. What does any man want?" Connor advanced, keeping Atalanta between himself and Saxen's grunt pair. One of the two might have a boot pistol. "Your boss wanted too big a leap. Greed may be useful, but too much of it in a man of his position gets people killed."

"My boss is on the up."

"On the way back down now." Elderson was two feet from the roof edge. Maybe if he dropped off of his own accord he'd catch onto a window ledge. Connor fired. His gunshot hit Elderson's left knee. He hissed and his leg shivered under him. His leathers, though, remained intact.

"Shields," Atalanta said in the background.

"I'd noticed. You'd think he would have thought of the possibility…" Connor fired again, same leg. This time it gave way. Blast pressure: sufficient. "I assume Saxen's are better."

"Until Gisele does a little discreet damage."

"She is discreet, isn't she?" Connor advanced. Elderson flung his rifle butt at Connor's face and launched himself upwards, pushing off from his unhurt right leg. Connor ducked missile and man both, and Elderson went sprawling.

"Your boss has a new business partner," Connor said, high above him feeling himself all the taller. "I don't think you're her type."

He flipped Elderson onto his back with one boot-toe. The man struck upwards with his right arm, aiming for Connor's knee joint. When he connected he drew his hand back with a cry. Yellow sparks, last trace of Éloise's gifts, trailed after him.

Connor staggered – the blow jarred right up his spine and came a feather from knocking him over – and reached down and grabbed Elderson's collar. "All for one Fed-bred runaway?" Elderson panted.

"Runaway and gone away," Connor answered, face an inch from the other man's, close enough to smell his overnight breath. "You were too late. Take note: if you reincarnate any time soon, don't kill any of mine next time. Even factory crew and cleaning staff." He released Elderson and shoved him backwards. Elderson landed on the roof edge and, his face grey with sudden terror, slipped backwards. For half a second his left hand's fingers gripped the guttering. Then they slipped free and he was gone.

Connor rose slowly and turned towards the merc pair. They'd stopped before the fire escape, staring at Connor in something close to horror, clinging together now for more than physical support. "You heard," Connor said, his voice harsh. He'd bitten his lip. Blood trickled down his throat, acid-sharp. "Your boss has a new business partner. I approve of her. Start obeying her."

He turned and strode towards the car. Arm, ribs and knee all ached abominably. Almost there. Saxen's deputies suborned, dead or running. Saxen's line staff, de Priet's.

If he could excise that burning look in Atalanta's eyes, he'd be laughing.

*

CHAPTER TWENTY-EIGHT

The *crack* of Atalanta's fist striking Connor's cheek sounded like broken partnerships. Instead of speaking, he explored his oral mucosa with his tongue. Blood, where his teeth had impacted on his mouth. He'd bled too much lately. The one minor plus was that she'd saved this till they got back to the office and into his study.

"Why I should have thought I could trust an undersider I don't know." Her accent had shifted, no longer a light Federation twang but distinctly more distant, and it had risen at least one social register at the same time. "I needed –"

"He didn't."

Sapphire blue eyes flinted a glare at him. "Your position –"

"My position in your affairs is as a bystander. You aren't my employee and neither am I yours. If money had changed hands in either direction, I would have at least considered doing what you wanted. You assumed. Assumptions are dangerous."

As was his assumption that if she'd wanted to kill him she would have already done so – but he didn't raise that point. Instead he watched her as he might watch a cat prowling round his study.

He could have a dozen people inside in thirty seconds. She could maim him in less than three. Her wings were beginning to glitter: thirteen spell-threads, all thirteen lethal if she were inventive enough. Why thirteen threads of the weave? Why not fourteen, or eleven, or a million?

"You'll survive this," he said, "at least when you eventually do find him and realise I've ensured he isn't a threat to the Federation. Far less of a threat, certainly, than Nerys had planned."

Still pacing, Atalanta spat to one side, a Septième gesture that didn't fit the rest of her demeanour. "I knew she was on the take."

"She wasn't. She was a loyal Union agent all along. I don't separate the interests of the UISS government from that of its major corporations – that's a pretty fiction for the UISS populace's benefit – after all, you don't separate the interests of the Federation from that of its weapon manufacturers. Why don't you merge Qinliang and Jürgenhoff, by the way? They're both nationalised."

"Specialisation," she answered, on automatic.

"Which makes it easier to hide their doings from each other – including trading that they can't afford to be seen doing – don't argue: I got a contract out of Jürgenhoff before I got one out of White Canyon." Admittedly it had been for Union equipment, but, still.

She stopped her pacing and stared him down again. "I shouldn't say a *word* to you –"

"Then don't. Keep your secrets and your integrity. Keep me clear of your machinations."

"I aim for the best interests of the *Septième* – and all the contested sectors – as well as the Federation."

Connor unbuckled his pistol belt in what he hoped was a sufficiently ostentatious motion, dropped it on his desk, sank into his chair and leant back. "Contested sectors. That's a phrase I've not heard since the last time I watched *Flight to Victory*. It was a bad feed: kept jumping around. Admittedly I was planet-hopping at the time in the back hold of some rustbucket Hamadryad. I think I was fourteen."

"Technological advance –"

"Keeps us all safe as long as nobody uses it. You know that. Just as I know that anything I sell to any given individual or corporation has done him, her or it its best job when it is never used."

"You can't stop history." She waved a hand at the city outside. "Think because you changed the future of one little planet you can affect the galaxy? You can't. Not unless you want to bring about another dark age – to invoke calamity. Saeed could have reconstructed his engine."

"Saeed maintains only idiocy stopped the whole thing working in the first place."

She nodded. "I believe that."

"And though you'd rebuild it quicker with him, you still have intelligent men and women – and the prototypes – and lacking him will just lose you a little time in recreating the work." Connor pulled his cigarette case from his upper drawer, slowly drew out a cigarette, and lit it. He didn't want the cigarette: he wanted another couple of seconds for thoughts to mature in his head. "It doesn't matter where he is. He is, ultimately, irrelevant. His invention would have fallen into Union hands in the end – they always do: unless you were planning an invasion in the interim?" He pretended to smile. Blood still stained his teeth, he knew. "I can't view that with equanimity. I know what happened to us last time."

She shook her head. "I don't know what our warhawks plan, as opposed to what they crow about in the media. I do know the thought of war is absurd."

"Unless your 'warhawks' thought your advantage were enough. A superior engine?" He shrugged. "What good will an engine do against a butt-ton of Circle Spellweavers? The Guild hasn't the manpower."

"Never presume. Never take us for granted. The Union doesn't, and neither does the Circle."

"I will never in my life take peace for granted, not of a city, an underside gang, a sector or any given jurisdiction. I repeat, I know what happens when peace fails."

She laughed, like a bird's caw. "An arms trader talking peace. You actually believe all that dung you're spouting? You, personally, have maimed and killed more people on the Septième than – for want of a better metaphor, than I have. You've propped up a dozen dictators – hells, you're propping up the next dictator here – and for why?"

He shrugged, cigarette dangling from his lower lip. "The money's good."

She hissed between her teeth, glaring at him as if he were a cockroach, and strode out of the study, slamming the door behind her. Connor waited five seconds, then ten, and then stood, cracked open the window behind his head, pitched out the cigarette and closed his eyes.

If she'd continued the conversation, she might have worked out where Saeed was hiding, or if he hadn't encouraged her temper to mount she might have been calm enough to ask him. Not that she wouldn't be able to calculate it on her own when she realised Yasmine was missing.

Connor frowned. A headache was starting to pull at his

forehead again. Even if Yasmine had already landed on Port Logis, she definitely wouldn't have had time yet to jettison Saeed in anything near safety and leave: Connor still had time to contact Éloise and tell her not to send her cousin back. He couldn't bring himself to trust Yasmine now.

He could at least cloak the decision in a little diplomacy. He pushed open the door to his bedroom – some servant had straightened the furnishings, changed his bedsheets and opened the window long enough for the Lagavulin fumes to fade – and pulled a tiny rucksack from the top of his wardrobe. He wouldn't need many clothes: just one change, and a couple of bits of equipment. With a light sigh, he pulled spare underclothes from their drawer and plucked a presentable shirt from the wardrobe.

Back in the study, the door to the corridor creaked, and pink-and-white movement in the corner of his eye meant Gisele was edging inside. "Running away?" she said.

"I understand Saxen's still alive. I need to visit Mina's daughter, but after that I can spend the next few days more profitably behind a desk on Port Logis than I can hiding in a broom cupboard here."

"Port Logis in the aftermath of a family election? You surprise me."

"Democracy's welcome after the last few days." He tossed a spare pistol into his bag and pulled the tie shut. "Éloise?"

"Yes. She'll have you babysitting a whole roomful of someone or other's toddlers."

"I'll welcome the comparative quiet. Thakar can cover me here until Saxen's safely dead, and I can hire a new bodyguard while I'm over there." Connor re-entered the study, dropping his rucksack on the floor by the bedroom door. "I'm surprised you left de Priet."

"I came back to pack. I'm most use if I move in with her for a week or two. There's rather a trust gap going on." She sighed, with some reproach in the sound. "Including here. You could have handled Atalanta better."

"She's too well-bred to harbour much of a grudge for long, and too intelligent. When she calms down she'll realise she can use this to lean on me for ten years."

Gisele closed the door to the corridor and sank down into

the comfortable client chair. "I confess, that went a little past me."

It was enough to make him laugh: the ghost of a sound, barely enough to stain the air. "I've done well if I've confused a telempath. I liked Saeed, what little I saw of him. He had the balls to travel quarter of the way round the galaxy – intending to up that to halfway round – at a woman's vague promise of safety, knowing that her promise wasn't worth a damn, because his superiors had offended his principles. He had that much respect for the soldiers and skymen sent to test his invention. Had the intelligence to trust the replacement girl, too."

"Replacement?"

"Merissa."

"But Nerys was Saeed's contact. She got him from the spaceport –"

"No. Nerys was meant to go to the 'port, but she stuck around in town to occupy Atalanta's attention: it was all our bad luck, especially hers, that Atalanta didn't start looking till too late. *Merissa* took Saeed off to hide, wearing Nerys's clothes. *Nerys* turned up dead in Merissa's flat and Merissa's clothes the next morning."

A long pause ensued. "Are you sure?" she said in the end, faint stress laid on the last word.

"The body's in the hospital morgue. Even if Cliff Enterprises doesn't have a record of Nerys's DNA pattern they're willing to send me, Aled was Nerys's first cousin: a DNA swab from him – however I have to get it – establishes relationship or lack thereof." Connor shrugged. "Nerys wouldn't have thought to hide in my warehouse vault. She almost certainly wouldn't have been able to get into it. Merissa, on the other hand, had access to all kinds of items with my fingerprints and DNA on them, and she could walk straight into the warehouse itself without attracting attention. They were very alike in build and colouring, though not at all facially, and not in hairstyle. I could buy – for instance – that if Nerys had wanted Merissa's clothes as a disguise and didn't want to pay her, or Merissa wanted to pinch Nerys's whole identity and run away out-sector, either could have killed the other as an initial step. But for two women to swap clothes *and* get busy with a set of hair straighteners on the one hand and curling tongs on the other, it's likely they both were alive and happy to do it.

"And then there were her fingers. Merissa had fingers broken many years ago: they set crooked. The dead body had fingers broken after death. Why, if not to disguise the fact that they weren't actually Merissa's? Then there was the whole issue of how the body – dead or alive at the time, probably alive – got into Merissa's flat. All we had to go on were the security camera images, which showed nothing. Nerys was immune to magic, and magic is a form of electromagnetic energy. Nulls don't show up on most security cameras either."

After a pause, Gisele said, "She didn't commit suicide, whichever she was."

"No."

"And Pritie told me that *no one* showed up on the security pictures."

"Something that was – and still is – immensely suspicious: it also never fitted a random Septième street tough murdering a drifter woman. No one would have taken that much trouble to cover up killing a drifter."

Gisele frowned, more in thought than disagreement. "Ilsa…"

"Yes?" Connor prompted when she didn't continue.

She rose. "Let me call her on your tangler."

"She headed off without leaving contact details." Taking with her any likelihood of a contract. *Damn* his luck.

"I have her private details," Gisele said as if to an impatient child, "but I don't have tangler service on my jack."

"She can't help us now."

"She can. Nerys, magic, lack thereof." She was still frowning, but in a more purposeful manner. "I wonder if it wasn't just her." She seated herself at the desk. "Is this thing on?"

"I don't know. Maybe not." Connor crossed behind his desk, opened the control unit on the wall and reached for the ON button.

The door creaked open again. "I'm busy, Marcello," Connor said without looking up.

A soft *phut*, and fire exploded across the tangler control unit, spitting hot metal into the air. Connor flung his left arm up to cover his eyes. Hot metal sparks slammed into his forearm. He dived backwards with his right hand out backwards, towards his gun belt.

"Freeze," said a soft voice from the door: a soft, cultured, Union voice, that of a man who could do exactly as he wished. Connor's extended right hand collided with the desk. The shock running up his arm jarred into his teeth. Still three useless feet from his gun, Connor lowered his arm, looked up slowly, and saw Aled.

Aled, Nerys's first cousin: holding a pistol as if he'd spent some hours on a shooting range. Not as many as Connor, likely, but given he was the only man in the room holding a gun, that didn't matter a ha'penny. Arm stinging, head aching, Connor straightened up and held his hands where Aled could see them. "So Mikhail's blood was tainted from the war. I thought so when I saw my bodyguard force him into a rabid mob."

"He was spineless and my cousin was an idiot."

"That doesn't explain why you stayed here to play his decoy. Or were you going to kill him too if he hadn't met another mischance?" Connor risked a glance sideways at Gisele. She was sitting statue-still in Connor's chair, a degree of shock Connor'd never seen in any Spellweaver spreading across her face. "What?" he said.

"I can't sense him. At all."

"Stay where you are," Aled said.

"I'm staying, I'm staying." Connor fought for a grip on himself. Gun out of reach. *Think, think.* To Gisele he said, "Devils save it, you're looking straight at him."

"He's another null." Her voice was tiny. "I was going to ask Ilsa…" She faded into silence, eloquent of a thousand tiny mistakes.

Connor's left arm was in spasm. He couldn't control it. Old pain, new pain. If he could reach the desk intercom, he'd be able to summon help. If he could reach his *jack phone*, he'd be able to summon help. He pressed his tongue against the side of his jaw. Nothing happened, just more blood, coursing down the inside of his cheek, from Atalanta's earlier slap.

Atalanta. Calad. *Call Calad*, he thought as loudly as he could, in the hope Gisele was listening and not just sitting frozen with stupefaction. To Aled he said, "What do you want? If you just wanted to shoot us you'd have done it already."

"I need to get off-planet. The ship Ilsa left is gone."

Connor could have kissed Yasmine at that, or flung her into an incinerator. "I wonder how that happened?"

Temper flared in Aled's eyes and subsided. "I can't get a ship at the 'port. There's too much going on. You can get me one: you can get anything. Those Cyclopes – Martinez's wife hasn't collected them all yet."

"At least two were destroyed."

"Four destroyed, one out of commission for months." *Four*? Connor restrained a whistle. Four Cyclopes down plus however many older ships: he'd give a nice handful of marks to look over Ilsa's ship weaponry. If he had any marks. If he didn't have a gun pointing at his chest. "Six are on duty or are being watched too closely. One is still shut down in dock. I need it."

Connor had definitely bled too much. The office was swimming: sound and light and a million thoughts cascading into each other, inescapable. "I can't help you to it. I'm an arms trader, not a hacker."

Aled smiled. "So you do know what's wrong with it." Connor winced. Mikhail's face swam from memory into the light. Connor might have liked Mikhail, maybe, if he'd had the opportunity and hadn't kept up his suspicion of the man. He'd done him an appalling turn at least twice over.

"Stand still," Aled barked. "Both of you."

"I am standing still," Connor said. His arm kept quivering of its own volition. Might be enough to set off Aled.

"When would I have learnt to shoot?" Gisele said. Her voice was steadier than it had any right to be. In her place Connor would have felt inclined to piss himself. Her one weapon, unusable.

"Mikhail changed that ship's dead-codes," he said. "He added a verbal password. I don't know what it was: he didn't tell me and I didn't ask. He died immediately afterwards." Another tiny link coruscated inside his brain. "You torched the temple of Beauty."

"The priest was drunk, as he had been all evening. A candle fell over."

"That's blasphemy," Gisele said.

Blasphemy, for him, for her, for all of them. "They got married. That night. They tossed the priest a hundred marks to marry them while Merissa went off to fetch Saeed." Aled didn't answer. "She took you to Merissa's flat for a joke and told you what they'd done, so you killed her."

Aled shrugged. "I loved my cousin. I love my mother more, and my brothers."

"And yourself."

"Yes, I'd have been killed too. Wouldn't you kill for your brother? Don't you see?" He took half a step towards Connor. "Throw an unstoppable fanatical mage-corps at me and what was I *meant* to do? Now – there's no proof of anything. Fine. No wedding. We're all safe. But I need to –"

The air sparked with a sudden *pop* in front of Connor's eyes. Aled blinked twice, and with a finality born of pure surprise, he crumpled to the floor, pistol falling with him.

Connor gripped the desk's edge, crisp wood under his fingers like a razor in a sheath, and looked down at Gisele. She was still sitting bolt upright in his desk chair, staring straight ahead, at the gap where Aled had been standing rather than at the heap he'd made on the ground. Connor's pistol was in her right hand.

"Dominic taught me to shoot," she said, in a voice that echoed beyond graves and beyond sanity. "Straight after we were married. He said I was too old to learn any other form of self-defence well enough to pass muster on the Neuvième, and he knew I would never let anyone else know I could do this – he knew from the day we first met that I never let anyone know anything until it was too late – we worked over and over at the firing ranges, whenever we had an excuse to go off together. Dominic…" The pistol slid to the floor, and she dropped her face into her hands and began to cry.

Connor, his left arm still burning, knelt beside her and embraced her with his right arm. She collapsed onto his shoulder, weeping down his neck. His eyes were sore. Last gift from Dominic, or first from Gisele: a second chance.

He took a few deep breaths till he trusted his voice not to quaver, and smacked the desk intercom with his left fist without opening his hand. "Cleaning staff to my study." Once that would have included Merissa, till she'd smiled at a foreign boy while she put her feet up after work. Four young faces in a photograph on the desk. Connor knocked the photo projection chip into range of his right hand, took it between finger and thumb, and crushed it.

As gently as he could, he eased Gisele to her feet and steered her into his bedroom. Now he could bless those fresh sheets. "You can cry in private here," he said, forcing sympathy into his voice. "One thing – Ilsa's private contact details…"

*

CHAPTER TWENTY-NINE

Aled's gunshot had shorted the tangler relays. Connor took a couple of minutes to calm Thakar down, then sent him to retrieve Joshua from the Bramhall estate, told Jack Priest and Pritie to find an electrician, and drove to the 'port, or more accurately had Marcello drive him as his left arm was a throbbing mess and his right hand was severely bruised. He'd had his first aiders dig the metal splinters out of his left arm rather than disturbing Calad. Atalanta having gone to pour her frustrations into her husband's ears, and possibly his genitals, had some bearing on Connor's decision.

He did not speak during the drive, just stared out of the window at the city damage already being repaired and the police forces – mingled already, albeit with some internal hostile glances – swarming every junction. Nods exchanged between police bikers and underside bikers buoyed him. A glimpse of understanding? Hardly, except in the cooperation between those police who had run on the gangland with Martinez and those undersiders who'd lived their whole lives on the Septième. But even a fragile peace formed a foundation.

Once at the 'port, he bypassed both the damage and the security teams' attempts to wave him down, and had Marcello drive him to *Shadowmark*'s hangar. "Stay outside," he advised his bodyguard as they pulled up alongside the ship. "She might not bite if she knew we had an audience."

Marcello pulled a face but nodded. "Want me to winnow applications while you're busy, Mister?"

Connor paused with his right leg outside the car and his left leg still in the footwell. "Applications for what?"

"A stack of protection rackets wanting your name on them. A couple of merc strings wanting to shift bosses. Forty or fifty petty merchants asking for your trade."

"No slaves, no drugs, and no whores who don't own their own brothels. I'll take everything else." He climbed out of the car, slapped the ship's ramp release and jogged inside the ship before he could stop and think about implications: that Marcello had taken it on himself to check Connor's business letterbox, or that Connor had received the letters at all.

The hatch lights came on automatically as Connor stepped inside. He headed straight to his study. Last time he'd been in here, he'd had Ilsa in front of him: maybe it was better that they now spoke separated by several thousand light years. If he saw her in person he would find it hard to keep his temper.

Gisele had hiccupped Ilsa's personal tangler code rather than reading it out straight. After a minor error caused by trying to switch on the tangler with his left hand, a subsequent pause for swearing, and the tangler's rejection of Connor's first code attempt as invalid, he deleted one of the duplicated numbers in the putative code, settled back in his chair and tried again.

Too late he realised he had no idea what planet and city Ilsa had gone to – the centres of Terra Nova and Sukli Ban were favourite, but she could have headed to any of a thousand planets – and therefore had no idea what time zone she would be in. He risked a grim smile at his own reflection in the panelling opposite. She'd inconvenienced him more than a little over the past few days: her turn now.

The tangler chimed its *connecting, connecting* buzz. Connor waited, drumming his good right fingers on the desk. He should have brewed some tea before he started. Coffee was starting to strike him as singularly uncivilised.

Click. Call terminated. Connor re-entered the code.

Buzz. Buzz. Call connected.

"This had better be urgent," Ilsa's voice floated out of the speakers. "No work calls on my personal line."

"Hello, Mistress Martins." Silence on the other end of the line. "I regret to inform you that I am alive and that I've located all the missing persons. Sorry to disappoint you on that regard. And if you cut me off I will call you back via a telempath who will bill you for the experience."

The ensuing silence was so deep that for a moment Connor wondered if she had cut the call, despite the tangler's lights maintaining their steady green flash. When he'd decided she wasn't going to answer him, Connor continued, "I really wanted to ask you... did you know she was playing away?

When you wiped your hands of her I was a little surprised, but it all makes so much more sense if you realised she'd done what would inevitably end up as an embarrassment. You're meant to be a trustworthy company, Cliff Enterprises. It would be very beneficial in the long run to host a spy keen on prising secrets out of the Federation – and would inevitably score you a few political points – but from a commercial perspective, and especially from that of maintaining your Federation trade, you couldn't have it publicly known, especially by anyone as distasteful or as talkative as a crowd of Septième riff-raff, that not only was Nerys spying via your company but relied on its protection. She did have a rather rare talent to assist her, I give her that."

"'Did'. I assume she's dead."

"Her cousin murdered her. I'm surprised, with your level of background checking, you didn't realise Mikhail's family had an interesting past. Or maybe you did. Maybe you worked out the whole thing, and saw you had an opportunity to try to rid yourself of both him and Aled by leaving them here." Connor allowed himself a light laugh. "The Circle might call to find out if you were hiding any more war criminals' sixty-times-great-grandchildren, if they thought it worthwhile... that's two. Shall we go for three?"

"You needn't."

"But I will anyway. Here goes. You realised from the outset there was something wrong with the Cyclops transaction. Otherwise you wouldn't have brought a full negotiating team along with the security team: the negotiations should have been over already. You went ahead with the transaction but kept all the dead-codes locked down – when ordinarily they would have been reset upon handover." He smiled at his empty office. His reflection in the metal wall-trim looked worn, aged, flecked with tiny scars. "What would your clients say if they knew you'd ever kept hold of a ship consignment's dead-codes?"

"They'd realise we'd taken appropriate precautions against being conned or being dragged into illegal activity."

"Appropriate precautions would have involved holding the deal till you had a string of warships in orbit, enough to outgun the sales goods. You couldn't do that because Nerys was pushing you to keep to the original schedule. You didn't ask her why… or maybe you knew. Did you, Mistress, know the details of the commercial espionage? Did you know she was planning to meet a Circle Spellweaver here –" one who'd been sidetracked by a domestic argument – "to help smooth Saeed's transfer into the Union? Does the Federation intelligence officer I have adjacent to my staff –" likely horizontally adjacent by now, unless she and Calad had gone out to find an open dance club as a form of foreplay, cheeks and chests pressing together in smoke-scented dawn as their feet carried them across sprung floorboards – "know that you were a party to spying? How's your *personal* security, Mistress?"

"What do you want?" she said, sounding aggrieved.

"I want to be named your export agent and reproduction contact for the Septième sector. Commercial basis, cuts back to you as standard, my capital at risk and so on. I have a range of credentials to prove I'm up to it."

"That's all?"

"Nearly. You destroyed or rendered utterly inoperable six of the twelve Cyclopes you sold to Rafael Martinez. His widow wants a refund on those six."

"Some of those *attacked us* on the way off-planet."

"They'd been stolen, which was possible only due to your negligence over the dead-codes – that negligence prevented Mister Martinez's employees from stopping the theft."

"We disabled *five* –"

"And your situation would have been worse if Mistress de Priet's employees hadn't been able to restart a couple that the thieves couldn't use." Connor's employees, on secondment, but he'd pass over that part. "One ship is on concrete unable to be unlocked. Mikhail nuked its dead-codes and set it to verbal password: I saw him do it. I also saw him die at a mob's hands less than fifteen minutes later. Your employee, Mistress: your responsibility."

"Six," she said with an air of resignation. "However many private wars you want to start under Cliff Enterprises' auspices, Mister, you will find the company does not approve of such activities."

"You'll be amazed to hear I don't plan on starting any.

Contract form?"

"In the morning."

"Now. You have standard contracts, I'm sure. I'll wait."

In her place he might have sworn a time or two. She did not. In the distance he heard her clattering about – possibly in a bedroom, whether or not shared with anyone else – and, after a moment, heard her writing.

"I've sent the contracts," she said a moment later. She sounded snippy but not entirely hostile. If she were smart she would be able to make a good profit out of him – if he were smart in his turn. "Anything *else*?"

"One minor issue. Aled pulled a gun on me in my office and was shot by one of my team for his pains. You'll get the repair bill shortly." He cut the line before she could object.

He closed his eyes for a long moment, listening to the ship's silence in a world of noise and fear. Maybe he should have saved that last speck of information until he needed it, rather than brandish an ill-chosen club at the close of a profitable conversation, but one more little hold he could keep over Ilsa might prove all he needed. Or he might have assassins sent after him... but he would have Éloise back soon enough.

The tangler beeped, contract received, and Connor diverted the document to his desk. He signed and returned it, and rose. As he reached to turn off the tangler, it flashed again, with a trio of new messages: compliance bulletin, corporate security policies, internal newsletter. He sent them to save to his jack – for bedtime reading – and left the tiny study.

As he stepped onto *Shadowmark*'s ramp he saw Marcello was still bending over the car's dashboard reading from notepads and, Connor guessed, his jack. He did not disturb the younger man, but walked out of the hangar into the 'port's connecting corridors.

Reject anyone a Circle Spellweaver found ideologically abhorrent. Anyone opposed to Zolde de Priet holding Mirqest: Meris Hardblade could swing it for now. Anyone starting a war... no, wars were fine so long as he armed both sides sufficiently to make each, independently, too afraid of the other to strike. Anything that would embarrass Éloise if it were brought up in parliament or family council. Anything that would prove harmful to Cliff Enterprises.

Last time he'd been here, drifters had raced past him heedless of consequence: now it seemed they slowed to a jog as they passed, stared a little more openly and with a little less bravado, despite the left arm that still dangled at his side. Connor plucked a coin from his belt and, without breaking stride, held it towards a girl barely into her teens. "Which hangar is the stalled Cyclops in?" he said. He knew already. He wanted to hear someone tell him the truth. *Never tangle with authority.* Maybe he could become authority.

"It's in C-181, Mister."

"Thank you." He tossed her the coin. She turned tail from her fellows and darted into a side corridor. Connor threaded through the youthful stampede that followed and into the C-hangars' commercial zone.

There was a cop on duty outside C-178, the home hangar for one of the surviving ships from the consignment: she nodded to Connor as he passed. "Everything OK with the new ships?" Connor said.

She nodded with an air of pride. "We'll get a proper sky force going soon enough. Half what we wanted till the repair crews are done, but we'll take it and grateful. Got spare parts for the shot-up one too."

"Wise way to think." Connor nodded, less than a bow, and headed into C-181.

Six ships. He stared up at the Cyclops in front of him, spindly stratification of space-based power, its arc-wings bristling with weaponry Connor could price with some accuracy – into the millions of marks for the twenty claw-cannons alone – and the central eye, the burst gun capable of such devastating attacks on petty shipping.

Six ships, the police and de Priet counted themselves as having, plus one requiring months of repairs, plus whatever salvage they could scrape together. They'd given up on this one. Connor lifted the neural access port at the ship's hatch. It showed signs of tampering, whether by random drifters or by de Priet's staff – or Saxen's – failing to gain entry. The attempt wasn't surprising, and nor was it surprising to find the ship still locked down: Cliff supplied quality anti-crypt and anti-intrusion measures, when it chose to use them.

He fired up the entrance command prompt. A string rippled across the screen, requesting codes. VERBAL BYPASS, he entered.

PASSWORD? prompted the AI.

Connor pursed his lips. One chance before the AI locked him out along with everyone else. Mikhail had grown up with overly romantic parents, and if they'd filled his ears with notions from far away…

"Nerys Chester," he said into the microphone.

A pause, and then the hatch unrolled in front of him and the screen flickered to welcome mode. CHANGE PASS CODE, Connor typed. The prompt arose obligingly.

He half-closed his eyes. "I'll be damned," he whispered to himself, and he meant it.

He filled in a new dead-code, and then up the ramp he walked. The hatch opened for him. He stood with one foot on the ramp and one inside the ship, staring at the blister-bright newness: a ship polished and clean and pristine, a far cry from the underside's usual reclaimed or rebuilt rustbuckets armed with whatever could be fitted to a handy gun port.

And he hadn't even had to kill anyone to get it.

"I'll call her *Nerys*," he said aloud to the silent air, as if in apology to Mikhail, but, in speaking, he knew he would buy an identical Cyclops as soon as he had the funds, and would name that one *Merissa*.

THE END

Elsewhen Press

an independent publisher specialising in Speculative Fiction

Visit the Elsewhen Press website at elsewhen.press for the latest information on all of our titles, authors and events; to read our blog; find out where to buy our books and ebooks; or to place an order.

Sign up for the Elsewhen Press InFlight Newsletter at elsewhen.press/newsletter

SAILOR TO A SIREN
ZOË SUMRA

Sailor to a Siren is a space opera novel with significant nods to the gangland thriller genre.

"If you like your space opera fast and violent, this book is for you"
– Jaine Fenn

When Connor and Logan Cardwain, a gangster's lieutenants, steal a shipment of high-grade narcotics on the orders of their boss, Connor dreams of diverting the profits and setting up in business for himself. His plans encounter a hurdle in the form of Éloise Falavière, Logan's former girlfriend, who has been hired by an interplanetary police force's vice squad.

Logan wants a family; Éloise wants to stop the drugs shipment from being sent to her home planet; Connor wants to gain independence without angering his boss. All of their plans are derailed, though, when they discover that the shipment was hiding a much deadlier secret – the prototype of a tiny superweapon powerful enough to destabilise galactic peace.

Crime lords, corrupt officials and interstellar magicians soon begin pursuing them, and Connor, Logan and Éloise realise they have to identify and confront the superweapon's smuggler in order to survive. But, when one by one their friends begin to betray them, their self-imposed mission transforms from difficult to near-impossible.

Sailor to a Siren is a great debut from Zoë Sumra and establishes her as a name to watch in epic space opera. These are stories that Zoë has been thinking about, preparing and crafting for many years; stories that deserve to be told, from a story-teller who deserves to be heard.

ISBN: 9781908168771 (epub, kindle) / ISBN: 9781908168672 (288pp paperback)

Visit bit.ly/SailorSiren

Don't Look Back

John Gribbin

"A real scientist writing science-fiction with real science – what more could one ask? John Gribbin is a visionary, and one heck of a good storyteller."
– **Robert J. Sawyer**
Hugo Award-winning author of QUANTUM NIGHT

Retrospective SF short story collection from the master science writer

John Gribbin, widely regarded as one of the best science writers of the 20th century, has also, unsurprisingly, been writing science fiction for many years. While his novels are well-known, his short stories are perhaps less so. He has also written under pseudonyms. Here, for the first time, is the definitive collection of John's short stories. Many were originally published in *Analog* and other magazines. Some were the seeds of subsequent novels. As well as 23 Science Fiction short stories, three of which John wrote with his son Ben, this collection includes two Science Fact essays on subjects beloved of science fiction authors and readers. In one essay, John provides scientifically accurate DIY instructions for creating a time machine; and in the other, he argues that the Moon is, in fact, a Babel Fish!

The stories, many written at a time when issues such as climate change were taken less seriously, now seem very relevant again in an age of dubious politicians. What underpins all of them, of course, is a grounding in solid science. But they are also laced with a dry and subtle wit, which will not come as a surprise to anyone who has ever met John at a science fiction convention or elsewhere. He is, however, not averse to a good pun, as evidenced by a song he co-wrote for the Bonzo Dog Doo Dah Band: *The Holey Cheeses of Nazareth.*

Despite the exhortation of this collection's title, this *is* a perfect opportunity to look back at John's short stories. If you've never read any of his fiction before, now you have the chance to acquaint yourself with a body of work that, while being very much of its time, is certainly not in any way out of date.

With a cover especially created by legendary space artist David A. Hardy.

ISBN: 9781911409182 (epub, kindle) / ISBN: 9781911409083 (272pp paperback)

Visit bit.ly/DontLookBackJohnGribbin

Existence is
Elsewhen

Twenty stories from twenty great authors
including
John Gribbin
Rhys Hughes
Christopher Nuttall
Douglas Thompson

The title *Existence is Elsewhen* paraphrases the last sentence of André Breton's 1924 *Manifesto of Surrealism*, perfectly summing up the intent behind this anthology of stories from a wonderful collection of authors. Different worlds... different times. It's what Elsewhen Press has been about since we launched our first title in 2011.

Here, we present twenty science fiction stories for you to enjoy. We are delighted that headlining this collection is the fantastic **John Gribbin,** with a worrying vision of medical research in the near future. Future global healthcare is the theme of **J A Christy's** story; while the ultimate in spare part surgery is where **Dave Weaver** takes us. **Edwin Hayward's** search for a renewable protein source turns out to be digital; and **Tanya Reimer's** story with characters we think we know gives us pause for thought about another food we take for granted. Evolution is examined too, with **Andy McKell's** chilling tale of what states could become if genetics are used to drive policy. Similarly, **Robin Moran's** story explores the societal impact of an undesirable evolutionary trend; while **Douglas Thompson** provides a truly surreal warning of an impending disaster that will reverse evolution, with dire consequences.

On a lighter note, we have satire from **Steve Harrison** discovering who really owns the Earth (and why); and **Ira Nayman,** who uses the surreal alternative realities of his *Transdimensional Authority* series as the setting for a detective story mash-up of Agatha Christie and Dashiel Hammett. Pursuing the crime-solving theme, **Peter Wolfe** explores life, and death, on a space station; while **Stefan Jackson** follows a police investigation into some bizarre cold-blooded murders in a cyberpunk future. Going into the past, albeit an 1831 set in the alternate Britain of his *Royal Sorceress* series, **Christopher Nuttall** reports on an investigation into a girl with strange powers.

Strange powers in the present-day is the theme for **Tej Turner,** who tells a poignant tale of how extra-sensory perception makes it easier for a husband to bear his dying wife's last few days. Difficult decisions are the theme of **Chloe Skye's** heart-rending story exploring personal sacrifice. Relationships aren't always so close, as **Susan Oke's** tale demonstrates, when sibling rivalry is taken to the limit. Relationships are the backdrop to **Peter R. Ellis's** story where a spectacular mid-winter event on a newly-colonised distant planet involves a Madonna and Child. Coming right back to Earth and in what feels like an almost imminent future, **Siobhan McVeigh** tells a cautionary tale for anyone thinking of using technology to deflect the blame for their actions. Building on the remarkable setting of Pera from her *LiGa* series, and developing Pera's legendary *Book of Shadow,* **Sanem Ozdural** spins the creation myth of the first light tree in a lyrical and poetic song. Also exploring language, the master of fantastika and absurdism, **Rhys Hughes,** extrapolates the way in which language changes over time, with an entertaining result.

ISBN: 9781908168955 (epub, kindle) / ISBN: 9781908168856 (320pp paperback)
Visit bit.ly/ExistenceIsElsewhen

Tej Turner

The Janus Cycle

The Janus Cycle can be described as gritty, surreal, urban fantasy… or sexy scifi. The over-arching story revolves around a nightclub called Janus, which is not merely a location but virtually a character in its own right. On the surface it appears to be a subcultural hub where the strange and disillusioned who feel alienated and oppressed by society escape to be free from convention; but underneath that façade is a surreal space in time where the very foundations of reality are twisted and distorted. But the special unique vibe of Janus is hijacked by a bandwagon of people who choose to conform to alternative lifestyles simply because it has become fashionable to be 'different', and this causes many of its original occupants to feel lost and disenchanted. We see the story of Janus unfold through the eyes of eight narrators, each with their own perspective and their own personal journey. A story in which the nightclub itself goes on a journey. But throughout, one character, a strange girl, briefly appears and reappears warning the narrators that their individual journeys are going to collide in a cataclysmic event. Is she just another one of the nightclub's denizens, a cynical mischief-maker out to create havoc or a time-traveller trying to prevent an impending disaster?

ISBN: 9781908168566 (epub, kindle) / ISBN: 9781908168467 (224pp paperback)
Visit bit.ly/JanusCycle

Dinnusos Rises

The vibe has soured somewhat after a violent clash in the Janus nightclub a few months ago, and since then Neal has opened a new establishment called 'Dinnusos'. Located on a derelict and forgotten side of town, it is not the sort of place you stumble upon by accident, but over time it enchants people, and soon becomes a nucleus for urban bohemians and a refuge for the city's lost souls. Rumour has it that it was once a grand hotel, many years ago, but no one is quite sure. Whilst mingling in the bar downstairs you might find yourself in the company of poets, dreamers, outsiders, and all manner of misfits and rebels. And if you're daring enough to explore its ghostly halls, there's a whole labyrinth of rooms on the upper floors to get lost in…

Now it seems that not just Neal's clientele, but the entire population of the city, begin to go crazy when beings, once thought mythological, enter the mortal realm to stir chaos as they sow the seeds of militancy.

Eight characters. Most of them friends, some of them strangers. Each with their own story to tell. All of them destined to cross paths in a surreal sequence of events which will change them forever.

ISBN: 9781911409137 (epub, kindle) / ISBN: 9781911409038 (280pp paperback)
visit bit.ly/DinnusosRises

About the Author

Zoë Sumra was born in London, but spent her later childhood living in Lancashire, where she started writing novels at the age of twelve due to extreme boredom. After completing the obligatory epic fantasy trilogy in her teens, she spent four years at the University of St Andrews, where she learnt to fence both foil and sabre and cemented her passion for space opera. She now lives in London with her husband, their daughter and a collection of swords. Zoë writes when she's not fencing, looking after her daughter, or working as a print controller for an advertising company. *Sailor to a Siren*, her first novel, was published by Elsewhen Press in July 2015.